A WEB OF DREAMS

Recent Titles by Tessa Barclay from Severn House

A BETTER CLASS OF PERSON
THE DALLANCY BEQUEST
FAREWELL PERFORMANCE
A FINAL DISCORD
A HANDFUL OF DUST
A LOVELY ILLUSION
THE SILVER LINING
STARTING OVER
A TRUE LIKENESS

A WEB OF DREAMS

Tessa Barclay

This edition published in Great Britain 2006 by
SEVERN HOUSE PUBLISHERS LTD of
9–15 High Street, Sutton, Surrey SM1 1DF.
First published in Great Britain only
in 1988 by W H Allen & Co.
This title first published in the USA 2006 by
SEVERN HOUSE PUBLISHERS INC of
595 Madison Avenue, New York, N.Y. 10022.

British Library Cataloguing in Publication Data

Barclay, Tessa
    A web of dreams
    1.   Scotland - History - 19th century - Fiction
    2.   Love stories
    I.   Title
    823.9'14 [F]

    ISBN-10: 0-7278-6306-1

Printed and bound in Great Britain by
MPG Books Ltd., Bodmin, Cornwall.

Author's Note

The background of this story – the weaving of Scottish tartan cloth – has always been interesting to me because I am by birth a Scot.

Queen Victoria and her husband Prince Albert fell in love with tartan the moment they saw it, so that it soon became high fashion not only in Britain but throughout the nineteenth century world. It seemed to me that a novel about a young woman who built a career out of the weaving of these wonderful patterns could be very appealing.

I hope that you will feel that I was right, and that my American readers in particular – many of whom share Scottish ancestry – will enjoy this book.

Chapter One

Captain Bobby Prentiss leaned his chair back as far as it would go without falling over, stared at the cracked ceiling of the makeshift room, and reflected that it might break the monotony if he fetched his shotgun and blew a hole through it.

On the other hand, it might not even be heard. There was so much distance between him and any other occupants of this godforsaken building that he might shoot not the ceiling but himself, and be unnoticed until nightfall.

Nightfall. Day had hardly even got started so how could night fall? The grey sky drizzled down on Balmoral Castle, dampness clothed the muddy surroundings in a dismal mist, some poor little bird piped from a tree at the far side of the rough lawn.

And for this, Captain Prentiss said to himself with some bitterness, I got myself sent away from my regiment as military attaché to the dullest embassies in Europe. I learned German, because the Prince Consort and the Queen like to have German-speaking staff around them. I actually sought an appointment to the Royal Household.

I will definitely go for my hunting rifle. I will shoot the glass out of the windows. I will shoot holes in the wall plaster. When they come to take me away, I will say I did it as a protest at the awful conditions under which the equerries are expected to exist in this damnable building, in this damnable country.

The captain hated Scotland. The cool climate irritated him, the grey skies depressed him. The people were taciturn and critical. Her Majesty might rhapsodise about the worthy folk of Deeside, but he thought them a bore. A bore, a dead bore, an utter and crashing bore.

With this last vehement surge of detestation, he gave a shove with his elegantly booted foot at the desk in front of him. The chair finally toppled over. He fell in a tangle of chairlegs, fluttering papers and inkpots.

'Damn,' he said, scrambling up. But then as he dusted himself off he had the grace to laugh ruefully. 'I've come to a pretty pass,' he muttered, 'when I can't even sit upright in a chair.'

He turned his head to the window. It hadn't been cleaned for weeks. During the remodelling of this 'pretty little castle', as Her Majesty was wont to call it, dust, grit and mud had been everywhere. The stone used for the new wings was of a very fine grain and very hard to work, so that a thin dust from the masonry had silted over the glass. The room in which he was standing was the best available for the equerries, though it was shabby, one wall only boards roughly plastered as a temporary measure.

To be sure, the main building was in better shape. The roofers were at work there, with slates carted across the hills from Strathbogie. The workmen from Cubitt's of London were putting in the plumbing for the hot and cold baths. In the rooms on the first floor of the west side, His Royal Highness the Prince Consort was at this moment conferring with the decorator over the subject of wallpaper and upholstery for the royal bedrooms.

Captain Prentiss couldn't understand why anyone should want to come to this dank, dreary place for any part of the summer or autumn. To judge by his experience, the temperature seldom rose above sixty degrees and usually it rained. Yet Victoria and Albert genuinely loved Scotland. They thought it 'romantic'.

Romantic! How could any place be romantic where the inhabitants had such stern moral principles?

Bobby Prentiss knew from experience that it was very hard indeed to awaken any romantic feelings in the young ladies of the neighbourhood. He was fairly adept at spotting those of a generous disposition, for he was often separated from his wife

Laura and you couldn't expect a man of his lively nature to go without feminine sympathy, now could you?

Alas, you only had to look hopefully at one of the pretty girls here to have her parents frowning and inquiring into your family. It was, of course, no use pretending he was a single man. The members of the Royal Household were subjects of great interest to the local gentry, and of course were expected to behave with as much circumspection as the royal couple themselves.

Which certainly put a curb on any 'romantic' notions Bobby might have, unless he were to go after a chambermaid or someone of that sort. But then they talked in such a peculiar way, almost a foreign language – how could you have any kind of fun with a girl like that? You could go to bed, of course – oh yes, easy enough, if you showed the glint of a silver coin. Yet his tours of duty abroad had taught Bobby that making love could have more to it than a florin's worth of physical relief.

Still, no use making himself miserable by thinking of the girls he'd known in France, the pretty little mistress he'd kept in Saxony. He was miserable enough, heaven knew, cooped up in this uncomfortable little office without even the possibility of getting out with a gun and a dog. He was on duty, a junior equerry – he must stay where he was.

He gazed out through the dusty panes. The drizzle had actually stopped! There was even a glimpse of watery sun on the downtrodden grass of what would be a sloping lawn. There was a sparkle on the leaves of the sad-looking bushes, struggling to stay alive among the piles of planks and the scaffolding.

And there, stealthily making her way among them, was a slender young lady!

Bobby couldn't believe his eyes. A girl! A girl of medium height, the hood of her mantelet dropped down to reveal very dark hair pulled back in a high chignon. In the faint silvery light of the September sunshine her face seemed very pale but she was gone before he could distinguish her features.

He blinked. Had he imagined her? He saw her at once in his mind's eye: the mantelet of dark cloth trimmed with something white – ermine, perhaps. The dark hair touched

7

with the gleam of moisture from the dripping trees. Her movements quick and supple. Yes, and secretive. She had been
skulking.

Skulking! And carrying a package!

He called it up again in his memory. A package in her arms
– something about a foot long and not quite so wide, wrapped
in dark strong paper or perhaps canvas.

A bomb?

The royal family weren't universally popular. Now and
again madmen leapt out to make attempts on their lives. Could
this neat little lady in the dark clothes by any chance be an
anarchist?

All this had taken a fraction of a second to pass through his
mind. Before the girl could have taken another step after she
disappeared among the building equipment, Bobby Prentiss
was out of the door and after her.

There was a pile of stone blocks immediately outside the
office. He crouched behind it, listened intently, and heard a
soft footfall some yards away. He moved without sound
towards it. At the end of the stone pile he glanced in the
direction the sound had come from. She was walking with a
gentle tread and with an anxious turning of her head towards
the open French windows of the drawingroom.

In two strides Bobby had overtaken her. He caught her by
the shoulder, swung her round. 'Hey!' he said. 'What d'you
think you're up to?'

She gave a little shriek of fright. She threw up her hands
to protect herself. The package fell from her grasp into the
wet mud.

'Oh, goodness!' she gasped. 'Now look what you've done!'

She seemed much more concerned about her package than
anything else. He stooped as she did, to recover it. It proved
to be yielding to the touch, not at all bomb-like. In fact, it
felt like a parcel of cloth.

They straightened together, the girl clutching the parcel to
her bosom. The mantelet proved to be of fine dark cloth but
edged with white felt, not ermine. Her features, now that he
could see them, were worth looking at. She had dark eyes,
almost Latin in their lambent blackness. Her eyebrows arched
over them with a strong, emphatic curve. Her mouth, now

8

half-open in alarm, revealed straight white teeth in her narrow jaw.

He knew in a moment that she wasn't what he thought of as a lady. She might perhaps be some kind of superior servant – a lady's maid, perhaps. But no, there was something about her as she glowered at him now – none of the acquired demureness or servility of the domestic employee.

'Who the devil are you?' he demanded. 'And what are you doing, creeping about in the grounds of Balmoral?'

'Creeping about? Who's creeping about? I'm going to see the Prince Consort.'

It was so unexpected that he gave a snort of laughter. 'The Prince Consort? Are you, indeed!'

'Yes, I am, and now look what you've done to my sample!'

'Your what?'

She hugged the parcel closer to her. 'It's got wet! Why did you jump out on me like that?'

'You're lucky I didn't shoot you on sight,' he declared. 'How did you get past the gates, anyway? Surely there's a guard – '

'The guard's only there to keep out bad people. I have an appointment with Prince Albert, so of course he let me pass.'

The more she said, the more he was convinced that despite her bright, intelligent face she was as mad as a hatter.

'Oh, so you've an appointment with Prince Albert, have you? Since when, may I ask?'

'Since the beginning of August, if it's any of your business.'

'That's very interesting. And for what hour was this appointment?'

'For any time after His Highness's lunch – naturally I wouldn't expect to know exactly when he'd be free but I said any time after two o'clock.'

'You said?' Captain Prentiss echoed. He felt a certain unease. 'You've talked to the Prince?'

'No, no, I said it in my letter.'

In the way she said, 'No, no,' there was a lilt of the Scottish speech which in general he found almost unintelligible. She was a local girl, perhaps, but not one of the thick-spoken country girls he'd heard among the shielings when Their Majesties went for a tour of the countryside.

9

'You wrote a letter to the Prince?'

'Am I not telling you I did? So you see you're keeping me from my appointment – '

'A moment, young lady,' the equerry said. 'I know all His Royal Highness's appointments for today, and I can assure you he has nothing in his diary about seeing you.'

'Well, that just shows how little you know,' she said, 'because I wrote to him on our printed notepaper on behalf of my father and you can be sure the appointment's there in his book if you just look to see – Miss Genevieve Corvill on behalf of William Corvill of Edinburgh.'

'So you wrote to him, Miss Corvill.' Despite himself, Bobby Prentiss was smiling. 'Did you receive a reply?'

'No, but then, of course, His Highness'll be too busy a man to reply to every letter he gets from those that want to do business with him – '

'Business! Miss Colville – what can you mean? What *are* you?'

'I'm a webster,' she said, drawing herself up to her full height at about the level of his shoulder. 'You'll not have heard of us, not being one that buys much cloth, I dare say – '

'A webster?'

She frowned, the dark brows coming together like a strong parenthesis. 'You're an Englishman, I suppose. A webster – you'd say, a weaver.'

'A *weaver?*'

'Aye, the best in Edinburgh.' There was a tilt of the chin that showed how strongly she believed it. 'William Corvill, my father, of Dean Village in Edinburgh. Ask anybody. They'll tell you – the finest cloth in the best patterns of anybody in Scotland. The cloth on the loom is the "web", you know, and those that make it are the websters – it's common as a surname even in England, I believe, though you don't seem to use it for the trade.'

Captain Prentiss forebore to tell her that he never concerned himself with trade of any kind, let alone weaving. 'My dear Miss Corvill, I've no doubt your father is foremost of his kind. But that makes no difference to the fact that you have no appointment with His Royal Highness for this afternoon or any other afternoon. I assure you – your name does not appear.'

She gave him a haughty stare. 'And how can you possibly know that, my good man?'

He kept a straight face. 'Because I'm a junior equerry to His Highness, and it's my role to know what his appointments are. Besides, my dear girl . . . ! Surely you know better than to think you have an engagement with the Prince just because you wrote to say you were coming?'

To tell the truth, this was a point which had troubled Miss Genevieve Corvill a little. Her father, always unwilling to be involved in anything new or unusual, had muttered that His Highness wouldn't want to be bothered with a visit from the likes of her.

To this she gave the same answer she now gave to the handsome equerry. 'The Prince Consort is known, is he not, for being a goodhearted man, very punctilious in his dealings with those beneath him. He'd have sent a message if he didn't wish to see me – he'd never have wanted me to come all the way from Edinburgh for nothing.'

There was just enough truth in this to perturb Bobby Prentiss. There should have been a letter telling her Their Majesties had no need of her services. But all the same . . .

'You must understand that the Queen and the Prince Consort have secretaries to deal with correspondence.' He pictured her letter, continually put to the bottom of the mahogany filing tray until finally the refusal was written and posted at the last moment. 'When did you set out from Edinburgh, Miss Corvill?'

'Yesterday morn.'

'Well then. The letter may have arrived after you set out.'

That was possible. But Miss Corvill had no intention of allowing it to be so. 'On the other hand, a letter may have arrived saying His Highness would be delighted to see the cloth we've made for him. It's well known that Their Majesties are very interested in Highland plaid designs, and my letter offered something particularly fine. You cannot deny, sir, that an acceptance is just as possible as a refusal.'

She saw uncertainty gaining ground in his blue eyes. She had been looking up at him with a confident, inquiring gaze, and now she tilted her head a little in unconscious coquetry.

11

She knew he liked her. There was something about the way his mouth kept curving towards a smile as he spoke to her.

She liked him. Apart from that first moment when he had scared the very hair upon her head as he whirled her round, she found him very pleasing.

He was quite unlike the sombrely-clad young men of the small Huguenot settlement to which she belonged. They were pale and quiet, weavers, mostly, like her father William and her brother Ned. She met them at the tiny Huguenot church, their Bibles held against their black-clad breasts. They walked her home with a sedate step.

One of them, in due time, would be selected by her father to pay court to her. He would be her husband.

But none of them gave her this faint flutter in the throat she felt now. The young equerry was tall, fairish, pink-complexioned. He had no beard, but a soft wide moustache above his smiling mouth and little curling sideburns down his cheek. She found herself, most unexpectedly, wishing to touch those curling sideburns with an approving finger.

'What is your name, sir?' she inquired, looking down.

'Captain Robert Prentiss of the Ninth Cavalry.'

She gave him a polite little curtsey. 'Sir, I'm sure you would wish to carry out your duties efficiently. It may well be that His Highness is expecting me at this very moment.'

It was unlikely in the extreme. The Prince had come to Balmoral to oversee the next stage in the rebuilding. He had appointments with the architect, Mr Smith of Aberdeen; the chief mason, Mr Beaton; various estate workers, such as the head dairyman and the wife of the gardener who cooked for the bothy-occupants; and of course the decorator and the upholsterer who were with him in the first floor rooms at present.

Into this crowded programme it was very unlikely the Prince or his secretaries had inserted a visit by an unknown little weaver from Edinburgh. A girl, at that – it was most unseemly.

'Did you come here unescorted, Miss Corvill?' Bobby asked, his tone reproving.

'Oh, no, captain, my brother was with me.' Colour edged up into the pale cheeks. 'He was taken a little unwell so I left

12

him at Crathie and walked up alone. I didn't want to be late, you see, for my appointment with Prince Albert.'

In the little laugh caused by that remark he forgot for the moment the embarrassment she had hidden about her brother. 'My dear young lady, you have no appointment with the Prince.'

'Oh, but I have!'

He shook his head. He really ought to call one of the staff and have her thrown out. Yet it seemed a pity to part with her. She had made a break in the hideous monotony of the grey day. Besides, she was exceptionally pretty, more like a French girl than a Scot, though some of the Scots with their fair complexions and tawny hair were stunning to look at even if hard to understand.

'Let me offer you a cup of tea before you leave,' he suggested.

For a moment he thought she was going to say, 'I won't leave.' But as the words were forming to be spoken she changed them. With a little bow she said, 'A cup of tea would be very welcome. And while I drink it you could no doubt speak to the Prince's secretary to check that I'm expected.'

The cheek of it! Yet, after all, what harm would it do?

'You're a very determined young lady,' he remarked, as he escorted her into the equerries' office.

'Yes, it's one of my great faults,' she agreed, in a demure tone that had hidden laughter in it. 'The minister is always telling me I have a stubborn spirit.'

When she had accepted the only other chair in the makeshift office, she set her precious parcel on the floor by her side. He rang the bell. The manservant from the equerries' mess raised his eyebrows when he came in. 'Yes, sir?'

'We'll have tea, Simpkins. And – ' with a glance at his guest ' – something to eat?' When she nodded he said, 'Some cake, or a biscuit.'

'Yes, sir.' Simpkins withdrew, blowing out his cheeks. He was a one, the captain. Where had he managed to find that nice little bit of skirt in the middle of this bivouac?

The nice little bit of skirt was looking about her with interest. The room was plain and tidy but there was a fine

13

film of dust over almost everything. The carpet bore the signs of mud from outdoors.

'There isn't much staff at the castle?' she deduced.

'Only enough in general to look after the builders, who've been housed in bothies and cottages in the grounds. His Royal Highness has brought his own bodyservants with him, of course, and his secretaries. The rest of us have to shift for ourselves mostly.' He glanced about. 'I'm sorry I can't offer you a more comfortable chair.'

'That's quite all right, captain.' She was looking at a leather-bound book which lay open on the desk. 'Is that His Highness's appointment book?'

'No, that's the day book of the equerries' office – but I assure you if you had been expected there would be a note of it here.' He held the book out to her, open, at a page with the date written at the top.

'Tuesday 12th September 1854,' she read. Below were brief notes of where HRH might be expected to go inside the castle and about the estate and who was to accompany him. The Equerry-in-Chief was at present with the Prince. A note in brackets caught her eye: 'Lunch 1.30 to 2, piper plays.' The Prince Consort's love of music was well known.

Simpkins arrived with a silver tray holding a service for two. Behind him came a page with a cake rack. She saw, to her astonishment, not one kind of cake but two. Cake for tea except at a celebration was unknown to her. *Two* kinds of cake was unheard-of.

The tray brought by Simpkins proved to have clever telescopic legs. He set it before her so that she could pour the tea. She began to do so, saying to Bobby Prentiss, 'Milk and sugar?'

'Neither, thank you.' He took his cup, gulped the tea down, selected a large slice of cake from the plate the page offered, and swallowed it in two mouthfuls. He was both hungry and thirsty. He'd been up since five-thirty, as was necessary to keep up with the Prince's rigorous schedule. Breakfast had been the detestable Scottish porridge, lunch for him had been at eleven-thirty so that he could go on duty at noon.

His guest looked at him over the rim of her raised tea cup.

'Well, captain, while I drink mine, perhaps you'd be so good as to check with the Prince's secretary about my appointment.'

He'd decided to fall in with the idea. And when he got back with his disappointing news, he'd spend a pleasant half hour or so consoling her. Officially he wasn't off duty until eight in the evening but if he could invent some excuse he might get the chance to walk her down to Crathie where the brother was awaiting her.

He said to the page, 'See that Miss Corvill has everything she wants,' took another piece of cake as he went out, and ate it as he threaded his way through the temporary covered passage to the main building. Here he came in at what would eventually be a side door. The Prince's secretary was in the old castle – he took a turret staircase and was crossing an upper landing when footsteps on the uncarpeted main stairway resounded and the Prince himself came into view.

'Ah, Captain Prentiss. Were you looking for me?'

'Er . . . no . . . that is . . .'

'What do you think of this wood sample, captain? It's for the staircase panelling.'

'It's . . . er . . . very fine, sir.'

'Rather dark, do you think? Yet oak . . . oak seems right for a northern castle.'

'Yes, sir.'

'We have been looking at the main bedrooms, Prentiss.' He turned to the man at his elbow. 'This is Mr McRae, from the paint firm. He suggests dove grey for the window frames and doors but I feel . . .'

'Your dove grey is a useful shade, Your Highness,' urged the paint-maker. 'Goes with anything – no matter what you choose for the wallpaper and the curtains, your dove grey will fit in.'

'But you see, McRae, I think of having tartan.'

'Tartan? Wallpaper?'

The Prince's pale features lit up. 'Is there tartan wallpaper?' he asked with eagerness. 'I had not heard of that.'

'Well . . . no, Your Highness. That's why I was a bit surprised. You'd mean tartan for the . . . the curtains, then?'

'Yes, and the carpet.'

'The carpet,' said Mr McRae faintly.

15

'Yes, most appropriate, you will agree. A Highland home should have Highland decoration.'

'Aye, no doubt, sir,' said McRae, who was himself a Highlander and had not a scrap of tartan in his house.

Another member of the Prince Consort's party moved forward. 'It should certainly be easy enough to find tartan fabrics, Your Highness. There are many cloth-makers who could – '

'Cloth-makers,' Captain Prentiss echoed, somewhat too loud in his surprise.

'What was that, captain?'

'Er . . . Sir . . .' Should he? Well, why not. 'Sir, a young lady called Miss Corvill has come to the castle with a sample of cloth to show you.'

'Indeed? I do not recall an arrangement?'

'No, sir, perhaps not. She is under a misapprehension, I think. Nevertheless, she's a weaver or at least represents a weaving firm – she says it's the best in Edinburgh – and she has a sample of cloth with her. I think she said it was plaid.'

'Corvill?' said the man who had first spoken about cloth. He was, Bobby guessed, the upholsterer. 'Yes, now, wait a minute . . . William Corvill . . . But they don't make furnishing fabric, they make fine cloth.'

'Something for the children's dresses, I expect,' put in the Equerry-in-Chief. 'Local people love to offer their products to the royal family, sir.'

'That is very kind of her. Prentiss, where is the young woman?'

'In the equerries' office, sir.'

The Equerry-in-Chief raised his eyebrows. Bobby avoided his eye by looking fixedly at the Prince Consort.

'That is most convenient. I have some free time, have I not, Harrington?'

'Not until this evening, sir,' the Equerry-in-Chief said repressively. 'Some of the local people are coming in to play and dance for you.'

'Very well, Prentiss. I will see her then.'

'Yes, Your Highness.'

'Good, good. Now, as to the paint, McRae. I seriously

doubt . . .' The royal voice faded as the royal progress continued towards the rooms intended for the royal children.

'Tartan carpets?' said McRae in a shocked voice to himself as he followed in the Prince's train. 'Tartan curtains?'

A problem now presented itself. HRH had expressed a wish to see Miss Corvill after dinner at the evening entertainment to be provided by the ghillies and their families. In the meantime Miss Corvill had to be bestowed somewhere. The housekeeper-elect of Balmoral was affronted at being asked to look after a mere weaver's daughter, and the footmen were trying to ogle her.

In the end she was put in a corner of the poky little library of the old building, with a fire for her comfort but no one for company. When Bobby glanced in on her at about four o'clock, he found to his astonishment that she was reading.

'Good afternoon, Miss Corvill. Is there anything you want?'

'No thank you, captain, not at present, though before I'm taken to see the Prince I should like to wash my face and get the mud off my shoes.' She stretched out her feet from under her skirts, ruefully surveying the brown-stained shoes.

She had taken off the mantelet, to reveal herself in a dark blue gown that fitted close to the waist and then swept out in the necessary layers of skirt and petticoat. A small collar of white lace was the only decoration. Yet the whole thing was elegant enough to have been the morning dress of a fine lady.

He came closer to find out what she was reading. There was nothing very lighthearted in the Prince's library, not even copies of the novels of Sir Walter Scott so greatly admired by the Queen. Seeing his curiosity, she held up the book. It was a fine volume of *Vestiarium Scoticum* by the brothers Sobieski-Stuart, the study of Scottish clan tartans published earlier in the century and cause of much argument about authenticity.

He was too surprised to say anything. He'd been startled to know she could read at all, and astounded to find her studying a learned book even if only to look at the illustrations.

'It's my business,' she said with a little shrug when she saw his expression.

'Yes . . .' In his opinion, pretty girls had better things to do than study old books. 'Would you like to be shown round the castle?'

17

'Oh, yes, if it's permitted.'

'This way, then.'

He offered his arm. Before taking it she carefully closed and set aside the book on the library table alongside her precious parcel of cloth.

He led her out of the little library, across the stone-flagged hall. He showed her the rooms occupied by the ladies of the Queen's Household when she was in residence, the dining-room now being prepared for the evening meal of the Prince and his staff, and up the main staircase to the suite used by the royal children and their governess.

Everything not in immediate use was swathed in dustsheets. The place was melancholy and felt chill. She was disappointed – where was the splendour of princes?

'It'll be better in the new building,' Bobby said. 'The Prince is very keen to make it handsome.'

'So we heard.'

'We? Who's we?'

'Ach, Prince Albert's plans for Balmoral are the talk of Scotland. Everybody wants to be part of it. All the furniture makers and the stonemasons and carpenters . . .'

Oh, she meant tradespeople. But there was something endearing in her earnestness.

'It's a long time,' she went on, glancing up at him as he opened yet another door for her, 'since a monarch showed any interest in this country. The Queen's very much liked for it.'

'The Queen would never spend any time in Scotland if her husband didn't enjoy it.'

'Oh, yes, him too – he's a grand man!' She smiled, her face flushed with excitement at the thought of meeting him. 'Is he as handsome as his pictures?'

That was a matter of opinion. Bobby thought him pale and insipid. Yet women seemed to swoon over him. Look at the Queen – absolutely besotted by him. Very odd. You'd think she'd prefer a more red-blooded man, being herself so bright and brisk.

'You'll soon see for yourself,' he remarked. He took out his watch. 'The Prince dines early – dinner will be about six-thirty, I expect, because the fiddlers and dancers are coming at seven-thirty. The idea was that they should dance outdoors but it's so confounded wet out there, they'll probably be in the hall. So I'll take you there at the first interval – that'll be about eight.'

'Yes. Thank you. What should I say?'

'Just answer when he speaks. You call him "sir" or "Your Highness". It'll be all right.' He was sure of that – Albert would work his usual magic on the girl. It was only those ladies who met him often who began to find him boring and stiff.

The tour of inspection ended in the conservatory added to the old building by the previous owner, Sir Robert Gordon. Here were more signs of neglect: the plants were alive but there was dust on their leaves, the glass needed cleaning in the rooflights.

He picked a sprig of white hoya, presenting it to her with a little bow. 'Wear it for luck, Miss Corvill.'

She drew back. Her first thought was that he ought not to pick the royal flowers. But when she saw the winning smile with which he offered it, she felt a little thrill of enjoyment. The delicate fragrance from the blossom drifted up to her. She took it, held it to her nostrils. 'It's lovely.'

'No lovelier than you.'

'Oh!' She heard warning bells ringing in her mind. But he was bending his head to be on a level with her, and next moment he was gently setting aside the blossom so as to kiss her on the lips.

It was a brief kiss, unemphatic, almost courtly. He drew back to look at her. She knew she should frown, should reprove him. But instead she moistened her lips as if savouring the kiss. There was innocence in the action, but also curiosity. No one had ever kissed her on the mouth before except for snatched attempts under the mistletoe.

When he put his arms about her and drew her close she made no attempt to stop him. She found him very attractive – alluring, almost, with his smooth skin and scented hair pomade. Something seemed to urge her towards him, some hitherto unknown need, some longing for physical contact.

When he let her go, he was flushed with triumph. 'Well,' he said.

She felt herself blushing. 'I shouldn't have let you do that.'

19

'Why not? You liked it, didn't you.'

'Yes, but – '

'You're not engaged, or anything?'

She shook her head.

'No harm in it, then.' He patted her cheek. 'What's your name – your first name?'

'Genevieve, but I'm called Jenny.'

'That's a pretty name. I'm just plain old ordinary Bobby.'

'Bobby . . . It suits you.'

He couldn't think why. But to her it meant something lighthearted and bright, like himself, a name for a man with no cares, a boyish man.

With a sigh he took her back towards the door. 'Come along, if you're going to make yourself prettier for HRH, you'd better be taken somewhere with a mirror and such.'

The housekeeper led her to one of the housemaids' rooms in the attic, lent her a comb and a face flannel, and sent a supply of hot water. First she cleaned her sturdy leather shoes, then she washed her face and tidied her hair. She pinched her cheeks to bring the colour into them. She pinned the sprig of hoya to the space between the points of her lace collar. Then, greatly daring, she unpinned it and threaded the stem into her hair at her temple.

It looked beautiful. But was it suitable?

She stared at herself in the mirror. Come, come, my lass, she said to herself, you've been in enough mischief for one day.

And with the commonsense for which she was noted in her family, she took the flowers out of her hair and pinned them back on her dress.

A tray with bread and butter and cold meat was brought to her but she couldn't eat. She had a long wait on a hard chair in the hall with the parcel on her lap. Then, as the light began to fail, people began to gather there, men in kilts and the light shoes of the dancer, women in their best frocks and white stockings. In a passage near the kitchens, a fiddler could be heard tuning up.

The Prince came into the hall. He was in Highland dress; a kilt of the Stewart tartan, a sealskin sporran, hose of the colours of the kilt, and a short dark green jacket with a plain white shirt. He was fully as handsome as his portraits promised.

Behind him came the gentlemen of his household. Bobby, she noted, was in mess jacket and dark trousers with a braided sideseam. He wasn't as handsome as the Prince, but he had his own charm.

Some of the tenants were presented. The Prince spoke kindly, stooping to be at eye level with the children. The entertainment opened with a Gaelic song, then the fiddler struck up a reel. The dancers stepped forward, threaded their pattern with lightness and gaiety. But Jenny could enjoy none of it. She was tense with expectancy.

It seemed hours later that Bobby came. He led her through the crowd to the Prince's side.

'Your Royal Highness, you were kind enough to say you would see Miss Corvill.'

'Indeed. You have come from Edinburgh, I hear?'

'Yes, Your Highness, on behalf of my father.' She heard her voice trembling with the anxiety of the moment. She must get a grip on herself. This, after all, was what she had come for. 'I brought with me, sir, some very fine cloth. If you'd permit me to show it to you I'd be very honoured.'

The long pale face was smiling indulgently. 'Please do so, Miss Corvill.'

She couldn't tell whether he was genuinely interested or simply being kind. She untied the tape on her parcel, folded back the paper, and with a flourish swept out the length of cloth.

It flashed momentarily in the lamplight as it fell across her arm. Red – scarlet – with black and azure blue across it, and white threads, and a touch of yellow. The bright tartan of the Royal Stewarts, the pattern she knew so well laid out on her father's loom: black, white, black, yellow, black, azure, red, azure, and so on, back to the four black threads that ended the check.

But woven exquisitely fine, exquisitely small. The tartan was here in miniature, rippling in folds across her arm.

'Your Highness,' she said, pride in her voice, 'my father heard you would be wanting fine tartans for your new castle at Balmoral, so he sends you a sample that perhaps you might like.'

She waited. The Prince leaned forward, took a fold of the cloth between his fingers.

'Why . . . it's wool!'

'Yes, sir. But so fine you could thread it through a wedding ring.'

He shook his head in wonder. 'But this is beautiful! Miss Corvill, I am very pleased you came.'

Chapter Two

For Jenny the next quarter of an hour passed in a haze of delight. The Prince admired the cloth, remarking that it was just the kind of thing he had been hoping to find for the bedhangings and curtains of the royal bedroom. Everyone nodded approval. His Royal Highness signalled to a secretary to make a note that fifty yards should be ordered at once with the option to order more should it be required.

He then inquired kindly into the circumstances of Jenny's family.

'My father and brother are the websters, sir – the weavers, I mean. My father sometimes hires others in our community – we're Huguenots, sir – from France by way of London and Norwich, but we've been in Edinburgh more than a hundred years now.'

Prince Albert was extremely interested. Items of historical note always caught his attention, and this was about Protestant refugees, originally forced to flee from France by religious persecution in the seventeenth century. Anything to do with the Protestant religion pleased the Prince; he was from a staunch Protestant principality.

'The Huguenots – ah yes – an admirable people, respectable and industrious. What a boon they have been to this country, gentlemen,' he remarked, glancing around at his entourage. They looked attentive, awaiting the little lecture he was sure to give. 'Louis Fourteenth, you know – he revoked the Edict of Nantes which had granted them the right to follow the Protestant religion. So they were driven out of France in – what? – 1680?'

'1685, Your Highness,' Jenny murmured automatically. To

23

her it was an old, old story, scarcely worth remembering except that it was sometimes useful in gaining customers. The Huguenot communities had the reputation of being sober, hardworking, reliable. People ordering goods liked to think that the work would be done well and to time.

The Prince talked on for a few minutes, giving the party the benefit of his knowledge of the politics of France in the late seventeenth century. Jenny, who knew it all, let her thoughts go back to the main point. An order for fifty yards from the royal family! And with an option to order more! It had been worth all the argument, all the effort.

Her father had been most unwilling to make the attempt. Oh, not to weave the cloth – anything fine and unusual was a challenge to his skill. But when she said she wanted to offer it to Their Majesties, he was aghast.

'Have you taken leave of your senses, girl? Approach the Queen?'

'And why not, may I ask? It's all the talk, how they adore everything to do with the Highlands. The scenery, and the pipe music, and deer-stalking – everything! And you've seen the photographs and paintings of them in the Highland clothes – the little Prince in full fig – why shouldn't we offer them the tartan?'

'But we've never done such a thing before.'

'That's no reason not to. There's nothing to be afraid of – they can't throw us in the Tower of London for offering them a bolt of cloth.'

Her mother intervened. 'Jenny, that's no way to speak to your father.'

'What way? What way am I speaking? I'm only telling him not to be *afraid* – '

'Your father's not afraid – '

'Yes I am, Millicent, mortal afraid. The very thought of weaving something fit for the Queen frightens me.'

'You mean you think you're a poor weaver?' asked his daughter.

His head came up in unconscious pride. 'No one would dare to say that to me!'

'You think that piece of tartan is really good?'

'It's the finest thing I've ever woven. When I set up the

merino threads, I thought then, they're spun fine as a spider's web, and I knew . . .' his voice became dreamy '. . . I knew it would be a beautiful piece of cloth.'

His pale lined face was peaceful as he thought of the bright plaid stretched on his loom. He had forgotten that it was all Jenny's idea.

Weavers sometimes bought thread for making cloth and sometimes had it spun by members of their own family. On this occasion, Jenny, ordering woollen yarn from a spinner in the village of Cramond to the north of Edinburgh, had seen some very fine merino ready-dyed and on the purn.

'What's yon?' she inquired.

'Ach, you don't want to bother about that. It's far too fine a thread for any practical purpose, Miss Corvill. I was asked to make it by a merchant who bought some merino wool in the fleece, him with a great idea to do something special with it and sell it to the big Yorkshire mills. But he couldn't find enough spinners to make it in quantity and he's pushed for money so he's no wanting it now, and I'm left with it taking up space on my shelves and after the expense of the dyeing!'

'Is it yours to sell, Mrs Hunter?'

Mrs Hunter pricked up her ears. 'Are you yourself interested in it, Miss Corvill?'

'Well . . .' It had already passed through her mind more than once that her father could weave any of the well-known tartan designs better than many she had seen in the merchants' warehouses. He, however, only set up work to order on his looms, work that had already been seen as a sample by the customer and was known to be wanted.

But this very fine thread, running like silk through her fingers . . . And the colours, so pure and clean. She looked at them, picturing in her mind the setting-up for one of the dozen or so famous tartans, now so unexpectedly fashionable because the royal family liked them.

Red, light blue, black, white . . . She saw it on the web in her mind's eye. All the colours were there for the Stewart check except yellow. 'Have you any of this thread in pale yellow?'

Mrs Hunter shook her head. But seeing that this customer was genuinely interested she said quickly, 'I can get the dyer

25

to mix some, and I've some of the yarn undyed – it would be no trouble to do it. That's if you have the firm mind to buy it, Miss Corvill.'

Jenny did sums in her head. So much yarn available, so many bobbins to be wound for the warp, so much for the weft. What was here on Mrs Hunter's shelves would make – what – six 'pieces' of about fifty yards.

It was fine merino wool, from Spain. The cost would be high. It was a terrible gamble. But if she could talk her father into it – and he would be pleased and charmed by the challenge – he would make a cloth of surpassing fineness. And if he made that, who else should have it but the royal family?

She made a provisional bargain with Mrs Hunter, that the yellow was to be dyed in the yarn and made ready for her inspection. She would be back in three days' time to clinch the deal.

The sample yarns she took with her were enough to catch her father in the snare. He wanted to see the threads wound for his loom. Almost before she'd finished explaining he was sitting down with pen and paper to draw the check as small as it ought to be for such a fine thread. A Stewart tartan in miniature, the surface of the cloth glinting with scarlet and azure blue, the handle of it soft as silk . . .

He was really happy only when he was at his loom. For William Corvill, life was a constant struggle. Though he made a good living and was well regarded in the small Huguenot colony of Edinburgh, he was always in apprehension.

He and his family were 'different'. Though they had been in this little enclave, the Dean Village, since the middle of the last century, the Huguenots had never quite been accepted. The children were sometimes set upon by street hooligans, names were called after them as they came from their little stone church by the river bank. Their clothes were too dark, their rules were too strict, they disapproved of whisky, they never came out to dance in the streets at Hogmanay.

Yet his daughter was now urging him to be even more 'different', to make the attempt to gain royal patronage with this piece of cloth he'd been tempted by pride into making.

'We can at least write, Father,' she begged. 'What harm

can that do? If they don't want to see the cloth all they have to do is refuse.'

Her brother Ned wrote the actual letter. Ned was a scholar, far too clever to be cooped up in a weaver's shed. Many weavers were cultured men, because the long hours at the loom alone tempted them to have a book by their side. But Ned was exceptional. It was one of his great dreams, shared only by Jenny, that one day he would get away from the loom to study at university.

The letter merely stated that the firm of William Corvill and Son had produced a particularly fine length of tartan which they begged to have the honour of showing to His Royal Highness on his forthcoming visit to Balmoral. It suggested the attendance of a member of the Corvill family on the afternoon of the 12th September and was signed, 'Your humble and faithful servant, Wm. Corvill.'

When no reply came, William was not surprised. 'I told you,' he muttered, 'it was an impertinent and foolish thing. What would they be doing with the likes of us? No, no, when they buy the tartan, they buy it from the big firms – '

'That's not true, they bought Macleod tartan from a woman in a cottage, Father – it said so in the Aberdeen paper. And I'm not surprised they didn't reply – why would they, when they have it there in front of them that we're coming? If they didn't want us, they'd write and say so.'

The discussion went on for days. But by the day before they must start on their journey to Balmoral, Jenny had worn down her father into agreement. He himself would not go – no, a team of wild horses wouldn't have dragged him to the train. Jenny was to represent them, because Jenny was the one with all the business sense and the least likely to miss the train connections. But of course Ned must go with her. It would be inconceivable to let a young woman travel from Edinburgh to Balmoral by herself.

Jenny was both pleased and displeased by the result. She wanted to represent her family on this great occasion. She accepted that she must have an escort. But she was very worried about Ned, because she knew something that her parents didn't even suspect.

Ned was addicted to drink.

The secret was well kept because she knew it would break her father's heart. He himself was not a total abstainer but the occasional glass of wine in which he toasted his French forebears was regarded as a great indulgence. Spirits he abhorred, and with good reason. Cheap bad whisky was the bane of Scotland. Drunkenness was one of the great problems in the weaving trade.

Ned, at twenty, was two years Jenny's senior. He had always been the leader in their childhood escapades. As a little girl she adored him, but as she grew older she began to grow aware of his faults.

He was clever, and he knew it. His mind ranged out and beyond anything the rest of his family could follow – his family and indeed the rest of the Huguenot community.

'There are other people in the world worth knowing, besides Huguenots,' he would grumble, when little parties or outings were planned.

'Aye, mebbe so,' nodded William, 'but I prefer those that are familiar to me, lad.'

Ned took to slipping off in his free time so as to mingle with the students at Edinburgh University. His father would have been horrified to know that these young men were generally to be found in the public houses in closes off the High Street. Many a long and interesting conversation Ned had with his student friends when the light had faded enough to make work impossible. Many a long conversation turned into a drinking session.

So far he had been able to conceal his failing. He managed on the whole to get home in good enough condition and if he had a headache next morning, well, headaches were common enough among weavers, due to the rattle of the loom.

Once he had come home very late. Jenny, lying awake for him, had opened the door and after taking off his boots, helped him up the steep little staircase to his room. Next morning she had tried to get him up and dressed, but the after-effects of the whisky were so bad he could hardly raise his head.

That was the first time she actually lied for him. 'He had an accident yesterday evening,' she told her mother. 'That's why he was so late home, he had a fall in Moray Place – '

'A fall? Is he badly hurt? Should we call the doctor?' Her mother turned from the fire she was coaxing into life for the morning porridge.

'No, no, but he's cut his forehead.' Now the cuts and bruises were nicely explained. 'One of his college friends looked after him and saw him home when he felt better – '

'But a blow to the head, Jenny – that could be serious.'

Mrs Corvill hurried up to her son's room. He was sitting up in bed, looking in all conscience pale and ill. She pressed him back among his pillows, brought him a cold compress, and was only restrained from calling Dr Bethune by the fact that at ten o'clock Ned was visibly improving.

'A slight concussion,' she sighed to her husband, when he complained that his son was away from his loom in the weaving shed. 'One day away from work, William – surely you can allow him that?'

William was no slave driver though he worked hard himself and expected others to do the same. Besides, Jenny had no spinning to occupy her at the moment – she could take her brother's place.

The parents were too innocent to recognise the after-effects of a drinking bout. Moreover, it was the last thing they expected from a member of their family. And so Ned's secret was safe, and had been unsuspected for nearly two years.

The thought of having him as her escort for a two-day trip away from home worried Jenny. And all the more so when, naturally, her father handed the funds for the journey to Ned. He was the man of the party, the escort; he must look after the money. But luckily both parents came to see them off at the railway station, so the return tickets at least were safely bought.

But the rest had gone on drink. It was too good an opportunity to miss: two days away from home, away from the eyes of his parents.

That was why Jenny had had to leave her brother at Crathie village. He was too drunk to come any further.

Dismissed now by His Royal Highness, she was delivered to Captain Prentiss to escort to Aboyne. There was a mail train at just after midnight, and since the unpredictable weather had turned fine, the drive of twenty-seven miles might be neatly accomplished in time for her to catch it.

'Thank you, Your Royal Highness,' she said, with her best curtsey.

'I wish you a safe journey home,' he said in his Germanic English. 'When will the tartan be ready?'

'In about three weeks, sir.'

'I shall be gone by then, but Captain Prentiss, whom you have become acquainted with, will be here. Send the parcels direct to him. Prentiss, you will see the upholsterer gets the cloth for the bed furniture as soon as it is delivered?'

'Certainly, sir. In fact, I will go to Edinburgh to see all goes well with the weaving.'

'Excellent, excellent. Goodbye, Miss Corvill.'

It appeared that no special orders needed to be given: carriages were always at the ready for royal use. A four-wheeled dogcart, suitable for the Highland roads, was awaiting Captain Prentiss when they came out into the fresh clear evening.

He handed her up and took the reins. He gave her a smile, only faintly visible in the lights of the carriage.

'Ready?' She nodded, sparkling with delight at the thrill of riding in a vehicle of the royal household. 'Then it's hey for Aboyne?'

'Yes – no – we must pick up my brother in Crathie first.'

That was a blow. He'd forgotten about the sickly brother. He'd been looking forward to a flirtatious drive, perhaps a pause in some quiet spot under the stars, a few more of those delicious kisses. But with a brother along, and a Huguenot at that . . . The Prince's little homily about the Huguenots had surprised him – Miss Corvill hadn't struck him as particularly reserved or staid.

He drew up by the post office in Crathie, opposite the iron bridge. It was the most likely place to find him, the natural stopping place. But there was no one there.

I left him sheltering from the drizzle under the clump of birches . . .'

Unwilling, he got down. But as he was about to set off down the road to the birches, the door of the post office opened. Light streamed out from a lamp held high.

30

'Who's there?'

'I'm looking for a Mr Corvill – '

'Oh, aye, come along in, but we were expecting a Miss Corvill?'

'I'm here,' Jenny called, jumping down unaided. She ran round the dogcart and in at the door under the raised arm of the postmaster.

Her brother was lying along a bench inside the stone-floored office. His eyes were closed.

'Has he had an attack?' asked Bobby in alarm.

'Oh aye,' said the postmaster, pulling his sandy whiskers. 'He's been taken by a weakness in the legs.'

Good God, thought Bobby. So much for the sober industrious Huguenot.

Jenny was stooping over the inert figure, tugging at his shoulder. 'Ned! Ned, wake up! Come on, Ned, we're ready to go home. Oh, wake *up!*'

With blunt kindness the postmaster said, 'I wouldna fash yourself trying to rouse him. He'll not open his eyes till he's slept it off.'

'I'm . . . er . . . much obliged to you for looking after him,' Bobby said. 'Would you give me a hand to load him aboard?'

'Certainly. I took him in, the poor soul, because he was getting drookit by the rain, but I was getting worried whether anybody would take him off my hands this night.'

Between them they hefted up the body, carried him out, and laid him on the back seat. Jenny hovered around, trying to ensure that her brother wasn't bumped or bruised in transit. The postmaster brought out a small valise, which obviously held toilet articles and other necessaries for a journey.

Suitably rewarded, he backed off, with a little salute. 'Thank you, sir, and safe driving.'

'Thank *you*,' Jenny said with fervour, her blushes hidden as she was helped to her seat.

Bobby shook up the horses. They pulled away, the postmaster holding up his lamp to light them past the church on their way east to Aboyne.

'You mustn't think,' Jenny began, finding her tongue thick and clumsy, 'that my brother . . . my brother . . .'

'It's all right, I've seen drunk men before.'

31

'But he . . . he doesn't . . .'

Bobby shrugged. If she liked to believe he didn't drink, let her. It might even be true. He might have taken a dram to steady his nerves for the proposed encounter with royalty and, if he wasn't used to it, succumbed. But Bobby didn't think so.

They passed one or two carriages, country gentlemen heading home from evening engagements. Behind her, Jenny heard her brother stir. 'Ned? Are you awake?'

A muffled groan.

'Stop a moment, so that I can go over to the back seat and look after him, captain.'

'He's all right,' Bobby said. He didn't want to lose her company. It was only a few miles to Aboyne and he still hadn't had the chance to draw in at the roadside for a little romantic conversation.

But now the brother was awakening and her attention was totally taken up with him. Bobby cursed the fellow under his breath. He was sorry for him, of course – fellow-feeling told him how wretched he felt. All the same, he wished the third member of the party could have slept soundly until he was pushed on the train.

Ned dragged himself up to a sitting posture. He pulled off his felt hat, held his head. 'Is it night-time?' he quavered.

'Yes, dear, and we're on our way for the train home.' She twisted on her seat, put a hand on his cheek. He was very hot. Perhaps he'd caught a fever, sitting out in the rain under the birch trees. She should never have left him . . . Yet what else could she do? He'd been rolling as he walked, impossible to present at the gates of the castle. And she'd been unwilling to ask if there was an inn where he could sit – at an inn there was more drink to be bought.

The little town was asleep as they drove into it past the castle. Only at Aboyne station were there lights and movement.

Sighing, Bobby Prentiss drew up at the entrance, handed the reins to a porter, and helped Jenny down.

Ned Corvill sat on the bench on the dogcart like a lump.

'Come on, I'll give you a hand down.' Bobby held out an arm.

Ned wavered towards him. It was clear to see that his head hurt terribly, every movement jolting through it like a blow.

Gingerly he edged to the side of the cart, put his feet down, slithered to the footboard, and as gingerly down to the ground. The moment he was standing there, everything began to swing round him.

Bobby held him up. 'Got the tickets?'

He made a feeble gesture towards an inner pocket.

'Right. On we go.' He put an arm under his elbow and steered him through the entrance. At the barrier the night stationmaster – the senior porter – was examining tickets.

Jenny brought up the rear. 'When is the mail train due?' she asked the porter.

'She's signalled now, miss.'

'Thank you.'

Aboyne was the end of the line. The train was coming in with the engine pulling but would go out with the engine pushing.

They had forgotten the little carpet bag with the travel articles. 'I'll fetch it,' Bobby said, and sprinted back to the carriage. As he reached it, he heard the train stop with a clanking and surging of steam. He hurried back.

The porter was putting mail sacks aboard at a carriage towards the end of the train. Jenny was struggling to open a compartment door for her brother, who was leaning helplessly against the side of the stationary train.

The smell of steam coal was strong in the night air. Bobby watched Ned Corvill look wildly about him. In a flash he understood what was coming and rushed him along to the end of the platform. There he was heartily and disgustingly sick.

'There now,' Bobby said, when at last the boy straightened up. 'You feel a lot better, don't you?'

The only answer was a groan. They walked back to the carriage door with which Jenny was still struggling. 'Are you all right, Ned?' she asked, alarmed by his sickly pale face.

Bobby handed her her valise. Then he opened the door of the compartment, turned for Ned, and found him slowly subsiding onto the platform.

'Damnation.' He bent, put two hands under his armpits, heaved him up, and thrust him in. Ned stumbled forward and landed head first on the floor between the seats. His hat went backwards out of the door and onto the platform.

Bobby picked it up and threw it after him. Ned, clambering up, caught the hat against his chest, then leaned out, holding on to the door for support. A whistle blew, the train began to move.

'Wait!' cried Jenny. But the cry was lost in the jud-jud-jud of the piston wheel slowly turning.

Ned pulled on the door to get his balance. It closed on him. The train moved on, steam billowing as the engine went by. In the dimness of the platform lights Jenny could be seen running, picking up her skirts with one hand and trying to catch at a door handle with the other.

She tripped over the valise and sprawled headlong. Bobby rushed to help her up.

He gathered her into his arms. 'Are you all right?'

She was gazing past his shoulder, where the rear lights of the train to Aberdeen could be seen vanishing down the line.

She couldn't believe it. She stared in helpless incredulity. 'Oh no . . .'

'Are you hurt? Can you stand up?'

'Oh!' She gave an impatient push, and clambered to her feet unaided. 'I'm perfectly all right, but Ned . . .'

'Well, *he's* all right,' Bobby said, busying himself brushing mud from her skirt front. 'He's safely on his way to Aberdeen.'

'But I've missed the train!'

'Never mind. You can take the next one.'

'But Ned will be – '

'Never mind your brother. He's too busy nursing his sore head to worry about you. I should think he might snooze again until he gets to Aberdeen – do him the world of good.'

'Oh, captain . . .' He seemed so unconcerned. How could she explain to him that Ned would hardly know how to get himself on to the Edinburgh train at Aberdeen?

She glanced around her at the station. There was a bench. She moved towards it. 'Thank you for all your help, captain. I truly appreciate it. But you can leave me now, I'll just sit here and wait for the next train.'

'You will?' Bobby said.

She saw that he was suppressing a smile.

'I'll be perfectly all right,' she said, shivering as she sank on to the damp wooden bench.

'Perhaps I'd better wait with you. I hardly like to leave you here on your own.'

'Oh, it's perfectly safe here, I'm sure.'

'A little draughty, perhaps. Wouldn't you do better to wait at the hotel?'

'The hotel?'

'The Huntly Arms – it's just a little way up the main road.'

'But, I don't know . . . it scarcely seems worth it. And besides, I might miss the next train if I go any distance away.'

'I assure you, you can be brought from the hotel in plenty of time for the train.'

'Well, I must admit, I should like a cup of hot tea . . .'

'And I'm sure there will be no problem getting you a room.'

'A room?' She sat erect on the station bench. 'Why would I need a room?'

'Well, of course, you can always take a nap in the common room. But I feel it would be more comfortable to have a room so that you can be at ease.'

Understanding began to dawn. 'When is the next train?'

'Twenty minutes to eight tomorrow morning.'

'Oh.'

It knocked the breath out of her. She allowed him to put a hand under her elbow and lead her out of the station. The porter said, 'Goodnight, mam, goodnight, sir,' and seemed to be jingling keys.

Bobby was urging her aboard the dogcart when she stiffened and turned back. 'Sir, I haven't any money for a room. My brother has it all – and my train ticket . . .'

'Oh, stuff, I have plenty of money.'

'But I couldn't possibly allow . . .'

'Now, didn't His Royal Highness tell me to see you safely aboard the train? Naturally I'll pay the expense of – '

'No, no, sir, I can't permit – '

Bobby knew when to sidestep. 'Very well, Miss Jenny. Think of it as a loan. You can send me the money at Balmoral when you send the parcel of cloth.'

She hesitated. But it was perfectly in order to do so. Her father would willingly meet the extra expense and besides,

35

now that they had the commission to weave the Royal Stewart tartan, there would be money coming in, and more commissions would follow when people heard of it.

'Very well, Captain Prentiss – '

'Oh, do please call me Bobby. I feel we are such friends already, don't you?'

She agreed, but a voice inside warned her not to say so aloud. Instead she mounted on the seat of the dogcart, looking forward with interest to seeing the Huntly Arms Hotel.

She had rarely been in a hotel and then only to meet some business acquaintance or customer in the salon. She was pleased and flattered by the attention they received when they alighted at the big stone building. A groom hurried out to take the dogcart, greeting Bobby by name. The hotel night clerk looked up in welcome as they came in.

'Good evening, captain. A pleasure to see you again.'

'Good evening, Anstruther. This young lady has had the misfortune to miss the last train to Aberdeen. I wonder if you can provide her first with a pot of tea and a snack, and then with a comfortable bed for the night?'

'Surely, surely.' He came from behind the desk in his serge uniform. 'This way, there's a fire still in the drawing-room. Let me take your bag, madam. The weather's cleared, I gather – a fine night outside.' Talking assiduously, he led them into a room lit by one lamp turned low and a glowing fire.

He turned up the light, offered an armchair to Jenny, knelt to poke the fire. A flame appeared. He fed a little shovel of coal to it, then got up to ring a bell by the side of the fireplace.

A waiter appeared, yawning.

'Tea and toast for the lady and gentleman, Davie. Or perhaps you'd like something stronger, sir?'

Bobby was about to say yes, but then he recalled the staggering figure of Ned Corvill. Jenny wouldn't like anything to remind her of that. 'No, tea will suit me fine,' he said, 'and if you could find a slice of pie or something of the kind, I'm sure we could both do justice to it.'

'Certainly, sir. You heard, Davie.' He shooed the waiter away. 'I'll just go and get the porter to light the fires in the rooms. It's chill enough, is it not.'

When the food came Jenny discovered that for the first time

36

that day she was hungry. She ate with appetite, and drank two cups of hot tea. By that time she was beginning to feel somewhat dazed: fatigue was catching up with her.

'If you would call the clerk, Bobby, I think I should like to be shown to my room.'

'Of course.'

He rang the bell, Anstruther hurried in. 'If you'll just sign the register, sir, madam . . . You've your usual room, captain, and I've had your portmanteau brought up from the store room.'

Jenny turned to him, puzzled, as they began to mount the stairs. 'He said your portmanteau?'

'Yes, I keep a few things here just in case. Going back and forth as I do, between here and Edinburgh and London, it's good to be able to tidy up before travelling on.'

'I see.' It made good sense. She stifled a yawn. Anstruther escorted her to a door on the first landing. 'Here you are, Miss Corvill.' He put the key in the door, and opened it. She was shown into a room lit by a softly shaded lamp and with a newly-lit fire sparking and spitting in the hearth. The bed was turned down invitingly.

He handed her the key. 'You'll wish to be wakened in good time for the morning train?'

'Yes, please.'

'Hot water at the door at seven. Goodnight, Miss Corvill.'

Beyond him, as she went out, she saw Bobby Prentiss waiting. He smiled and called, 'Goodnight.' As she closed the door, she saw him head along the passage while Anstruther turned to go downstairs.

She had her valise, but it contained only a few articles: comb, washflannel and towel for herself, razor, hairbrush and clean stiff collar for Ned. They had slept in the night train from Edinburgh to Aberdeen on their way north and had intended to sleep in the train again on their way south. Extending the trip by staying in the luxurious surroundings of a hotel had never occurred to her.

As she began to undress, she found the sprig of white hoya in the top buttonhole of her bodice, wilting now, but still sweetly fragrant. *He* had plucked it for her. She took it out with gentle fingers, to put it under the pillow.

As she climbed into bed in her fine lawn chemise she was saying to herself: If we're going to do business with the likes of the royal family, we'll have to think about staying in hotels. It's agreeable . . .

She was very tired, but too strung up to sleep, especially in a strange bed. It was comfortable enough, far wider than her little cot at home and with softer pillows. The sheets, stiff with starch, smelt of laundry soap. The fire crackled and sighed as the coals shifted. The light from its dwindling flames danced on the ceiling.

What a day it had been. She had succeeded where all the rest of her family were sure she'd fail – she had seen Prince Albert, she had sold the Stewart tartan to the Royal Household. And she had been helped by such a handsome young man. So tall, so well groomed, so kind and well-mannered . . .

She turned over, gathering a pillow to hug in her arms. She found the sprig of hoya blossoms. Her fingers closed around it. He had been so helpful to her. And he had kissed her, among the strange plants. That had been wonderful. A strange, wild experience, like nothing she had ever known. Would such a thing ever happen again?

She became wide awake. She had heard a sound at the door. She sat up. In the red light from the fire she saw the door handle slowly turning.

She snatched the sheet up to her breast. Her heart leapt into her throat. She had forgotten – oh, she had not even thought of it – to lock the door.

It opened. Her breath died in her throat.

Someone stepped inside. She saw the firelight glint on strands of fair hair, smelt the familiar pomade. He moved forward.

'Jenny?'

She could distinguish his figure now. He was clad in a rich silk dressing-gown of figured black and gold. One hand was outstretched.

'Bobby,' she whispered, and caught his hand in hers.

'Ah, I knew you'd be awake,' he said, sitting on the side of the bed. He leaned over her. His head came down so that he blotted out the firelight.

She felt his lips on hers. She put her arm around his shoulders. She felt the pattern of the silk, she stroked it, felt the muscles underneath as he bent over her.

They were kissing, and he was close to her, body against body, only the flimsy lawn of her chemise and the thick silk of the dressing-gown in the way.

Soon even that was gone, and they were together in a closeness beyond anything she had ever imagined.

Chapter Three

The journey home was uneventful. But even had the train been attacked by wild Highlanders waving claymores, Jenny would scarcely have noticed.

Her mind and her heart were too full of other things.

Chief among these was the wonder and delight of being in love. Never in her wildest dreams had she imagined anything so alluring as the ecstasy of physical passion. And Bobby had been a good teacher. The first experience had wounded and frightened her. But he had held her close afterwards, soothing her and wiping away her tears, assuring her that it was always so for a woman, that he didn't blame her for being hurt, that he only loved her the more for it. She had scarcely dared to believe him, but she was sure that he knew everything, that he spoke the truth.

A little later, when the caresses with which he had soothed her were changing to something more, she had responded openly, willingly. And though she didn't experience the bliss that Bobby had found before he at last lowered himself to her side again, still there had been the beginnings of something that came after the initial eagerness.

They fell asleep in each other's arms. Then, very early, as the grey September dawn of the Highlands was beginning to outline the curtains at the window, he had wakened her by kisses and murmurings of love.

Half-asleep, half-awake, she turned to him, arms and legs wide, body soft to his mouth that seemed to touch every responsive curve and crease. She wound herself about him as he took her, answering his need with her own.

Splendour, joy, delight . . . 'A bundle of myrrh is my well-beloved unto me: he shall lie all night betwixt my breasts. My beloved is unto me as a cluster of camphire in the vineyards of Engedi . . .' Now at last she understood the Song of Solomon, that mysterious book of the Bible which the minister seemed so reluctant to discuss. Not about the heavenly love between God and the people of Israel, not about the union of Christ with his church, but about man and woman, body and body, physical love.

She felt herself colouring up as she thought of it. She turned up the collar of her mantelet in case the other passengers noticed. But it wasn't shame or remorse that made her blush, it was longing, physical desire to be with Bobby again.

He had bought her ticket and put her aboard the train without even so much as a kiss. He had shaken hands, stood back, given a slight salute. At her look of reproach he said in an undertone, 'Must be discreet, my darling. Staff from the castle might be about. Wouldn't do for HRH to hear of this.'

'Oh yes. I understand.' She leaned out of the open window. 'Shall I see you again?'

His smile reassured her. 'Of course. Have to oversee the production of that wonderful tartan cloth, don't I?'

'When, Bobby, when?'

'Soon as HRH leaves Balmoral – four days' time.'

'Our house, the weaving shed, it's down the brae at the west end of the town, by the Water of Leith. Anyone will direct you.'

'Leave it all to me, my dear.'

So she would see him soon. And by hook or by crook, she would find time to be with him alone somewhere. He would arrange it all – he was so clever, so experienced.

One thing above all – she must never let her parents know. It wasn't that she was ashamed or felt she had done anything wrong, simply that she knew they would be upset. She didn't want to be in discord with them over what had been the most wonderful thing in her life. She didn't want to hear them talking about wantonness or sin. How could it be a sin when it had seemed so right, so perfect? If God had not intended the human body to enjoy physical love, why had he created it with the powers to give and receive pleasure?

Her parents would say: only within the bounds of marriage.

Perhaps so. Perhaps she should have resisted Bobby's advances. She was certain if she had pushed him away or threatened to cry out, he would have left her room at once. That had been impossible for her to do. She had been lying there dreaming of him, longing for him. He had come like a dream made flesh. She couldn't believe she was wicked in having embraced the dream.

When she reached home, she was braced for all kinds of anxious accusations, and ready to lie her way out of it. Yes, she would lie: she found she had enough intent to deceive, enough hardihood, to do it. She found there was scarcely any need.

Ned's story was that he had been taken ill with a stomach upset at Crathie, that Jenny had gone to the castle without him and later sent him home while she returned to Balmoral in a further attempt to see the Prince Consort. It had never for a moment occurred to him that she had been successful.

Any gaps in his story had been passed over as due to his being too unwell to pay attention. Jenny supported this tale with enthusiasm, saying she had been asked to stay overnight at the castle.

'In Balmoral Castle?' gasped Mrs Corvill in awe. 'Under the same roof where the Queen has slept?'

'Aye, indeed – but only in one of the maid's rooms, of course.'

'What like of a room does a maid have in a castle?' wondered her mother.

Jenny was able to give a minute description of the attic room – the sprigged wallpaper, the white iron bedstead, the basin and ewer with a portrait of Old Balmoral on the side, the hand towel embroidered with 'VR'.

Enthralling. But even more enthralling was the news that she had an order for the Stewart tartan, that both her father and her brother must set it up on the looms at once and weave the pieces, each of fifty yards, one to fill the immediate order and one to be ready if extra were needed.

'But what if it's not wanted, child?' protested William.

'Och, father, do you think we'll have any trouble selling a piece of cloth that the Prince Consort has admired?'

'But it'll be wanted exclusively by the Royal Household,'

he said. 'They'll not want all and sundry having the same cloth as themselves.'

To be sure. She should have thought of that. 'Then we'll put it on display. There can be no harm in that. "As designed for Their Majesties" – wouldn't that be a good advertisement for us, eh?'

In the amazement and delight of her news, any doubts about her conduct were totally forgotten. She had done wonders – she, alone face to face with the husband of the reigning monarch, had spoken up for their work, had sold the cloth to the most prestigious customer in the land.

Even her father, usually alarmed at anything out of the ordinary, smiled and nodded. 'I'm well pleased. Yon's a fine tartan, it deserved a special fate. And I expect you asked for a fine price?'

She was startled. Not once had she thought to talk about money. But she recovered at once. 'It wasn't discussed, father. But if we ask for what's fair, you can be sure the Prince is not going to quibble.'

What she really meant was, Bobby will help me with all that.

She overestimated Bobby Prentiss's interest in cloth-weaving. When, five days later, he came to the Village of Dean ostensibly to see how matters were going, he gave only the most cursory glance at the work.

Truth to tell, he found it embarrassing and almost distasteful. The weaving shed attached to William Corvill's cottage wasn't an agreeable place. It was, in truth, a shed, with large windows so that good light could fall on the web. The floor was of stone. He didn't know enough to understand that this was the shed of a prosperous handloom weaver, that others had only earth floors, and no stool for the weaver to rest when he wished. Other weavers didn't have the fine standard bearing two paraffin lamps of the latest design, because other weavers had no call to work by artificial light – their work wasn't sufficiently in demand.

'Yes, yes, excellent, splendid,' he said, giving the cloth half a glance. 'May I pass on the news to the upholsterer that the cloth will soon be ready?'

'Certainly, sir, certainly.' William Corvill was trembling

43

with awe and eagerness before this handsome young gentleman in his fine morning suit. He was the richest-looking person William had ever encountered face to face. 'I'll put it on the train for Balmoral myself, in about two weeks time – '

'Good, good. You have a special label, no doubt, for urgent or special goods?'

'Er . . .'

'Yes, captain,' Jenny intervened. They had no special label – in fact, any labels were handwritten on pasted paper for each parcel. But for the Prince Consort's tartan, she would ensure that a special label was purchased. She had seen them in the stationer's shops. Better yet, she would have one specially printed. For by all the signs, they would be needing printed labels. The news of the personal interest of the Queen's husband had brought a flock of customers to the Corvills' cottage.

'We've had to put this new extra work out among some of our fellow-websters,' she explained to Bobby, when they were alone together that afternoon. 'My father scarcely knows whether he's on his head or his heels.'

Bobby wasn't paying attention to what she said. It was her bright laughing face that held his attention, the sparkling black eyes.

'Of course the tartans are to our own design. He supervises the work carefully. And the finishing is done by the Suchetts as usual. It's as if he'd made the cloth in his own shed – you understand?'

'Oh, don't let's talk about cloth-making, Jenny.'

'No, of course; that's of no interest to you, my love, you being no kind of a webster!' She smiled and took his hand. 'Oh, my world has totally changed since the moment you stepped up behind me among all the building implements outside the castle! I didn't think then that it was the least romantic, but now . . .'

'Yes, now?' he coaxed.

'I think it was the most wonderful good luck, that you were on duty that afternoon. Bobby, what if it had been that tall gaunt man – the Equerry-in-Chief?'

'He'd have had you escorted out of the grounds as fast as you could trot. But then, he's got no discrimination.' He enfolded her in his arms, dropping little kisses on top of her head. She snuggled against him adoringly.

'You know, even if I weren't so in love with you, I'd always be grateful to you because of what you've done for Ned.'

'For Ned?' He had difficulty for a moment placing Ned. Of course, the drunken brother whom he'd seen sitting solemnly at one of the looms this morning.

'He's going to the university! What do you think of that?'

'Good for him,' said Bobby, thinking that he'd been happy to miss that part of a gentleman's education by going straight into the army.

'You see, it's not just that we're going to make more money. We can afford now to take another weaver into father's shed in his place, and pay him a wage. One of the big problems of letting Ned go to college, you see, was always how my father could manage without him. We could perhaps *just* have managed the fees, but we couldn't manage without his earnings, nor could we afford to pay a substitute, so we'd have had to let the new man take a percentage of – '

She broke off. Bobby, instead of paying attention, was unbuttoning the front of her bodice. Blushing furiously, she caught his hands. 'Bobby – don't – '

'But my darling, what is it?'

'You mustn't . . . I mean, I can't . . . Not with the daylight streaming in . . .'

They were in an apartment leased to him by a friend who was off to spend the winter inspecting the antiquities of Egypt. The tall Georgian windows faced out south on to the handsome square, the afternoon light of a bright September day gleamed on gilt mirrors, satin chair covers, porcelain ornaments.

'Sweet girl! Between people who love each other as we do, there's no need for modesty.'

'But . . . it seems so shameless . . .'

'We have nothing to be ashamed of, my angel. We belong to each other, don't we?'

'Yes.'

'Then what we do is right and good.'

She allowed herself to be persuaded, the more so as his touch upon her breasts was making her shiver with the anticipation of pleasure. Between kisses, he undressed her and then

45

laughingly picked her up to carry her into the bedroom. There Mr McArthur's fine fourposter was awaiting them, the covers already thrown back to be the more ready. He laid her down among the white pillows.

She sat up, rosy with embarrassment yet full of a strange courage. 'No, she said, 'let me – it's only fair!' But she was so unaccustomed to the buttons and studs of a man's clothes that he couldn't wait. In a few moments they were together in the big bed, and the slanting light from the windows no longer perturbed Jenny Corvill.

His visits were what she lived for. Soon he was recalled from Balmoral to resume his duties at Buckingham Palace, and then their meetings were fewer. But he was good at suggesting reasons to the equerries' office for travelling north – arrangements to be made for some improvements in the royal apartments at Holyrood, or the hiring of a carriage-maker to refurbish the royal carriages used in the Highlands.

As for Jenny, it was easy enough to get away to meet him in the daytime. Her parents would have forbidden any unescorted outings at night, but it was quite usual for Jenny to walk about the city of Edinburgh on business for her father. Moreover, she could always say, if she were late home, that she'd been chatting with her brother.

Ned was now a student, though still living at home. He had wanted to take rooms near the colleges but Jenny hadn't given him her support in this. She was afraid that if he lived away from home he would drink far too much.

In this, she sometimes accused herself of double standards. If it was wrong for Ned to take drink, why was it right for her to take a lover? She would quieten her conscience by saying that it was totally different; she and Bobby loved each other, they made life wonderful for each other. Whereas the whisky injured Ned; took away his self-respect and was bad for his health.

If a voice within her whispered 'Hypocrite!' she stifled it. She would do all she could for Ned – help to make the money that kept him at university, reassure her parents when they worried about the way their cosy family life was changed with a stranger in their weaving shed.

And certainly the world of the Corvills was different now.

They had suddenly become all the rage. Cloth merchants sought them out, and were disappointed when William explained that even if he extended his business with all his Huguenot colleagues working for him at their looms, it was still impossible to produce cloth in the amounts they asked for.

Instead, he preferred to concentrate on special customers. Jenny had a great talent for designing plaids with all the rich colours of the old tartans. There was a vogue for tartans – genuine tartans and invented designs. Jenny would paint a new check on paper and then set up a sample on the loom. Her father would weave a yard or two. When it was finished and handled in the daylight, it looked 'authentic' – the tartan of some old clan.

Customers came not only from the surrounding area but from London, from abroad, even. The Empress of Russia sent a lady-in-waiting who happened to be in Britain visiting relatives. The Countess Velikilova looked through the pattern book that William kept in the cottage parlour, sipped tea out of his new china, and then asked to see what Jenny was currently working on.

Jenny led her to the weaving shed. On her father's loom was a tartan of which there was only as yet about twelve inches in existence. It was of a purplish-blue, with a black and a red over-check.

'But that is extremely beautiful!' exclaimed Madame Velikilova, her diamond earrings asparkle as she bent to study it. 'What tartan is that?'

'It's a variation of the Montgomery plaid, madame. The Montgomerys are a Lowland clan – their tartans are little known.' Newly invented, she might have said. There had been a Montgomery tartan known in Ulster, but here in Scotland Jenny had never seen it worn. Moreover, the tartan she'd heard described was not really the one she had just designed.

'You say it is a variation?'

'Exactly – it's not the true Montgomery. I think of calling it Langside – the last of the original Montgomerys was killed at the Battle of Langside nearly three hundred years ago.'

'How sad,' murmured the countess. 'Do you tell me that no one has bought this tartan as yet?'

'No one has even seen it, madame.'

'That is very pleasing. Her Imperial Majesty would prefer that if I order a dress length, it should be unique. If I order a length of this Langside, do you guarantee that no one else shall have it?'

William was about to utter an eager agreement. Jenny said smartly, 'Well, but, Your Excellency, that would be a big loss to us. This is a pretty tartan – I thought to sell it to ladies throughout the country.'

'No, no – Her Imperial Majesty would not be pleased at that.'

Jenny was inclined to do business with this Russian lady. The Crimean War was still going on, though the Russians were losing and the old iron-handed Tsar, Nicholas I, had just died. The Countess was lady-in-waiting to the new, young Tsarina. From what Bobby had told her, Jenny expected the new Tsar to give up the fighting in the Crimea very soon, in which case Britain and Russia would no longer be enemies and in a few weeks or months it would be possible to boast that the Corvills had sold cloth to an Empress as well as a Queen.

She let the Countess admire the cloth a while longer, promised to bring a piece to her hotel in a day or two when they had a length worth handling, and saw her to her carriage at the top of the steep hill above the Water of Leith.

Her father said, 'Why did you not agree at once to letting her have it exclusively for the Empress?'

'Because they've millions of money, the Russian royal family, and I want her to pay a good price for it.' She shrugged. 'Don't forget, if the war goes on, we won't want to be telling anybody we've sold goods to the enemy – '

'I never thought of that.'

'But, on the other hand, if the war ends soon – and I hear it may – then we can have the benefit of a very good price and a great achievement to add to the others.'

'You've a head on you, lass,' William said with puzzled admiration. 'I don't know where you get it from . . .'

Three days later Jenny took a finished sample of Langside tartan to the Douglas Hotel. The countess was even more attracted to it when she saw it folded against Jenny's arm. The bright March day picked up the soft colours admirably.

'I should like you to make twenty yards of this tartan for Her Imperial Majesty.'

'Certainly, madame. But if we are not to make any other lengths, we shall have to make a high charge for this one length.'

The countess never haggled over money. And besides, it was much more important to bring home to Her Imperial Majesty a piece of this suddenly so-fashionable cloth than to bother about a few guineas here or there. 'How much?' she said with a shrug.

Jenny calculated the realistic price which an exclusive merchant would charge. Then crossing her fingers behind her back, she doubled it and said, 'We should have to charge you twenty guineas the yard, madame. That's to say, four hundred guineas for a dress length.'

She held her breath. Twenty guineas a yard! If the woman had any sense, she'd throw Jenny out there and then.

But Countess Velikilova had no idea of costs. Her gowns were made, the bills came in, her husband paid, and that was that. 'Very well,' she murmured, nodding at her paid companion, an English lady who had the task of easing her path in every way. Mrs Simpkins duly made a note in the pocketbook she carried with her everywhere, and likewise noted the proposed date of delivery at their temporary London address.

Jenny went down the stairs to the lobby in high spirits. True, it was a pity to lose such a pretty tartan, just the kind the ladies would have loved for their autumn dresses and cloaks next winter. But to sell to an Empress!

Moreover, there was an additional and more important reason to be happy. Bobby was waiting for her in his rooms in Charlotte Square.

She rang the downstairs bell, then ran up the beautiful curving stone staircase. Bobby was awaiting her on the landing of the second floor, the door of the apartment open behind him. He took her inside, taking from her the parcel of sample cloth and throwing it on a chair.

49

'How is it that almost every time I meet you, you're carrying parcels around?'

'Oh, Bobby, it's wonderful to see you again! It's been such a long time! Almost a whole month since we met.'

'And you're even prettier than ever.' He tilted up her face to him. 'Come now, tell me what you've been up to. I can see you've just done something clever or special – you're all alight with it.'

'What do you think, Bobby! I've just sold some cloth to an Empress!'

'An Empress?' He laughed. 'Come, my pet, there are no Empresses in Edinburgh.'

'No, well, I mean, to one of her ladies-in-waiting – just imagine, the Russian Empress herself. She'll be wearing a gown made of Corvill cloth before long.'

'Never mind her, you're my empress,' Bobby told her. 'Come along in, I got Stephenson to make us some tea before he left.' Stephenson was the servant who went with the set of rooms. 'How long can you stay?'

'Oh, certainly until six o'clock – I'll just say that the Russian lady kept me waiting.'

'Little minx,' Bobby said in admiration.

He was really very fond of her. She flew to his arms like a joyous bird, which was always so very flattering, and she had proved an apt pupil in the art of love under his tutelage. However, he found her enthusiasm about business matters rather a bore and, to tell the truth, he wished she hadn't been mixed up in the weaving trade.

He was accustomed to boasting to his friends about 'My little German actress' or 'my little shop girl'. It hardly sounded right to talk about 'my little weaver' – there was something not very chic about it. But he was proud enough of Jenny to have told one or two cronies how much he enjoyed his trips to the cold and dismal northland.

As they sat together on the sofa with the tea tray in front of the bright fire Stephenson had kindled, he was looking forward to a very enjoyable afternoon. Jenny had taken off her bonnet and cloak, to reveal herself in a neat gown of blue and black check, with a blue silk edging. As she poured the second cup of tea, he began what had become a little tradition with them: untying the blue ribbon bow at her neck and unbuttoning the front of her gown, so that the white broderie edging of her camisole could be seen. The next move would be to slip his hand inside that crisp white linen, to fondle the warm curves underneath.

He had just moved closer to her on the sofa and was pushing her back against its headboard when an unexpected sound made him pause.

Someone was turning a key in the outer door.

God damn it, if Stephenson had come back for the tea tray at this inappropriate moment, he'd skin him alive.

Jenny too sat up. She hadn't heard the sound, but she saw that something had startled Bobby.

'What is it, darling?' she asked.

'I'll tell you what it is, *darling*,' said a harsh voice from the door of the drawing room, 'you have a visitor.'

Bobby had jumped to his feet. Jenny sat erect, fumbling together the edges of her bodice. 'Who . . . who on earth are you?' she faltered.

'Who did you expect?' said the very fashionable lady who was glaring at her with fury. 'I'm Mrs Robert Prentiss.'

Chapter Four

The world stood still. Her heart gave a great lurch and ceased to beat. The moment lasted for eternity.

Then Bobby's wife broke the spell with her loud, angry voice. 'Well? Aren't you going to introduce me to your friend, Bobby?'

'Laura,' he gasped.

'Yes, Laura! What am I doing here, you ask. Catching you with your latest trollop, that's what! You fool – did you think I couldn't read the signs?'

'Laura, you misunderstand – '

'Not I! I've seen you creeping off all sleek with expectation too often to make a mistake. This time I decided I'd meet the slut – '

'Laura, you're being very – '

'I'm not a slut,' Jenny said, her voice suddenly coming back in a broken whisper.

'By no means! A respectable daughter of the vicarage, no doubt. Or from a local convent.'

'I'm a weaver – '

'A weaver? A weaver? My God, Bobby, I thought you had more taste than to take up with a comman mill girl.'

'Now look here, Laura – '

'Oh, hold your tongue! And you, girl – do up your clothes, you look disgusting.'

Certainly it was no contest between them. Mrs Robert Prentiss was dressed in the height of fashion: a crinoline gown of figured heavy silk under a fur cape, a small bonnet trimmed with matching fur, a muff of fur and ruched black ribbon.

52

She had light brown hair exquisitely dressed in ringlets, and her hazel eyes were blazing with anger.

With trembling fingers Jenny buttoned her dress, tied the bow at the neck. She wanted to stand up, to be less at a disadvantage before this tall, elegant woman, but her knees were too weak to support her.

'You shouldn't have come here, Laura,' mumbled Bobby, standing hunched and wretched to one side. 'It's very . . . very unseemly.'

'I wouldn't have had to come here if you'd only behave decently! Why you have to sneak off to play the fool with pretty dolls – '

'You don't understand,' Jenny cried. She couldn't bear to hear this harsh voice smearing something that was beautiful. 'We love each other!'

Laura stared at her, her mouth coming open. 'What did she say?' she demanded, turning to her husband.

'Listen, Laura, it's not what you think – '

'We love each other,' Jenny repeated, her conviction giving strength to the words.

'Oh, do we?' Laura sneered. She glared at Bobby. 'Do we love each other, my dear? That's something new, at any rate. The others were in it for the money, I suppose.'

'The others?' Jenny said faintly.

Laura laughed; a hard, bitter sound. 'You didn't imagine you were the first, did you? I think you're the fourth, although there may be others I haven't known about. Oh, my poor child, my husband isn't one to be mean with his favours. He even bestows them on me, from time to time. But presumably you "love each other" so much that you don't care about his wife.'

Jenny was scarlet with shame and humiliation. 'I . . . I didn't know . . . he was married.'

How could she have been so foolish, so wickedly uncaring? She ought to have known – a man of twenty-nine, in the service of the royal family – of course he was married, the Queen and the Prince Consort preferrred to have family men about them.

But Bobby had never said a word that would raise such a thought, never given so much as a hint. He was great fun to listen to, with a store of anecdotes about royal circles and the work he did. He talked about himself a lot but the narration was always about something amusing that had happened, someone he had met, some foolish bureaucracy in the equerries' office.

But if the truth were told, they didn't meet to talk. They met to make love. And the thought made her cheeks burn with self-condemnation. She had not thought to ask if Bobby had a wife – and if she had, and he had told her about Laura, would it have made any difference?

He had taught her to know desire. While he was away she dreamed about him – but it was his touch, his caresses, that she remembered. The dreams always ended with the thought of herself in his arms again, his body moulded against hers, her soul taking wing as they reached their climax.

She turned to him now, willing him to speak up for her, for their love. Surely he must feel as she did? That ecstasy they had shared must mean as much to him as to her.

But no. Bobby was standing, hangdog, enduring until his wife's anger should have spent itself.

It was Laura who spoke into the pause. 'Well, now you know. And so you can just put on your bonnet and shawl and take yourself off back to your mill.'

'Don't talk to me like that! You can't order me about like a mere – '

'Like a servant? What else are you? A paid servant, to come and give my husband an hour's enjoyment – '

'How dare you! I've never been paid – '

'No?' Laura gave her husband a glance of contempt. 'Great heavens, you really are a cad, Bobby! You mean to say you've got this girl to bed without paying out a penny?'

'Don't!' Jenny cried. It came out a strangled sob. 'Don't say things like that! I love him, and he loves me!'

'Don't be silly. Bobby doesn't love anybody – except himself. Isn't that right, dear?'

'Oh, come on, now, Laura, you're being really rotten – '

'How mean and selfish of me. I apologise.' She nodded her head at Jenny. 'Get out. And don't come back.'

'I won't go!' Jenny cried. 'Bobby, tell her – '

'Tell me what? That you share a great love and you're

willing to give up everything for each other? What do you expect him to do – run off with you to France? Poor little idiot! Bobby isn't going to give up one iota of his comfort for the likes of you – '

'Laura . . . dear . . . I do wish you'd moderate your – '

'You feel some concern for her, do you?' His wife paused. 'Maybe there is something more between you than I imagined . . . But that doesn't make – '

'She's a nice child, Laura. She – '

'She's a hussy, and if she doesn't leave here this minute I'll go to the owner of the mill and get him to throw her out!'

'I don't work in a mill! My father is a master webster! How dare you talk to me as if I were nothing!'

'Hoity-toity! So your father is a master of something or other, is he? And he brought up his daughter to be a mistress – mistress of a double-dealing fool – '

'You're horrible,' Jenny exclaimed. 'You don't care what you say. No wonder Bobby goes to other women if you – '

Laura made a movement towards her. Bobby stepped between the two women, fearing literally that his wife would rend Jenny. He eyed her muff with alarm – she might even have a knife in there. She was capable of anything. Her temper was awesome.

'Now, now, Laura,' he soothed. 'Do try to calm down. You know you'll only give yourself the headache. And tomorrow you'll be in tears all day and sorry for what you've said.'

'No I won't! You're the one that'll be sorry!'

'I *am* sorry, Lolly, I really am. I never meant you to find out. I can't imagine how you come to be here in the first place.'

'I knew you were going to see her. It was all in the way you were smiling to yourself. And when you said you were going on official business to Edinburgh I knew I'd find you here at Robbie's place.' She gestured with a gloved hand towards the window. 'I've been sitting in a closed carriage across the square, watching the doorway. After *she* arrived I just gave you time to get comfortable with one another before I got the servant to let me in.'

By making her explain herself, Bobby had brought some

calm to the situation. Laura's anger was ebbing a little, but not her determination to deal with the affaire.

'You,' she said, turning with a sweep of her crinoline towards Jenny, 'take yourself off.'

Jenny wasn't even looking at her. Her gaze was on Bobby. 'Bobby, explain to her – '

'What is there to explain, girl? He's a married man who likes to philander. The more fool you not to make any money out of him.'

'Bobby, don't let her spoil it like this – '

'I'll do worse than that. I'll put you out of a job, I'll see you never find anyone to take you on again – '

'Now, now, Lolly, there's no need for all this. Just let's sort it out and clear it away – '

'Clear it away?' Jenny echoed. 'End it between us, you mean? Just because she – '

'I suppose you have some sort of reputation to preserve, haven't you? If your father is a man of some worth, as you seem to imply? You'd better get out of this as fast as you can, or I'll make your name mud – '

All at once Jenny had had enough. 'Be quiet!' she said.

'What?' Laura Prentiss was astounded.

'Be quiet! You come here and scream and shout and behave as if you were the Empress of Everywhere! Be quiet and behave like a decent woman.'

'How dare you – '

'Oh, I dare!' Strength and determination had come into Jenny's spirit. Taken by surprise at first, weighted down by guilt and shame, she had been utterly at a disadvantage. Moreover, her belief that Bobby loved her and would save her from this termagant had made her weak.

But now she was strong. She saw that Bobby had deserted her. His love, if he had felt any, wasn't proof against the righteous anger of his lawful wife. Very well, she would fight her own fight.

And she would deal hardly with this woman who had wrecked her dream and, in doing so, had tried to grind her into the dust.

'First of all, we'll have everything out in the open,' Jenny said. 'I didn't know Bobby was married. He never mentioned you.'

'And I'm sure you took care never to ask him!'

'It never occurred to me – '

'The more fool you.'

'I agree. I think I've been a fool from first to last. But not any more. I believed Bobby loved me and for that reason I was happy' – her voice trembled momentarily, but she recovered – 'I was happy just to exist so that I could come to him when he wanted me. Now I understand I was deceiving myself. I blame myself, but if you think I am going to let *you* blame me – threaten me – you're mistaken.'

Laura was frowning at her in perplexity. 'You don't speak like a mill girl . . .'

'What I am is neither here nor there. What I can do is much more to the point. You threatened me. Let me return the favour. I threaten you.'

Laura stared.

Bobby said, 'Oh, now, Jenny . . .'

Jenny held up her hand. 'Don't say anything to me, Captain Prentiss. If you were going to say I ought to let your wife escape scot free after the things she's said to me, save your breath.'

'But Jenny – '

'You made a fool of me!' she burst out. 'You took me like a silly little pigeon you saw in the sights of your gun! And your wife is just as bad – she thinks that because I fell in love with you I must be a slut or a fool. Well, I'm neither.'

'I think, young woman, you had better guard your tongue. Otherwise – '

'Otherwise, what? You'll hound me out of work, you'll turn my friends against me? But you, of course, will take the train back to your fine friends in London and go on just as you did before, and your husband will pretend to be sorry and it will all be forgotten.' Jenny shook her head with emphasis. 'Oh, no. I can speak my mind too, you see. I can make things known to friends, I can say a word in the right ear so that someone else's job might be in danger.'

Laura looked her husband. 'What does she mean? Is she mad?'

To her surprise he wasn't making reassuring gestures or giving a little smile of tolerance. Instead he was looking almost scared. 'She's talking about putting my career in danger,' he groaned.

'Your career? How could a common creature like this endanger – '

'She's met the Prince,' said Bobby. 'He took an interest in her. She could – she just *could* – get his attention.'

'Don't have any doubts on that score, Captain. I am, after all, a little Huguenot girl with whom His Highness discussed religion – remember?'

'Oh, lord,' moaned the captain.

'Met the Prince? What do you mean?' Laura asked sharply. 'How could such a girl as this meet the Prince?'

'It's too complicated to explain – '

'All you need to know,' Jenny interrupted, facing the other woman with cold antagonism, 'is that I can threaten just as harshly as you. I can have your husband dismissed his post – '

'What nonsense! You vain little liar – '

'Laura, for God's sake! Don't speak to her like that! Can't you see the harm you're doing?'

'No, she can't see. She's too blinded by her own self-importance.' Jenny pointed at her. 'Look at her – just because she has money and position she thinks she can come here and – '

'Listen, Jenny, you have to forgive her. She's angry and upset – '

'Don't *plead* with that creature!' Laura stormed. 'Tell her to get out – '

'I shall go,' said Jenny, 'when I'm ready. I at least was invited here by your precious husband. He certainly didn't want you to come.'

'Why, you – '

'Jenny, Jenny,' begged Captain Prentiss. 'I understand you're angry, I understand you feel I've let you down – '

'How can you take her side?' his wife broke in. 'She's a wicked, immoral slut and as if that isn't bad enough she invents stories about the Prince Consort – '

'It isn't invention, Mrs Prentiss. You're going to find that out. I'm going to write to the palace this very evening, to tell His Highness the kind of man he has on his personal staff – '

58

'No, Jenny! No, please!'

Laura stared from one to the other. She saw the angry determination on the girl's face and the rank fear on her husband's.

'She could really do this?' she said, on an indrawn breath.

'She could indeed, and be listened to!'

'It would be her word against yours.'

'True enough, Mrs Prentiss. But my story would be very convincing and very damning. What do you think of this? Your husband took me straight from a conversation with the Prince Consort at Balmoral to an inn at Aboyne, where he seduced me – '

'No – '

'It's true,' Jenny said cruelly. 'What's more he arranged things so that my brother, who was my escort and protector, went on the train to Aberdeen and left me at his mercy.'

'No, good God!'

'It frightens you? It ought to! Now you know what it's like, don't you?'

Laura pulled herself together. She closed her gaping mouth, straightened her shoulders. 'What do you want, then? Money, I suppose. How much?'

Until that moment Jenny's only impulse had been to strike back at Laura Prentiss for the contempt with which she'd been treated. She wanted only to see the other woman brought to a standstill, made to understand she wasn't dealing with a nobody.

Money? She didn't want money.

And yet . . .

Why should Captain Prentiss and his shrewish wife walk away from the affair with only a bad scare? Bobby had wounded Jenny deeply, by his cowardice and his lack of concern for her. Love . . . Well, she'd been a fool to think he loved her, she understood that now. So he had deceived her, made a fool of her, treated her just as his wife described – as a slut, a prostitute.

Such women were paid for their trouble. It seemed Bobby's other lovers had been paid. Why should she fail to profit, even if only financially, from their liaison? There was nothing else worth saving from the wreck.

She said to Mrs Prentiss, 'I should expect to be well rewarded for my silence.'

'Jenny!' Bobby gasped.

She glanced at him. He looked stricken. She knew he was shocked by the thought that she might take money. He knew her as generous in the deepest sense, giving herself without stint. For him that had been the greatest charm of the affair – the fact that she expected nothing but his love.

'How much?' Laura repeated. 'A hundred pounds?'

'A hundred!' said Jenny. 'For the hurt I've suffered, for the things you've said, and for keeping my silence with the palace – a paltry hundred?'

'Two?' said Laura. 'Two hundred.'

Only yesterday Jenny would have thought two hundred pounds a very large sum. But the negligence with which the Countess Velikilova had agreed to the cost of the dress length had taught her something. Sums that seemed huge to hard-working tradesmen were nothing at all to the rich.

'I'll take five hundred pounds,' she said, in a very calm, cool tone.

'Jenny, what's got into you?' Bobby implored, making a move almost as if he would take her arm.

'Stay away from that girl!' blazed his wife. 'You weak, stupid fool! Haven't you done enough?' She was thinking of the years she had helped him with his career, the boring hours at Court listening to German music or the little lectures of the Prince. She thought of the money they had spent on clothes and carriages and entertaining.

Her sights had been set on seeing Bobby at last made a Viceroy – or at least, on being herself a Vicereine. She had pictured herself in gowns of the finest satin, receiving the homage of Indian princes in jewelled turbans, mounting howdahs decked with gold, entering palaces with lapis-lazuli domes.

But one breath of scandal, one whisper that her husband's morals were suspect, and he would be closed out by the royal family. Victoria and Albert were sternly upright. They might extend Christian charity to those who had 'fallen', but they would never employ them in high office.

And then, when all was said and done, she loved him. He

had married her for her fortune, she knew that – but he had taught her to love him, to need him physically.

So . . . It was going to cost hard cash to preserve their life. And she could see it was no use trying to haggle with this hard little girl. Besides, it was beneath her dignity. And after all, what was five hundred pounds compared with the money already poured out to get Bobby this far?

'Very well,' she said. 'I will send you a banker's draft. Give me your address.'

Jenny's mind raced. A letter, a banker's draft . . . it would cause comment in their household. The passing of it through the bank account of William Corvill and Son presented no problem; she'd had the keeping of the books since she was fifteen and her father scarcely glanced at them. But a letter . . . her father, as head of the house, opened all correspondence. 'I'll have cash,' she said.

'Cash!'

'Five hundred golden sovereigns. And I'll have them now.'

'But . . . but . . . gracious heavens, girl, no one carries that sort of money about.'

Jenny smiled. 'There's a bank on the corner of the square,' she pointed out. 'I'm sure Captain Prentiss, a junior equerry of the Royal Household, would have no difficulty getting cash against an order on his own bank.'

'But – '

'I'll wait,' Jenny said. The tea tray with its silver service still sat on the little table before the fire. 'A cup of tea?' she inquired, taking up the cold teapot.

Laura almost ran to the door. 'Get her her money!' she cried to Bobby as she wrenched it open. 'Pay her and get rid of her! I'll never forgive you, Bobby, for submitting me to this humiliation.'

The door crashed shut behind her. There was a silence.

Then Bobby came to sit beside her on the sofa. 'Jenny,' he said, 'you don't really mean all this.'

He put out a hand as if to take hers.

'Don't touch me,' she said.

'Jenny!'

'Go and get the money.'

'But . . . but . . . you don't really want it?'

61

She drew a deep breath. 'What I really want is beyond you to give. So I'll take the money instead.'

'But it's so unlike you – '

She got up quickly, to put distance between them. She couldn't bear to have him near, to smell the familiar and once loved pomade he put on his hair, the scent of his shaving soap, the savour of sandalwood that always seemed to linger about his body.

'You don't know me,' she said. 'You never bothered to get to know me. So go and fetch the money, and let's be quit of one another.'

He picked up hat and gloves and went out without looking back. Twenty long minutes later he returned bearing a small chamois leather pouch which chinked.

'Five hundred gold sovereigns,' he said angrily. 'I hope they make you happy.'

She took them without a word. As she picked up her cloak he said, struck by sudden alarm, 'Jenny, you'll keep your word? You won't say anything to the Palace?'

'I never want to speak of you or hear of you again,' was her bitter reply.

Late that night, Millicent Corvill was awakened by small sounds downstairs in the cottage. She was sure as she woke that it was her beloved Ned, coming home late. With a shawl over her shoulders, she went quickly downstairs to offer a hot drink, soup, whatever he might need.

Even as she went down the steep staircase she knew it couldn't be Ned. The sounds had been of someone opening the dampers on the kitchen range, to bring the fire to life. Ned had no more idea how to handle the controls of the range than fly – he had never in his life had to lift a finger in the house.

And as her husband was sound asleep in their bed, it must be Jenny. But what could Jenny be doing, downstairs at this time of night?

Her daughter was sitting in the wooden armchair by the hearth. She was in her nightgown with her dressing-gown thrown around her. She was curled up in the chair, her head supported on her hand. In the low red light from the fire it was possible to see that she was staring into its depths but not to distinguish the glisten of tears.

'Gracious lord, lassie,' exclaimed Millicent, though in a loud whisper so as not to disturb the sleeping menfolk. 'What are you doing out of bed?'

With reluctance Jenny stirred. 'I couldn't sleep, mother.'

'Are you ill? Have you the cramps?'

'No, nothing like that. I just couldn't sleep.' And couldn't stay in bed: restless, angry, full of pent-up energy caused by reaction to the scenes of the day.

A common mill girl. The words stung and rankled. Though they were untrue in every sense, the reasoning behind them had foundation.

Compared with Laura Prentiss she was a nothing. Proud though she might be of her father's abilities, of her own talents as designer, of a brother at the university, she knew she had no worth in the eyes of Bobby's wife.

It had never perturbed her hitherto. The Corvills were having success enough, she had thought.

But now pride and something that might be ambition were gnawing at her. She had tossed and turned for hours before finally rising to steal downstairs, to pace the stone-floored kitchen until at last she had felt chilly enough to rouse the fire.

'Surely you should be getting your sleep, child. You're so busy all the while, and today you've been out and about and done so well . . .'

'Have I done well, mother?'

'What a question! Four hundred guineas from the Russian lady!' Mrs Corvill took up the poker, gave the embers a little stir. 'Will I make you a cup of tea? Or a hot drink with the raspberry cordial?'

Jenny shook her head. 'What will we do with the money, mother?' she demanded.

'What?'

'How shall we use it?'

'Use it?'

'Father will tell me to give it to the bankers, to have it entered in their ledgers to our account. But what then?'

Mrs Corvill had no idea. Moreover, the trend of the conversation worried her. It sounded so strange, so impatient. Her daughter's mind was clearly full of financial concerns, and Mrs Corvill lived in dread that one of her children would, through excessive use of their minds, develop the mysterious illness called brain fever. What exactly it was, she didn't know. But clever people often succumbed to it, so she heard.

'You shouldn't worry your head on that,' she scolded gently. 'It's not fitting. Your father is the one to deal with money matters.'

'Really?' Jenny said in a tone her mother had never heard from her before. It sounded almost like disdain. 'The only way he knows to deal with money is to earn it. Once earned, he never uses it.'

'Of course he uses it. What do you think we live on, but the money he earns?'

'He earns much more than a mere livelihood. There's money now in the bank, and there'll be more when we get the price of the dress piece for the Russian lady. There'll be a lot of money, mother. And it just sits there in the bank, doing nothing.'

Mrs Corvill made a great mental effort. 'Doesn't it . . . doesn't it earn interest?'

'Oh, interest! Two-and-a-half per cent! We could do far better than that.'

'Could we?' She didn't want to talk about it. She had no idea what two-and-a-half per cent meant. 'I think I'll make a cup of cocoa,' she said.

'Mother!' But Jenny bit back her impatience. Cocoa and toast, tea and biscuits, beef broth and thin gruel – these had been the remedies for every ailment, the responses to every crisis in the Corvill family.

Millicent took a saucepan from a hook, poured in milk from an earthenware jug, and moved towards the range.

'What would you say if I told you we ought to move?' Jenny demanded.

Her mother started, so that the milk in a tidal wave escaped from the pan to make a splash on the hooked rug. 'Move? Leave the Dean Village?'

'Leave Edinburgh.'

To ward off the words, Millicent went to fetch a cloth. She

mopped at the stain on the rug. Then she rinsed the cloth, hung it on its accustomed hook, and poured more milk into the saucepan. 'There won't be enough for breakfast,' she lamented. 'I'll have to go out to Wilson's Dairy at six.'

'We should move to the Borders,' Jenny said, following her own line of reasoning. 'That's where all the fine woollens are being made these days. We should take a mill, or part of a mill – '

'Jenny!' her mother cried, forced at last to take heed. 'You're over-excited. It's all this talking to foreign ladies and – '

'It's the next logical step. We're getting far too much work to handle ourselves – '

'But your father factors it out.'

'It'll soon be too much to do on handlooms, even if he employs every webster he knows. Besides, it's so inefficient, trotting up and down the village supervising what they're doing. Either we have to get them all together in one place and go over to water power – which would cost the earth – or we have to move somewhere else, where the power and the accommodation already exist.'

'No,' said her mother. 'No, Jenny, don't talk like this.'

'At the moment we buy our yarn as we need it and so far we've done well enough, the dyeing has been good and we've always got what we wanted. But we ought to have control of the dyeing, we ought to have control of the spinning to ensure the thread's fine enough. And as to the finishing afterwards . . .' She nodded to herself. 'We've been lucky so far, Meldwick's been able to take every piece and finish to a high standard. But the time's coming when we'll have to go to a second finisher. And who could do it well enough to please us?'

'That's for your father to say.'

'Besides, we ought to do our own finishing. We ought to have it all in our hands, from start to finish. That way we could *plan*, do you understand, mother?'

'No,' said Millicent faintly. She snatched the saucepan off the range as the milk hissed up in a slow boil. She realised, to her consternation, that she'd forgotten to mix the cocoa in the cups. She felt frightened, at a loss.

65

'It's time the Corvills were mill owners, mother. What do you think?'

Millicent gasped, and burst into tears. 'I think you're mad!'

That was the reaction of Jenny's father when she put the plan to him after breakfast.

'Move? Where to?'

'To the Borders.'

'But that would cost a fortune – '

'No, if you look in the newspaper you'll see that there are mills to let – '

'Don't talk nonsense!'

'It's not nonsense. It's time we thought about the future. We have so much work – '

'God will look after the future, my lass,' he told her with some sternness. 'It's not for us to question His intentions.'

'His intentions for us are quite clear,' Jenny riposted. 'He's given us this talent to make fine cloth, and we must use it.'

William was struck. The parable of the talents . . . Could it be true that they were meant to grow into a mill-owning firm, that God, who looked with approval on those who exerted themselves in the sphere in which it had pleased Him to place them, wanted them to move on?

Mrs Corvill was terrified by the idea and called in her son to support her. To her dismay, Ned was on Jenny's side in the days of discussion that followed.

'In this life you either go forward or you go back,' he said. 'You can't stand still.'

Since he was a scholar, taking philosophy at the university, no one dared argue with him. That he had his own reasons for wanting the family business to expand, his parents didn't guess.

Ned was enjoying life as a student. He was actually drinking less because there seemed fewer frustrations in his world. But one had proved inescapable.

In matters of intellect there was a great democracy at the university. But when it came to making friends and belonging to groups, some were accepted and some were not. And Ned had found that to some, he was not acceptable.

The son of the poorest country minister would be welcomed to the social round. A lawyer's son could be invited to parties in Charlotte Square. But the son of a mere webster could never be a gentleman.

That apart, there was the humiliation of coming home to the cottage and its clacking loom-shed. He couldn't invite friends here. And in the Christmas vacation his father had actually expected him to sit to his loom again. Impossible!

Ned threw his weight behind Jenny's plan. As to the actual financial investment, that was up to her. She said they had the money or could borrow if need be. She had put the five hundred gold sovereigns in the bank, together with the draft for four hundred guineas from the Countess Velikilova and other monies that fell due on quarter day. No one thought to question the bank balance, which was very healthy.

'We have the money,' she said, at the end of one of the long arguments that seemed to dominate their lives these days. 'We have the skills, we have the reputation, we have royal patronage, we have a great future before us. All we need is the courage.'

There was a long silence round their kitchen table. Mrs Corvill picked at the edge of her apron. Ned and Jenny looked at their father.

'Very well,' he said at last. 'You can look in the newspapers for the agents of property in the Borders.'

Chapter Five

This was a time when many men were making the step from self-employment to the employment of others. Engineers who had built or mended machines for factories hired others to build them, navvies who had helped construct the railways got contracts from the railway owners to supervise the building of new lines.

In the cloth trade, it was usually the fullers and dyers who organised a factory. Fullers were the men who finished woollen cloth after it was woven, thickening and shrinking it to the requirements of the cloth merchant. Dyers sometimes handled the woven cloth, sometimes the spun yarn.

Their work needed premises big enough for dye vats and the machinery invented for the finishing, the fulling stocks. In the area known as the Scottish Borders, the buildings also housed the new water-driven weaving looms. The woollen industry needed water for power but, almost more importantly, for the dyeing and cleaning and processing of the cloth. Pure water, soft water – that was the great need, so that the dyes shouldn't be altered by lime or other elements, so that nothing should harm the fine wool fibres.

Along the rivers of the Borders, woollen mills had sprung up. Some of the rivers were tributaries of the river Tweed. And by a happy accident a name had been invented for the cloth made there.

Woollen cloth sent to London merchants was referred to in the invoices as 'tweel' – the Scottish form of the word twill, referring to the manner in which it was woven. Invoices were, of course, hand-written, copper-plate.

But one invoice clerk's writing wasn't copper-plate enough,

as it happened. The merchant read 'tweel' as 'tweed', took it to mean the cloth was specific to the area where the river ran, and the name of the fabric was invented. Tweed: the handsome, hardwearing, exclusive all-wool cloth made in Scotland.

Jenny knew the story. It had happened a few years before she was born and had been part of her upbringing. Her father had made tweed for customers who 'bespoke' it, but what he loved most was to make the plaid, the tartan of the clans, which called out all his artistry as a weaver.

In finding premises for their new venture, Jenny had to bear in mind that they would need a master dyer. He would be given charge of a dye-room capable of producing subtle colours. It was almost more important to find this man than to find the building.

The agent met her at the railway station of Galashiels. 'Good morning, Miss Corvill,' he said, politeness demanding that he greet the lady first. But he imagined that the head of the firm would be the gentleman of the party, and to him he turned with his hand outstretched. 'Good morning and welcome to Galashiels, Mr Corvill.'

He was surprised by the youth of the pair. He knew something of the firm of Corvill and Son, for there had been reports in the newspapers about their success with the Stewart tartan and others of their own design. The inhabitants of Galashiels took an avid interest in anything to do with the promotion of the sale of cloth. He had supposed that William Corvill was a middle-aged man. A moment's thought suggested that this was 'and Son'.

'Your father?' Mr Kennet said, glancing at the train as the porters slammed doors in preparation for departure.

'My father has given us full powers,' said the young lady, moving towards the exit. 'You've taken rooms for us at the hotel?'

'Certainly, Miss Corvill . . . er . . . The Abbotsford Inn, directly across from the station. If you'll walk this way.'

It was a fine morning in the first week of June. The cobblestones of the station yard glistened from an earlier shower. At the goods entrance a wagon was drawn up, the tarpaulin frame cover painted neatly with the name 'Buckie's Mills'. The heavy horses had their noses in feedbags, the wagoner and his mate were lounging against the wheels, awaiting a goods train that would bring in bales of wool from the stapler's warehouse.

A station porter came behind Jenny and Ned carrying their portmanteaux. A vast difference, thought Jenny to herself, from the trip to Balmoral, when she and Ned had been under instructions to save money at every turn. On that occasion – only ten months ago – they had had a few articles in a small carpet bag. They had slept in the train to save on hotel bills.

The Abbotsford Inn was more used to commercial travellers than the pair who now presented themselves under the escort of the lawyer. The young lady knew she was being inspected by the manager's wife, but felt no qualms. Black and blue checked silk carriage dress, matching cape, straw bonnet with pink and blue flowers, fine kid gloves, tiny leather boots peeping from beneath the flounces of the skirt – she had chosen her outfit to impress two facts: that she had money and that she wasn't a flibbertigibbet.

She had supervised Ned's clothes also. He was always rather careless, but his jacket was of a very fine cloth woven by the family, and his trousers were the very latest navy and brown plaid. His black silk top hat sat rather far back on his untidy brown hair, but that apart, he looked tolerably like a man of business.

Jenny's father had declined to come. He hated travel, was afraid of steam trains, and had no wish to be involved in financial chat with Mr Kennet. 'I'll rely on your views,' he said, as he waved them off at Edinburgh station. 'You've the business head, Jenny, and Ned has the training.'

If both Ned and Jenny thought privately that the study of philosophy was poor training for renting a woollen mill, they kept the thought to themselves. Both were eager to succeed in their enterprise.

After a short pause while they tidied themselves and were offered refreshments, they set off in Mr Kennet's carriage to inspect the mill premises on offer. There were two, both on what was known as the Mill Lead. The river, the Gala Water, had been diverted to provide power to turn the machinery of the mills, each of which was named by Kennet as they drove by.

'Leitch's, Brown's, William Fairgrieve . . . Fairgrieve has

the main part of the building, William Gray has the northern
extension, but Fairgrieve's brother has the mill against the
Cuddie Green, that's yon open space. Beyond that – do you
see the chimneys, sir? – that's Stirling's, but they've a problem
with the water supply there, it's a wee bit far from the Lead.'

Jenny had no objections to the lawyer's addressing his
remarks to her brother. He probably took it for granted that
she acted as amanuensis or note-taker to the menfolk. She
knew that Ned would acquit himself well enough because he
was interested, for his own reasons, in seeing the family translate itself to a more important sphere. So long as he asked the
right questions and got reasonable answers, she was content
to remain in the background.

The mill Mr Kennet wished them to lease was a dark, rather
dreary place, built like a house only taller, three storeys high
with small, inadequate windows. Ned exchanged a glance with
his sister. 'This looks very inefficient, Mr Kennet.'

'Not at all, sir. I assure you it's been a successful mill, the
owner's product simply went out of fashion.'

'Shawls, I suppose,' said Jenny.

'Why, yes. Ah, the ladies,' Mr Kennet said with arch
approval. 'They know all about such things. Yes, the vogue
for shawls began to go out some seven or eight years ago,
although Ballantyne's continued to do quite well with them
until, I believe, the last two or three.' He smiled at Jenny.
'You young ladies like a shaped coat or jacket these days. I
remember my mother . . . the dear soul had four or five
shawls, and one heavy cloak, not a single coat.'

They had got out of the carriage and were being ushered
towards the mill. Jenny put a restraining hand under Ned's
elbow. He paused. 'I think we needn't go in, sir,' he said.

'But, I assure you, it's a fine sturdy building – some looms
still in place which you could purchase at a bargain – '

'It's badly designed for the flow of work,' said Ned. 'And
it's too dark.'

'Oh, as to the dark, you'll find employees have more sense
than to complain of that – '

Jenny said, 'My brother and I are websters, our father too.
Good light is needed not only for good work but for good
humour.'

71

'Good humour? But, my dear Miss Corvill, the *humour* of employees is surely not to be considered?'

Jenny thought otherwise. She contented herself with turning back to the carriage and waiting to be helped up. Mr Kennet followed, shaking his head to himself. Foolish girl! Why had Mr Corvill brought her with him?

The next site was much better. It was a large mill of four storeys with a separate stair tower peaked by a bell and a clock. The bell was to summon the workers and to ring the hour of going home. The clock was to note their lateness and ensure money was docked.

The water from the Mill Lead was pouring through the channels. From the building came the unmistakeable sound of the power loom at work. A cart was pulling away from the loading yard.

Ned was taken aback. He was about to say, 'You're offering us a going concern?' but Jenny spoke first to prevent the blunder which would have revealed not only his inexperience but his naivete.

'How much of this is to let?'

'At present you can have four carding sets if you wish, ma'am, with ancillary processes, and more should you need to expand.'

'With whom should we be sharing?'

'The other sets are in operation under the firm of Begg & Hailes, a very respectable and reliable company, but not in any way in competition with your father's goods. They make plain cloth, a very good cloth, for covert coats and carriage capes, outdoor cloth, you understand me.'

Mr Kennet found himself addressing Miss Corvill without even being aware he had sensed her importance. He watched her as they were welcomed at the door of the entrance hall by the manager.

'Miss Corvill and Mr Corvill, may I present Mr Gaines.'

Greetings were exchanged. They had all to speak a little louder because the sound of the looms was already growing although they had not entered the main works. Here in the hall was the desk of the chief clerk, who took and booked orders and received prospective customers. His domain was as far as possible from the wool-shed and the smelly scouring and drying department.

'We'll go straight to the carding engines, if that will suit you,' Gaines said. He was an elderly man, sober-suited. 'Mind these steps, ma'am.' He was looking at Jenny from under bushy brows. What did Kennet think he was up to, bringing a lady in all her finery into the dust and noise of a weaving shed?

They bypassed sets in action. Each set consisted of four machines, the scribbler, the second carder, the piecing machine and the slubbing billy. Jenny had seen them at work before, in mills she had visited in the Edinburgh area, but she was still overawed by the speed and dexterity with which the endless apron of raw wool was turned into a rope that became in the end a spread of fine filaments to be spun into yarn.

The far side of the big room had four carding sets standing silent. 'Mr Begg thinks of bringing in the new "condensers",' Gaines explained. 'They'll replace the piecing and the billy. It's faster and, if you've seen it, sir, you'll agree it gives a more even thread.'

'Yes,' said Ned, who had never seen a condenser and would not have recognised one if he had.

The tour of the premises took two hours. The amount of walking was tiring, since it involved mounting to upper floors for the actual making of the cloth, the fulling, the cropping, and the pressing. The noise was a fatigue in itself.

The girls tending the machines eyed them as they walked by or paused. Ned smiled at one or two, but they kept themselves from acknowledging him. He was a stranger, a gentleman, he spoke with a strange accent quite unlike their Border dialect. As for 'the young leddy', she was the subject of envy. Her dress alone must have cost the equivalent of six months' wages. They weren't to know that it had been made and paid for, with great trepidation on Jenny's part, purposely to impress the Borders mill owners.

They adjourned for lunch at two. Mr Kennet was in something of a quandary. He'd expected the female secretary to be left at the hotel for a ladylike collation, while he took the gentleman off for a dram and a substantial meal of Border mutton with potatoes.

But this young lady seemed to be the brains of the pair, so he sent a message by the office boy to his wife, to say that he'd be bringing home two guests for a luncheon. Mrs Kennet nearly sent the boy back with a message that her husband must be out of his mind to expect her to provide a meal at half-past-two when all decent respectable households ate at noon. But instead, suspecting these were important clients, she had her cook send to the dining-room hot soup and potato scones, cold pork pie and salad greens, and the trifle intended for the evening meal.

With it Mr Kennet provided an excellent Chablis, which Miss Corvill scarcely touched but which proved much to the taste of her brother. Afterwards there was coffee and port, which Mr Corvill seemed to enjoy. The result was that he became rather somnolent during the discussion that followed. That was all to the good, because it was about money, which he understood scarcely at all.

About four o'clock they went to the office to look at a map of the town of Galashiels and consider where, supposing Jenny leased part of the mill of Begg & Hailes, they might rent a house.

'You'd be bringing your own furniture?'

She shook her head. When she thought of the solid, cottage furniture of her home, she knew it would suit badly with any house they might take as 'mill owners'. 'It would be convenient to take something furnished for the time being.'

'I have clients who have an upper floor to let, capacious, on the corner of Simes Place near the Gala Bridge.'

A moment's thought told her that her mother would hate having to share a house with anyone else. She was too set in her ways, too insecure. 'I should prefer a furnished house. It need not be very large.'

'But, Miss Corvill, the Corvill family can scarcely live in a webster's cottage.'

That was true. They would have a position to keep up. 'We had better leave this point for the moment. Perhaps you could make enquiries.' What she meant was that he wasn't the only solicitor in Galashiels, that other firms might have clients with houses to rent. He took the point perfectly.

They parted at six, when Mr Kennet habitually went home

74

to the meal the English might call either supper or dinner, but which he called high tea. He debated whether to invite the Corvills again but Jenny prevented it by saying she and her brother were very tired, would eat at the hotel and have an early night. The truth was that Ned needed a nap to sleep off the port.

They had their meal served privately and rather late in the parlour that separated their two bedrooms. Ned had woken up enough to take an interest. 'What was all that you and Kennet were chatting about?'

'Somewhere to live.'

'You've decided to take the mill, then?'

'Oh, yes, though I haven't told Kennet yet. It's a great opportunity.'

'It is?'

'Of course. We can make a good start and then we have the chance to buy the new carding machines with condensers at a reasonable price.'

Her brother looked baffled. 'How do you make that out, Jenny?'

'Weren't you listening? Mr Kennet said we could lease premises with four carding sets with the possibility of expansion – that can only mean that Begg & Hailes think of going soon. Then their manager remarked that Mr Begg was bringing in the new condensers – he'll be trying them out there. When they eventually move, to some more modern place, perhaps, with new machines installed, they'll leave the carding sets that are in place and we'll be able to buy them secondhand.'

There was a long pause. 'My word!' sighed Ned. 'What a head you have, Jenny.'

She laughed. 'You ought to argue, point out the flaws. For all I know, Mr Begg may intend to take his new condensers with him. But even if he does, I'll have had a close look at them and I'll know whether we should invest in them.'

The maid came in to mend the fire and to clear away the remains of their meal. Ned stretched out his legs to the warmth, for it was cool now that night was drawing on. He had taken off his jacket and unbuttoned his check waistcoat.

Jenny, too, had replaced her fine carriage gown with a house dress of poplin.

'You're planning a long way ahead,' he murmured. 'Buying new machinery – and we aren't even in the place yet.'

'If you want to make the best cloth you have to have the best machinery.'

'Jenny . . .'

'Yes?'

'Do you think . . . are we right in making the change?'

She sat up in surprise. 'What d'you mean? Why else are we here?'

'It was when I spent the morning in the mill . . . Those machines . . . Father will never come to terms with them.'

'I don't understand you. Father doesn't have to do anything with the carding engines or the power looms. He only has to oversee them.'

'I don't know whether he wants to do that, Jenny. All he really wants is to make good cloth. Himself, with his own hands.'

'But good heavens, Ned! The days of the handloom are over.'

'Not for him.' Ned pulled at his chin, then said, 'I wonder if we wouldn't be better just to go on as we are? Father's happy, after all – '

'You agreed! You said it yourself! You have to go either forward or backward, you can't stand still.'

'I know, I know. I still think that. But Father would be happier just working at the loom and supervising the work he puts out to the other handlooms.'

'But we're turning away orders, Ned! We could have sold nearly four times our present output – '

'Money isn't everything, after all.'

She leapt to her feet in irritation. 'It's money that keeps you at the university, brother! It's money that made it possible to bring in a man to use your loom so that you could listen to lectures on Plato and Aristotle.'

'Yes, well, you see, that proves my point. We made enough for that without uprooting Father and Mother – '

'And so that makes it perfect! You're catered for, Father and Mother are content.'

'It isn't a bad situation.'

'It is for me!' she interrupted. 'Have you ever thought about me?'

He stared up at her. The parlour was dimly lit by the long summer twilight. He couldn't quite distinguish her expression. 'You, Jenny? But you'll marry soon and – '

'No, I won't. If you really imagine I'm going to let Father marry me off to some straitlaced Huguenot – '

'But what else can happen, sister? That's always been the plan.'

'I'm not going to stay in the Dean Village and be married off to Walter Chambron! Even if he wasn't such a hypocrite I'd still refuse.'

Ned got up. He took her hands. To his surprise he discovered she was trembling. So all this was deeply felt, long suppressed.

'I didn't know you disliked Walter?'

'He knows full well that gluttony is one of the seven deadly sins yet he eats like a pig. He'll be as fat as a feather bed by the time he's thirty.'

'Well, you don't have to take Walter. James Leclare is interested in you.'

'Stop it.' She snatched her hands away. 'I'm not going to stay at home in the Dean Village and be a Huguenot wife. I'm going to run a mill in Galashiels and be a somebody.'

It was the first time he had even thought that she had ambitions for herself. Until now it had always been taken for granted that she was working and planning only for the family, for the good of Corvill and Son and thus, for Ned and his future. It shocked him to think she had ambitions of her own.

'This is very unwomanly, Jenny.'

'Oh, don't prate at me! If you were perfect yourself I might listen, but we both know, brother, that you have faults. Don't desert me now because you were frightened by the machines.'

'I wasn't!'

'Yes you were, don't deny it. You hadn't thought beyond the idea of being "the son of a mill owner". When you saw those engines in action you suddenly understood what it meant. But no one is asking you to deal with the mill, Ned. You know that full well. *I* will handle all that.'

'But you've never dealt with the making of cloth by power.'

'I'm not going to do it myself, you idiot! I'm going to hire others. After all, Mr Begg's mill is managed for him. I shall have a foreman and a master dyer and Father shall be the master webster to check the cloth when it comes out at the end. It can be done, Ned, and I've already contacted London merchants who want to market our wares, and I've got orders from customers in Edinburgh and Glasgow, and I'll write to the palace to tell Their Majesties we can supply tartans in any quantity – '

'Jenny, Jenny!' Her enthusiasm frightened him. He wasn't sure it wasn't all some wild dream.

The maid came in after a tap at the door, bringing the lamps. She drew the curtains. When she had gone, Ned pulled up the worn but comfortable sofa to the fire and brought his sister to sit there beside him.

One of the things that Jenny loved about Ned was that he was tolerant, open-minded. It was also one of his weaknesses. He could always see all sides of every argument. This morning he had suddenly seen how his conservative father would react to the bustle and clatter of the mill. Now he saw how important the project was to his sister.

'Is it just to get away from marrying Walter or James?' he asked gently. 'If it is, it's too big a counter-attack. All you have to do is say no to them.'

She understood that the time had come to give him her side of the matter. She wasn't a girl who confided for the sake of giving confidences; she'd never been one to exchange little secrets with other girls. But now she must make Ned understand how she felt about moving from Edinburgh.

'I want us to make the best cloth in Scotland,' she began. 'And the best cloth is being made here, in Galashiels. That gives us an added cachet. We have a good reputation already, and moreover we have royal patronage – I believe if we work at it we might even get a royal patent in time. Ned, we could have one of the finest cloth-making firms *in the world* – but we can never do it on a small scale with ten or twelve handlooms.'

It was breathtaking, almost like Alexander planning to conquer a continent. 'But it would cost a fortune in investment, wouldn't it?'

'It wouldn't happen all at once. I've put my target at five years. In five years, you'll be able to go into a shop in the United States and ask for cloth by Corvill and Son – and get it.'

'It's . . . I don't know what to say . . .'

'Just think, Ned. Your name will be known throughout the country, throughout the world, in time. You'll have money, you can travel, study . . .'

She knew how to entrap him. The vista she spread before him was irresistible. The genuine concern he'd felt for his father faded in the glow of the future splendours Jenny conjured up. He went to bed a firm ally of his sister.

Next morning Jenny had early interviews with three or four men who came by appointment to ask for a job with the new mill owners. She was relatively pleased with Robert Ritchie, whose references described him as being competent, honest and fully trained in the use of power-driven wool-carding machinery. Mr Kennet arrived at eleven to show them living accommodation. For the first time they had a chance to make a closer acquaintance with Galashiels, which proved to be a workaday little town. Cloth-making had brought change, not entirely approved of by Dorothy, sister of the poet Wordsworth. She had lamented the 'ugly stone houses' that were replacing the romantic dark-thatched cottages, but the weavers probably preferred slate roofs and dry floors to the damp huts of former years.

There was little of architectural interest. The finest residence was Gala House, the property of John Scott, Laird of Gala. The Hall, home of Mr Haldane the brewer, was prosperous-looking and the town cross stood across the green from it. There were two or three good inns, and a carriage bridge across the Gala Water leading to the High Street. Further upstream there was a narrow bridge at Wildhaugh.

The river itself was pretty enough, with rushes and kingcups at the edge of the ale-coloured water. It flowed smoothly on to join the Tweed, where stood Abbotsford, home of Sir Walter Scott, almost a place of pilgrimage now for admirers of his novels.

'You yourself may feel like paying homage,' Mr Kennet

said with playful jocularity. 'He seems to have invented the tartan industry single-handed.'

'You mean because of popularising the shepherd's plaid for trousers.'

'Certainly we noticed a great increase in orders for that cloth when he began to wear it.'

'But the vogue for tartan comes from the pleasure shown by Their Majesties in wearing it,' Jenny said.

'And greatly appreciated, of course. But you know,' Kennet went on, determined to show his erudition, 'Sir Walter once remarked of tartan that "most of the designs owed their origins to the mercantile ingenuity of the Edinburgh merchants".'

'Wherever the designs come from,' Jenny replied, 'I'm sure we agree that what is important is that they should be beautiful and well made.'

'Indeed,' said Kennet, thinking that it was very difficult indeed to impress this young lady.

They had inspected the apartment in Simes Place and a house on the north side of the river badly in need of repair. They now drew up on a corner of the old road from Peebles, where several houses had been recently erected in clearings on the estate of the Laird of Gala.

'This house was brought to my attention,' said Kennet, meaning that he had spent all yesterday evening visiting his colleagues to see what they had on their books.

'Isn't it rather far out of the town?' Ned objected.

'Far? Why, sir, it's only a quarter of an hour's walk to the High Street and another ten from there to the mill. Say half an hour at most, excellent exercise for a man on a fine morning.'

'And if it rains or snows?'

'You'll have your carriage, of course.'

'Of course.' The idea of owning a carriage delighted Ned so much that he had no further objections to make.

Mr Kennet led them on foot up a rather steep drive. He did this on purpose because the most successful surprise was obtained this way. The house came into view round the curve.

'Good gracious!' said Jenny.

'Delightful, is it not?' said Kennet.

It looked like a miniature abbey, built in a warm reddish stone. Designed, no doubt, under the influence of the novels of Sir Walter Scott, it had a romantic, gothic appearance and yet wasn't sombre. The windows were all mullioned. There was a hexagonal turret on the roof between the main wing and the gabled north end. The entrance was in a little bay with castellations and arched church-like windows.

The garden bloomed with the last of the spring tulips, and roses coming into bud. A lawn ran down the slope to mature trees left untouched to give shelter from wind and weather. There was a coach house at the entrance gates, behind which could be glimpsed the kitchen gardens.

'This way,' said Mr Kennet, smiling to himself. He produced a large key to unlock the nail-studded entrance door. He paused. 'The house is called Gatesmuir,' he announced. 'Because, as you can see, it is at the edge of the moor on what used to be the only road across it.'

They walked into a hall floored with the coloured granite of Scotland, dark red and dark grey, highly polished. The arched window shed a bright, clear light.

Most of the furniture was draped in dust sheets which Kennet twitched back. The drawing-room on one side, the dining-room on the other, had rather heavy chairs and tables of oak, well in keeping with the architecture. Upstairs a very pretty sitting-room was flooded with noon sunshine, then beyond that bedrooms with white wainscoting and tester beds without hangings. There was even a bathroom, with a bath edged with mahogany and two taps which ran water into the tub.

'Hot water comes from the boiler in the kitchen,' said Mr Kennet. 'This way.'

The kitchen was as big as the ground floor of the cottage at home. Though other parts of the house were attractive, it was here that Jenny could picture her mother, bustling around, supervising the cooking – for of course they must have a cook, and a maid. At home they had only a woman who came in daily, but in this house they would need permanent staff. 'There's a woman comes in once a week to keep things tidy,' Kennet said in answer to her query, 'and to light fires against the damp in winter. She'd be glad to be kept on, I imagine. An honest woman, Annie Dacre.'

'How long has the place stood empty?'

'Ah. Ten months. Colonel Anderson married about three years ago, built this house for his retirement, but his wife proved to have a delicate constitution so they've gone to live in Portugal. He's willing to sell or let, furnished or unfurnished, I gather.'

'Is he likely to return to Galashiels?'

'To live, you mean?' Kennet shook his head. 'If they come back to Britain it will be to one of the softer regions – the West country, perhaps.'

'That is reassuring,' Jenny said, in cool tone. 'One wouldn't wish to settle in and then find the owner wanting his property back at the end of a year's lease.'

Her coolness hid a deep excitement. The moment she'd seen the house, she knew it was for her. Its charm, its warmth, its capaciousness – they drew her as if she had found what she'd been looking for all her life. But she took good care not to let Kennet see it. If he did, the rent would go up.

They went on to look at other properties. Ned, bored, cried off at midday, saying he would look round the town. Jenny tried to keep him with her, knowing full well he would head for the nearest tavern, but he shook off her hand.

She and Mr Kennet parted in mid-afternoon. She went back to the hotel, tired enough to want to take off her elegant boots and put her feet up. As she entered the lobby, a man came forward.

'Miss Corvill?'

'Yes?'

'I hear you're hiring for your new mill.'

'Do you, indeed? How did you come to hear that?'

'Och, in a small place like this, we only have one topic of conversation – cloth-making. News gets round.'

'I see. Well, what do you want?'

'I'd like to offer for a position.'

She took a look at him, unhurried. He was tall, angular, well dressed enough to advertise the fact that he was a superior workman. He had reddish hair which hinted at an inheritance from the Danish raiders of long ago. His age, she thought, would be about thirty.

'What is your name?'

'Ronald Armstrong.'

82

'Well, Mr Armstrong, I'm very tired and I've had nothing to eat since six in the morning. I want to rest and eat. Perhaps you could come back – '

'I'll wait,' he said.

She was both taken aback and interested. Good workers were at a premium in the cloth trade. He had no need to cool his heels in a hotel lobby for a job. She hesitated. 'Perhaps . . . I'll order a snack and while I wait for it, we could converse?'

'That'd suit me.'

She nodded, and turned to the hotel manager at his desk. 'I should like hot tea and cold meat sandwiches in my parlour as soon as possible.'

'Certainly, ma'am. For two?'

'For one.'

She saw out of the corner of her eye that Ronald Armstrong hid a smile at this demonstration of their relative positions. And she thought to herself, After all, I'm not a mill owner *yet*. Over her shoulder she said, 'Unless you'd like a cup, Mr Armstrong?'

'I'd like it fine, Miss Corvill.'

She led the way to her parlour. He took her key from her, unlocked the door, then stood back to allow her to go first. He stood gazing out of the window while she went into her bedroom to take off her bonnet and gloves. For the moment she kept on her walking boots – she felt it would be beneath her dignity to appear in house shoes.

'Well, Mr Armstrong,' she said as she re-entered the parlour. 'What do you do?'

'I'm a master dyer.'

'Are you employed at present?'

'No.'

'How did you come to leave your last post? Did you give notice or were you dismissed?'

'I was dismissed.'

She raised her eyebrows. 'On what grounds?'

'Impertinence.'

'Oh,' she said, trying to remain impassive. Impertinence . . . She studied him. He was standing looking rather demure, as if secretly amused. 'What does that mean, impertinence?'

'I told the mill owner that he was a fool if he thought his cheap mid-magenta would prove fast. He gave me the sack on the spot. He asked me to come back when I was proved right, but I can't be doing with fools.'

'Well,' she said, 'I take it you have no reference from *him*.'

'But I have. Do you want to see it?'

'Yes please.'

He brought from his pocket a manila envelope. Inside there were others of various kinds. He held it out. 'Mr Cairns's is the one on top. The others are previous employers.'

She went to a chair, gesturing to another at the opposite side of the parlour table. 'Sit down.' He obeyed. She opened the reference from Mr Cairns.

'Ronald Armstrong has worked for me for fourteen months,' she read. 'His work as a dyer is excellent but he has a high opinion of himself. Signed, yours faithfully, Herbert Cairns.'

She looked up. 'Is that true, Mr Armstrong? Do you have a high opinion of yourself?'

'It's been said.'

'But is it true?'

'I have a high opinion of my abilities. I know how to produce good colour.'

'Very well.' She read the other references of which there were three. He had worked in Galashiels, in Glasgow, and in Perth at the premises of Mr Pullar, the dye expert. 'This is quite impressive. You could get a job anywhere. Why are you hanging about asking for a job with a mill that hasn't even started?'

'I have enough to live on for a while, I'm not desperate for a wage-tin. I've seen the cloth your father makes, Miss Corvill. I'd like to work for him.'

'You've seen our cloth?'

'Of course. Anyone who takes an interest in cloth-making has taken the trouble to see it. I went to Renfrew on purpose to see a piece you'd made for a merchant there.'

'The green plaid?'

'That one.'

'What did you think of it?'

'Too much Helindone-yellow. The dyer was Swintons of Edinburgh, I take it.'

'How did you know that?'

'He's heavy-handed on yarn. He can dye and finish whole cloth but he never calculates lightly enough for yarn.'

Jenny was impressed, too impressed to hide the fact. And she was filled with a sudden exultation.

She had found the one man, the lynchpin without which the wheel would never have turned smoothly. Here was the master of dyes who would translate her designs from dream to reality. Here was the man who would bring colour to life in the wool.

The maid knocked on the door before entering with a laden tray.

'Have some tea, Mr Armstrong,' Jenny said, thinking she should have offered him nectar and gold.

Chapter Six

William Corvill always kept as far away from the thundering machinery as he could. He set up a handloom in a disused office on the first floor of the mill, where he would weave sample pieces of new designs to see if they were attractive when translated from water-colour on graph paper to living cloth. To him from time to time samples of the newly-spun yarn were brought, for his approval as to weight and regularity. He took a keen interest in the dye samples.

To the workforce he was a figure of mystery and awe, seldom seen. The moving spirit in the section of the mill run by the Corvills was the young Miss Corvill. Section foremen reported directly to her, the manager of the carding department and the dye master were often in conference in her comfortable office.

The mill girls couldn't come to terms with the idea of a boss who was a 'miss'. In addressing her they used the old Scottish term, 'mistress', the equivalent of the English Mrs when attached to a name, but also the equivalent of 'madam'. In the course of the first winter in their new premises the question would be, 'Have you asked the mistress about it?' or 'We'd better leave it for the mistress to see.'

Jenny was more relieved than she could say to watch her father settle down to life in Galashiels. Her brother's accusations had disturbed her more than she let him see. Was she uprooting a plant that would die out of its usual setting?

If a term could have been invented to suit the role William played, he would perhaps have been called Artistic Director. It was due to him that the cloth made by William Corvill and Son continued to own its good name for beauty and quality.

No one knew that it was Jenny who designed most of the new checks and tartans that came from their looms. They thought of her as the business head, that strange prodigy of the Corvill family, a 'businesswoman'.

Most of William's time was taken up by religion or, more properly, theology. He brought all his books with him to Galashiels and with the money that began to flow in he bought more. He joined and became a leading member of the United Secession Church, which had its being on the road opposite Gala House and prided itself on its upright Protestantism. Mrs Corvill also attended, was embraced with open arms, and devoted herself to good works carried out by the ladies of the congregation in Galashiels and surrounding villages.

'So you see,' Jenny said to Ned, when he came from Edinburgh for the Christmas vacation, 'your misgivings were mistaken. Mother and Father are quite happy.'

'And are you?' he asked, studying her. She was thinner than formerly, her pale skin seemed stretched tighter over her high cheekbones, her dark eyes glowed bigger than ever in her face. 'Aren't you overworking?'

'Oh, it's only until we get really established. We're doing well – orders are rolling in. Our designs for next spring were all taken up and the samples for next winter are out now and getting a lot of approval, especially on the Continent. Oh, Ned, you don't *know* how wonderful it is to see the bales of cloth going out labelled for London and Paris and Hamburg!'

Well, she seemed happy, if finely drawn. 'Just don't overdo it,' he urged. 'You told me you were going to get other people to do the actual work, yet it seems to me you spend all day in the mill.'

'But I love it!'

'But, Jenny . . . After all, if you're shut up there, you're not meeting people.' He meant, not meeting any men suitable to marry.

She understood him quite well. 'I've accepted almost every invitation that's come in for parties at Christmas and New Year, Ned, and we've taken tickets for the Assemby Ball at the Ordnance Arms. We've only mixed in Galashiels society to the extent of tea parties and morning visits so far, but the family will get right into the swing of everything in the coming month, I promise. And when I've got the hang of what people expect, we'll have a party here – perhaps a Burns Night party.'

'A Burns Night!' He was surprised and pleased. There was something literary and intellectual about the notion. The habit was growing to give a dinner on the anniversary of the poet's birth, with toasts and music, and recitations of the more famous works. 'I could give a speech,' he offered. 'About the influence of Burns on the Scottish language – '

'We'll see, Ned, we'll see.' Jenny had no desire for a long dinner with too many whisky toasts and a static set of dinner companions. What she had in mind was a party – not a ball, because she had no confidence in her own ability to deal with one nor in her mother's. But a party, based on the notion of old country dances, the singing and playing of the songs Robert Burns had written, perhaps games or charades . . . She read about such things in the fashion magazines.

The morning visits and the leaving of cards had brought the Corvills a large circle of acquaintance. Most of the initial calls had been from the wives of other cloth-makers or those connected with the cloth trade. The wife of the headmaster of the Subscription School, and the wives of the town's two doctors had also left cards, besides those of most of the town councillors.

Working her way painstakingly through the necessary return calls, Jenny's mother had at first needed Jenny's company as moral support. But she soon discovered that it was quite easy to pass fifteen minutes in polite conversation, that even the wife of a town councillor liked to talk about recipes and crochet, and that – to her own surprise – she was regarded as very 'interesting' because of her speech. All the Corvills were thought to speak in a very genteel manner, due to their Huguenot background. In fact, her fear that she might be looked down upon because she was really only a weaver's wife was unfounded: in the Borders, where new mills were springing up every month, families were welcomed if they brought prosperity to the district, no matter what their origins.

To the Assembly Ball they went as a family party. Jenny and her mother had new gowns for the occasion, Jenny in a copy of a French model in rose pink silk with rows of tassels on the crinoline skirt and a pretty latticed front-bodice, Millicent in dark blue with a frilled bertha edged in yellow and a matching yellow fan. Ned was looking handsome in black broadcloth and a silk shirt with a soft black bow. Even William, who thought this frivolity rather lax, was in a new evening suit of charcoal grey with a plain satin waistcoat.

Jenny learned several important things at the ball. The first was that families of standing didn't arrive at the time printed on the tickets – that was much too early. The second was that Ronald Armstrong was present with a young woman on his arm. Well, why not? Anyone who could afford the price of the ticket could attend. The third was that Jenny herself was very attractive to men.

It might be thought she had learned this through her affair with Bobby. Quite the contrary. For months she had been haunted by the idea that she had been taken by an experienced hunter, like a deer by a lion. He'd gone to bed with her because she'd been easily gulled, and easily available. Why had he continued the affair after that first night? Well, that was more difficult, but she'd thought it was perhaps because on his journeys to and fro on behalf of the Royal Household, he'd been too busy to find anyone better.

But at the Assembly Ball she had assurance that it wasn't so. Her programme for the first half was filled almost from the moment she had left her wrap in the cloakroom, and so she was spared the indignity of dancing more than one dance with her brother. Men already known to her through the family visiting were the first to approach, but it was soon clear that acquaintances were being asked to introduce others.

'Miss Corvill, may I present Mr Archibald Brunton, of Bowden and the Mains Farm. Archie, Miss Corvill of Gatesmuir.'

'Delighted.' And it was clearly true. This tallish, darkish man with the smiling blue eyes was delighted to meet her. 'May I have the honour of a dance with you, Miss Corvill?'

'Oh, sir, I'm afraid . . . Not until after supper.'

'Must I wait so long in anguish?' he said, laughing.

'Na, na, Archie,' said Mr Cairns, 'You were too slow off your stool. Miss Corvill, I won't ask you to waste your time with an old fellow like me, but I beg to be of your party in the supper room.'

'That will be a great pleasure.'

'And when may I claim you after supper?' Archie Brunton insisted.

'Shall we say the eightsome reel?'

He bowed and perforce moved aside as her partner claimed her for the next dance, a quadrille. She took the arm of Mr Hailes, the sleeping partner of Mr Begg of Begg & Hailes, a rather elderly, gossipy man who collected butterflies. 'Let you not get too smitten with Archie Brunton,' he said with a wink as he led her on the floor. 'He's the gay dog, is Archie.'

'Mr Hailes, I've only just bowed to the man for the first time.'

'That's no guarantee you won't be in his arms the next. Half the young women of the Borders have been in love with him. And half of that crew have succumbed to more than bows and curtseys, I hear.'

'Mr Hailes!'

He chuckled, handing her across to the ladies' side. 'Only joking,' he said.

Later she talked Mr Cairns, the mill owner who had dismissed Ronald Armstrong for impertinence. As they stood waiting by their partners while the set formed and the fiddlers tuned up, she said in idle tones, 'Did I see Mr Armstrong here with his wife?'

'He's not married,' Cairns said shortly. The matter clearly still rankled.

'Oh? I thought the lady with him was his wife, perhaps.'

'I'm not the least interested in Armstrong's doings,' he said. And then, realising how impolite he had been, he coloured, his face glowing between his soft brown cheek whiskers. 'Ach, I made an idiot of myself over the man,' he said. 'And naturally you're interested because you were lucky enough to get him after I'd lost him by my own daftness. I think the lady with him is the sister of his landlady.'

'Ah. He's danced with quite a few others, I notice.'

Mr Cairns looked as if he were a little surprised she should be so curious. 'Oh, yes, he has a fair acquaintance among the ladies. He's regarded as a respectable escort – a widower, you see.'

'Oh. I didn't know that.'

'No, well, he's not like to tell you himself. I heard it in a roundabout way. Lost his wife and child in a cholera epidemic in Glasgow.'

The orchestra struck a chord, the ladies and gentlemen bowed and curtseyed, the cotillion began. And that was the most Jenny was able to learn about Ronald Armstrong for that evening.

The long cotillion led on to supper. She rejoined Ned and her parents, bringing her partner with her as etiquette demanded and being introduced to a young lady whom Ned had partnered. Her relatives joined them, and Mr Brunton appeared. They were able to commandeer a large table in a corner, where the ladies sat fanning themselves in the heat from too many gaslights, and the men went to fetch refreshments.

Ned's dance partner couldn't make up her mind whether she wanted to fascinate Ned or Archie Brunton. Archie soon solved her dilemma by devoting himself to Jenny.

'I hear wonderful things about you, Miss Corvill,' he began. 'You run your father's mill for him, I hear.'

'You use wonderful in its old sense of strange or unusual, I suppose.'

He blinked. He had thought she would demur, because to tell the truth he'd only just heard this piece of gossip in the course of trying to find out more about this exceedingly pretty girl. He hadn't for a moment thought it was the truth.

'Is it actually so, then?' he asked, deciding to be open and frank about it.

'It is actually so. Where do you live, Mr Brunton?'

'My estate is at the village of Bowden, some miles to the south. You must come and – '

'I only inquire because the place must be at the back of beyond. Everyone in Galashiels – perhaps in the Scottish Borders – knows about this strange species of woman who manages a cloth mill.'

She was warning him on two scores: first that if he wanted a flirtation she wasn't easy game and secondly that if he was interested in a more serious friendship, she wasn't like the other women he had met.

She wanted him to know it from the outset. Ned had

reminded her she must think about marriage, and Archie would be considered a very suitable match – a bachelor, of course, well-educated, with a great estate consisting of many farms let out to successful sheep farmers.

The gentlemen were rejoicing in the fall of Sebastopol, certain news of which had just appeared in *The Times*. Discussion ensued about whether the Russians would now agree to a peace conference to end a war in which they were failing so miserably.

'Poor souls, they were badly advised ever to get into it,' Mr Cairns remarked. 'I suppose, having put Napoleon to flight forty years or so ago, they thought they could do the same with France and Britain. Very foolish.'

'The Tsar, I hear, is a very well-educated man,' said Ned.

'Aye, aye, probably better educated than his generals . . .' To the party, it all sounded a very long way away, in a world they knew nothing of.

'We sold a gown piece to the Tsarina,' remarked Jenny, trying it out for the first time in public.

'You did? You sent patterns to her?'

'No, a lady-in-waiting came to our premises.'

'My word,' sighed Ned's dancing partner in envy. 'You actually met a member of the Russian court?'

'Yes, a very elegant lady. She seemed very rich.' Into Jenny's mind flashed another picture, of another rich and elegant lady she had met that day – Mrs Bobby Prentiss. She felt herself colour up, but the attention of the party was elsewhere, fortunately.

'And did the Tsarina like the gown piece?'

'We received a very appreciative letter,' William Corvill said with pride. 'Her Imperial Majesty was so good as to say the colour was superb.'

A murmur of awe and appreciation followed. Archie Brunton said in Jenny's ear, 'I had no idea you had such notable customers.'

'Oh, yes, and we have supplied tartan to the Queen and Prince Consort which they greatly liked. We think of having their letters framed and hung in a little room at the mill where we may receive buyers and visitors.'

'The tartan for the royal family was ordered by a lady-in-waiting too?'

'No, I met His Royal Highness personally.'

Archie was impressed. Jenny couldn't be sure whether it was good or bad to impress him so much. It might frighten him off. On the other hand, it might counterbalance the idea of a woman who went to work daily in a mill.

She was aware that she wanted to cultivate his acquaintance. After all, she would soon be twenty. She couldn't go on for ever without a husband. The term 'old maid' might not be applied to her, but to continue too long unmarried and in business would build up an idea that she was odd.

Archie was by no means the only man she'd met since settling in Galashiels. But he was the richest . . .

It was only politeness for her new acquaintances of the ball to further the friendship by a visit in the next few days. Unfortunately a spell of bad weather made this less possible. There was snow on the hills encircling the little town, roads became slippery although not bad enough to prevent goods being moved on heavy wagons. But if a man wanted an excuse not to take out his carriage for a journey from Bowden into Galashiels, the weather provided it.

Instead a polite note came from Mr Brunton to Jenny's mother, remarking on the pleasure of having made her acquaintance and that of her family. 'We'll invite him to the Burns Night party,' said Mrs Corvill.

'He won't come,' said Jenny.

'Why would he not?'

'It's not elegant enough for him. A friendly party with country dances and hot punch – it's not what he enjoys.'

'How can you possibly know that?' Millicent wondered. 'You only met him the once.'

Jenny didn't reply. She was fairly sure Archie Brunton had found her a little alarming. It was a pity, because he was much the most entertaining man in the district.

Other young men came. If Jenny had wanted merely to be a married woman, she could have achieved the status within the first year. She had two formal offers, which she as formally refused. And there was Mr Gables, a mill manager who loved her both for her looks and for the fact that she was a member of a family that was making money. This suitor she seriously considered: he shared a common interest and was a lively enough fellow, though bumptious. But when in the end she said she thought she would like to remain single a while longer, he left in a huff for the Yorkshire woollen mills.

Naturally, everyone in Galashiels took an interest. So it was Ronald Armstrong, the manager of the dyeing department, who told her that Hector Gables had accepted a post in Leeds.

'You hadn't heard?' he asked, seeing her surprise.

She shrugged. 'I daresay someone would have told me soon enough. When did he accept?'

'Posted the letter yesterday, as far as I can gather.'

'My word! News travels fast.'

'Well, he's making a great thing of it. It's a promotion, of course – he's going to manage Macclethorpe Mill. Besides . . .'

'What, Mr Armstrong?'

'I expect he wants everyone to know he can succeed in his career even if he fails elsewhere.'

She looked at the long, tranquil face. She had a feeling he was laughing inwardly. There was some slight glint in the hazel eyes that seemed to say so.

'Well, Mr Armstrong, what are we going to do about this fugitive beige?' she inquired, to show him that as far as she was concerned the affairs of Mr Gables were of no importance.

'The mordant will have to be changed, that's all. You're sure you really want beige for a background?'

She made no reply to this, for it deserved none. He had the graph before him, with its colours set out. All the same, perhaps it was unusual to want to make a tartan with a beige background.

She answered the question he had not asked. 'It will be good in a heavy weight,' she explained. 'For men's capes and winter riding coats. We need to get a sample made as soon as possible to offer it in the pattern books for next winter.'

He twitched his sample of yarn to and fro in his hands. 'Aye,' he sighed, 'one thing about the weaving world – you never seem to live in today, it's always next season, next summer, next winter . . . And life's going by all the while.'

She felt an impulse of sympathy. She had thought the same

94

thing herself more than once. ' "The world is too much with us; late and soon, Getting and spending" – '

' "We lay waste our powers",' he took up the quotation, regret in his voice.

'Do you think you're wasted here, Mr Armstrong?' she asked. 'In fact, now I come to think of it, I wonder you've never started up on your own.'

'Oh, I thought of it, mistress . . . There was a time . . . But it seems pointless, doing it for yourself alone.'

She knew he was thinking of his lost wife and child. They had never spoken of it, never in fact exchanged more than the politenesses of daily life. She was on the verge of inquiring if he had ever thought of remarrying, but something prevented her – a respect she felt for him, for his privacy. 'Ah, we're melancholy today,' she said in a teasing tone.

'It's not for anyone as young as you, Mistress Corvill,' he said in the same manner. 'Melancholy is for old men like me – and it doesn't help solve the problem of this exasperating shade of beige. I'll away and have a think about it.'

The conversation recurred to her again on the day of her twentieth birthday. On an impulse she took time off from the mill, ordered out the dogcart, and decided to amuse herself with a morning's driving, a newly acquired skill.

The sturdy cob, Downie, clopped his way with pleasure along the dusty road out of Galashiels eastwards towards Melrose and into the sun of the August morning. It was a journey of some five miles along the north of the Tweed with the slopes of Easter Hill and Camp Knowe on her left and the green river valley on her right.

She was wearing a new capote hat, a birthday present from her mother. It had nodding pink roses and broad pink ribbons tying under her chin. Her gown, rather less hooped than usual because she had chosen to drive the dogcart, was of glazed cotton, cream sprigged with pink rosebuds, with cream gauze undersleeves which came down to meet the white kid gloves. She had thought that morning that she looked rather well – the soft blush of colour suited her dark features.

She had wanted time to herself, to think. She was twenty years old today. Though she enjoyed her life, she heard again Ronald Armstrong's voice: 'Life's going by all the while . . .'

Recently she had been troubled by a restlessness, a nameless longing that made her want to move about without purpose or kept her awake at night. Sometimes, at an evening party when one of the gentlemen was rendering a sentimental song or a young lady playing a piece by Mendelssohn on the pianoforte, a chord would strike her as poignant, a phrase would bring tears to her eyes.

It was a foolishness. But it existed, it was a factor in her life. She wanted to examine it.

As she drove along she now and again passed a vehicle driven by someone she knew. She raised her whip in greeting. At a crossroads before Melrose she noticed a young couple standing hand in hand by a church gate, smiling at each other. They were unknown to her, but she was given a moment of recognition, a moment of envy.

The thing that troubled her was loneliness. Though she had her parents and, when he was at home, her brother . . . Though she had a host of friends and acquaintances in the town . . . Though at the mills she was surrounded by people . . . She was lonely.

She wanted someone for herself. Someone to be to her what Bobby Prentiss had been. Her own soul-companion, her lover, the one person to whom she was more important than the world – the man who would assuage this longing that was of the body as well as the spirit.

She pulled the reins to bring Downie to a standstill. For some moments she sat in the shade of a roadside tree, gazing with unseeing eyes over the meadow where sheep grazed on lush grass.

She had refused or eluded four suitors. There had been reasons why they hadn't pleased her. But it was time to be sensible. She at last understood that she had physical needs. Her affair with Bobby had given her experience beyond what most girls of her age were allowed – and she didn't regret it, she knew she had been blessed in the sensual pleasure of that happy time.

But having once known it, she knew how empty her life was. She felt like Eve locked out of Paradise. Paradise was unlikely to be regained, but she could find some lesser happiness.

By and by she drove on again and into the town of Melrose. The ancient settlement had grown up around the gates of St Mary's Abbey, which still dominated the town with its extraordinary splendour of Decorated Gothic, its flamboyant tracery at windows and gables. A ruin for centuries, it was a place of romantic interest to many because Sir Walter Scott had praised it.

Jenny handed the reins to a groom at the George and Abbotsford Inn. It was a little after ten. She paused to drink some cooling lemonade at a rustic table in the garden before sauntering on to look at St Mary's.

And there, strolling on the lawn, she found Archibald Brunton with a group of friends.

He saw her and came towards her, recognition and pleasure in his eyes. Then she saw a slight hesitation. It was as if he suddenly thought that he ought not to seem too pleased to see her.

But she was looking very pretty and very elegant, and he was with people who were very dowdy and very boring, friends of his mother's, from Edinburgh.

'Miss Corvill,' he said, smiling. 'What a surprise.'

'Good morning, Mr Brunton.'

'Your parents are with you?'

'No, I'm alone.'

'Alone!' He thought this unseemly, but said nothing. His companions drifted up. 'Mother, let me present Miss Corvill, of Gatesmuir in Galashiels.'

Mrs Brunton, rather stout in black poplin and a straw bonnet, bowed. Her friends were introduced, the party resumed its stroll in the sunshine around St Mary's.

When it became clear that Miss Corvill was of a family in manufacture, there was a slight cooling off in the interest of the Edinburgh friends. But when it became known that Corvill and Son had sold cloth to royalty, the coldness evaporated.

Jenny invited the visitors to come to Galashiels if they had time during their holiday. It would be a pleasure to show them round the mill.

'Should we see the tartan you sold to Her Majesty?' inquired the youngest lady in the group.

'Only a small sample is left, but yes, it's on view. Also the one we sold to the Tsarina. And others, of course – we have many clients among the nobility and gentry.'

It was too enticing. An arrangement was made. Mrs Brunton nodded and smiled, and was encouraging. She too would like to come. She too would like to partake of the luncheon Miss Corvill would offer.

Jenny wasn't one who thought of things as 'meant', who believed that Providence intervened in the personal lives of mortals. But finding Archie here on the very day she had made up her mind she must marry was too apt a coincidence to ignore.

Of all the men she had met since coming to Galashiels, he was the one she liked best. And now she had decided.

She needed a husband. Archie Brunton was the man.

Chapter Seven

The difficulty soon became clear. Archie Brunton had no intention of dwindling into a husband.

He was a 26–year-old bachelor who very much enjoyed his life. True, he must marry some day, to ensure an heir for the estate, otherwise it would all go to a hateful cousin in Berwick. But he had good looks, good manners, good health: any time up to the age of fifty he had only to crook his finger and a suitable girl or young woman would come running.

In the meantime everything was for the best in the best of all possible worlds. He could flirt with all the pretty girls in his neighbourhood, and when he wanted something more satisfying there were always ladies available in the lanes around the markets, or in Glasgow or Edinburgh at the hotels. He could spend his money to please himself, not on the upbringing of children or at the behest of a wife. He liked to play cards a little, to back horses a little, to travel a little, to buy fashionable carriages, see the latest plays, and be admired as a gentleman of taste.

Jenny wasn't the first young lady who had set out to capture him. It was, of course, incumbent on every mother of a marriageable girl to get a good husband for her, so plans had been made and seiges laid for Archie Brunton ever since he came home from Fettes College. He was an old hand at avoiding the quotable declaration, the compromising situation, from which there was no escape for a man of honour except to offer his hand in marriage.

Jenny understood this without having to be told. And her plan, if she had one, was simply to make herself such a pleasant companion that Archie would miss her sorely if they had to part. She didn't imagine he could be made to fall passionately in love with her, and she was right. Archie had a poor opinion of love. He saw that it landed his friends in very dull marriages, and felt that love was bad for the brain.

Jenny had an ally, unacknowledged and unannounced, yet powerful. Mrs Brunton wanted her son to settle down.

She knew more about his activities than he guessed. An elderly male friend had murmured once that the boy had been seen in an unsavoury area of Newcastle, and on another occasion when supervising the sending of some of his clothes to be cleaned, she had found revealing hotel bills in his pockets.

There had been other girls, more suitable than Genevieve Corvill, whom Mrs Brunton would have preferred as a daughter-in-law. But they had married other men and were mothers of young families now. Moreover, as she grew to know Miss Corvill, Mrs Brunton began to like her.

It was true she managed the mill for her father. It was true she went almost every day to the office and conferred with workmen. It was true that she spoke with more assurance than was quite elegant in a girl so young. On the other hand, she was level-headed, intelligent, patient. She knew how to handle her own menfolk – presumably she would know how to handle Archie.

And, widowed, Mrs Brunton knew that Archie needed handling. Whether he would ever be a faithful husband might depend very much on how much work his wife would put into keeping him faithful.

She took an important step to bring the Corvills and the Bruntons closer. She invited them to her New Year Ball.

'It's so kind of her!' cried Millicent Corvill when she took the invitation out of its stiff envelope. 'Mrs Wylie was only saying the other day that it's a great privilege to be invited.'

'She likes you,' her husband said, seeing it in simple terms. 'I've seen you chatting together quite often.'

'She's very amiable,' agreed his wife. But her mind was working, and she had understood the unspoken message, which was: let us bring Archie and Jenny together.

Jenny understood it too, and made a very special effort on her appearance at the ball. Excitement and resolve had brought colour to her pale skin. Her hair was piled high in a coronet of ringlets threaded with pale blue ribbon. Her gown of cornflower silk was nipped in at the waist with silver braid which matched her fan.

She was such a success that Archie Brunton almost failed to get on to her dance ticket. He was in quite a huff about it. After all, it was *his* house and she was *his* guest, and if anyone were to partner her it should be the host. He became quite possessive about her for an hour or two.

Jenny noted it as one more step on the road on which she was coaxing him. And when the Corvills gave their January ball in return, she made sure that Archie was made to feel important. It was the first ball the Corvills had given at home, causing much terror to her mother, but with good caterers and a careful reprise of what they had seen at other houses, all went well.

And it became the first of a series of enjoyable entertainments at Gatesmuir. From January into June, the house became the centre of social activity in Galashiels. Archie found himself looking forward to the parties, the at homes, the dances, formal or informal dinners.

He began to be quite happy in this web the womenfolk were spinning around him. He found the Corvills agreeable enough, if only they had not been cloth manufacturers. Jenny's brother Ned, for example, was quite the gentleman, and when you got away from the rather Quaker-ish home influence, quite good fun to go about with.

On a June day Archie arranged a picnic outing to the banks of the Tweed where the view was considered to be very charming. It was to be a *tour de force* of organisation, with the food provided by the first-rate cook at the Mains, transported separately and of a very special standard – pies kept hot in a hay-box, early strawberries and cream.

Unfortunately the weather, which had been beautiful, turned cool. Archie's new carriage developed trouble with the springs after he had left the Mains Farm and he had to accept a lift from Walter Hailes. The food was late arriving at the rendezvous. All in all, he was in a bad temper by the time lunch was served on the rather chilly knoll which had seemed so inviting when he first spied it out.

The conversation turned to the new transatlantic telegraph

cable which had just begun to be laid amid speculation about its ever being successful.

'It will be a great impetus to trade between Britain and the United States if it works,' Jenny said.

'The achievement itself is more important than any results to trade,' said Archie.

'Oh, come now, Brunton – '

'Yes, think what you're saying, my boy. Science is the handmaiden of industry.'

'More's the pity! Pure science should be our chief interest. I sometimes think,' Archie said, with a tilt of his handsome head towards the heavens, 'that I should like to devote the rest of my life to astronomy.'

'You'd have a hard time doing that without the money to finance it,' said Mr Hailes. 'And any money that is made available for science *must* come from trade.'

'Quite untrue. If I took up astronomy I should use my own money, which has not been sullied by mere commerce.'

Jenny glanced across at him, and caught a glint in his blue eyes that spoke of irritation with the occasion and the wish to vent it on someone. Sometimes he was very like a spoiled child.

'I can't see,' she said, 'that taking rents from farmers is uncommercial.'

He sat up. 'Money isn't the first priority in land management, as it is in industry.'

'But land management is an industry, Archie.'

'Not at all! How can you say so?'

'You rent land to farmers, who produce wool, which they sell, and from the proceeds they pay rent. If that isn't an industry, I don't know what else it is.'

'It's a relationship,' Archie insisted sharply. 'A relationship with people known to my family for generations. Not like in trade, where you have to deal with any rogue or vagabond who comes in off the pavement with money to pay for goods.'

There was an uneasy pause. The party exchanged glances.

'You seem to be saying,' Jenny remarked, very cool, 'that among the customers of Corvill and Son there are people you would find deplorable.'

102

Too late, Archie saw where his ill-temper had led him. He said uncertainly, 'No, I didn't quite intend that . . .'

Jenny gave her hand to Tom Simpson to be helped to her feet. She moved away, saying in a low voice to Archie as she passed, 'Perhaps you should begin to think what you do intend.'

She avoided him for the rest of the day, which was not a success in any sense. What was worse, she continued to avoid him. She ensured that her mother refused an invitation from Mrs Brunton to a concert in St Boswells, and also that the Bruntons were not invited to a midsummer lantern-party in the garden at Gatesmuir.

A month went by. It was known that Ned Corvill would soon be down from university for good and that a dance would probably be given to celebrate his homecoming. No invitation or message came to the Mains.

'Archie, what have you done to offend the Corvills?' Mrs Brunton inquired when he came home from a few days at Peebles for the spa waters.

'I? I've done nothing.'

'Tell me the truth, my lad. Did you say or do something at that picnic last month?'

'The picnic? Why do you ask?'

'Because you came home in a gey bad mood, and there's been a coolness ever since from the side of the Corvills.'

'Well, let them be cool! I don't care if they turn into icicles!'

'Don't be a fool, Archie. You've been drifting about like a lost soul the last few weeks, ever since they stopped inviting us.' His mother fixed him with a sharp blue gaze, like his own but colder. 'What's up?'

'Nothing. It's just . . .'

'What?'

'I don't like it when a woman takes it on herself to argue!' he burst out. 'Who does she think she is?'

Mrs Brunton laid aside her tapestry. 'Archie, I'll tell you who she is,' she said. 'She's the best chance you've had at a wife who could keep you in order. And if like a gomeril you've put her off, I'll never forgive you.'

'Mother, I'm not thinking about taking a wife.'

103

'The more fool you! How will you feel when she marries someone else?'

'What?' gasped Archie.

'Do you imagine she's going to cool her heels forever waiting for you? I estimate,' Mrs Brunton remarked, 'that the girl is going on twenty-one this year. She'll want to be a married woman before she gets to twenty-two – it stands to reason. If Tom Simpson – '

'Tom Simpson!' he said in scorn. 'She'd never take Tom Simpson – '

'She'll take you if you ask her,' his mother said. 'But I think you'd better make up your differences first.'

'I've nothing to apologise for, if that's what you're suggesting.'

'Archie, Archie . . .' she sighed. 'If you can't do anything more constructive, at least ring for tea.'

And she dropped the subject.

But he knew she was right. It would be galling if Jenny Corvill married anyone else. He would be shut out from her friendship, from her lively world, from her pretty ways . . .

He sent a bouquet of choice flowers from the garden of the Mains together with a note suggesting that there had been some misunderstanding between them. She replied saying she wasn't aware of any misunderstanding but suggesting they hadn't seen each other because she had been so very busy. Her father's firm was buying out Begg & Hailes at the mill: it was taking up a lot of her attention.

Her note was nicely calculated to tell him that she was ready to forgive him for his bad manners but that he mustn't think he came first in her life. Chastened, he accepted the implied rebuke. He had missed her more than he expected.

The friendship was resumed. Mrs Brunton beamed on her son. Though nothing had been said she thought she could hear wedding bells in the offing.

Jenny's mother, too, was pleased. She had gone along with Jenny's insistence that they should stand off from the Bruntons, but her mind misgave her at the time. She'll lose him, she told herself, she'll lose the best husband in the district. But no, once again her clever daughter had been proved right.

Archie had returned to the fold. And, like Mrs Brunton, Mrs Corvill thought she could smell orange blossoms.

The party for Ned's homecoming was the great event. He had not come back to Galashiels immediately on taking his finals but had waited to see the results posted. He had done well, a first class degree. So when he wrote that he would like to stay a few weeks more in Edinburgh with friends it had seemed only fair to let him celebrate.

He was expected on the Wednesday of the last week of September. Mrs Corvill ordered a special dinner, had his bedroom aired, put fresh flowers on the high-boy, and badgered her husband to be sure to come home early from a meeting of the elders of the United Secession Church.

Archie had called, to say 'welcome home' to a pleasant drinking companion. He was walking with Jenny in the garden of Gatesmuir when they heard the carriage come up the steep drive.

Jenny eagerly picked up her skirts and ran round to the front of the house. The early evening sun was turning the trunks of the birch trees a silvery pink. The hackney that had brought Ned from the station stood on the gravel before the door, the steps already down.

Ned leapt out. Jenny flew towards him to hug him in greeting. But he turned to hand someone down from the carriage.

It was a pretty girl of about Jenny's own age in a stylish travelling costume of gold moiré and velvet. She put out a little gloved hand, which Ned took tenderly.

Jenny had stopped, transfixed at this unexpected newcomer. Her mother, slower to move, appeared from the drawing-room as the housemaid opened the outside door.

'Ned! Dearest lad!' She bustled down the shallow steps.

'Mother,' he said in a tone of deep affection. 'Mother dear, I want you to welcome my wife.'

Chapter Eight

Archie's mother wouldn't believe him at first when Archie got home and told her of it.

'Mother, I assure you, it's the truth! You know I was supposed to stay for dinner but they were so . . . so *stunnert* I had to bow out and let them recover.'

'Married? And they knew nothing about it?'

'They looked as if the heavens had fallen in on them.'

Mrs Brunton shook her head. 'That means she is utterly unsuitable, or why else should he make such a secret of it?' She played with a ribbon of her widow's cap. 'What like is she? Some little fortune-hunter?'

'A sweet little thing, from the glimpse or two I saw of her.'

'A sweet little thing,' she repeated scornfully. 'She's pretty, I take it, then. But is she a lady?'

'Very genteel, I would have said. Prettily dressed, looked nervous – '

'Well she might! Did you discover who she is?'

'The daughter of his landlady.'

'Ach!' It was a snort of triumph. The worst kind of fool was a young man who married his landlady's daughter. 'I take it then that they had to get married.'

'No, in this case I believe it may not be the usual foolishness. Ned explained that the mother – Mrs Morrison – was a widow lady of good birth. She had been reduced to letting rooms through sheer necessity.'

'A likely tale,' said Mrs Brunton.

She was extremely vexed. If Ned Corvill had made a scandalous alliance it was useless to expect a marriage between

106

Archie and Jenny. The Bruntons couldn't allow themselves to be related to anyone without breeding.

'Well, it is a bit strange,' Archie murmured. Ned's escapade only strengthened his opinion – falling in love meant a softening of the brain. 'But I must say that to my eyes at any rate the young Mrs Corvill seems every inch a lady.'

'Seems is easy enough, laddie,' said his mother. 'What's the truth, that's what I want to know. Why marry in secret?'

This was what Ned was now trying to explain away to his stricken parents. 'I thought you might try to prevent it,' he said. 'At least, Lucy felt sure you would, because, of course, she has no dowry.'

'My son, money isn't the first thing we would have thought of. What is her education? Do they have religious conviction? Is her mother well-thought-of?'

Ned said stiffly, 'As to her education, I should think you could judge that by her speech and manner since we arrived. And Mrs Morrison would have come with us today, except that she has to run the boarding-house.'

'The boarding-house!' groaned Mrs Corvill.

'Well, after all, we started off with a weaving shed! Are we so much better?' cried her son in anger.

'Ned,' said Jenny softly. 'Ned, nothing is going to be gained by shouting at Mother. She's upset, and no wonder.'

'I don't see anything to cry over, when I bring home the girl I love.'

Jenny could have said, What she's crying over is the deceit, the surprise. But what was the point? The marriage was valid, both parties were of age and had resided in the parish in which the banns were called for far longer than the requisite three weeks. Nothing that anyone could do would change it now.

She said to her mother, 'We had better rearrange the rooms. There is only a single bed in Ned's room – '

Mrs Corvill threw her gauze apron over her face to stifle her sobs.

'Mother, they are married. They need a bedroom fit for a married couple.'

William Corvill got stiffly to his feet to ring the bell at the fireplace. When the housemaid came in he said, 'Get Daniel to move Mr Ned's belongings to . . . which room, Millicent?'

107

'The gardenside bedroom.'

The housemaid curtseyed. 'Yes, mistress. And the young mistress?' Then recollecting herself, for 'the young mistress' meant Miss Corvill, she amended; 'I mean, the young Mrs Corvill?'

'Her luggage is to be taken up to the gardenside room. Put stone jars in the bed to air it. Make sure there are enough hangers and that there is fresh lavender in the drawers.'

'Yes, mistress.'

Ned knew he had won as the door closed on the maid. He said, 'I'm sure Lucy will want to change into a fresh dress for the evening. Shall we meet for supper in half an hour?'

His mother looked at the clock. 'Aye, supper in half an hour.' Her hand flew to her mouth. 'My God, what happened to Archie?'

'He rode off home.'

'I never even saw him go. What must he think of us?'

'Never mind that for the moment, Mother.' That's the least of our worries, thought Jenny. Let's see what this girl is really like.

The young woman who came in on Ned's arm at eight o'clock was in every respect a model of respectability and demureness. She was wearing a soft print dress with many flounces and a large soft gauze collar, against which her pale prettiness was almost fey. She was fair, with a creamy skin and pink lips. Her voice was soft and sweet.

The Corvills were trying very hard to like her, and to tell the truth there seemed no reason why they should not, except for the unorthodox introduction. She seemed just the kind of girl that Ned should have married: rather shy, anxious to please, genteel.

Jenny found herself unbending. And she would have gone to bed that night much easier in her mind except for one thing. As the meal ended, the maid had stood by Lucy's chair with a tray bearing the silver table equipment – trellis bread-basket, sauceboats, water bowls. Jenny could have sworn that Lucy was trying very hard to ascertain whether the items were silver or electroplate.

That shrewd sideways glance haunted her dreams. Next morning, after she had dealt with the urgent items at the office, she wrote a letter to the lawyer in Edinburgh who dealt with the Corvills' affairs. She despised herself for doing so, but she asked for information about Mrs Morrison of Lochend Close, Cannongate.

The reply came about eighteen days later. In the meantime Jenny tried very hard to become friends with Lucy, and found it impossible. The girl seemed to have no opinions of her own. She agreed with anyone over anything, apparently more eager to please than to be truthful. It was true she had good manners, spoke well, and knew how to dress. But something was lacking. The lawyer's letter explained what it was.

'Mrs Morrison is a widow of good appearance and standing. She seems to have no large debts though she is known to let bills go as long as she can before paying. Her husband was Lamont Morrison, a character actor in the travelling company McAyre's Players, known for their performances in the holiday resorts of the west coast. He was killed in an accident with some stage equipment on tour. I am told he specialised in playing roles such as vicars, lawyers, country squires. With the compensation for his death Mrs Morrison was able to rent and set up the house in Lochend Close. It may be that she herself trod the boards but she seems to have left the theatre on the birth of her child, Lucy.'

Under this report the lawyer had added in his own hand, 'The word is that she runs a respectable lodging house but is not greatly liked by her neighbours because of a rather grasping nature.'

The story according to Lucy was rather different. Prompted by Ned, she had shyly explained her family background. Her father, she said, was a younger son of the Morrisons of Linlithgow, a well-known family. Her mother had been Miss Alice Howe, daughter of a lawyer. They had run away to be married against family opposition. Lamont Morrison had died with the China Squadron in the action of October 1839 in the Opium War.

'Mama was prostrated with grief, so I was told – though of course I was only a young child at the time. She's been so brave, you know . . . only the tiniest naval pension and yet she managed to bring me up with all the refinements she herself had been used to . . .'

Lucy offered proofs of this as opportunity occurred. She could sketch a little, play easy pieces on the piano, read French from a book. Jenny's parents were pleased with her, and even a little respectful of these displays of superior upbringing.

Jenny saw it differently. Lucy was the daughter of an actor and an actress, a quick study – she had learned to play the part of a lady.

There was nothing so very bad in that. Jenny herself had done it, had adopted the manner and lifestyle of the class in which she now lived. What was different in Lucy was that she denied her origins.

But there was no point in telling her parents what she'd found out. At the moment the first shock had died away, letters of friendship had been exchanged between the Corvills and Mrs Morrison, Lucy had been quietly introduced into Galashiels society and, after a day or two of gossip, as quietly accepted.

In October the Corvill family went to Edinburgh to see Ned receive his degree. Mrs Morrison of course joined the party. She proved to be very like her daughter in looks except that the pale fair hair of Lucy was a little brighter in her mother – helped no doubt by dyestuffs Ronald Armstrong could have named. She was dressed in a new gown of the very highest fashion, bought with money Lucy had sent as soon as she received her dress allowance from the Corvill coffers.

'They were very naughty to marry without letting us know,' she said with a mannered tilt of her head, so that she could look under her lashes at William. 'But Mr Corvill, one must be kind to young love, must one not?'

William said that the young married couple must be helped in every way to settle down to a proper happy life. He remained immune to Mrs Morrison's attempts to fascinate him into close friendship. The truth was, he didn't entirely understand what she was at. He thought of her as another middleaged parent like himself. She thought of herself, Jenny could see, as a mature woman of great charm.

The celebration dinner after the ceremony was held in the Douglas Hotel. To it came two or three of Ned's lecturers and several university friends who had also received their degrees.

One of these proved a very sensible young man, with whom Jenny took the trouble to have a private word.

'Did you know of the proposed wedding, Mr Summers?'

'Not a word! When he moved from the lodgings we shared to go and live at the Morrisons, I thought nothing of it.' He glanced across the room, where mother and daughter were sitting on a sofa with a man on either side – Ned holding Lucy's hand, Ned's tutor offering bonbons to Mrs Morrison. He added in a very careful voice, 'Marriage was not what I expected.' He looked at Jenny to see if she understood.

'I gather he met her at the Assembly Halls,' she rejoined, to let him know she was following the sense of his words.

'Quite likely. You know the variety of events that go on there. Ned . . . er . . . liked to go about . . .'

She nodded. 'I know my brother's foibles, Mr Summers.'

He relaxed. 'In that case I can say, Lucy was acquainted with quite a few university men. But none of us wanted to be . . . er . . . taken seriously.'

'You mean she was a flirt?'

'She was looking for a husband. Quite within her rights, of course.'

'Yes.'

'But you know, they *are* fond of each other.'

'It seems so. Thank you, Mr Summers.'

So Lucy had been on the hunt. But then, how could she be reproached for that? Jenny herself was on the hunt, after Archie Brunton.

The Corvills parted next day from Mrs Morrison. Jenny had seen that there was no great love lost between mother and daughter, which was a relief to her because it meant that Mrs Morrison would not visit them often. Her affectation of elegance and fine breeding was very hard to bear.

Back in Galashiels the daily round resumed, the small gaieties of country society. Hallowe'en came with its boisterous parties and dressing-up. The men went out shooting. The last apples and pears were picked, preserve-making was supervised. Jenny began sketching the new cloths for the spring pattern books.

She was at work in her comfortable office at the mill when she was surprised by a visit from Lucy. Her sister-in-law had come once before, been shown round the mill, announced that the noise gave her the headache, and then avoided the place.

'Lucy, what a pleasure,' Jenny said, rising to greet her. She laid aside the board with its graph paper on which she had been lining up the colours for a new country check.

'I thought I'd drop in as I was passing,' said Lucy.

Most unlikely. There was nothing by the Mill Lead of the Gala except mills. So the girl was here for a purpose.

'Sit down, Lucy – wait, I'll clear the chair for you.' She took up some sample pieces her father had woven the previous week, which were now under consideration for the spring. 'Would you like tea?'

'Er, yes . . . why not?' She clearly expected it to be brought in a tin mug, and was surprised when in response to Jenny's orders a pretty tray with sprigged china appeared.

'Now, Lucy, what can I show you? The mill is a different world to you, I know, but if you'd like to see the new winter cloths – '

'No, thank you, I really prefer to wear velvet and velours, Jenny. No, I didn't have any particular reason for calling . . .'

'Ned isn't with you?'

'No, he's gone shooting with Charlie Linton. He . . . er . . . doesn't have to come to work in any regular way?'

'Father and I would be delighted if he did, Lucy, but he doesn't show much taste for business as yet. Of course, he's entitled to some leisure after so many years of study.'

'But he will be the owner of the mill in time, won't he?'

'Of course. He's a junior partner already – William Corvill *and* Son.'

'He . . . The mill . . . It makes a lot of money?'

'Quite a lot,' Jenny said, smiling to herself. Now the reason for the visit was about to appear.

'It's just that I was thinking . . . you know . . . he was a little bit put out when I asked him what his income was. He didn't seem to know.'

'Well,' said Jenny, sipping her tea, 'his income varies. He gets a percentage of the profits, and the profits change from year to year.'

'A percentage?' Lucy's ladylike education hadn't equipped her to understand percentages.

112

'Well, let's put it in fractions. Ned gets a fraction of the profits.'

Fractions were even less accessible than percentages. Lucy's pink lips pursed over the word. She stirred her tea thoughtfully. 'What I really wanted to know was . . . whether I could have an allowance made over to me from his money.'

'But you have an allowance, Lucy.'

'A dress allowance. It's not much, really.'

'But you can order anything you need, of course. We have accounts with all the shops in Galashiels – '

'Galashiels! It's not the height of fashion, is it?'

'Oh, I see . . .' It was true. Compared with Edinburgh, Galashiels was a dowdy little town. Most of the shops were scarcely more than displays in the downstairs parlour of a house. Bank Street was regarded as the fashionable shopping thoroughfare but even there, only a few plate glass windows had appeared, only a few sun blinds to protect fragile goods.

'Well, if you don't see what you like in the town, you can always send for it. You could probably get anything by train within a day or two – '

'But that's not the way I like to shop. I like to see things, compare, choose . . .'

'I see. In that case, perhaps you could have goods sent on approval. The big firms probably would send a selection.'

Lucy shrugged with something like impatience. 'If Ned doesn't take much part in the running of the firm, is there any reason why he has to live here?'

Jenny was startled. 'Where else would he live?' she asked.

'We could go to Glasgow. Glasgow's full of life, I hear.'

'But Lucy, Ned's been away from home for three years, taking his degree. Mother and Father would never agree to parting with him again so soon.'

Lucy looked as if she were going to say that Mother and Father were a bore, but thought better of it and smiled with daughterly understanding. 'Of course. How selfish you must think me! I don't mean to complain in any way, Jenny darling. It's just that . . . life is so different here.'

'Different from Edinburgh, I quite understand. I was brought up there too, you know. I remember the hustle and bustle, the feeling of something going on all the time. All the same, I enjoy it here.'

'But you have the mill to occupy you,' Lucy pointed out, setting down her cup and saucer with a little bang. 'I just sit and twiddle my thumbs. Ned goes off to shoot grouse or see friends – '

'You've made friends here too, Lucy.'

'They all seem engrossed in cloth-making! It's all they ever talk about!'

'Well, it is our livelihood, you know. And the women do talk about other things: fashion, family matters – '

'Housekeeping, how to make apple jelly, whether wintergreen is good for the chest.'

Jenny didn't know what to say. What had her sister-in-law expected? They were living in a provincial town, with provincial interests.

At the beginning, Jenny had thought that there would soon be a baby. She had almost taken it for granted that it was the reason for the hasty, secretive wedding. But no baby was on the way. There wasn't even the prospect of a young family to keep Lucy occupied.

'If Mother would just let me take over the house,' Lucy went on in an injured tone. 'She's not young any more, after all, and some of her ways are so oldfashioned! I have some ideas that would make the place look so much *à la mode* . . .'

Jenny shook her head. 'In the first place, the house isn't ours to change – '

'Good heavens! You mean it's only rented?'

'Yes.'

'But that's . . . that's . . . I took it for granted it was ours!'

'Well, I hope it will be, some day soon. I instituted a special fund, putting money aside to buy the house. Quite soon, I hope, it will be ours.'

'But we own the mill?'

'No, that too is only rented.'

Lucy's unguarded face was a study. Her forget-me-not blue eyes were hard with anger, her mouth was a thin line, her fair brows were drawn together in a shadowy line. 'Ned never told me that! I thought you owned everything!'

'There's no need to own it, Lucy. That isn't good business.

It's better to rent and then, if we want to expand, we can move to bigger premises. We haven't been in production here long, you see. We still have a long way to go.' She rose, to come and stand looking down at her sister-in-law. 'Don't worry, Lucy. There's plenty of money and in time you'll settle down to the life we lead. It's not like Edinburgh, I admit – but you can make it very agreeable once you come to terms with it.'

She put a friendly hand on Lucy's shoulder. She very much wanted the girl to feel that she understood her frustration and disappointment. The Corvills weren't what she expected; she'd perhaps pictured a grand country estate, a fleet of footmen, entertaining in candle-lit halls. Everything was on a smaller, more workaday scale. But it could be a happy setting for her, if she could only accept it.

Lucy got up. Jenny sensed that she did so to avoid her touch. She thought, She dislikes me. It was a revelation.

She drew back, but hid her startled realisation under a friendly smile as she showed her out. A hackney had been called for her. It was waiting on the paved yard outside. She helped her in, waved as it drew away. Lucy didn't wave back.

She really dislikes me, thought Jenny, as she went back to her work. Why? I've never given her the slightest hint that I know her real background. I've kept her secret, taken her at face value, tried to be friends. Why should she dislike me so much that she draws away from my touch?

For the next few days the question kept recurring. In the end she thought she understood. Lucy was envious of her. She had come to Galashiels as the bride of a rich young cloth-maker, expecting to take over the running of his house and to see him running his business. She had expected to be queen of her castle.

But that role was already filled. Jenny Corvill was in command at the mill and, through her mother who did little without consulting her, at Gatesmuir.

Jenny's first impulse was one of irritation. Let her get on with it, she thought. We're not what she was hoping for – too bad.

Yet in a day or two basic good nature was making her rethink the situation. How would she feel in Lucy's place?

Brought up in a city where something was always going on, where cheap entertainment was everywhere, educated by a mother who probably filled her head with silly notions . . . And then trapped in a family whose head felt that even a simple evening game of cards had something sinful in it, in a town still lacking many of the amenities taken for granted in the capital – nowhere to go except to visit the same people, nothing to do except walk or drive along country roads . . .

Jenny said to her mother, 'I get the feeling Lucy finds life pretty dull. Could you do something to include her in the swing of things more?'

'Well, dear,' said Millicent with a little frown, 'I did ask her to join the Ladies Charitable Sewing Circle so we could get the flannel shirts finished before the cold weather – '

'Oh, Mother!' Jenny stifled her laughter. 'That's not the kind of thing that would appeal to Lucy.'

'I don't know why not, dear. The poor appreciate it so and we have such good chat while we work – '

'No, no, I meant something that's more fun. The St Andrew's Day party, for instance.'

'Yes, the one we're having the musicians from Peebles – '

'Could you let Lucy choose the flowers, decide on the food?'

'But, my pet, I can do it twice as quickly as Lucy. She takes so long to make up her mind about anything.'

'That's not the point, Mother. It would be a kindness to give her something to do that she might really enjoy.'

Unfortunately when Millicent handed the task over to Lucy, she told her daughter-in-law it was at Jenny's suggestion. Lucy at once felt she was being patronised. From being simply bored and restless, she became angry. Who did they think they were, this bunch of country mice? Just because they'd been lucky with their stupid tartans, and nobody of any taste would ever think them so wonderful, they were nothing compared with French cloth like velours or gaberdine.

Worse was to come. A letter arrived from Buckingham Palace, inviting a member of the firm of Corvill and Son to attend on a matter of business at three o'clock on 8th January 1858, if convenient.

'Ned must go,' Lucy said at once, when the letter was read

out with surprise and acclamation at the Gatesmuir breakfast table.

'Me?' said Ned. The idea didn't appeal, especially since he had a headache due to too much whisky the night before. A long train journey . . . bowing and scraping before some royal secretary . . .

'Well,' mused William, 'you see it says "on a matter of business" and, as it happens, Ned hasn't come to grips with the business yet.'

'Good gracious, they're not going to discuss how to run a cloth mill!' Lucy cried. 'They just want to look at patterns of tartan to dress up the children again, that's all.'

'Jenny ought to go,' Ned said. 'Jenny knows how to go about it – she went to Balmoral.'

'It's a long way,' Mrs Corvill lamented. 'A very tiring journey – '

'Not if you stay overnight in Edinburgh on the way. Ned, we could both go. I should so much enjoy – '

'Whoever goes,' William went on, following his own thoughts regardless of his daughter-in-law's fervent interventions, 'ought to take the opportunity of calling in on Wilson.'

'Who's Wilson?'

'Our factor in London, Lucy.'

Lucy was just as much at a loss as before. She had no idea what a factor did.

'I agree it would be a good idea to meet him face to face,' Jenny said, speaking for the first time since exclaiming in pleasure over the invitation. 'I think he's been behaving a wee bit trickily for a while now.'

'The man's a villain,' William said. 'It's time someone saw him and told him outright that the price he's buying at is daylight robbery.'

'What price is he paying?' asked Ned.

'There you are,' said his father, 'that's the point, lad, you don't even know, so clearly you're not the right person to speak to him. And as for me . . .' he sighed. 'I've no mind to go to a place like London. I hear it's even worse than Edinburgh for show and vanity.'

So in the end it was decided, to Lucy's great chagrin, that Jenny must go.

This time, as befitted her station, she would take their lady's maid with her as escort. This was another matter to make Lucy sulk. Mrs Corvill might manage very well without Baird to do her hair, but in the few months since her marriage Lucy had become accustomed to having someone else do all the wearisome chores that went with an elegant turn-out.

If Jenny were to be in London on 8th January it meant leaving Galashiels on the 6th. Christmas and New Year behind them, it was time to make preparations for the trip. First of all, a new and very smart pattern book must be prepared in case the royal family wished to see some samples. Then some sketches of designs for next winter, not yet in production, must be mounted on board.

'You're fair busy,' Ronald Armstrong commented as he came into Jenny's office for a discussion of heather shades for the next dye vat. 'Did the letter actually say they wanted to look at new designs?'

'No, it simply said a matter of business. But I feel I'd better take a few things . . . Mr Armstrong, what do you think of this?' She held out a water-colour design of grey and white on black paper.

'Mournful.'

She laughed. 'It's for gentlemen's suiting.'

'For a mournful gentleman.'

'I wondered if I should take it? It might interest HRH for London wear.'

'I wouldn't think that's in prospect, mistress. As far as the Palace is concerned, Corvill and Son are great for the tartan. I don't think they're asking you to call so they can talk about gentlemen's suiting.' He paused. 'How long d'you think you'll be gone, Mistress Corvill?'

'A week? Not much more. Why?'

'I'm going to try out the new German blues in the dye vat. I thought you'd like to see them.'

'They'll still be here when I get back, surely? The samples, I mean.'

'I usually throw out the poor results.'

118

'Well, this time keep them,' she said, puzzled. 'A few hanks of yarn won't take up much room.'

'That's true,' he said. 'It's just that you're usually *here* . . . Ah well, if you're happy with this heather shade I'll away to my work.'

She shook her head as the door closed on him. It wasn't like Ronald Armstrong to be hanging about asking for opinions.

Still, it was good to know that she'd be missed . . .

Archie Brunton's reaction to the news was even more positive. 'Going to London?' he exclaimed. 'Good heavens, why on earth doesn't Ned go?'

'Because Ned knows nothing about anything and we can't make fools of ourselves at the Palace.'

Archie scowled. It was true that Ned paid no heed to the mills, as Archie knew only too well, because it was with Archie that Ned spent a lot of his time. The two of them would be off together, meeting companions in Selkirk, fishing for salmon at Berwick on Tweed, going to the races.

'I don't think it's seemly,' he said.

'In what way?'

'A woman shouldn't be travelling about the country doing business – it's not right.'

'Archie, I'm not going to "travel about the country". I'm making a trip to London at the request of the royal family.'

'I'm sure they don't expect a woman to represent the firm – '

'They may very well. I represented us before, when I went to Balmoral.'

'*You* went?'

'Yes, I thought you'd heard about it. When we sold them the first piece of tartan.'

He was very put out. 'I hope you're not going to make a habit of it,' he remarked, his expression mirroring the bewildered exasperation he felt.

'No, I hope not. There's no reason. In general we deal through the factor, like everyone else. This is different, though. A royal summons!' She was trying to make it sound playful. 'I hope I shall always be ready to answer a royal command.'

'Always?' he echoed. There was a pause. 'You're not

thinking of . . . being concerned in the business . . . all your life?'

All at once there was a great question hanging in the air above them. It was something she had always avoided thinking about when she considered her life as a married woman.

If Archie asked her, she was going to say yes. She had put too much time and energy into catching him, and had known something like despair when Ned's extraordinary marriage almost wrecked things. Lucy had been gingerly inspected by Archie's mother, and Jenny knew it had been touch and go whether Mrs Brunton would accept her.

In the end, however, good sense had prevailed. Lucy might not be quite what she pretended to be, but she made a good enough impression, was very anxious to please, and, after all, Mrs Brunton's only son need have very little to do with her once he was married to Jenny.

So everything resumed as before. Archie often spoke as if it were a matter of course that he and Jenny would be living at the Mains by and by. All that was needed was a positive declaration.

That had been put off, partly because Archie couldn't bring himself to give up his freedom and partly because Jenny didn't want to drive him to the final word. Though in her own view being married need not stop her from carrying on her role as the controlling genius of Corvill and Son, she knew instinctively Archie wouldn't agree.

Now the question hovered. And she felt she ought to say at least something to make her views clear.

'I can't foresee a time when I wouldn't be interested in the business, Archie. You know it's my designs that we use, mostly. I would always want to take part in the designing if nothing else. And since I *am* good at the financial side, it seems silly not to – '

'But surely Ned,' said Archie, choosing his words, 'Ned is going to take over?'

She made a sound, half a laugh and half a sigh. 'Do you see any signs of it?'

'Well, I . . . . I took it for granted. He's the heir, after all.'

'Quite true. But he seems to have no interest in business.'

'He could always put in a manager.'

120

'Yes. That was what we intended, at first. Only, you see, I'm good at it.'

'But it's so unsuitable!'

'I think most people are quite used to it by now, Archie. They don't see anything wrong in it.'

'But that's only because you're Miss Corvill. If . . . if things changed . . . What I mean is, if you married, you could hardly go on in the same way.'

She said nothing. She almost held her breath. If she were to utter the words that had sprung to her lips she'd have said, 'It's *my* firm. I made it what it is. Why should I give it up just to suit the conventions?' But one wrong word now and Archie would go away. And perhaps he wouldn't come back.

For the moment they let it lie. But she could tell, during the next few days, that he was displeased with her.

London proved overwhelming at first. As she and Baird walked in the wake of the porter out of the station, the noise and activity outside almost made Jenny recoil. Baird, however, was made of sterner stuff. She'd seen London before. A widow, neat in person, plain in speech, she'd been with a shipping merchant's family in Glasgow before her marriage. With them she had travelled to London, she knew good hotels and respectable restaurants.

A hackney took them to the Hyde Park Hotel, near Marble Arch. On the drive there, Jenny thought they would collide with other vehicles, the roads were so crowded. The day was very cold, the horses slid on the icy cobbles, the drivers swore at each other and used their whips. 'Heaven preserve us,' muttered Jenny. Her maid smiled grimly. It was worse, she recalled, at morning and evening.

But the hotel itself pleased Jenny; spacious, well-carpeted, full of palms in highly polished brass containers. Her little suite of rooms had a beautiful view of the park. She sank into an armchair with thankfulness. From here, it would be a pleasure to look out in the morning. She might almost believe she was at home in her own bedroom gazing out at the lower slopes of Meigle Hill.

She spent the next morning having her hair done at a fashionable salon in Belgrave Street. When the hairdresser stepped back, curling tongs swinging loose, hand raised in

121

appeal, Jenny had to admit she looked rather fine. It seemed almost a pity to hide the effect under the fur-trimmed bonnet called for by the January weather.

Baird made her eat a light lunch in the suite. 'Now, now, my lass, you have to eat something. I ken fine you feel too high-strung at the thought of going to the Palace but you'll likely faint if you don't have something in your stomach.'

True enough. She felt faint every time she thought of the prospect. But at a quarter after two she went downstairs to the private carriage she had ordered, stepped inside in her fur wrap and her new gown of dark blue plaid, and was on her way.

The carriage driver knew what was expected. She'd thought she'd go bowling in at the main entrance but no, he took her to the side. There the carriage went in as at a stable yard, drove between short rows of buildings where other carriages could be glimpsed, and drew up at a door which, for a side entrance, was stately enough. She gave her name, saying – quite accurately this time – that she was expected.

'From Corvill and Son, quite so. Please to wait.' She was ushered into a room with chairs and some periodicals on a table, with a stand on which she could leave her fur wrap and bonnet. After a short pause she was conducted along a corridor, through what looked like a main hall, up some stairs, along a mile of corridor, and asked once more to wait. She sat on the edge of a crimson plush chair, clutching the portfolio of patterns to her chest. Lunch or no lunch, she felt faint.

The footman returned. 'Her Majesty will see you now.'

Jenny rose, then sat down again. 'Her Majesty?'

'Certainly. This way.'

'But . . . but . . . I thought I would see a secretary, or an official?'

The footman gave a very faint shrug. 'Her Majesty is waiting,' he said.

With shaking knees Jenny got up again to follow him.

The room into which she was shown had large windows letting in the cold light of the January afternoon. The Queen was sitting in a chair with a low padded back, and had before her a sloping table on which a sketchbook lay. In her hand was a charcoal pencil.

She looked round as Jenny was shown in.

'Miss Corvill, Ma'am.'

'Miss Corvill, please come in. How do you do?'

Jenny curtseyed, the room wavering around her as she did so. She was relieved to find she could regain her upright posture without swaying about. Her heart was going like a carding-engine.

She was face to face with the Queen of England!

Victoria wore a warm dress of fine brown wool checked with white, and a white woollen shawl so fine it looked like lace. Her hair was plainly dressed, parted in the middle with ringlets at the side. A white lace cap set near the back of her head echoed the soft white of the shawl. Her only ornaments were a jewelled watch hanging from a lover's knot bow on her bodice, and the wedding and engagement rings on her left hand.

'Well, Miss Corvill, you see me making good use of a little spare time. Do you draw, my dear?'

'Er, not to say draw . . . I . . . er, design the checks and tartans made by our firm.'

'Ah, so it is to you that we owe so many delightful patterns? How interesting. I see you have brought a sketchbook. Sit down. Miss Rowland, settle Miss Corvill.'

A young lady, unnoticed until now, stepped forward. She set a chair for Jenny, who thankfully sank down. Miss Rowland took the pattern book from Jenny's hands to take to the Queen.

Victoria laid the book on top of her own on the table, opened it, and glanced through the patterns until she came to the water-colour designs on board at the back. 'Ah yes, I see, so that is how it is done? And then the patterns are tried out on the loom?'

'Yes, Ma'am. My father makes a sample piece on a handloom.'

'And the thread – how do you decide on the thread? I am interested, you know, Miss Corvill. I am a spinster – a spinner – myself.' She nodded towards a corner. To Jenny's surprise, a spinning wheel stood there, its well-used wood gleaming in the light from the bright fire. 'A very soothing occupation,' Victoria said, with a faint smile.

'A great change from affairs of state, Ma'am,' Jenny said, greatly daring.

'Not so different, my dear! Deftness and patience – those are things of great use in statecraft. Well, now, these designs are delightful, but it wasn't for this that I asked you to come.' She paused. 'To tell the truth, I expected someone older. How old are you, Miss Corvill?'

'Twenty-one, Your Majesty.'

The Queen tilted her head. She didn't say, How does it come about that a girl of twenty-one is the representative of an important weaving firm? For she herself had been in charge of the entire country from an even younger age.

'Miss Rowland, please bring the drawings.'

'Yes, Ma'am.' The lady-in-waiting went to a bureau, opened it, and took out a large envelope. She brought it to Jenny.

As Jenny opened the envelope the Queen said, 'We've seen some very fine tartans in the Highlands, worn by tenants and gamekeepers – particularly that worn by the employees of the Countess of Seafield.'

'Ah yes,' said Jenny, 'the Glenurquart . . .'

'There are others.'

'Yes, what are known as the District Checks – not belonging to a clan and not for dress occasions.'

'What we might call workaday tartans, more like the shepherds' plaid of the Borders.'

'Exactly, Ma'am.' By this time Jenny had the contents out of the envelope. There were two designs, one large, one small, done in crayon on cartridge paper.

The check was unusual, rather dignified and subdued, but handsome. The background was grey, the main square was black, with lesser lines of grey and black, all overchecked with thin lines of tan.

'Ma'am, this is a very good design,' Jenny said, without pausing to think.

To her amazement, Victoria coloured and smiled with delight. 'You think so?'

'Very fine! It would be very good for indoor wear, but also, on a hillside, it would fade into a stony background – excellent for a stalker. I take it one of the ghillies made this?'

124

'I am very pleased with your verdict, Miss Corvill. My husband designed that himself.'

'The Prince?'

'Yes, he takes a great interest in applied art. He and I have felt for some time that it would be pleasant to have a tartan other than the Stewart, for use by our household. And that is why I sent for you. The Prince was pleased with your work on a previous occasion. I want your firm to make this for us.'

Jenny drew in her breath. 'Madam, it would be an honour.'

'What is the usual procedure? How soon could we see it in the cloth?'

'The greys are no problem, we have grey yarns in stock now that are almost an exact match, although of course we shall adjust the shade if need be. The tan . . . my dye-master can reproduce the tan in a few days once he sees the sketch. Then my father will produce a sample on a handloom. Tell me, Ma'am, what weight would you wish to have?'

'I think, two kinds – the usual kilt weight, and perhaps something lighter for women's gowns, although I'm not sure if we shall put the women servants into tartan. Can you let me see two samples?'

'Certainly. Might I suggest, Ma'am, another – a heavy enough weight for a jacket but less than the kilt. It might be a handsome effect, to have a plaid jacket and plain trousers?'

'I had not thought of that. Why not? Yes, let us see something along those lines.'

Jenny bowed acquiescence. She was alight with excitement and enthusiasm. Another order from the royal family – and this time, the Prince's own design. What a triumph, what an honour . . .

'Tartans have a name, as a rule, do they not?'

'Yes, indeed. Have you thought of a name for this one?'

'The Prince and I have considered it, but nothing seems right. I wish to call it the Prince Albert, but my husband feels that would be wrong – he feels only Scotsmen should have tartans named after them.' She smiled in loving tolerance at her husband's sensitivity. 'I thought, perhaps, Royal Highland . . . Or Highland Grey?' But she looked dubious as she said it.

Jenny pondered. 'District Checks usually take the name of a district, of course.'

'Deeside?' suggested the Queen.

Deeside . . . Not bad. But perhaps a little too general. To Jenny Deeside meant only one place. 'What do you think,' Jenny said, 'of . . . Balmoral?'

Victoria's face lit up. Any reference to that well-loved home made her remember happy times. 'Miss Corvill, that is an excellent idea! Why did we not think of that? Balmoral, of course – our Highland home. That shall be the name.'

The Queen's approval made Jenny feel light-headed. She sensed that the interview was ending, and rose to her feet. Moving to the Queen's table, she began to reclaim her portfolio. In doing so she uncovered the drawings on which the Queen had been working.

They were surprisingly lively little figures in country costume, standing out from the page in stark black and white. One that caught the eye was a woman in a black dress, with white apron and headdress, holding a baby.

'That must be a national costume, surely?' Jenny remarked, for a moment forgetting she must not speak unless spoken to.

'Quite right. Can you guess where?' the Queen said in amusement.

Jenny blushed, suddenly embarrassed. 'I beg Your Majesty's pardon. I didn't mean . . .'

'No, tell me, where do you think this sketch was made?'

'I have never been abroad, Ma'am, but I think . . . France?'

'Very good. These are some sketches I made during our little visit there last summer. It was so charming, we were incognito, in a little Normandy village. See, here are the starched caps in more detail. I asked how they kept them on in a high wind but they wouldn't tell me.'

For another five minutes Jenny stood by the Queen's side while Victoria went back and forth among the sketches on her drawing table. Then, at last, she closed the book with a sigh. 'Such a happy time,' she sighed. Then, coming back to the present, to the handsome room in the cold palace in January London, 'I look forward to seeing the cloth, Miss Corvill.'

'I shall bring it myself, if you permit me, Ma'am.'

'Excellent. Until then, Miss Corvill.'

A maidservant was waiting to help her on with her wrap in the downstairs anteroom. She gathered up portfolio, reticule and gloves. She was being led down a long corridor to the porte cochere when a door at the far end opened. A woman came out, momentarily silhouetted in the light from the room.

Jenny checked her stride. Could it be . . . ? To her, it was an unforgettable figure, engraved on her memory with a steel tool. Laura, Mrs Robert Prentiss.

The maid was leading on. Jenny shook her head. Nonsense – she was imagining things.

The woman spoke over her shoulder to those in the room. 'Remember, my friends, I'm expecting him home in good time to change for the opera.' There was laughter and teasing disagreement from within.

Unmistakeable. The voice of Laura Prentiss. Jenny turned, ready for flight.

The maid escorting her looked back. 'Ma'am?'

'I've forgotten my gloves,' Jenny said.

'No, miss, you have them in your hand.'

Trapped, Jenny trod the stone corridor, hearing the footsteps of her former vanquisher come towards her. The light in the corridor was dim, from gas-brackets on the walls. If she kept her head turned away . . . ?

It wasn't to be. As they came abreast Laura Prentiss said to the maid, in a hearty, friend-of-long-standing tone, 'Who have we here, Maisie? A lucky visitor to the royal parlour?'

'Miss Corvill, ma'am,' said the maid, bobbing a curtsey as she went past.

Jenny drew herself up. She saw the puzzlement in Laura's face giving way to incredulous recognition.

'Good afternoon, Mrs Prentiss,' Jenny said calmly through stiff lips, and walked on.

In the carriage going back to the hotel she sat huddled in a corner. She had had nightmares about perhaps seeing Captain Prentiss, but had banished the thought – by this time his tour of duty would be over, she was sure the royal family tried to ring the changes on the young men available for service in the Royal Household. Never in her wildest dreams had she thought she might see Laura. Nor had she thought it would affect her so deeply. She was trembling, she felt sick, her head seemed to be going round.

When she came into the parlour of the hotel suite, Baird leapt upon her, taking her sketchbook in her bony hands, helping her off with her wrap, fussing around like a lanky old hen. 'Did everything go off well, then, Miss Corvill? You look gey queasy.'

'It was a bit frightening.' She had to account for her state, she saw, as Baird stared anxiously into her pale face. 'I actually met the Queen, Baird.'

'The Queen?' breathed the maidservant.

How strange and sad that her moment of greatest triumph should be blotted out by that unexpected encounter with the enemy of years ago.

Chapter Nine

The reaction of everyone in Galashiels was the same as Baird's: 'You met the Queen? You actually spoke to her?'

Jenny was asked again and again what Her Majesty was wearing, how she looked, whether she was agreeable. Her patient replies conveyed exactly her impression: the Queen was a goodlooking woman of thirty-nine, dressed for warmth rather than elegance, kind in manner and with a sense of humour. Nobody seemed quite to believe it. Surely there was some grandeur, some regal disdain?

'You make her sound quite ordinary!' Lucy said crossly.

'I don't think I've said that,' murmured Jenny. 'But she certainly wasn't wearing a crown nor wielding a sceptre, if that's what you hope to hear.'

Lucy shrugged and smiled to herself. She seemed to be implying that if she had been the one invited to the Palace, she'd have better things to report than chat about cloth and sketching. Jenny, she seemed to be saying, lacked sensitivity for the finer points.

Archie Brunton, too, was dissatisfied over the London trip. It was bad enough that she had gone to the Palace, but to meet the Queen herself – it was too much. How could he hope to keep Jenny in her proper place as a provincial wife if she were going to meet the Queen from time to time?

'I don't see any need for you to go back in person with the cloth,' he grumbled. 'You could send it – '

'I promised I'd take it myself.'

'Oh, no doubt,' Lucy put in. 'Too good a chance to miss, to hobnob with Her Majesty again.'

'It was only respectful to offer,' Jenny's father said. 'I think it was the right thing. And Jenny, when you go, I think it would be fitting to take a gift of some other tartan, just as a mark of our appreciation for the honour.'

Archie made a sound, half annoyance, half disgust. 'By all means seize every opportunity to promote your goods – '

'It's simply to show we're grateful, Archie,' Jenny soothed.

'I should think the royal family are bored to death with having things showered on them to "show appreciation".'

Jenny sighed to herself. It was almost as if he wanted to pick a quarrel with her. And sometimes, in the fortnight that elapsed before she made the return trip to London, she felt it would be a good thing to quarrel and be done with it.

Her encounter with Laura Prentiss had taught her one thing. Whatever might have been wrong in her love affair with Bobby Prentiss, there had been real feeling. She had genuinely loved and wanted him.

The comparison with what she felt for Archie made her uncomfortable. Archie, the man she had decided on as a husband, was tolerable – handsome, amiable when in a good temper – someone she felt she could rub along with for the years to come. But she didn't love him, and she knew it, and he knew it.

Yet they were more or less committed to each other now. Their families and all their acquaintances were awaiting the announcement of their engagement. She must bring him to the point soon – as soon as she got back from London again. They should have an Easter wedding. It really must be so, because she must be an established married woman by her twenty-second birthday or she would be an old maid.

Everyone in Galashiels pressed the Corvills to show the new tartan. William refused. 'It's the royal family's tartan, they must be the first to see it,' he said.

Ronald Armstrong had had no problems finding the right dye for the tan check over the grey. He even teased Jenny about it. 'You should have put a tan line in that one you were showing me before you went to London,' he told her. 'Your grey gentleman's suiting would have been livened up by that touch of colour.'

'Mr Armstrong, you know very well I wasn't trying to design a tartan. I wanted a quiet businessman's check.'

'I thought afterwards, you could have shown it to Wilson. How did you get on with him, Mistress Corvill?'

She sighed. 'There's no doubt the man's a rogue,' she said. 'But he's an impressive rogue. That warehouse of his in Cheapside is full of bales of cloth. And while I was there I met a buyer from Paris, and heard there was one from Vienna. We really can't afford to lose him as our factor.'

They were sitting quietly together in the office. There had been a little conference of all foremen and department managers about how quickly the Balmoral tartan could be fitted into production if the Queen wished it to go ahead, and if so, how much they could produce without disrupting their other schedules.

The conference had ended with tea and seedcake. Armstrong had lingered afterwards to chat. His long figure was leaning by the window, strands of wool in his hands – he was seldom without some sample of new colour to show.

'Was Wilson impolite to you?' he asked.

Jenny was surprised. 'No, indeed. He'd expected a man, since we'd written to say our representative would call. But he recovered quickly and was amiable enough, though full of complaints about our cloth – in hopes we would lower our prices to him.' She paused a moment. 'What made you ask such a question?'

'I hardly know. Since you came back you've been different, somehow.'

'Surely I'm allowed to be "different" after speaking to the Queen,' she said, laughing.

'No, it's not that; it's more as if you'd had something worrying . . . alarming . . . happen to you.'

'No, I assure you.' It occurred to her how shrewd he was. He had noticed what others had missed. She *was* different – preoccupied, a little shadowed by the memory of the emotion she'd felt when she saw Laura Prentiss.

'Can I ask – is it about your marriage?'

She coloured. Never before had they touched on personal matters. She said with some stiffness, 'Certainly not.' And then, recovering herself, 'What marriage, in any case?'

'Och, it's the talk of the town you're going to wed Archie

131

Brunton. The workers here are wagering it will be before the summer now.'

'Mr Armstrong!' She was offended. 'I would prefer not to have my personal affairs discussed.'

'Right, you are,' he agreed, straightening from his lounging attitude at the window. 'Have you definitely decided on taking the Old Stewart as a gift to Their Majesties?'

'I shall take two yards as a sample piece and if they like it, I'll say the full piece will come to the Palace by carrier.' She retreated gratefully into business matters. 'Why do you ask?'

'It's a darkish green. If they remark on it, you can say I can produce a mossier shade – there's no historical precedent to say that the main colour has to be pine-tree green. I was thinking, if you offer it for the children's clothes, mebbe Her Majesty would prefer something a bit lighter.'

'Thank you, Mr Armstrong. That's a good thought.'

'Aye, well . . . Good afternoon, Mistress Corvill.' When he got to the door he turned back a little. 'Everybody takes it for granted it's a match between you and Archie Brunton. If it's still in debate . . . mebbe you should think twice about it.'

With that he was out of the door and away. She sat at her desk with her mouth open in astonishment. She was angry a moment later, but then she was puzzled. What did he mean? He was the first person who had ever said anything to suggest that marrying Archie would be less than perfect for her.

But she had no time to worry about odd ideas from a member of her workforce. She had to conclude the preparations for her journey, ensure that the samples of tartan were neatly wrapped, first in tissue and then in stiff blue paper, see her trunk packed, and book her hotel rooms again.

She had written to the Palace to say that she would be at the Hyde Park Hotel with the sample of Balmoral tartan as from 2nd February, and would await a summons to deliver it. When she reached her hotel, an envelope was awaiting her, a stiff envelope with the royal arms embossed. She was asked to come to the Palace next day at eleven-thirty.

'Baird, make sure the skirt of my brocatelle gown is pressed – you see how creased it's become in the trunk. Since the weather is so mild, I shall wear the short cashmere jacket with it. You'll have to do my hair in the morning, there's no time to see a professional coiffeur – '

'Mistress, mistress, dinna fash yourself – I'll see to it all, you'll look as pretty as ever when you set out.'

She couldn't tell her maid that she was dressing not only for the Queen, but in case she had another encounter with Laura Prentiss.

When she was ushered through the ground floor of the entrance wing next morning, she saw a figure sitting on a chair in the main hall. Instinct told her that it was Laura. She held her head high, knowing that though she was very pale she looked attractive and elegant – certainly not like a 'mill girl'.

As they crossed the hall to the staircase, Laura rose. 'Good morning, Miss Corvill. I heard you were coming today.'

'Good morning, Mrs Prentiss. How kind of you to take an interest.'

'I was, indeed, very interested,' said Laura, with a flash of hidden annoyance. 'I hear the Queen has mentioned you more than once.'

'I'm gratified. Do you spend much time at the Palace, Mrs Prentiss?'

'Oh yes,' Laura said, with triumphant satisfaction. 'My husband – you may remember him? – Captain Prentiss concluded his turn of duty as equerry but his new post at the War Office allows us to be here as often as we are wanted.' She gave Jenny a warning look. 'We have many friends here.'

'How delightful,' said Jenny. She moved a little towards the footman who was leading the way, and who now glanced back as if to say, Remember we're being waited for.

'Perhaps I shall see you again, Miss Corvill.'

'I greatly doubt it. I seldom visit London.'

'Ah.' There was relief in the sound. 'Perhaps that is all for the best, Miss Corvill. Unless one knows one's way about, it's easy to . . . shall we say . . . find oneself in a difficult situation.'

'That must surely be true even for those familiar with the palace,' Jenny riposted. 'But good sense helps in every situation. Good morning, Mrs Prentiss.'

The other woman stood back to allow her to proceed. Jenny followed the footman up the staircase with legs that trembled.

133

Veiled threats, animosity scarcely hidden – Laura Prentiss was in a position to harm her if ever she wanted to. But then 'having friends at the Palace' didn't necessarily mean that Laura was often in the Queen's company. Part of what she'd said was bluff, she felt sure.

She was shown into a different room this time, a larger room with more furniture and massive paintings on the brocaded walls. There were heavy armchairs near the great fireplace. From one a figure rose as she entered. The Prince Consort!

'Good morning, Miss Corvill. We met before, when you were on a similar errand, if I remember rightly.' The infallible royal memory, the kindly royal manner. And still a handsome man, though his hair was receding fast from the lofty brow.

Two little boys in sailor suits scrambled up from behind a sofa, one carrying a toy boat. They converged on Jenny as she was curtseying, almost bowling her over.

'Mama, is this the young lady who's making our new tartan?'

'Hush, boys, mind your manners!' said a voice.

Jenny, led by the Prince, was brought to the other armchair where the Queen sat facing the fire but with a mesh screen to keep its warmth from her cheeks. She laid aside a document to give her attention to her visitor. 'Good morning, my dear. I hope you don't mind my two young ones making up the party. They so much wanted to see their father's design made into cloth.'

Jenny realised these must be Prince Arthur and Prince Leopold, about seven and four years old. The smaller boy was intensely eager, coming to pull at the parcel she was holding.

'Let me do it,' said the Prince, taking it from her. He put it on an inlaid table and with a few deft tugs had undone the tape.

'This packet, sir,' she said, taking up the one that held the Balmoral plaid. She unfolded the tissue paper, caught hold of a corner of the cloth, and with a practised throw laid it across her arm.

The Prince leaned close to study it. Jenny bent forward so that the Queen could see it without having to get up.

Prince Leopold craned on tiptoe. 'Is it nice, Papa? May I see?'

'Surely, my boy – here is the pretty cloth the young lady has brought.'

Prompted thus by his father, the little boy said solemnly, 'It's very pretty.'

'You see there are three samples,' Jenny pointed out. 'Her Majesty asked to have weights suitable for kilts and woman's gowns. I suggested – '

'Yes, yes, for jackets, I understand. What do you think, my dear?'

Victoria was looking at her husband, not the cloth. She could see he was smiling. 'Most pleasing, Miss Corvill. We are very satisfied with what you have produced. But what is in the other package?'

Jenny produced the Old Stewart, explained that Corvill and Son wished to offer it as a gift in any length Their Majesties might choose. She passed on Ronald Armstrong's suggestions about the shade of green. 'We thought that if you wished to use it for the children – '

'A very kind thought. We are happy to accept.'

The two little boys, hearing that the green tartan was primarily intended for them, asked to be allowed to hold it. In a moment or two they were draping it over each other and saluting, as if on parade. Jenny laughed, then checked in embarrassment, but the royal parents were indulgent for the moment.

A short conversation ensued, about how much of the Balmoral tartan should be woven. Jenny produced notebook and pencil, and jotted down the requirements.

'May I mention one thing, Your Majesty?' she ventured. 'About the Old Stewart. That is an old clan tartan. As such, the pattern is in the public domain and anyone can wear it.'

'How does it come,' Albert inquired, 'that Old Stewart is so very different from the other?'

'The reason is lost in history, sir, but the legend goes that when Mary Stuart came home to rule Scotland in the middle of the sixteenth century, she was shown her family tartan. Having been brought up in the French court she found it too countrified, and so the red check – you see it, sir? – was

135

increased to make it look brighter. In the course of another century or so, the red overcame the green. That's the story, although I cannot vouch for it.'

'I like it as a story,' Albert said, with a faint smile. 'The ladies, you know . . . they are always the leaders in fashion.'

'Even the name of the cloth, sir, perhaps we owe that too to Mary Queen of Scots. It's supposed to come from the French, *tirletane*. It's said that the French courtiers thought the cloth worn by the Scottish nobles was barbarous and referred to it as *tirletane*, which seems to have meant linsey-woolsey.'

'Linsey-woolsey – this I do not know?'

'It's an old name for a cloth of mixed linen and wool, which a rich Frenchman might have thought very inferior.'

'Miss Corvill, you are quite a student!' said the Queen.

'Not at all, Ma'am, it's simply that I'm interested in anything to do with cloth. Which brings me back to what I intended to say, if I may?' At a nod from the Queen she went on: 'The two Stewart tartans can be worn by anyone descended from the Stewart clan – and I'm afraid by anyone who likes them and wishes to wear them, because there is nothing to prevent it. But the Balmoral tartan, Ma'am – that could be kept exclusively for royal use. Corvill and Son will never make it except at your orders, if you wish it so.'

There was a little pause. She saw the Queen lay her hand on her husband's sleeve and press it gently. The Prince said, 'Miss Corvill, you have very good understanding. That would please the Queen and myself very much.'

Her chief purpose accomplished, Jenny allowed herself a few days' relaxation in London before returning home. She went shopping with Baird, to view what was available in the dressmakers, the milliners, and the tailors. Men's fashions interested her as much as women's – the colours were still drab, with brightness focused on the waistcoat. Checks for waistcoats could be bright, although checks for trousers seemed to be growing more sombre every year. But plaids for overcoats could be rich in colour, she noted in her notebook.

She bought a round felt hat as a present for Ned: 'New from Paris,' proclaimed the copper-plate card beside it in the hatter's window, 'suitable for country wear.' She found some ready-made shirts for her father, with the new starched cuffs – she thought they would go well with his habitual black. For her mother she bought a lace bertha, and for Lucy stockings made of very fine silk in a lacy pattern.

She stood for a long time before a window showing fishing tackle, looking for a gift for Archie. Was it proper to give him a present? They weren't yet officially engaged. But when she got back she would have a word with Archie's mother and hint to her that it would be convenient for him to offer for her hand as soon as possible, so that the Easter wedding could be planned. And as soon as all that was in train, she could give Archie the fine cane fishing rod.

Her gifts were received with pleasure in the family, but even more so her account of her interview with the royal parents and children. She had to go over it a dozen times to please her mother. 'And what kind of clothes did the children wear? Did they have shoes or boots? And the young one still had his ringlets?'

It was now 9th February. St Valentine's Day was approaching. She decided it would be pleasant to have Archie make his declaration on that romantic day. She must take the next opportunity of speaking to Mrs Brunton, which would be in two days' time at a birthday party in the home of Mrs Balfour of Hermont.

The day before the party, Jenny felt unusually restless. Once she spoke to Mrs Brunton, the die was cast. Archie would ask her the following Sunday, she would say yes, and within seven weeks she'd be a married woman.

The thought filled her with a strange mixture of feelings. There was reluctance – reluctance to give up her freedom, reluctance to commit herself to Archie, reluctance to face the arguments that must ensue when he discovered she couldn't settle down to be a dull provincial wife. Yet there was eagerness, too. As a married woman she could know again the pleasures of physical love. She couldn't deny to herself that she had often longed for that – to have a man's body melting with hers into that perfect unity of enjoyment.

She knew, however, that most of the married women in her circle were less than transported over their love life. Whispered conversations, immediately broken off if she entered the room, had conveyed enough – phrases caught, expressions glimpsed. 'I can't imagine why he finds pleasure in it,' or, 'But men insist on that kind of thing,' – murmurs that implied distaste rather than joy.

Needing to clear her head, Jenny took the afternoon off from the office and went for a walk in the hills. The weather was still exceedingly mild for February. The snow had melted, leaving the brownish green of the winter grass to gleam, warmly tinted, under the sun. The burns were full of clear brown water, rushing over the stones with a sound like children laughing.

She trudged up the slope, holding up the skirts of her gown to keep them from the mud of the path. When she reached Wallace's Stone, she turned to look back. Sheep were moving dreamily on the hill, their fleeces still heavy with winter wool. The larch and birch had a haze of green, new growth tempted out by the soft early spring. Far below her the town straggled, mill chimneys like fingers pointing up to the robin's-egg blue of the sky. The Gala Water glinted between the houses, touched here and there with creamy-beige foam – colours suitable for a plaid coat, she told herself.

She watched a heavy wagon, tiny at this distance, drag its way to the railway. Off to the north she could see the steam of the approaching train though the folds of the land hid it from view.

If she stood very still, on the wind she could hear the hum of sound that meant the town was busy – traffic in the streets, carding engines and looms at work, steam boilers heating dye vats, people calling to each other, the whole world busy about its affairs.

She loved the town. She was suddenly aware of it. The hard-working, bustling, thriving little town – it had claimed her and made her its own.

Must she leave it to live at the Mains with Archie and his mother?

Well, it isn't so very far off, she told herself. It's only a short drive from Bowden to Galashiels, less than eight miles, a little over an hour's drive in good weather.

Yes, but what if the weather's bad?

And what if Archie won't let me come?

She put her hands up to her cheeks, closing her eyes, squeezing them shut to prevent the daunting picture – Archie with his back to the door of his house, barring her way to her carriage.

She must persuade him. Before they were married she must make it clear to him that though she of course couldn't attend to the day-to-day problems at Corvill and Son, yet she must, she absolutely must be at the mill two or three times in each week. Otherwise everything would dwindle away, everything would lose impetus. Her father was afraid of the mill, her brother had no taste for it. A manager, yes, they could bring in a manager but why should they, when Jenny Corvill could do the job better?

The sun began to sink behind Miegle Hill. She made her way down to the path leading to Gatesmuir. Unwilling to face her family, she sat for half an hour in the summerhouse overlooking the newly constructed paved walk. On either side the beds of tulips showed green shoots in the brown earth. But soon they were indistinguishable in the dusk. With nothing resolved, she went indoors.

She was quiet that evening through supper and the pastimes that followed – a game of draughts with her father, a reading by Ned from the *Edinburgh Review*. She went to bed physically tired by her walk but mentally too alert for sleep.

The mild weather made her bedclothes seem heavy. She felt smothered by them. She thrust them off. But then, soon after she dropped asleep, she was too cold. She sat up to draw the covers over her again, but found herself too wide awake to settle down.

She got out of bed. The moon was riding high in the sky. Soft clouds from the west diffused the light, spreading a milky glow over the garden. She opened her casement window to look out, to see the barn owl from the coach house tower flit on wings like grey velvet into the trees.

She breathed the cool air. How still the night was, how tranquil. If only her mind and spirit were as calm . . .

She heard a sound, the faint screech of a door hinge, from the side of the house. She leaned out a little, startled.

A figure came from the side of the path, across the little terrace, down the step to the paved walk. A woman, in a dark thick cloak. One of the servants? But where was she going, at this hour?

The figure halted. A froth of lace at the hem of a nightgown was visible in the opening of the cloak. Not a servant, then. She put up a hand to tuck back a fair curl. It was Lucy, Ned's wife. Gasping with disbelief, Jenny drew back from the casement.

A movement among the trees drew her gaze. A man stepped out into the moonlight. He crossed the lawn in rapid strides, took the woman in his arms. She threw herself into his embrace, they kissed with an urgent passion. With one arm about her shoulders, he led her along the paved walk, towards the summerhouse where Jenny had sat a few hours earlier.

Jenny let her head droop against the cold stone surround of her window. She felt stifled, unable to breathe.

The man who had come to meet Lucy was Archie Brunton.

Chapter Ten

Jenny excused herself from the party at the Balfours' next evening by saying she felt a bad cold coming on. Her mother immediately said she would stay at home to keep her company and her father, who never enjoyed parties, did likewise. He spent the evening with his books in the library, while Jenny, in shawl and slippers to keep up the fiction, sat with her mother in Jenny's bedroom.

By and by Millicent's suggested remedies had been endured. Jenny began to be restless. She found a book, laid it aside, longed to look through some business papers but knew her mother would object.

At about nine o'clock Millicent, having eyed her for some time, asked, 'What was the real reason for staying at home, daughter?'

'Mother!'

'Well, you're not unwell. Is it the same as last time – you want to give some sort of rebuff to Archie?'

'No,' Jenny said slowly. 'I've decided to put an end to anything between Archie and myself.'

Millicent nodded, saying nothing.

'You don't protest?' asked Jenny.

'Well . . . If God had meant it to be, it would have come to pass by now, daughter.'

Jenny considered the idea. She didn't share her parents' strong and simple faith, but she respected it.

'What changed your mind, Jenny?'

'Oh . . . I hardly know . . .' During a sleepless night she had decided to say nothing of what she'd seen in the garden. So now she had to account for her apparent fickleness. 'He's so unwilling, Mother. I began to think . . . perhaps it's best not to drag him to the altar.'

'Aye. To tell the truth, your father never quite approved of our doings. And lately he's heard things. The church elders have spoken to him about Archie . . . The long and short of it is, your father would have accepted Archie Brunton as a son-in-law in the hope that marriage might reform him, but without great optimism on that score.'

'What has he heard, Mother?' Jenny asked in alarm.

'Nothing fit for your ears, my dear.' But there was a calmness in her manner that told Jenny the gossip had had nothing to do with Lucy.

'I'm glad you're not disappointed. It seems to me we had better avoid the Bruntons for a month or two.'

'Very well, Jenny.'

This meant that invitations from the Bruntons were met with a polite refusal, none were extended to them, and though calls were still exchanged between the elder ladies, they were on a purely formal basis.

It took two or three weeks for Lucy to become aware of the fact. She was sitting one evening in the drawing-room, painstakingly writing invitations for an Easter outing, when she glanced up from Mrs Corvill's list. 'Mother, the Bruntons have been forgotten.'

'No, dear, I left them out on purpose.'

There was a tiny pause. 'I don't understand,' Lucy said. 'We're not *dropping* the Bruntons?'

'For the moment, yes.'

'But . . . but . . . we can't do that!'

William Corvill looked up from his book. 'We can choose our friends, I think.'

Lucy never liked to oppose her father-in-law openly. After a moment's thought she said, 'It seems a shame not to be on good terms with the Bruntons. Mrs Brunton is a very agreeable lady.'

'Certainly. I have nothing against *Mrs* Brunton.'

The slight emphasis on the name was enough to show Lucy where the problem lay. After a moment she visibly gathered her courage to ask, 'Has there been some new gossip to set you against Archie?'

142

'Lucy, don't concern yourself with it,' said Mrs Corvill patiently. 'It's not worth your notice.'

A flash of relief. Then Lucy said, 'All the same, Mother, if we cut ourselves off from the Bruntons, it will look very odd. People will say . . .'

She glanced at Jenny, who was sitting under the lamp amusing herself with some pencil sketches of a new check she wanted to try.

'Never mind what people will say,' Mrs Corvill said.

' "If any man among you seem to be religious, and bridleth not his tongue, but deceiveth his own heart, this man's religion is vain",' quoted William.

Lucy was silenced for the moment. But after a while she rose, to drift towards Jenny at her table. She sat down beside her. 'Everyone'll think he's jilted you,' she murmured.

'Very likely.'

'You don't care?'

'Not much.'

Lucy played with the pen in her hand. 'Have you had a quarrel with Archie?'

'I haven't exchanged a word with him since I got back from London.'

'Then what's it about?'

Jenny looked up from her sketching. 'Lucy,' she said, 'don't ask questions to which you might get very unpleasant answers.'

She saw her sister-in-law go very pale. For a moment there was a dreadful, beating silence between them. She feared Lucy might burst out in angry denial. But luckily the drawing-room door opened to admit Ned, fresh from an evening's conviviality at the Galashiels Gentlemen's Club.

He told them it had turned colder again, Mr Nash had bought a roan colt, and the Church of Scotland minister was having floral decorations for Easter.

'Papal fashions,' said William, whose Secession Church would allow nothing but a plain deal table for an altar and no kneelers for prayers.

'Did you see Archie Brunton at the Club?' Lucy asked, greatly daring.

'No, but there was great crack about him,' said Ned, who

143

had been once or twice to the whisky bottle at the Club. 'What do you think? They say he sent out half a dozen Valentine cards with declarations of undying love! Got his groom to write the envelopes so the young ladies wouldn't know who sent them.'

Mrs Corvill smothered a laugh, Jenny smiled, Lucy looked vexed. William Corvill shook his head. ' "Let no man deceive you with vain words",' he said.

'He's a great one for a joke, is Archie,' Ned murmured in mitigation. 'There was no harm in it.'

'He's not a man I think highly of,' his father replied. 'I'd prefer it, laddie, if you would keep your distance from the likes of him.'

'Father, he and I are friends!'

Lucy flashed a glance at Jenny. There was defiance in it, almost as if she were daring Jenny to speak out. How ironic, that Ned should be claiming friendship with his wife's lover . . .

Jenny held her peace. Nothing could be gained from causing an open scandal. The best she could hope for was to keep the two families apart as much as possible until Lucy's infatuation died away.

On an afternoon at the end of March, a visitor was announced at the door of Jenny's office in the mill. 'Mrs Brunton,' said the chief clerk.

Taken aback, Jenny was about to say, 'Tell her I'm engaged,' but the lady herself swept in before she could utter the words.

'Good afternoon, Miss Corvill. I hope you can spare me a few moments.'

'Certainly, Mrs Brunton.' Jenny stifled a sigh. She had a fair idea what was coming. 'Pray sit down.'

Archie's mother settled her stout person on the straight-backed chair. 'Now,' she said, 'tell me what's amiss between you and my son.'

Jenny smiled. 'Would you like some tea, Mrs Brunton?'

'No, I would not like some tea. I'd like an answer to my question.' She waited.

Jenny shrugged.

'I spoke to Archie,' his mother said. 'Last time, when the

pair of you cooled off, he admitted he'd upset you and I got him to write a wee note. But this time . . . This time he gets flustered and embarrassed. He says he doesn't know what to write and apologise *about*.'

'Archie's embarrassment is his own affair.'

'Nothing of the kind! If it means he's losing you, it's my affair.' She made a snorting, sighing sound. 'I've looked forward to having you as a daughter-in-law, my dear. I can't give up the idea so easily.'

'I'm sorry.'

'You're saying . . . it's off?'

Jenny said nothing.

'But why? Why?' She hesitated. 'Was it the Valentines? I tried to stop him but he would do it . . .'

'I'm not perturbed about the Valentines, Mrs Brunton.'

'Then what is it?' She almost glared at Jenny. 'I'm not leaving this office until you tell me what's wrong so I can put it right.'

She settled herself more firmly on the uncomfortable chair, folding her arms like a soldier.

There was no help for it. Jenny said, with great reluctance, 'Archie is involved with another woman.'

'Ach!' sighed Mrs Brunton. Then she gathered herself together. 'But come now, Miss Corvill – you've always known there were other women. His reputation is no secret. And one of the things I felt happy about was that I knew you could handle him.'

'This is something I can only handle by putting an end to our relationship – if there ever was one.'

'You make it sound very serious. I wonder at you! What does it matter if Archie exchanges a kiss or two with a girl at a party?'

'This wasn't at a party. It was in a secret meeting – '

'Come now, how could you possibly be present – '

'I would rather not go into it.'

'You saw him in some underhand situation with another woman?'

'Yes.'

'I insist on knowing what you mean. You're slandering my son.'

145

Jenny sighed. 'Very well. The woman was my sister-in-law.'

Archie's mother went very red. 'That girl . . .' she muttered. 'I knew she spelt trouble, the moment Archie came home to say your brother had brought back a "sweet little thing" from Edinburgh.'

'Mrs Brunton, it takes two to make the kind of trouble we're speaking of.'

'What exactly are we speaking of? If they had some foolish rendezvous that you happened upon, there's no need to take it too seriously. Archie will flirt with anyone at the least encouragement.'

'It was the middle of the night. And Lucy was in her nightclothes.'

Mrs Brunton began to gasp for breath. Jenny leapt up to attend to her, but she waved her aside, gasping and choking, but in the end coming to herself. Jenny brought her a glass of water from the desk carafe.

She sipped it, put it down. 'The damned young fool,' she groaned. 'I knew he was up to his tricks. He was out in the middle of the night . . . He thinks I don't know, but I hear him come in so stealthily. But Lucy! How could he have been daft enough to fall into Lucy's clutches?'

Jenny shook her head. 'I think Lucy is very bored with life in the Borders,' she suggested.

'And very eager to score off you if she can! Why does the child dislike you so, Miss Corvill?'

'Who knows? I don't pretend to understand her. But the situation being as it is, you can see that any notion of a match between your son and me is out of the question.'

'Aye, you could hardly feel happy with a man who might creep out of your bed and into your sister-in-law's . . . Damn him, he hasn't the brains of a hen! He's lost the best wife he could ever have had!'

'I wonder if that's true,' said Jenny. 'I know from my own reactions to the mess that I never have loved Archie. A wife should love her husband.'

'He'll play the braw gallant until he's forty and then some cold-hearted little snip will catch him and lead him a dog's life . . .' She got heavily to her feet. 'Ach, Miss Corvill, this is a sorry ending to my visit. I thought to mend matters and see you my daughter-in-law by June.'

'I'm sorry.'

'Have you told anyone else what you saw?'

'No, no one. Ned still thinks of Lucy as some perfect little porcelain ornament that must be kept in a glass cabinet, you see. I couldn't hurt him needlessly. And my parents would be so shocked.'

'You say nothing of yourself. Let me ask you this – what will you do now? There's almost no one else in the district worthy of you. You wouldn't think of taking Tom Simpson?' And at Jenny's quick shake of the head, 'Of course not, I shouldn't have even suggested it. But then there's only Hector Bruce, but you deserve better than a tenant farmer. Or Ainsworth – but he has a vile temper, I hear.'

'Don't worry about it, Mrs Brunton,' Jenny responded with hidden amusement. 'I can survive a while more without a husband.'

'But it will look gey strange – unmarried and well past twenty. Before you make this break final, Miss Corvill, reflect! For all his faults, Archie is a great catch.'

Jenny almost said, I don't even like him any more. But there was no point in hurting his mother more than had been unavoidable. 'I'm prepared to face the prospect of seeming gey strange. I want to be able to love and respect my husband.'

'Aye, that's understandable. I felt like that about Archie's father – the finest man that ever stepped. And the unhappiest day of my life was when I lost him. Today's almost a match to that, now I lose you, my dear child.' The older woman came to kiss Jenny on the brow. 'Goodbye.'

She moved to the door. There she paused. 'Is there anything I can do to help matters?'

Jenny siezed the chance. 'There is one thing . . . If you could make sure that Archie and Lucy don't get a chance to meet?'

'I'll see he never gets within a mile of that little white cat. Rely on me, my dear.'

She was as good as her word. News came by the end of the week that Archibald Brunton Esquire had left for a year's visit to distant cousins in Canada.

Only someone who knew the whole story would have seen the shock and disappointment on Lucy's face. Then she gave a little trill of laughter. 'That has a look of desperation,' she cried. 'People will say he had to leave the country to escape you, Jenny!'

Even Ned was startled at the sharpness of her tone. 'My love! If anyone says any such thing, I hope you'll set them right.'

'Of course.'

The population of Galashiels were of a totally different opinion. 'She wouldna have him,' mourned the porter at the mill loading bay as he paid up on his bets.

'She's got too much sense,' Ronald Armstrong said, watching the transaction with amusement. 'How could you have thought the mistress would take a man like that, Rob? He's got a head as full as a well-washed jug.'

Some of the mill girls had come out to eat their midday 'pieces' in the spring sun. 'What better could she want than Mr Brunton?' one of them said wistfully. 'Rich and handsome . . . I'd gie my soul for one like him.'

'And that's why you're tending a carding machine and the mistress is managing the works,' Ronald said.

'What does that mean, Mr Armstrong?'

'It means she knows what's really important, Maisie.' With a little nod for emphasis, he went back into the mill.

Maisie looked after him, still pursuing her romantic notions. 'If she werena so far above him, *he'd* think of her,' she remarked.

'Think of her? What way?'

'For his wife.'

'Dinna be sae daft, Maisie.'

'He'll never hear a word against her. I tell ye, he thinks of her.'

'Och, havers,' said the porter, and went back to work.

If it were true that Ronald had some special feeling for Miss Corvill, the feeling must have been enhanced when, a few days later, she called him into her office. 'Mr Armstrong, do you ever go fishing?'

'Fishing?'

'For trout.'

'Oh, well . . . Aye, often enough, when I have the time.'
He was looking at her in bewilderment.

'I'm pleased to hear it. I'd like you to have this rod.'

'Eh?' he said, his mouth actually falling open a little.

'It's in token of my appreciation for the work you did on
the Balmoral tartan.'

'But . . . but that was just in the line of work . . .'

'All the same, that tan line was a difficult shade to catch.
And you did it so quickly. I hope you'll accept this in the
spirit in which it's meant.'

He took the long parcel from her in stunned silence. And
then a beam of pleasure split his long face. 'Why, I . . . I
don't know what to say . . . I never expected . . . It's very
good of you, Miss Corvill.'

'It's nothing.'

If he had known that in fact it was less than nothing, that
it was something she wanted to be rid of, he would have been
less delighted. He would have wanted nothing to do with
presents originally intended for Archibald Brunton.

Her conscience troubled her a little when she saw how
pleased he was. Yet, after all, he was a valuable colleague, an
expert workman – he deserved something as a reward. She
reproached herself that she hadn't thought to buy him something specially.

But, if one thought about it sensibly, the reward an
employee liked best was a rise in wages. Perhaps, at New
Year, she would offer a bonus if sales continued to go up in
this steady fashion.

For after it became known that the mill had had a direct
commission from the Palace, orders rolled in. They were
working at full stretch. It was a most satisfactory situation.

If only it could have been as happy at home . . .

Archie's desertion hurt Lucy. He hadn't even sent her a
note, got any kind of message to her – he had just gone, as if
she meant nothing to him. Somehow Lucy was sure it was all
Jenny's doing. Without any evidence, she knew it was so.

She became restless, irritable. She practised long and noisily
on the piano, attempting to master a ballade by Chopin that
was quite beyond her, drowning out the reading aloud that
had always been part of the family's evening amusement. She

scolded the servants over nothing. Her manner to occasional business guests of Jenny's was less than cordial.

Jenny thought about it, and came to the conclusion that Lucy needed something to occupy her. Since apparently no children were on the way, Lucy would have to be given a role to play.

A week or two of thought provided the answer – an answer that made a lot of sense. Jenny had understood very well that by dismissing Archibald Brunton she had perhaps condemned herself to spinsterhood. That being so, she might stay at Gatesmuir for the rest of her life.

The house didn't belong to the family. But it would be easy enough to buy it outright. She asked Mr Kennet the lawyer to get in touch with Colonel Anderson in Portugal. In about a month it was arranged, Kennet had power of attorney to act for the absent owner, papers were drawn up, Gatesmuir became the property of William Corvill of the Waterside Mill.

William had been bemused at the notion of owning such a fine house. But he accepted Jenny's reasoning. 'Aye, lassie, if you're not to find a husband, I see you want to be sure of a roof over your head. Only, I wonder that you think marriage so unlikely. I could ask among the menfolk at the church – a respectable young man with good principles, not like yon Brunton . . .'

'No, Father, thank you,' Jenny said hastily. It amazed her to recall how she would have accepted some dark-clad, sedate young Huguenot only four years ago. She was well beyond that now. No one except herself should ever choose her husband. And there was no one she found to her liking.

Now that Gatesmuir belonged to them, they could undertake work other than repairs. To Lucy Jenny gave the task of supervising the redecorations. Afterwards, when she was engaged in wrangles about expense, she wondered at her own stupidity. But there was no doubt it brightened her sister-in-law's outlook in the most extraordinary way to be looking through pattern books for curtain fabrics, discussing paint shades with the decorator, and driving to Selkirk or Peebles to look at carpets.

It was going to cost money. And the result might well be a

house not exactly to Jenny's taste. But if it restored Lucy to good humour, it was worth it.

High summer came, and the wool sales began. Jenny had a lot of anxiety over wool supplies to take her mind off Lucy's great redecorating schemes.

Wool for the Border mills came from two sources, by direct buying from local growers or through an agent known as a stapler. Until about ten years previously, Border mills had used Border wool.

But Scottish sheep farmers clung to old-fashioned methods. They daubed their sheep with tar or butter to prevent infestation of the fleece. When the fleece was clipped, the wool was stained with these unwanted blemishes. Sheep-washing was supposed to clean the fleece before clipping but in fact it was impossible to use the wool at the mill until after expensive cleaning.

As a result, wool imported from Australia was much in favour. Cross-bred sheep on the vast grasslands grew a purer, whiter wool. When Corvill and Son began production in Galashiels, it was often Australian Botany that went through their machines, for the heavier cloth.

But two things made it important for Corvill and Son to find other sources. First, Australian wool was going up in price. And second, for the very fine grades of cloth for which the Waterside Mill had become famous, an even better wool was needed – Saxony of the highest grade, or Merino.

The wool brokers were in difficulties in finding what Jenny wanted, at a price she was willing to pay. She had been growing impatient even last year with the excuses and prevarications she received from them.

So this summer she decided to go herself to the wool fairs.

'Go yourself?' Ronald Armstrong said, when she told him her plan.

'It's the best way to make sure we buy the right wool.'

'You can't go to the wool fairs, Mistress Corvill! Indeed, you can't!'

'Why not?'

'It's no place for a lady! You'd make yourself a puppy-show!'

'Och, you mean the men would stare at me? Well, let them.'

151

'Let them? Let them stare, and say the kind of – ' Ronald broke off. 'Mistress, the language at a wool fair is not fit to be heard by Miss Corvill of Gatesmuir.'

'But as it will be in a foreign tongue, I shan't be perturbed by it.'

'A foreign tongue?' he echoed, utterly at a loss.

'I'm going to Hamburg.'

'Hamburg? You can't go to Hamburg!'

'Why not?'

'Because . . . because . . . It's unheard-of!'

'Nonsense.' There was a sparkle in the black eyes that told him she was looking forward to it enormously.

Instinct told him she would go whatever objections he put forward. And it also told him that she needed to go, that the breaking-off with Brunton had damaged her self-esteem, diminished her own view of herself, so that she needed somehow to restore it.

'At least tell me you're not going alone.'

'Of course not. I'm taking my brother with me.'

'Your brother.' The total lack of enthusiasm hid his opinion of Edward Corvill, which was the opinion shared by the rest of Galashiels. Ned liked either to play the fool with the rich young men of the area, or to play the scholar with a pile of books at his desk. But he had no role in business.

'My father's the one who knows most about wool,' Jenny acknowledged, 'but asking him to go aboard a ship is useless. The idea terrifies him.'

'He has some justification. Yon passage across the North Sea is no great pleasure.'

She was surprised. 'You've been abroad?'

'Aye, I went to Berlin, it would be about six years ago, to see what they were doing at the University with the new dyes from coal tar.'

'Indeed.' She eyed him with respect, but then laughed. 'And you lived to tell the tale! So you see, all this alarm about foreign travel is foolishness.'

She was proved wrong on the passage from Newcastle. The steam packet was buffeted along by a brisk south-westerly, which caused Ned to retire to his cabin with a whisky flask for comfort. Jenny stayed on deck thinking fresh air was best, but was glad when nightfall allowed her to seek honourable refuge in her bunkbed.

The docks at Hamburg were intimidating, tall gantries moving great loads on the end of chains, masts and funnels obscuring the front of the Seewarte and the warehouses. Much had been destroyed in a great fire about a quarter of a century before, but much had been rebuilt, and finely rebuilt.

Herr Guttmann, waiting to greet them as they came down the gangplank, was somewhat taken aback. He had had a letter from a London wool merchant asking him to extend politeness to the son of the famous cloth-maker, William Corvill, but who was the young lady? How annoying of Mr Corvill to bring a wife! Women were such a hindrance in business.

No, she wasn't a wife. 'My sister, Miss Corvill,' said Ned.

'Delighted to meet you,' lied Guttmann in excellent English. The young lady had come along for the pleasure of visiting the Continent, no doubt. Very well, he'd get rid of her into the care of his wife.

Not in the least. When he had seen the couple to the Hotel Kastanhof and helped them register, the young lady refused to be taken out at ten next morning to go sightseeing with Frau Guttmann. 'Thank you, no,' she said. 'At what hour does the dealing open at the Wool Fair?'

'Eight o'clock,' Guttmann said, in a faint voice.

'Very well. How do we ask a hackney driver to take us to the hall?'

'You . . . er . . . *you* intend to come, Fraulein?'

'Yes indeed.'

'I . . . I don't advise it.'

'Herr Guttmann, I've come to Hamburg to buy wool. I am certainly coming to the Fair.'

'Er . . . in that case I'll call for you at seven-thirty.'

Their entry into the great barn of a hall caused something of a sensation. Business didn't exactly cease, but heads turned and conversation slackened as he threaded his way through with the slight feminine figure in dark blue silk at his elbow.

Before an hour had passed, they had collected quite a following. Word had gone round that the two *Englanders* were members of the Corvill family, owners of Corvill and Son, the famous cloth-maker.

'My mother and my wife both have gowns made from your tartans, Herr Corvill,' said a young man to Ned.

Jenny leaned round Ned to reply. 'Which tartans, sir?' She was always keen to know who liked what.

'My wife has the Rob Roy tartan and my mother – it is a dark blue design with a red check – I do not recall the name.'

'Eliot?'

'Right!' He smiled at her. She was a great novelty – a woman at the Wool Fair. 'Allow me to present myself. Franz Lennhardt, a buyer for Jener and Schlieber of Berlin.'

'Jener and Schlieber! Of course! Ned, Jener and Schlieber is the firm who took a big order of the Coigach plaid.'

Since Ned could only just picture the Coigach plaid and had no recollection of who had ordered what, he could contribute very little to the conversation. By and by it became clear to all that the young man couldn't talk business. Guttmann had to smother a snort of laughter when he heard Lennhardt say in German to some friends, 'Don't bother with the brother, he scarcely knows whether he's wearing a hat or not. The girl is the one with all the sense.'

At lunchtime many of the men resorted to a beer parlour for hearty quaffings of ale and hot meals on large plates. Luckily it was a fine August day, so the problem of what to do about Jenny was solved by young Herr Lennhardt. 'There is a very pleasant little park just along the road,' he suggested. 'We can have what you call a pic-a-nic with bread and cheese and wine, yes?'

'Picnic,' Jenny said. 'Yes, that would be very pleasant.'

'*Sehr gut*, Franz,' Guttmann breathed with gratitude into the young man's ear.

'*Nichts*,' said Franz. He was delighted to stay close to this pretty, black-haired girl who sparkled with life and enjoyment in the dusty wool hall.

By mid-afternoon even Jenny's pleasure was dimmed. The noise, the smell of the wool, the heat, the cigar smoke, even the after-effects of the unaccustomed wine was making her dizzy.

A trolley piled with great canvas-wrapped loads of wool was

154

being pulled by a sweating porter through the hall. He had to stop as his way was blocked by a crowd of chaffering dealers, so that when he started again he had to tug and wrench at the drawbar. The pile on his vehicle swayed. The top bale began to tilt.

'*Achtung!*' he shouted despairingly as it fell towards a group of buyers.

Jenny felt a pair of strong arms come around her. She was lifted off her feet and pulled to one side. She fell against a muscular chest. Her cheek rested on a poplin-clad shoulder. A great brown bundle weighing forty pounds went toppling past.

Confusion reigned. Shouts and consternation. 'Are you all right, Fräulein?'

'Jenny, did it hit you?' Ned cried.

'No . . . No . . . I'm all right.' She drew away from her saviour. She looked up into two dark blue eyes that were smiling with relief and pleasure. 'Thank you, Herr Lennhardt.'

'Delighted to be of use,' he said.

Their eyes held. The smile of politeness faded a little. Something passed between them, a silent message, an acknowledgement.

'Delighted,' he said again, in a slightly different tone.

Herr Guttmann was very upset. What if his precious charge had been hurt? He owed a considerable debt of gratitude to· young Lennhardt. So, of course, when trying to arrange entertainment for the evening – entertainment suitable for a respectable young lady as well as her amiable brother – he included Lennhardt in the party. It was agreed they would go to a *Weingarten,* a well-known venue where bourgeois citizens of Hamburg could take their wives and daughters of a summer evening.

The dinner party was made up of Herr Guttmann and his wife, Franz and his wife Elsa, and the Corvills. The restaurant was near St Catherine's Church. It was a revelation to Jenny. The room had decorations of red and gold, with. swags of green garlands on a trellis leading out to a paved garden. The tables were covered with white cloths that sparkled in the dusk. There was a little orchestra which played sentimental

155

songs in which the diners would join from time to time. And when there was no singing, the customers would rise from their tables and dance on a flagstoned space under a bower of rambling roses.

When Franz Lennhardt asked Jenny to dance, she was so surprised that she was stricken speechless. He took her hand, pulled her to her feet, led her on to the little dance floor, and whirled her into a waltz.

Fully two minutes went by before she recovered from the shock. The thrill of movement to music in the arms of a stranger quite overpowered her. This was different from the stately cotillions of the Assembly Ball or the country dances of an evening party – this was face to face with a handsome young man, whose brown head bent a little towards her, whose hand rested warmly in the small of her back. She could feel its warmth through the satin of her gown and the whalebone and linen of her stays.

Franz was singing the words of the song to himself as they danced. 'What does it mean?' she asked, looking up at him.

'Oh, it's about moonlight, and lovers . . . "Though the moon wanes, my dear, my darling, Love still remains, my heart, my joy" . . .'

'That's very beautiful,' sighed Jenny.

'*You* are very beautiful, Fräulein Jenny.'

'What?' In the lilt of the music, she could scarcely hear him.

'Nothing. How long are you staying, Fräulein?'

'Only until the day after tomorrow.'

'What a pity,' he breathed. The music ended, he led her back to their table. His wife was watching them approach. She said something to Franz in German. He smiled and shrugged. One must be polite to foreign guests, his manner implied.

Next day was busy with contracts and instructions for shipping Jenny's purchases. She invited the Guttmanns and the Lennhardts to dine at the hotel in the evening. There was music here too, a little trio that played Schubert, but no room for dancing. Nothing could have been more sedate. Even so, some magic seemed to flow between Jenny and Franz. When

156

she glanced up, he was looking at her. When they were silent, they seemed to be speaking to each other.

As she brushed her hair that night she leaned forward to stare at herself in the mirror. 'You're a fool,' she said. Her reflection made no contradiction. But neither did it offer any help.

She and Ned went aboard the steam packet for Newcastle at about half-past nine next morning. There was a little party of wellwishers to see them off – Herr Guttmann, Franz, and the merchant from whom Jenny had bought the wool. The men pumped each others' hands, promised to meet again next year.

While Ned was chatting with Guttmann, Franz took Jenny's gloved hand in his. She thought they were going to shake hands. Instead he bore it towards his lips. But, as he bent his head towards it, he peeled back the white kid glove and turned her wrist. On the bare skin of the palm of her hand, he imprinted a kiss.

'Goodbye, *mein Leibling*,' he murmured.

At the touch of his lips, a frisson went through her. She felt herself go pale. She almost swayed from the intensity of her reaction. At that moment Ned turned, took her by the elbow. 'Time to get aboard,' he said.

'Yes.'

They went up the gangplank. Already sailors were throwing ropes, the engine of the steam packet was throbbing urgently as the vessel prepared to move out of its berth.

Jenny stood at the rail to wave as the *Eisenkranz* slowly backed away from the quay. Within a few minutes the figures smiling and calling to them began to grow smaller, then they were hidden from view as the packet steamer edged between the great cargo ships and headed out of the Elbe.

Slowly the spires of Hamburg disappeared from view in the shimmer of smoke and heat haze. Goodbye, goodbye, Jenny said within herself. Her throat ached, she could only nod or shake her head when Ned spoke to her.

She had come to Hamburg to prove to herself she could do without Archie Brunton, be a person in her own right. She had done well, she had carried out the business for which she'd come, she had made a good impression.

And she was lonely, lonely, lonely . . .

157

Chapter Eleven

Lucy's redecorations were finished when Ned and Jenny reached home. Going through the front door was more like stepping into a ballroom than an entrance hall. It glimmered with metallic brocades and crystal-hung gasoliers. The quiet drawing-room carpet had been replaced with a swirling pattern of roses in baskets. The dining-room chairs had been reseated in crimson satin with curtains to match.

Jenny had expected changes but not quite to that extent. Her sister-in-law, however, took it for granted the changes were all for the better. Jenny dutifully admired, grateful only that her bedroom had been altered very little because of the plain wainscoted walls. She felt she could live with the bedspread and curtains patterned with yellow and brown flowers of uncertain species.

'Do you really like it?' her mother asked, looking round when she came in for a bedtime chat.

'Not much. But it's better than the drawing-room.'

'Those shiny new sofas . . . She threw out your poor father's favourite armchair!'

'We'll get it back, Mother.'

'It'll look gey queer in the middle of all those roses. Jenny, why ever did you let her do it?'

'I thought it might help to amuse her. She seemed . . . cast down.'

'Cast down? She was wound up all the while you were away – determined to have everything finished to show you when you got back. I kept saying to her, "There's no rush," but she would go at it hammer and tongs . . . And I must say I think it was because she knew you'd stop her.'

'Never mind, Mother. We'll tone it all down gradually.'

'You know what she wants next?' Millicent Corvill went on without heeding Jenny. 'She wants to give a Grand Ball to show off the new furnishings. Your father thinks it's mere ostentation.'

'Oh dear.'

'I wouldn't let her start on it, not without your say-so, dear. But she's gone a long way with the planning – she said she wanted it to be one of the opening events of the winter season.'

'The winter season? Since when has Galashiels had a winter season?'

Millicent sighed. 'She's a strange one,' she said. 'Not nearly as quiet and sweet as she seemed at first.'

Jenny had no wish to condemn Lucy for that. She knew – who better – that we all play a part to some extent. To her parents she was a dutiful, clever and hardworking daughter. They were quite unaware of that other Jenny who lived behind that quiet facade, who had loved a man to the fullest extent, who had been sinful according to their lights, and who had kept her passionate secret from them in mere pity for the grief it would cause them.

That girl went on Sunday with them to the kirk, knelt on the hard floor to pray, listened meekly to the minister. But that was not the real Jenny. The real Jenny was the girl who had felt her whole being leap in response when Franz Lennhardt kissed the palm of her hand.

'I suppose we all have different faces we show to different people, Mother. When Lucy first arrived, she wanted you and Father to like her so she . . .'

'She pretended.'

'Oh, I didn't mean that exactly – '

'It's what it amounts to.' Millicent shook her head. 'Your father says she has a restless soul. Well, we must take her for what she is, for she's one of the family now, after all.'

'Yes, that's right, Mother – '

'But your father shakes his head over her a lot, Jenny. An awful lot.'

And how much more, if he only knew the truth about Lucy. The lies about her family and background, the foolish affair with Archie Brunton . . .

159

The family peace had to be preserved. If Lucy wanted a Grand Ball, why not let her have it? They could afford it, after all. And it was better perhaps to have Lucy busy about things of that kind than bored and ready for mischief.

With Jenny's agreement and Ned's fond approval, Lucy launched into action. Being in charge of the redecorations had brought home to her how easy it was to spend money in the name of the Corvills.

She hired a well-known group of musicians for the dancing. She called in caterers and florists to whom she showed her plans for the event. For a week the house was full of men measuring the rooms and discussing whether to serve the supper in the drawing-room or the parlour. Ned absented himself to the Gentlemen's Club, his father bore it in baffled silence.

To have a special new gown made for the ball, Lucy sent for an expensive dressmaker from Glasgow, who came to stay at Gatesmuir complete with bolts of silk and satin and a scared little apprentice. Books of dress illustrations, paper patterns, lengths of ribbon and braid overflowed out of Lucy's bedroom on to the landing.

Jenny came home at lunchtime one Thursday with a splitting headache from the thundery weather and a long spell in the weaving shed. One of the machines had been causing trouble. She longed for half an hour's peace and quiet, a headache powder, and a good strong cup of tea.

Instead she found uproar. Madame Adair, the dressmaker, was in a furious quarrel with Baird, the personal maid.

'If you dare to tidy away my work again, I shall complain to your mistress,' Madame Adair was declaring. 'You folded the silk after I'd had my girl press it – '

'And she used my iron to do it! Without even asking! And if you so much as touch my hussif again, I'll have the head off you,' Baird said menacingly as she towered over the stout little dressmaker, who was facing up to her like a pouter pigeon.

'Good gracious, if a person can't borrow a paper of pins – '

'You're a dressmaker, aren't you? You should have your own pins! And, anyway, you didn't only take pins out of my hussif. Where are my buttonhole scissors, tell me that? You've taken those as well, and all the silks are gone – '

'Well, I had to have something to tack up the skirt seams – '

'You used my good silk threads for tacking? And without even asking?'

'Baird!' Jenny interrupted. 'Baird, that's enough. Madame Adair, if you need anything, please ask.'

Madame Adair had spent the four days of her residence closeted with Lucy, who seemed to give the orders and certainly spoke to her with the air of being the mistress of the house. She therefore felt safe in taking a high tone with this interfering young lady who, she gathered, was the old-maid daughter of twenty-two.

'My good woman, *ask* – I tried asking *this person* yesterday and got nothing for my pains – '

'Buckram – how on earth am I supposed to have buckram? I only do mending, I don't do dressmaking. Mistress Corvill, tell her to leave my things alone, I'm fair sick of having them turned upside down – '

Lucy came out of her bedroom holding a piece of sky-blue silk to which was tacked the paper pattern for the bodice of her gown. 'Who folded this up? It's got creases all over it – '

'Lucy, I think you ought to keep things within bounds – '

'Oh! Jenny!' Lucy had just realised Jenny had come home. She'd thought the argument was only between the maid and the dressmaker.

'I think if you're going to have a new ballgown made, you ought to be able to do it without turning the house upside down.'

'If I may say so, young lady,' said the dressmaker, completely misunderstanding the situation, 'it would be a great deal easier to get things done if other people would not interfere in what doesn't concern them.'

Jenny turned a cold glance upon her. 'Madame Adair!'

'Yes?'

'You will please pack up all your paraphernalia and be out of this house in an hour.'

'Eh?' said Madame Adair inelegantly.

'Pack up and go.'

'You tell me to pack up and go?'

'You heard me.'

'Who are you to dare – '

'You'll find out soon enough.'

'But . . . but . . . Mrs Corvill, I appeal to you!'

'Don't appeal to Mrs Corvill,' Jenny said, quite at the end of her tether. 'I am the one who settles the bills in this family. If you are not out of this house in an hour I will deduct ten per cent off your total, because of the nuisance you have caused.'

'Mrs Corvill!' cried the dressmaker, looking in dismay at Lucy.

Lucy trembled on the verge of defying Jenny openly. But so far she had always shied away from that. Now she clutched the piece of cut-out balldress to her breast and burst into tears. 'Oh, how can you, Jenny, how can you shame me so in front of the servants!'

'Oh, for heaven's sake, Lucy, don't carry on as if it were a tragedy.'

'You let me work myself to a shadow refurbishing this dull old house – '

'What's that got to do with it?'

'And this is all the thanks I get!'

'Am I to go or stay, madam?' asked Madame Adair, raising her voice to make herself heard.

A door across the landing opened and William Corvill came out, a book in his hands with his place kept by a finger in the pages. 'What is all this noise?' he demanded.

Jenny was vexed and embarrassed. 'Father, I'm sorry, it's just a silly upset. We'll be quiet.'

'Quiet! Why should I be quiet over injustice?' Lucy cried. 'After all I've done, to be treated like this!'

'Like what, lassie?'

'Oh, Father,' wept Lucy, woebegone, 'I only wanted to have everything perfect for the ball – '

'Lucy, please don't drag Father into this. Madame Adair, if you'll get your goods packed up and get ready to leave, I'll pay you in cash.'

'No!' cried Lucy. 'Who'll finish my balldress? Father, I have my rights! Tell Jenny not to treat me like a child!'

'What in the name of heaven is this all about?' William said, gazing round at the group of angry women on the landing.

'Sir, I only want to be treated with the respect due to me,' Madame Adair said, deciding it was time to put these provincial nobodies in their proper place. 'I am well-known in Galsgow, the Provost's wife has her clothes made by me! I will not be ordered about like a servant.'

'You're the dressmaker, I think?'

'I am a *modiste*, sir.' She flounced across the landing, twitched a length of bright pink cloth from a chair just inside Lucy's room, and spread it dramatically along the carpeting for William's inspection. 'I supply only the finest Parisian silks. The cost is high, but the finished gown is a work of art. My designs are recognised to be completely *de bon gout*.'

'You see, Father?' Lucy urged. 'It's not right to turn such a woman out of the house on an hour's notice.'

'She should never have been let in here,' Baird said, very sour. 'Her and her apprentice, fu' o' airs and graces, making free with my equipment and demanding meals at all hours of the day and night – '

'You hold your tongue!' Lucy said hotly. 'You take far too much on yourself – '

'Silence!' roared William.

Silence followed.

'Vanity of vanities, all is vanity!' he went on, using a quotation that had trembled on his lips often in the past few weeks as he watched Lucy at work. 'You should be ashamed to waste your thoughts on finery and frippery when you should be thinking of your immortal soul – '

'Father, I apologise,' Jenny put in. She had seen her father in this mood before, troubled more than he could bear over the trappings of society. Lucy, with her insistence on making a show for their neighbours, had tried his patience greatly. 'I'll see to Madame Adair's departure and then you won't hear another sound – '

'Sir, if you are the master of the house, I appeal to you,' the dressmaker interrupted. 'I will not be turned out at an hour's notice – '

'I am trying to read Mr Schaff's *History of the Apostolic Church!* How can I give my mind to it when the house is full of this unquiet spirit?' He glared with contempt at the sumptuous silk spread out for his approval, at the cut piece Lucy still held.

He twitched it out of her hand. 'Remember the fate of the man who was clothed in purple and fine linen! Give your mind to higher things!'

He crumpled the piece, cloth and paper, in his free hand and threw it contemptuously from him. It went towards the stairs in a loose parabola. Lucy uttered a cry of consternation, throwing herself forward to catch it. Her foot caught in the length of silk spread out on the floor, jerking it unexpectedly. William, who had stepped onto it to snatch the piece from Lucy's hands, lost his balance.

He staggered against the balustrade, his legs went from under him, he went headlong down the stairs.

'Maister!' screamed Baird, and threw herself forward to catch him. Her hand missed his jacket sleeve by a fraction. His heavy body thudded on the treads, he made a compulsive gesture to grasp the rails, missed.

Next moment he was a sprawl at the foot of the staircase.

Jenny picked up her skirts and ran down. He was lying head down, his legs somehow caught in the banister rail. She knelt beside him.

'Father!'

She put out a hand to raise his head. Then it struck her how unnatural it was, at how crooked an angle it lay.

She sat back on her heels, cold with horror.

William Corvill had broken his neck.

Chapter Twelve

After the first shock of regret and the excitement of the funeral, the chief interest in Galashiels was in the will. Corvill and Son was a chief employer in the town, and likely to have expanded considerably under the management of Miss Corvill. But now . . . ?

The terms of the will became known. A hundred pounds and his theological books to the United Secessionist Church. A hundred pounds to the Huguenot Church of Edinburgh. Five thousand pounds and a one-third share each in the house, Gatesmuir, to his wife and daughter. Thus having ensured they always had a roof over their head and an income if worst came to worst, he left everything else to his son, Edward Corvill.

'It's a damned shame,' Ronald Armstrong remarked to friends, over a glass of ale in the saloon of the Abbotsford Inn. 'She made the firm what it is. It should have been left to her.'

'Aye, but you canna expect a man to leave a business to a lassie,' came the objection from Hanson, the lawyer's clerk. 'It isn't fitting.'

'Fitting! Do you see any of the men and women the mill employs, refusing to work for her because it isn't fitting?'

Heads wagged or nodded. 'What d'you think'll happen now, Ronald?'

'He'll sell up. He's no interest in it. I'm told he was a weaver once himself but he prefers to forget that now, among his high-toned friends. Him and that little Dresden china wife of his . . . If he'd the slightest mind to go on with the mill, his wife'd put a stop to it.'

165

Here he was wrong, for since her father-in-law's death, Lucy Corvill had learnt a lot. The interest aroused by the funeral had startled her. Everyone who was anyone had come to it – all the members of the town council and the Manufacturers' Corporation, all the local landowners, elders of all the churches besides the Secessionist, every other cloth-maker in the Scottish Borders, to say nothing of the workforce, which came in its entirety as a mark of respect.

Letters of condolence began to come in from all over the world – from wool merchants and selling agents in Australia, New Zealand, Germany and Spain: from cloth warehousemen in London, Paris, Berlin, Madrid, New York, New Orleans, Sidney and Wellington. From fashion houses, from famous shops, from young William Morris the poet, from Scottish writers. Most impressive of all, there were letters from members of the nobility and, on the stiff unmistakeable paper of Buckingham Palace, a note in the very hand of the Prince Consort himself.

This had borne in upon Lucy something she'd never believed – that the Corvills were people of consequence. Their rather simple way of life, the gentle pursuits of country living, had misled her to think that they were of no importance. The mill, which had always been something that made her rather ashamed, now became a thing of value.

So when her husband muttered that it would be as well to be rid of it as soon as possible, to his astonishment Lucy demurred.

'But I thought you'd jump at the idea – '

'No, Ned dearest, we ought to think very carefully. Your father wouldn't have wanted you to sell up.'

'No . . . But then, what did he expect me to do?'

'He wanted you to run the mill, of course.'

This may in fact have been an accurate reading of the will. Ned's father had been worrying for some months about his son's feckless life. He had been a long way from suspecting Ned's addiction to the bottle, but he had sensed a lack of seriousness, a lack of direction. Ned had been down from university long enough now to have settled to work. But still he had avoided going to the mill to play his part.

The will had been William's way of forcing his son to face

the real world. A man of twenty-three ought to have chosen his career and started upon it – and the mill must be Ned's career.

Ned detested the mill. He had hated his loom when he had been a humble handweaver, and he hated the factory with its noisy engines and its smell of raw wool and dyes.

However, coaxed by Lucy, he went to the place on the Monday after the funeral. Ten days had gone by since his father's death. Jenny, broken with grief and guilt, had been nowhere near it. Everything was still going on in a lack-lustre way – cloth was being made, orders were being packed. But there was no feeling of purpose in it.

Ned walked round, accepting the little nods and half-curt-seys of the workforce. He spoke to the foremen of the carding department and the weaving sheds. He came at length to the dye works. He had heard Jenny speak with respect of Ronald Armstrong. 'Corvill's have two secrets of success,' she would sometimes say, 'the perfection of the weaving and the subtlety of the colours. Father is responsible for the first and Mr Armstrong for the second.'

Mr Armstrong greeted his new boss with politeness. He had scarcely ever said a word to him, except to pay his respects at the funeral.

'Ah, Armstrong,' Ned began. 'I've dropped by to have a chat about the future of the mill.'

'Oh aye?'

'As you know, my father left it to me.'

'So I heard.'

'I myself have never played any part in the running of the place.'

'That's a fact,' observed Ronald, pulling at his chin to prevent a sardonic smile.

'I think of putting in a manager.'

'A manager.'

'Yes, because if the truth be known, I've no head for business. I was trained as a scholar, you know.'

'Oh, aye, Plato and Heraclitus.'

Ned was startled. 'You take an interest in philosophy?'

'I've read a bit. And what I've read tells me that it's no

167

grounding for running a cloth mill. So you're bringing in a manager.'

'Yes. I'm going to look around for one.'

'Look around?' said Ronald in a sharp tone. 'Why do you need to look further than your own house?'

'I beg your pardon?'

'I'm speaking of your sister. She's the best manager you could ever have.'

'Excuse me, I don't think you understand. I never thought it seemly that my sister should – '

'You didn't? But you lived on the money she brought in, I take it?'

Ned was so taken aback that he actually gaped at the tall, loose-limbed, aproned figure draped at ease on a tall stool by his bench. 'Look here, Armstrong – '

'What? You think I'm impertinent? All right, sack me. But I'll save you the trouble. If you put anyone else in Miss Corvill's rightful place, I'll walk out of this mill. And so will every other department head – and believe me, we'll get jobs with the opposition the day after, for anyone that ever worked for Corvill's will be welcomed with open arms.'

This was delivered in a tone of complete calm. Ned wrestled with a desire to order the man out on the instant, and a feeling that he was being told something he ought to pay attention to.

'I . . . er . . . you express yourself very cogently . . .'

'The English language lends itself to cogent speech. What I'm trying to tell you, Ned Corvill, is that if you don't let your sister go on with her work here at Waterside Mill you'll be doing her a great injustice and dealing yourself a foolish handicap.'

'But a man would be more suitable – '

'Suitable to whom? For what? Would anyone else have the gift of designing new plaids? Have you any idea how many successful new designs your sister has put in our pattern books?'

'Well, I . . . She has a knack, I do of course appreciate . . .'

'Show your appreciation by leaving her where she belongs – in the office on the ground floor.'

'But you don't understand! My father left the mill to *me!*'

'For what reason, only God knows. Very well, carry out his purpose – run the mill. And if you can't, leave the job to the one who can. The mistress is the best manager you'd find in a long day's journey, and if you want a frank opinion it's simple wrongheadedness to hire someone else.'

'I don't like your tone, Armstrong.'

'Aye, well, I don't like yours either. That makes us quits. Now, if you'll excuse me, this tincture is about to lose its power so I'll say good afternoon.'

'See here, Armstrong – '

'Excuse me, Mr Corvill; people talking to me when I've a red dye in my hand make me very nervous.' Ronald twitched the test tube in his hands as if it were going to fly off in Ned's direction. Ned beat a retreat.

He stamped out of the mill furiously angry, but on the walk home to Gatesmuir he began to have second thoughts. The fellow might be totally insubordinate but he had a great talent as dye-master and if he walked out, he would find a job next day – and with a competitor. Moreover, if one could just overcome one's antipathy to having a woman as manager, it was true that Jenny was extraordinarily good at the job.

Lucy was awaiting him. She had the silver tea service on a table by the drawing-room fire. Sitting behind it, all aglow in her rose-coloured velvet gown, she was a picture. Ned felt his irritability drain away. When she offered him his teacup and asked how he had fared at the mill, he told her of his encounter with Ronald but in a modified version.

'Leave Jenny in control?' his wife cried. 'Oh, that's not a good idea, Ned!'

'Why not?'

'Because *you* are the Corvill of Corvill and Son, now your father is gone. It's up to you to take your rightful place.'

'Dear, I don't really want to go to the mill every day and fiddle about with yarns and tensions – '

'But if you have a manager – '

'The fact is, dearest, Jenny is the best person for the post.'

Lucy was adamantly opposed to the idea. Since William's death, Jenny had taken no part in anything except the care of her mother, who was prostrated with grief. Lucy had reigned supreme. After the reading of the will, her powers seemed to have been extended even further than the house – she would be the wife of the mill owner, wife to the great Corgill whose cloth was in demand by important people all over the world.

If Jenny were to be reinstated, Jenny would be the controlling power. That was not at all what Lucy wanted.

'Well, all I can tell you, Lucy dear, is that I was given the strong impression the entire staff would walk out if I brought in a stranger to take over the management.'

'Good God, are you going to allow yourself to be ruled by the work people?'

'Some of them are irreplaceable, Lucy. Good weavers and dyers can go anywhere and get good wages, but even in that category, Ronald Armstrong is exceptional. You know Jenny sometimes said – '

'Oh yes, yes, your father and Armstrong – it was because of them the cloth was so superior.'

'Then don't you see? We've lost Father; we can't afford to lose Armstrong.'

'You're not going to submit to blackmail?'

'Darling, I don't want to get involved in a lot of unpleasantness and uncertainty. I mean to say, you know I don't really want to be involved in running the place at all. I really think Armstrong may be right. Jenny ought to be left to go on as before.'

Lucy argued, grew quite heated. Ned, puzzled, said, 'I don't know why you take it so personally, my love. You almost sound as if you would do anything to keep Jenny out of – '

'No, no, how can you be so silly, Ned? I'm only thinking of what would be best, and of course, darling, you know best. We'll do whatever you say.' It was no part of her wish to have her dislike of his sister out in the open. It might give rise to questions – questions she couldn't answer either to him or to herself.

Her antagonism to Jenny had been heightened by the manner of William's death. Jenny had moaned, 'It's our fault!' as she knelt by the twisted body. Lucy knew – she *knew* – she was in no way to blame. Madame Adair agreed with her. The old gentleman had lost his footing and tumbled downstairs – not uncommon in elderly people, a sudden onset of giddiness. As to the quarrel that had brought him out on to the landing – well, if he hadn't interfered, he wouldn't have been there.

Jenny's view was that she herself should have handled the quarrel better, should have soothed ruffled feathers and got rid of the upstart dressmaker later, without a fuss. She should never have let Lucy run wild in the first place. She should have dealt with the problem of Lucy's boredom in some other way than allowing her to spend money and behave like a provincial version of a London hostess.

Her mother claimed all Jenny's attention. Millicent seemed stunned. For all that Madame Adair spoke of William as 'the old gentleman', he had been only fifty, with twenty of his three score years and ten still to come. Millicent simply couldn't believe that he had been taken from her.

So Waterside Mill had been left to look after itself. When Ned at last came to ask her to go back to work, Jenny was almost startled. It had all drifted away from her. It seemed quite unimportant.

'Well, if you don't want to go back, I'll have to start looking for a manager,' Ned told her in perplexity.

'A manager?' That was different.

Two weeks after the funeral, Mistress Corvill was seen coming in through the front entrance of Waterside Mill. A sigh of relief seemed to go through the building. It was November. It was time to be planning and experimenting for the spring patterns. New tartans should have been forming on William's handloom as specimens, Jenny's sketchbook should have been full of graphs and charts, Ronald Armstrong should have been holding skeins of yarn up to the light to examine new shades. So far nothing had been done. But now the mistress was back. All would be well.

And so it was, on the whole, except that young Mr Corvill would come from time to time with his wife, to stroll through the place and give opinions. Mr Corvill was somewhat of a fool and often more than a little drunk. Mrs Corvill, though sober, was a sore trial. She complained if she got dust on her white gloves, expected a chair to be placed for her wherever she happened to be, and caused one of the girls to lose her concentration so that a machine seized up.

'Please, Lucy, don't talk to the girls – '

171

'But I'm sure they like me to take an interest. After all, I am the owner's wife.'

'It took Maisie four hours to undo the damage you caused – '

'*I* caused? Don't be absurd, Jenny. You do like to make a fuss about every little thing!'

A stream of buyers and agents came to the mill to look at the new designs. Sometimes, if they were important customers, Jenny would invite them home for dinner. These were the occasions when Lucy loved to shine. The table would be dressed with an épergne full of flowers, crystal and silver would glitter on the table, the meal would run to at least eight courses.

Lucy would chat. 'My husband's plans to extend the mill next spring . . . My husband's cloth has been bought by the Viceroy . . . My husband expects some Japanese agents to pay a visit next year . . .'

Ned would smile and pass the wine. After dinner Lucy would play the piano. The guest would stifle his yawns, eager to get away to his comfortable bed at the inn.

Mr Tyler of Pickersville and Thomas in Chicago made his escape before coffee on the grounds that he expected a message by the new telegraph system which had just been connected to Galashiels. He was so embarrassed by his own lies that he left early next morning without placing an order.

Despite the legend that only women gossip, men pass on malicious little stories. Word got round that it was better to escape the pains of being entertained at Gatesmuir. When Jenny had received three quick refusals of her invitations, she decided to speak to Lucy.

'Lucy, I think it would be better if you entertained on a smaller scale for the men who come on business. You know, they're tired, and all they want is a hearty meal and a cigar and then an early bed.'

'If you don't mind, my dear, I'll run the house while you run the mill. I know what's expected of the wife of Edward Corvill.'

'But I assure you, Lucy, it's not necessary to go to such lengths. In fact, it would be preferable to be more . . . more welcoming and less imposing.'

172

Lucy bridled. 'Only a very ignorant person would mistake elegance for ostentation.'

'Lucy dear, don't let's argue; after all, we only do it for the good of the business – '

'That's not my view! I do it because it's expected of a great firm like Corvill's – '

'What's expected is hospitality and suitability, not a performance like a grand opera.'

'Grand opera!'

Jenny was at once sorry. 'I didn't mean that. But all that silver and so forth, and having a musical soiree when all the poor men want is a quiet chat – '

'If you will allow me to run my house the way I see fit, I'll be obliged!'

Jenny could see it was useless. So when the next buyer from abroad called, she entertained him to supper at the Abbotsford Inn, with her lawyer and his wife as makeweights to prevent any censure about dining alone with a stranger.

Lucy was furious. An almight row ensued the moment Jenny got home at ten-thirty. Next morning Lucy had in revenge given orders to hold breakfast back by half an hour so that when Jenny came down, nothing was ready. Lucy descended at the new time to find Jenny finishing bread and butter in the kitchen.

'Please have the goodness not to eat with the servants! It lowers the tone of the house.'

'But if I had waited for breakfast in the dining-room I'd have been late at the works – '

'If you wish to breakfast at seven-thirty alone, I'll leave instructions to that effect.'

'But that means having the servants do it all twice!'

'The servants are my concern, thank you.'

It was too much. Jenny went away quickly, wrapping her tweed cape closely around her against the December morning, and fumed all day.

That evening she took Ned into the room that had been her father's study, now seldom used. 'Ned, things have got to change. I cannot put up with Lucy's interference any more.'

'Jenny!'

'I'm sorry. Lucy's notions of how to run the house are quite

173

wrong. She doesn't seem to understand that part of the thing is to help with our business needs. She makes our business guests uncomfortable, she went out of her way this morning to upset my routine. And when she comes to the mill she puts everyone's back up. It's got to stop.'

Ned had been having a pre-dinner dram or two. He had been feeling full of goodwill towards the entire world. Now he felt baffled. 'But Lucy's such a sweet wee thing, Jenny. You've only to tell her what you want – '

'I've tried that. It doesn't work. I want things on a new footing.'

'Well, I'm sure, just say the word.'

'You'll agree to a change?'

'Certainly, certainly,' Ned said, with an expansive wave.

'I want you and Lucy to move out.'

'Wha'?' That was a facer. After a moment he sobered up a little. 'Move out? Where to?'

'Wherever you like. You have plenty of income and I'd imagine you could amuse yourselves perfectly well in some other place than Galashiels. Talk to Lucy about it. She might very well like to go back to Edinburgh to be near her mother – or to Glasgow, where there's always a lot going on.'

'Really? You think we ought to go and live in Glasgow?'

'Why not? You don't really like the mill, so there's nothing to keep you here, and Lucy could give parties and entertain to her heart's content.'

Lucy was stunned when Ned put the idea to her. At first she grasped the opportunity, then she saw she was being got rid of and wanted to resist, and then in the end she saw that it was possible to act the part of the wife of the rich and important mill owner to perfection in a city. After a week of argument and discussion, it was agreed.

Lucy favoured Glasgow as her new home. She had no desire to live close to her interfering mother. And Ned, who hoped never to set foot in Waterside Mill again if he could help it, pictured himself really getting down to his treatise on *The Influence of Greek Culture on Scottish Society* in some pleasant little apartment close to Glasgow University.

A wagon from the mill was used to take their trunks to the station the day they left. The mill workers were going home for their lunchtime mutton broth. Ronald Armstrong leaned on the big iron gate to watch it trundle by. Jenny had come out too, to see her brother and sister-in-law off on the train.

'So you got rid of her,' he said to Jenny as she paused to let the way clear.

'Mr Armstrong!'

He grinned. 'Come on now, don't deny it. There isn't a soul at the mill who isn't cheering today. She was as much help to anybody as treacle toffee on the hair.'

'I think you're being overfamiliar, Mr Armstrong,' Jenny reproved, trying not to return his smile.

'Maybe I am. That's because I feel a great interest in everything concerning you.'

'Indeed!'

'Of course. Whatever concerns you concerns the mill.'

'Oh, I see.' She was glad the remark hadn't been as personal as it sounded, and yet she was a little disappointed.

Lucy's departure seemed to give Millicent Corvill a new impulse to take hold on life. Since William's death she had kept more or less to her room, emerging only to go to church. But, urged now by Jenny, she took hold of the reins of the household. 'If you don't do it, Mother, I shall have to hire a housekeeper – and neither of us would like that.'

'No, dear, it's bad enough having to let someone else do the cooking,' her mother agreed. She always had the feeling that the cook was extravagant and wasteful, particularly under the regime of Lucy.

Millicent descended to the kitchen, had a long chat with the domestic staff, and almost at once began to restore the former appearance of the rooms. Out went all the spindly new furniture Lucy had bought. Down came all the shiny curtains. Gradually Millicent found plain, comfortable replacements and the house began to seem quiet and homelike again.

For her part, Jenny was busy. Her plan to extend Waterside Mill was put into execution. She had a railway line laid so that wagons could be shunted to the very door of the loading bay to take the big bales of cloth, thus cutting out the time-wasting loading of horse wagons.

With the extension of the passenger rail network throughout the Borders, visitors became frequent. One manufacturer came after a promising correspondence: he made raincoats and capes from the rubberised cloth invented by Charles Mackintosh some twenty years previously. 'My thought is this: the cloth itself is cold and unpleasant to the touch so the usual practice is to line it with a softer material,' he had written. 'As most of the garments are, of course, sold to people for outdoor use, it would make sense to have a hardwearing, outdoors fabric for a lining.'

They spent an afternoon going through the pattern books. He chose two designs, the plaid adopted by the American Gun Club for its especial use and now popular throughout the world, and a dark green tartan. He left after giving a substantial order.

Jenny was still smiling to herself with pleasure at this coup when next day another visitor was announced. 'Mr Ross, representing Dudovsky of Moscow,' said the chief clerk, showing in a middle-aged man of ample girth.

'Mr Ross.' She rose to greet him.

'Miss Corvill. I come to introduce myself. I hope we shall meet often. My firm has hitherto contented itself with a man in London, but the demand for new tartans in the Russian wholesale houses has caused them to place me here, in Galashiels.'

'Here? You mean you are going to *live* here?'

'Precisely. I shall of course travel to Selkirk and Hawick and Walkerburn – my brief is to look at tweeds as well as tartans. I hope we shall have a very profitable relationship, Miss Corvill. Ah . . .' He hesitated. 'It would make my task much easier if you would be so . . . ah . . . so kind as to let me have first sight of any new designs you bring out.'

'First sight? You mean, give you favourable treatment?'

'Miss Corvill, it would be greatly to your advantage. The market in Russia is enormous. Since the Tsarina followed the example of our royal family and took up the tartans, the entire Russian court has followed suit, for informal wear, you understand.'

'I know the Tsarina likes Scottish tartans. I have had the pleasure of supplying them more than once.'

'Not only Her Imperial Majesty, I assure you. I have visited Moscow and Leningrad and I may say that at the moment *la mode d'Ecosse* is all the rage, particularly for spring and autumn, those periods between the extreme cold of winter and the enervating heat of summer.'

Jenny let him have half an hour of her time, said she would consider giving him first approval of Corvill's new designs, and eventually signed an agreement that he should be given favourable treatment on condition he spent at least five hundred pounds per annum with her. It seemed to her a sensible arrangement – there was no other agent for the Russian market with whom he was in competition.

But Mr Ross was the harbinger of others. A French gentleman, M Lamotte, set up an office in rooms on the ground floor of the Old Commercial Hotel. She heard that a 'spy' from Yorkshire had taken premises in Hawick. All the cloth merchants, it seemed, wanted to have early knowledge of the new designs in the Borders so as to be first in the field at the fashion houses in Paris and London.

'We'll have to put the mill on an extra shift,' Jenny told a meeting of her foremen. 'It may not last beyond the year, but we must take advantage of this upsurge in business while it lasts. Can you get me extra scribblers and spinners, Mr Ritchie?'

'I'll do my best. What wages will you be offering, mistress?'

'We'll offer a shilling above the norm, so as to be sure to get them. Sixteen shillings a week as compared to fifteen. And as the mending department is short of staff already, we'll offer another sixpence a week for menders – that'll bring the wage to sixteen and six.'

'Miss Corvill . . .'

'Yes, Mr Armstrong?'

'This won't make you very popular with the Manufacturers' Corporation.'

She flashed him a smile. 'Why should that bother me, since I am not a member of that all-male association?'

The department foremen exchanged glances. She could make a lot of enemies if she wasn't careful.

'Come, come,' Jenny said, with a little motion of her hands that waved away difficulties, 'we're all in the same boat, all starved for mill hands to take advantage of the market. We'll all have to offer increased wages – you'll see, there'll be nothing unusual in it by the end of the month.'

She was proved correct. But having moved fastest, she had enough people to extend production and meet all her orders in good time.

One evening she went home earlier than usual. Waterside Mill was still running, and would continue to do so until midnight, but her presence wasn't required. It was fine July weather, the hills gleaming in sunshine, the heather just beginning to tint the slopes with that soft purple like the glow of a pure amethyst.

Jenny walked up the slope through the town, nodding to acquaintances. She saw the carriage in the distance but paid no heed until she saw it go in at the entrance to Gatesmuir. She quickened her step. A visitor, in a hackney from the railway station?

She came up with the carriage as it was turning to go back down the drive. The passenger had descended and was waiting for the house door to be opened. It was a man in a light dustcoat and a pale top hat.

She came up to the door. At the sound of her step he turned politely. The light of recognition flooded across his face. He raised his hat.

'Fräulein Corvill?'

She went hot and cold with surprise. It was Franz Lennhardt from Hamburg.

Chapter Thirteen

In dreams Jenny had sometimes lived through this moment. Through the dappled shade of some sunlit glade a figure, indistinct in the half-light, would walk towards her. He would hold out his hand. When she stretched out and touched him, every nerve in her body would leap in recognition.

In real life it was otherwise. The housemaid opened the house door, looked surprised at finding Jenny on the doorstep as well as a visitor, stepped back, and Jenny ushered Franz in, saying, 'How do you do, Herr Lennhardt.'

The maid took his hat and linen topcoat. Jenny said, 'Is my mother in the drawing-room?'

'No, mistress, she's upstairs. Shall I – '

'No, I'll tell her. Please bring Mr Lennhardt some refreshments.' With a slight bow she left him, to go up and tidy herself. After a day at the works she was hot and a little dusty, her mourning dress made her feel dowdy, her hair needed smoothing down after her walk. She was vexed. What did he mean, turning up here at such an awkward hour?

She tapped on her mother's door. 'Can you come down, dear? We have a visitor.'

'Just a minute, Jenny.' Her mother opened the door, revealing that she was in a wrapper. 'I'm changing for dinner, pet. Is it Mrs Kennet about the Braw Lads Gathering?'

'No, it's a gentleman from Hamburg.'

'Hamburg?' She might just as well have said, From the moon. 'Ach dear me! Well . . . I'll be a minute or two yet.'

Jenny went downstairs, uncertain how she was going to handle it and what exactly it was she was feeling. Delight? Consternation?

After she got home from Hamburg, she had banished thoughts of Franz from her waking hours. He was a married man. She had no right to feel this perturbation over his merest touch.

When her father died, every other emotion was swamped by grief and guilt. Day and night the picture was in her mind – William's crooked body at the foot of the staircase, lifeless, cast there because he had stepped in among a band of silly, quarrelling women.

The need to take charge again at Waterside had pushed the memory from her waking hours, but it haunted her dreams to the exclusion of all others. She would wake in a sweat, wrestling with the sheets, knowing she had tried to throw out her arms to catch him and break his fall – but in the nightmare some iron band had been fixed about her, preventing any movement.

Gradually, after Lucy went and life became more relaxed at home, the nightmares had ended. Everything had been going along quietly, the day's work, the evening's innocent amusements, an occasional meeting of friends and neighbours, the refreshment of eight hours' good sleep . . .

The past, she had told herself, was behind her. A stupid, unnecessary accident had robbed her of her father. Could blame be laid at her door? She couldn't tell, but tried to forgive herself because otherwise the feeling of guilt would cripple her.

As to Franz and what might have been, she ought to be glad her stay in Hamburg had been so short. Franz belonged with that other memory, Bobby Prentiss, better never dwelt upon.

Yet here he was, behind the door of the drawing-room.

She drew a deep breath and went in.

He was sitting on a dark oak settle in the window, drinking iced lemonade and looking out at the garden. He began to stand up as she came in but she waved him to remain seated, taking a chair near the low table on which the carafe stood. She poured cool lemonade for herself, wondering if she ought to have offered him something stronger. But wine was only for parties and special occasions in her mother's house, beer was unknown, and since Ned's departure the whisky decanter was seldom in use.

'What brings you here, Herr Lennhardt?'

'How good it is to see you again!' he burst out, smiling at her with evident pleasure. He was faintly tanned, which went well with the light brown hair and the dark blue eyes. 'I was so delighted when I was offered this post, Fräulein! To renew acquaintance with you – '

'What post is that, mein Herr?' she asked hastily.

'I am no longer with Jener and Schlieber. Promotion was slow there and it was time to move on. I was offered this post with Gebel's, a good promotion and with considerable responsibility, so I – do you say, jumped at it?'

'That's what we say,' she agreed, sipping. 'But what post exactly? Are you a traveller for Gebel's? They usually buy through Wilson's in London.'

'No, no, my travelling will be very little. I am based here in the Borders. I can choose where to make my home and – need I tell you, dear lady – I have decided to make it here in Galashiels.'

'You will be . . . living in Galashiels? Permanently?'

'I have a year's contract which can be renewed indefinitely. Now, isn't that wonderful? We can be sure of seeing each other often.'

She stifled a gasp. It was so blatant. 'How is your wife, Herr Lennhardt?' she inquired, in a very level tone.

'Elsa? You met her, of course, at the restaurant. She is well. Very taken up with her new baby.'

Jenny bent her head and closed her eyes.

'Fräulein? Are you unwell?' Franz had risen and hurried towards her.

She looked up. 'Just tired, that's all. I never enjoy hot weather.'

He took her hand in his. She drew it back at once. The door opened, and her mother came in wearing a good black gown, rather better than she would have worn for an evening alone with Jenny. She had heard about these important people her son and daughter had met in Hamburg.

'Good evening, sir.'

'May I present Mr Lennhardt – he is representing Gebel's Warehouses. My mother.'

'Mrs Corvill, let me offer my sincerest sympathies on your loss. At the time I was employed by Jener and Schlieber – I believe you received a letter from them?'

'Yes, indeed, many kind letters. I appreciated them. You're very welcome in Galashiels, Mr Lennhardt. When did you arrive?'

'I just stepped off the train half an hour ago, Mrs Corvill. I left my luggage at the hotel, then came straight here to renew acquaintance with your son – '

'Ah! Ned has gone to Glasgow.'

'Gone? On holiday?' He was uncertain of the meaning.

'No, sir, he has gone to live there. He is writing a book, you know.'

'No, indeed, I had not heard that. A book?'

'About the Greeks. He needed access to libraries and places of learning, so he and my daughter-in-law are now living in Glasgow.'

Jenny saw that their visitor was surprised by the news, baffled, almost. 'I recall that Mr Corvill did not seem to take a great interest in the Wool Fair . . . He plays no part at all in the running of Corvill's?'

'No, my son's a scholar, always was.'

'Then who . . .' His eyes went to Jenny. 'Who runs Waterside Mill?'

'It'll surprise you when you hear,' Mrs Corvill said, with a smile. 'Gentlemen are always amazed. My daughter manages the mill, sir. She's in complete charge. It was an understanding between her and Ned so that he could get on with his book.' This was the fiction given to Ned's mother. She fully believed it.

'I see.' Franz paused. 'You have no other family, Mrs Corvill?'

'What? You mean, who else lives in our fine house? A strange thing, is it not? Just the two of us, Mr Lennhardt. Ah, little did we know when we bought it that it would empty so soon . . .'

'The local children say, "A widow and an old maid, Clinging like ivy in the shade," ' Jenny told him, smiling.

182

He frowned. 'That is unkind.'

'But it's true. Children often speak aloud things that adults only think.'

There was a melancholy in the air that he didn't like. He set himself to chase it away, with so much success that when he said he must be going, Mrs Corvill protested. 'But you must stay to dinner, Mr Lennhardt.'

'Oh, I couldn't impose – '

'Nonsense, nonsense, to let you spend your first evening in Galashiels on your own – that would be a cold thing! No, no, if you're prepared to take pot luck with us, we should love to have you.'

Mother, Mother, you don't know what you're doing, Jenny said within herself. She wanted Franz gone, kept at arm's length. But Millicent thought of him as a friend of her son's, alone in a strange land. She must befriend him.

To keep matters straight, Jenny talked stoutly about their visit to Hamburg and Franz's wife. Mrs Corvill took an interest, heard there was a baby, and after the meal asked if he had a photograph. Of course he had. He produced from his pocketbook two tinted portraits, one of a baby in lace shawls enthroned in many cushions, the other of a thickset young woman holding the child in her arms and staring transfixed at the camera.

'A very fine child,' said Millicent. 'A boy?'

'Yes, three months old.'

'You must have been very sad to leave them,' she sympathised.

Laughing, he said that men were not much wanted when there was a new baby around, and gave some humorous examples of how he had been at a loss in his role of father. Millicent laughed and told him he was pretending but she knew he would be lonely for them.

'You must come and see us whenever you feel like that. Ned told me how kind you were to Jenny and him when he was in your homeland.'

'I hope you mean it, Mrs Corvill, for nothing would give me greater pleasure.'

When he had gone Jenny tried to put up barricades. 'Mother, we can't single him out for special favour. He's here to buy cloth – the other agents would be very annoyed if he had freedom to come and go here.'

'Oh, really, dear? I never thought of that.'

'You mustn't encourage him to drop in. If he comes without invitation, you must arrange not to be at home.'

'I couldn't send a message that I wasn't at home if I *was*, Jenny. You know your father disapproved of white lies.'

'Very well, I'll see to it.'

She instructed the housemaid that if Mr Lennhardt called unexpectedly, he was to be told Mrs Corvill was not at home.

'She wants to fend him off,' the housemaid remarked to the kitchen staff. 'I wonder why?'

'Never bother your head about it,' Mrs Baird said crossly.

'He's a handsome lad,' said the kitchenmaid. 'I had a peep at him as he left. I'd be glad if he came a-calling at my house.'

'He's a married man,' Baird said, in a tone that put an end to all tittle-tattle.

Jenny might arrange for Franz not to be admitted beyond the hall of Gatesmuir, but she couldn't prevent him from calling regularly at the mill. Even when she was busy elsewhere, he was known to be in the visitors' parlour looking at the pattern books. He contrived matters so that they came across each other in the High Street. He made a large circle of acquaintance so that he was often at events that Jenny attended.

She wasn't surprised to see him at the Braw Lads Gathering. He edged nearer in the crowd to ask the significance of the event. 'It's a haphazard summer celebration, commemorating the marriage of Margaret Tudor to James IV of Scotland in 1503,' she explained politely.

'Was that particularly pleasing to Galashiels?'

'The nearby Forest of Ettrick was granted as a bride-gift.'

'Folklore is very interesting, is it not?' he remarked.

A procession of young people went round the outskirts of the borough, a king and queen of the summer were crowned with leafy coronets.

'This is surely of pagan origin,' Franz hazarded.

'Oh, aye,' said Mr Hailes, joining them, 'you've hit it, sir. The same kind of thing happens all over Europe in summer.

But it's a grand excuse for a day's holiday in which to get drunk.'

'Ah, that is universal.'

Mr Hailes dug him in the ribs, grinned at him, and told him he had a particularly fine bottle of whisky at home he'd be delighted to share with him that evening. At that moment the uncertain weather decided to cut the festival short. The rain came down. Everyone dashed for shelter. Most people rushed into Haldane's brewery in the yard of which trestle tables had been set up under a canopy. Jenny saw her mother escorted into the lobby of the inn. She herself was being guided elsewhere.

She knew she should have wrenched herself free and run after her mother and Mr Hailes. But the holiday spirit, the high summer madness, was in her. And his hand was on her arm.

They came to rest in the doorway of the block of offices next to the Bank of Scotland. He pulled her back into its shadows. He put his arms about her, held her trapped, her body between his and the wall behind her. He kissed her so fiercely that her lips hurt.

She made a sound of protest. He released her only a fraction, simply so that his tongue could part her lips and dart into her mouth. Sweetness rose up on her palate as if honey had been dripped there. Her head tilted back against the stones of the wall. He put one hand on her stretching throat, and caressed it with the tips of his fingers while his mouth moved on hers.

'I will resist, I will resist,' her mind was saying. But her body was melting under the glowing assault of touch and taste.

Running footsteps and laughter on the pavement outside brought her back to her senses. Any moment someone might come in, seeking shelter from the rain. Franz too relaxed his hold, looking towards the doorway. She slipped from him, hurrying towards the street.

No one came in but she saw a group of young people running by. Franz caught her arm from behind.

'Jenny!'

She tried to free herself. 'Let me go!'

'Jenny, don't run away – '

'Let me go this minute or I'll never speak to you again.'

185

His hand fell away. He joined her near the entry, standing innocently at her side, two people sheltering from the summer downpour so common in hill country. The decorated carts of the Braw Lads procession could be seen at the top of the hill, the horses tossing their heads impatiently as they waited to be taken to shelter. Beyond that there was the sound of fiddle and melodion as the merriment at the brewery yard continued under the canopy.

'I love you, Jenny,' Franz said, his voice low, his lips close to her ear.

'No!'

'You know it is so. I love you and you love me.'

'No!' She flung up her hands to cover her ears, to shut out the words.

'Jenny – ' He put an arm about her shoulders.

She ran out into the street, into the rain, anywhere, to escape the dangers that would engulf her if she stayed near him. She ran up the hill towards the carts, round a corner – and straight into a group of men carrying baskets with bottles and wrapped dishes.

'Hi! Mind where you're going! Oh, it's you, mistress!' They fell back respectfully.

She knew them, they were her employees. Then a well-known voice said, 'My, you're getting drenched! Here, take this.' Ronald Armstrong took off his jacket to hold over her head and shoulders like a tent.

'What are you doing here, mistress?' someone asked. 'The notables are all at the brewery wi' the mutton pies and the Forfar bridies.'

'I made a mistake, looking for shelter . . .'

'Come on then, lassie, we'll escort ye back to the celebrations.' Laughing and joking, they turned on their steps to lead her back to the party of important townsfolk. One of them began to sing, 'Braw, braw lads of Gala Water, Bonnie lads of Gala Water . . .' They were all a little tipsy, but full of good intentions.

'Where were you off to?' she asked, to keep them from asking why she'd left her mother's side.

'Where else but the well in Rye Haugh – for a wee revelry

186

of our own, with the requisite provisions.' They flourished the baskets.

'I wish you joy,' she said, as they delivered her to the brewery gates.

There was something in her tone that made Ronald look at her with attention. 'You're not enjoying the day, mistress?'

'Oh, of course I am. It's lovely.' She ducked out from under his jacket and handed it to him. It was soaked. 'Mr Armstrong, you'll catch your death of cold if you sit around the edge of Rye Haugh Well in that!'

'Na, na,' cried a wag, 'he'll have a warmth within to dry him.'

'Besides, it's clearing up, he can spread it out to dry.'

'Mistress Corvill, are you all right?' Ronald asked, disregarding the joviality around him.

'Fine, thanks.'

'Because if you're not, I'll see you home.'

She longed to say, Yes, take me home, let me hide from all temptations in the safety of Gatesmuir. But she knew she couldn't withdraw from the festivities. This was a great day in Galashiels, a commemoration of a happy time, apart from Sundays the one day except New Year when the mills were quiet.

She shook her head, trying to smile at Ronald Armstrong. He studied her. He wasn't sure that the drops on her cheeks were rain – they might even have been tears.

His companions claimed him, he nodded farewell and left her to join her mother, who scolded her for running off and getting wet. The rain didn't clear. Under the canopy the mutton pies and the Forfar bridies, the shortbread and the thick cake, the whisky and the ale and the fruit cordials were sprinkled with blowing moisture. Even the bravest spirits had to agree that it was best to give up the thought of an al fresco celebration.

On Braw Lads Day open house was kept by everyone. Buffet food was spread out in the Gatesmuir dining-room from five in the evening onwards, and a continual stream of visitors came to dance to the fiddle of John Graham the coachman. The ladies changed into a lesser form of mourning – dark purple with a gold mourning brooch for Mrs Corvill, dove grey for Jenny.

Jenny knew Franz would come. It was inevitable. She had escaped from him but he would pursue. She recognised something in him that wouldn't be denied.

He came with Mr Hailes, about eight o'clock. A boisterous game of forfeits was in progress at the time. Mr Hailes was a little enthused by generous samplings of the excellent bottle of whisky he had mentioned. Franz was entirely sober, and proved it by sitting by Mrs Corvill in quiet conversation. Only his occasional glance told Jenny he was watching her.

She moved about, playing hostess, greeting newcomers, saying farewells to those who were moving on to other parties. The drenched garden glittered in a belated evening sunshine. Carriages of laughing people came and went, guests arrived on foot bearing flowers traditional to the day – rose and iris and veronica. But at last the gathering began to thin out, the dishes of food on the buffet table were almost empty, the wine had been drunk, the whisky decanter held only a shallow golden puddle.

Mr Hailes was still in the drawing-room, looking through a collection of tinted engravings. Franz was still chatting with Mrs Corvill.

Jenny had perforce to join them. Her mother was saying, 'We have a copy of the book, it came by the Edinburgh train a few days ago. But you know, Mr Lennhardt, we have no one to read to us these days.' Her hand touched her mourning brooch. 'My husband . . . but he read mostly sermons. It was my son who used to read Mr Dickens's works.'

'Dear lady, if you can put up with my imperfect English, I should be delighted to read for you.'

'Oh, Mr Lennhardt, your English is very good indeed, excellent. And it would be such a kindness . . .'

Jenny's heart sank. The copy of *A Tale of Two Cities* had been ordered as soon as published. There was nothing to stop her mother reading it for herself. But Millicent had been brought up to believe that 'Satan finds some mischief still, For idle hands to do'. So she preferred to be read to, while she sewed or mended or knitted. Jenny would often read to her, but she found it tiring. And besides, she often wanted to think about new designs, to try out colours, in the evenings at home.

Millicent looked to her daughter. She remembered that they weren't supposed to single out Mr Lennhardt. Jenny shook her head slightly. Millicent, obedient, said, 'Thank you, sir, but it would be expecting too much when you have had a day's work. Jenny will read it for me.'

'But I should be glad to – '

'You are very kind, but I think we must decline.'

'Let me at least read you a chapter now – a perfect ending to a day of holiday.' He picked up the copy, opened it at the bookmark, and began to read about the reunion of Dr Manette with Lucie. His slight German accent fitted somehow with the 'foreign' aspect of the story. Mrs Corvill listened, enchanted.

Mr Hailes toddled towards the hall. 'I'll away,' he said. 'Young Franz can find his way home from here, I daresay. Thank you for a pleasant party, Jenny.'

'Don't go yet, Mr Hailes – '

'Aye, I must go, dear lassie, I've had too much to drink and I'm hardly able to keep my eyes open.' He kissed her on the cheek and trotted unsteadily out, singing, 'Braw braw lads,' out of tune.

That was at half-past nine. At ten o'clock Franz was still reading and Mrs Corvill was still listening, although her eyelids were beginning to droop. At length her head nodded. Waking with a start and in embarrassment, she said she thought she would go to her bed. Smiling, she shook hands with Franz, and kissed Jenny goodnight.

The door closed behind her. Franz laid aside the book. 'You must go, Franz,' Jenny said, standing close to the door through which her mother had gone.

'Not before we have had a talk.'

'What is there to talk about? You must go!'

'It's foolish to turn your back on it. We love each other.'

'No!'

He got up, came to her, and quite gently led her to a sofa where he sat down with her. 'Jenny, I've held you in my arms. I know you want me as much as I want you.'

'No, it's not so – '

'I knew it the very first moment I touched you – remember, at the Wool Fair, when the load nearly fell on you?'

'I don't know what you thought, what you imagined – you were wrong.'

'No, I was right. And this afternoon, when I kissed you – '

'You had no right!' she cried. 'You're a married man!'

He sat back against the sofa cushions, almost laughing. 'Is that it? You worry about Elsa? You need not, my darling. Elsa doesn't care what I do.'

'How can you say – '

'Listen, I'll explain. Elsa and I . . . we don't love each other, never did. Our families were friends, it was taken for granted we would get married. You know how these things are?'

Unwillingly, she nodded. She remembered the grave young Huguenot she might have married if she had stayed in Edinburgh.

'Elsa very much wanted to be a married lady and I . . . I hadn't met anyone I cared about more, so I agreed, we were married. And then when I met you I knew I should have . . . oh, I should have waited, I should have been free to ask for your hand, my dearest!'

He leaned forward, captured her hand, and carried it to his lips. He kissed it fervently, and she reproached herself that she didn't snatch it away at once.

'What you're saying is that you're sorry you're a married man,' she said bluntly. 'But you made an oath to be faithful when you married your wife. You can't just go back on it.'

'I would keep my oath if Elsa would keep hers!' he cried, his dark blue eyes flashing with anger. 'She promised to love and honour me – but she didn't like being a married woman, although she was "dutiful". It was like being married to a statue. You don't know, Jenny, how awful it is to turn to someone for warmth and comfort, and find – only a marble coldness.'

She said nothing. She didn't know how to reply. She was sorry for him, but to let him see it would be fatal.

'Our child was born at the end of March. Elsa has made it clear that he is to be the centre of her world from now on. She scarcely seems to know I exist any more.'

'But . . . but . . . Franz, that's quite common, I believe. It's only temporary, it's to do with having to think of the baby, its welfare, its needs – '

'It's not that. When I told her I was applying for this position in Scotland her relief – ! It was plain she was glad to be rid of me, so that she could spend all her love on Wilhelm without feeling guilty. So you see, my dear one, you needn't think of Elsa.'

'I can't look at it like that. You're speaking as if she doesn't exist, but she does, and how would she feel if – '

'She need never know – how *could* she know, Jenny? She's in Hamburg, and we are here. We wouldn't be hurting her in any way.'

'No, don't, you're confusing me. I know it would be wrong – '

His face took on a look of gaunt desperation. 'Don't turn your back on me, Jenny,' he begged. 'I've come such a long way to find you again.'

'Oh, Franz . . . my dear . . . don't, I'm so sorry . . .'

'You see? You love me, don't deny it – '

'I don't know whether it's love,' she said, almost wildly, turning away from him. 'You make me feel . . . as if I'm being pulled apart!'

He was silent. Then he quoted, ' "A widow and an old maid . . . " You are not an old maid, my darling. When I touch you I feel your heart beating with the same longing that fills me. You have known love. That's so, isn't it?'

She remained turned away from him, silent, full of guilt.

'If you could love *him*, why can't you love me?'

'It was different – you don't know – I was young, silly, and he . . . he . . . I didn't know he was married.'

'Well,' Franz said, in a voice that broke with emotion, 'you know I am married. I am being honest with you, utterly, completely honest. I can only offer you myself – my longing, my need of you – but that can bring happiness, because you need me too. We belong to each other, Jenny. Don't deny it.'

She was clenching and unclenching her hands in her lap. She wanted to turn to him, throw herself into his arms, let his caresses blot out her fears.

The room door opened. Thirley, the housemaid, came in.

191

'Shall I lock up – Oh!' She stopped, taken aback. 'I'm sorry, mistress, I thought everyone had gone.'

Jenny got to her feet. 'Mr Lennhardt is just leaving,' she said. 'Goodnight, Mr Lennhardt.'

It was a moment before he could respond. He couldn't school his features. He went out to the hall, took his hat from Thirley, and with a bow left the house.

'Shall I lock up now, Mistress Corvill?' the maid said, looking at her with curiosity.

'Yes, thank you, Thirley.'

With dragging feet she climbed the stairs to her room. Baird was waiting to help her to bed. She shook her head, dismissing her. 'I shan't need you, Baird.'

Slowly she heard the house settle down for the night. Rain clouds flew across the sky again, the drops spattered on the panes. She knelt on the window-seat, staring out, seeing the leaves on the trees shiver in the summer storm, hearing the owl call as she hunted to feed her brood.

It was a long time before she sought her bed.

Next day the town went back to work, and Miss Corvill of the Waterside Mill did likewise. She filled the hours with business. She kept herself from thinking about Franz. That day went by, and the next. Franz came to the mill, a trade inquiry. She arranged to be busy elsewhere. He left a sealed note on her desk: 'Please don't evade me, we must meet. I will come again tomorrow.'

She went to Selkirk next day, to look at some new machinery in use at a mill there.

But she couldn't go on avoiding him for ever. She must make up her mind what to do.

She found refuge in the room on the first floor of the mill, where her father's handloom still stood. She used it from time to time to set up patterns. She wasn't as good a weaver as her father or Ned, and when she wanted a really expert effect she called in an old man too crippled with rheumatism to work for long but happy to do special small pieces for the mistress.

She was sitting at the loom, throwing the shuttle deftly but automatically, taking comfort in the 'rickle-tick' of the old machine as the pattern grew on the bed. She heard a sound behind her, and paused.

'I wanted to ask you if you'd decided – ' It was her master dyer. He stopped in mid-sentence. 'Jenny lass, what ails you?' he gasped.

She shook her head. 'I'm all right.' She didn't even notice he had called her by her first name.

'You look sick and sore-hearted. What's troubling you?' He waited but she said nothing. 'Is it what I hear, that you're thinking of buying the premises outright instead of leasing? Because if it's that, it's not worth worrying yourself sick over. You can always – '

'It's not that . . . It's something I can't . . . If only there was someone I could confide in . . .'

She turned on the stool to look at him. He was staring down at her, his long face full of kindly concern, the grey eyes watchful. Could she confide in Ronald Armstrong? He was a good man, steady, sensible. She thought of him as a friend.

But he would be so shocked. And it was such a personal matter.

'You miss your father,' he suggested. 'It's a hard thing, for a lassie your age to have so much responsibility on her shoulders. Not that he understood the money side, but he was a rare man for the cloth.'

'I miss him,' she admitted. She felt tears rising within her. She missed her father, but there was a greater gap in her life, the gap left by having no one of her own to love.

Hastily she rose, passing Ronald to the door. 'I haven't time for being silly,' she said. 'What was it you wanted me for?'

But the moment stayed in her mind all day. When she got home, she settled herself with a sketchblock in the window-seat while her mother wrote a letter to her daughter-in-law, who had sent word she was expecting a baby.

Jenny thought about Ronald Armstrong, and she thought about herself.

She was twenty-three years old in two weeks' time. She was in the greatest danger of beginning a liaison with a married man.

If she did that, she would be no better than her sister-in-law Lucy had been when she was involved with Archie Brunton. She might excuse herself by saying she was free to do as she wished, she had no husband to betray. But Franz

193

had a wife. No matter how he rationalised it, to go to bed with Franz was a betrayal of Elsa. It was wrong.

Yet she longed for him. Her body ached with longing for him. She felt she had only to see him alone once more and she would throw herself into his arms. Her defences weren't as strong as her own physical desire.

The evening of Braw Lads Day had been a warning. Perhaps only Thirley's entrance had saved her from committing herself to Franz. And Thirley . . . She remembered the expression of avid curiosity on the maid's face. Was this what lay before her? To be a scandal, a cause of gossip, in the town where hitherto she had been respected?

The solution was to have a man of her own. She ought to be a married woman with a husband who would treasure her, partner her in need and love to reach that soft bliss of the body she remembered so well.

Even in her most earnest pursuit of Archibald Brunton, she had never imagined herself transported with physical delight in his bed. But Ronald Armstrong . . .

He was strong, forceful, a man sure of himself. She could imagine he would be a kind lover, experienced and considerate.

As to what people would say . . . True, it would cause a sensation if she married Ronald. He was a workman, although a skilled one. She was the daughter of the mill-owning family.

People would say they had had to get married, that she had been 'caught'. But what did it matter? In the end gossip would die away, people would accept Ronald. And he would be a good husband in more than the physical sense. He would be a partner in work. He knew all there was to know about cloth-making. She could talk to him, discuss with him, confide in him.

For forty-eight hours she came back to the thought, banished it, resurrected it, and finally reached the conclusion that it was an excellent idea. It was the solution to her dilemma, the way out of her torture. She would have a husband. She would be protected.

She sent for Ronald to her office. She had dressed with special care when she went home at lunchtime, changing into a summer gown of black muslin embroidered with a pattern of leaves. Above it her dark hair and black eyes seemed part of the scheme, as did the soft cap trimmed with obligatory mourning ribbons. The effect was demure, reticent, delicate, but very attractive.

She had tea brought in the best china, and told her chief clerk she wasn't to be disturbed until she rang her bell.

Ronald came in, bearing strands of newly-dyed yarn. He expected a discussion about the tartan she was trying out for the spring season, a grey and lilac check of which he had great doubts.

She listened to what he had to say about the fading of alizarin with too small an iron mix.

'Very well, Mr Armstrong, I leave it to you to try again. But it was something else I wanted to talk about.'

'Yes?'

She poured tea with a trembling hand. She almost decided not to go on with her plan. She handed him his cup. He took it, a little puzzled. Generally she didn't provide refreshments except at a meeting of all foremen and department heads.

'I wanted to talk to you about something personal. You know I . . . I shall be twenty-three in ten days time?'

'Is that a fact? No, I cannot say I knew that.'

'I . . . er, you know what the children sing as they skip: "A widow and an old maid, Clinging together in the shade." '

'Oh, aye,' he said, laughing, 'I've heard them, the rascals!'

'Mr Armstrong, I don't want to be an old maid.'

He frowned. 'That's easy enough to remedy, mistress.'

'Not so easy!' she rejoined. She managed a wry smile. 'Remember Archibald Brunton.'

'Oh, him . . .' He sipped his tea. 'Why did you show him the door? I've always been curious.'

'I can't tell you that. Just let's say I discovered it would be terribly unwise to marry him.'

'Truly said. I always knew you'd come to your senses before you tied the knot – if I can say so without offending you. The marvel to me was that you spent so much time on him in the first place.'

His frankness took her aback. She hesitated. Then she said, 'You take an interest in what I do?'

'Why would I not? Whatever you do affects the mill.'

'If I were to tell you now that I have a man in mind . . .'

It was his turn to be surprised at the frankness of their talk. He said after an indrawn breath, 'Well, I'd wish you luck with all my heart. Who is the man?'

'You are, Mr Armstrong.'

A flush ran under his pale skin to reach his tawny hair. Then it slowly receded, leaving him pale, almost white.

'What did you say?'

'It would make good sense, don't you see? You and I get on very well together, we share a lot of interests because of the mill. And I need a husband . . .'

'Is this a joke?' He set down the fine china cup on her desk with a movement that rattled it in its saucer.

'No, certainly not. I am asking you very definitely, Mr Armstrong. Will you marry me?'

Slowly he stood up. He stared at her from eyes that looked like grey coals in a hot fire.

'You must be out of your mind.'

'No, I've thought it all through – '

'Not far enough! Jenny Corvill, when I want a wife, I'll find the girl and ask her myself. Good day to you.'

'Wait!' she cried, suddenly in horror at having somehow mishandled the situation. 'Wait, you must listen – '

'I've heard enough. I heard the question, clearest of all. And the answer, Miss Corvill, is no.'

Chapter Fourteen

The latch of the office door clicked behind him.

Shocked, stunned, Jenny tried to call him back. Her voice failed her. She sat dumbstruck. The room wheeled around her.

She had been rejected. *Rejected.*

She should have said more, explained the whole thing. She hadn't made it clear, he hadn't understood.

Her feet pushed against the floor, she heaved herself up. She got to the door, hurried out towards the dyeing department.

In the room Ronald used as a laboratory only his assistant was to be seen, stirring dubiously in a small dye vat with a pair of wooden tongs. 'Where is Mr Armstrong?'

'Mr Armstrong? You sent for him to the office.'

'He hasn't been back?'

The young man shook his head.

She threw herself out the door again, going quickly to all the places in the works where he might be found. No sign of him.

She went back to the entry hall. The chief clerk who sat at the desk looked up.

'Where did Mr Armstrong go when he left my office?'

'Straight out the front entrance, mistress.'

Left the building? She looked at the watch pinned to the bodice of her dress. A few minutes past four o'clock.

He must have gone home. He must have decided to put distance between them. It was understandable – he was angry, embarrassed.

She would send him a note. She went to her desk, picked up a pen, began to write.

But what could she write? Dear Mr Armstrong, You left before I could explain. I intend to make you Manager of Waterside Mill, taking only the design department and the overseeing of the books for myself.

Before she could even pen the words she knew they sounded like a bribe. She was saying, You refused me as a woman but as a business proposition you will take me.

She still couldn't believe it. Why had he reacted so angrily? He was a sensible man, a shrewd man. She had offered him the best catch in the district, Miss Genevieve Corvill of Corvill and Son, the best cloth-makers in Galashiels.

It wasn't that he didn't like her. She was sure there had been something almost of affection in his manner to her in the past.

She sat staring at the few words she had written. No, she couldn't put matters right by telling him that marriage would bring him position, power, money.

She should have said that she liked him well, that he was a man in whom she had confidence. She should have explained that she needed his protection. She should have appeared more womanly.

Perhaps her forthrightness had simply . . . scared him off.

But when she saw him again she would start on a different footing. Instead of being totally frank and honest she would use some feminine wiles. She would explain that she had been very nervous about speaking to him – after all, what she had done had taken courage, a shameless thing, and if she expressed herself badly he must forgive it.

The chief clerk tapped on the door. 'Mistress Corvill, is it all right to interrupt now?'

'What? Of course.'

'The head packer wants to know when the freight car will be sent from the railway yard to take the order for the north?'

'Isn't it here? It was supposed to arrive by four.'

'If it's no here soon, Harrison says he'll never get the goods on it for the night train.'

'Send the boy to the railway yard. Tell him to say – no, wait, I'll write a message for him.'

The day resumed around her. The goods car came, late, and every spare hand was needed to help load. The packing and labelling had been done but in the hurry the goods were loaded in the wrong order for easy unloading. It all had to be done again.

At seven, exhausted, she went home. She walked slowly, full of a fatigue that was more than physical. By going only slightly out of her way, she could pass Ronald's lodgings. Should she knock on the door, ask to speak to him?

She knew she was too weary to face him, too dazed to do herself justice. She dragged herself home, to the meal her mother had kept waiting for her.

Afterwards she went early to bed. She slept quickly, worn out by a day that had gone wrong in every possible way. She woke very early, the sun of a late-August morning spreading joyfully into her room. She lay watching the light catching on the hangings of the half-tester, hearing the crowing of the cock from the farm on the hill.

A new day. A new beginning. She would start all over again, go to seek out Ronald instead of summoning him to her office, beg him to listen to what she had to say, speak as a woman should in the mild, beseeching tones he might think fitting.

Once more she dressed with care. She sighed at the mourning gowns which she couldn't avoid – two more months before the year was up. She chose a gown that had lightness and softness again, a voile dress with lace at the neck and wrists, more suitable for afternoon visiting than a day at the works. But she knew what she was doing. She wanted to be all melting femininity as she presented herself to Ronald Armstrong.

Her clerk had put the morning post on her desk as usual. On top was a letter without a stamp and addressed merely, Miss Corvill. Her heart gave a lurch. She recognised the writing.

'Miss Corvill, This is to tender my resignation starting immediately. I understand that in so doing I forfeit any wages due to me. All the work of the dye department is up to date – test results are on file and notes referring to work in progress are in folders separately marked. Signed, R. Armstrong.'

Dismay flooded her mind so as to blot out everything else. She started up, forgetting even to take the bonnet she had just untied. She ran out of the office, out of the building, ran to

Scotts Place and then, because she was running out of breath and because people were turning to stare, she slowed. She came into Eliot Lane. She knocked with desperate anxiety on the door of Number Four.

A plain-faced middle-aged woman in an apron opened. 'Can I speak to Mr Armstrong?' she asked, still half gasping for breath.

'Mr Armstrong packed up and left last night.'

Jenny stood at the doorstep, aghast. 'Left?'

'On the eight o'clock train for Edinburgh.'

'Where – Did he leave an address?'

'No, Mistress Corvill, he didna. He paid up to me for the rest of the month and a bit over, and he telt me he was away, and wouldna be back.'

'Did he – did he say anything?'

'Scarce a word. Grim as death, he was.' Mrs Graham looked at Jenny with unfriendly curiosity. 'You gave him the sack, did you? And now you've changed your mind.'

'No – no, I didn't – I – I – '

'Well, whatever you did, you did it thoroughly. He's away, and sorry I am to lose him – a decent, good man and the best lodger I ever had in the house. Good morning to you, mistress.' She stepped back, the door closed.

It was too much to take in. Too harsh, too awful.

She had thought to give him a golden opportunity to better himself. Instead she had driven him out of Galashiels.

With slow steps she made her way to the banks of the Gala. It was half-past eight. The work of the town was well under way. The clatter of hooves and the crying of carters overrode the steady hum of sound that was the water driving the mills.

The Gala flowed past, sparkling brown like polished sard. The sun shone. Wood pigeons cooed from the slopes of Forebrae.

There was shade and solitude under a leafy willow. She sank down, wrapped her arms about her knees, put her head down, and let her misery have full rein.

By the waters of Babylon, we sat down and wept.

She didn't weep, but her whole being was suffused with regret and remorse. And as she let her mind go over yesterday,

200

understanding at last began to come to her. How could she have been so crass?

She had never once thought of the matter from the point of view of Ronald Armstrong. She had miscalculated his feelings. Worst of all, she had disregarded his pride. She should have known he would never look at a woman who made an offer in that way. To him it was an affront, a total insult.

She had made it impossible for him to work for her any longer. He could never see her, they could never come face to face again. She was a person he would avoid for the rest of his life because she had shown she had scant respect for him. And now he had no respect for her. She knew – from the outset she had known – he could never work with people he didn't respect.

She'd been telling herself she'd been honest with him. But she should have said, I'm afraid, afraid of myself and my loneliness. I can't go on any more without someone of my own to love and to love me. You and I could learn to love each other.

She recalled what Archie Brunton's mother had said: Who is worthy of you? Worthy of her! What an absurd view!

Her confidence in herself as a woman had been utterly destroyed by the events of yesterday. It seemed she had no judgement, no intuition. Every man to whom she turned had been somehow wrong – Bobby Prentiss, Archie Brunton, Ronald Armstrong. And . . . Franz.

It was only to escape the fatal attraction of Franz that she'd made a fool of herself in front of Ronald. Only because of a weakness in herself. It was *her* problem, she should have found a way to solve it without dragging in Ronald.

Too late now to see it with clear eyes. Too late, he was gone – and with an opinion of her that could only be low. That hurt. Yet she had to admit he would be right to think her a fool, a self-centred, grasping, insensitive idiot.

The clever, efficient Miss Genevieve Corvill of Gatesmuir . . . If the world only knew.

At length the height of the sun told her it was past mid-morning. She emerged from among the trailing boughs of willow, because she couldn't hide for ever and work had to go on.

She found the mill humming as usual, but her head clerk was in a state bordering on hysteria. 'Mistress, where have you been? You had an appointment with Mr Goveley of Hunter's at nine-thirty, and we're waiting for your signature to get cash from the bank for the wages.'

'Yes. I'm sorry. I needed some fresh air.'

For a moment he paused, studied her. 'Aye,' he said, 'you look as if you have the headache . . . Can I get you anything, mistress? Tea? A wee dram?'

'Nothing, thank you. Let's catch up with all this work.'

Next day was Sunday, always a very quiet day at Gatesmuir. Millicent had returned to the regime imposed by William Corvill at the outset of his marriage: church in the morning, a light meal at midday so as not to involve anyone in more work than necessary on this day of rest, the afternoon spent with worthy books or in doing acts of charity, then evening service. After that, a substantial supper because with the end of evening service it was felt the Sabbath had been given its due. But visitors, even after supper, were never encouraged.

Jenny's excuse that she didn't feel very well was readily accepted by her mother. 'You've looked poorly for a few days now, my dear. Perhaps you're sickening for a summer cold?'

'I'm all right, dear, I'm only tired.'

Mrs Corvill sighed and acknowledged it. She went alone to morning service at the United Secession Church.

The day was a typical Borders day – a strong wind blowing from the hills bringing with it the scent of the heather, clouds racing across the blue summer sky. Jenny went out for a walk, but only in the grounds as it was against her mother's principles to go to the town on a Sunday unless in an emergency.

The garden around Gatesmuir was extensive enough to need a gardener and a boy, though compared with, for instance, the estate around the laird's house it was small. The trees on the west side were always a great pleasure to Jenny. There among the fallen leaves and the woodland flowers she often found inspiration for new colour designs.

This morning, in the fleeting sunshine between the scudding clouds, she watched a butterfly spread its wings to catch the warmth. A pretty thing, not as bright as some but speckled green on brown – she remembered a conversation with the collector Mr Hailes, which had led her to think it might be some kind of fritillary. A beautiful colour scheme, but too sombre for a fashionable tartan. It was a tweed blend – some day, she thought, we may start to make tweeds as well as tartans.

On the slope above the house she came out of the shelter of the trees. The wind whipped her skirts against her body. She stood looking at the view – colours, shades, a thousand ways of combining them to catch the light.

A horseman was turning in at the drive of Gatesmuir. She was surprised, for most inhabitants of Galeshiels knew the Corvills didn't willingly receive on Sunday.

Then she recognised the rider. It was Franz Lennhardt. He, of course, wasn't familiar yet with the customs of all the families in the district. She watched him dismount, tie the reins to the post, and walk to the door. There was a long wait after his knock. Thirley was probably astounded at being summoned to answer the door on a Sunday morning.

She saw the short conversation. Franz withdrew, remounted, and rode away. Her throat began to ache with unshed tears. He looked so lonely, riding away. He loved her, and she avoided him, and now he had come to see her and was going away. Franz, Franz – she called him silently, wanting the comfort of his uncritical love.

But she knew that would be wrong.

Half an hour later she saw her mother returning from church. Lunch would be already laid in the dining-room: soup, bread and butter, plain cake for dessert, milk to drink. She returned to the house. Thirley spoke to her as she came down from her room after putting away her bonnet.

'Mistress Corvill, a gentleman called, Mr Lennhardt.'

'Yes?'

'He left a message. He said . . .' Thirley screwed up her forehead as she repeated exact words, 'he had had no reply to his note and begged the favour of a word from you.'

His note had said: Please don't evade me, we must meet.

'I see. Thank you, Thirley.'

'Business?' Mrs Corvill said, shocked. 'On a Sunday?'

'You know other people aren't as strict as we are, Mother.'

203

'Yes . . . And he's a foreigner, of course. Well, my dear, you missed a good sermon today.'

Through the meal Millicent related the main points of the Reverend Dr Dall's homily. Jenny paid only surface attention. Her thoughts were with Franz.

What did he do on these long dull Scottish Sundays? A stranger in a strange land . . . He might go to church, following an unfamiliar service in a foreign tongue. Then there were one or two of the gentlemen who allowed themselves the luxury of afternoon pursuits – chess games, even cards, though not for money, or simple casual conversation. Perhaps Franz joined them. Whether it was as agreeable as Sunday in his homeland, she had no idea. But from the depth of her own loneliness, Jenny felt a true sympathy for him.

She spent the afternoon reading to her mother – a tiresome, admonitory book called *The Philosophy of the Active and Moral Powers of Man* by one Dugald Stewart, much admired by her late father. What did he know, she asked herself as she read. What had he ever *felt?* The power of the senses could not be so easily denied as he seemed to imply.

When church time came she excused herself again. 'All right, dear – I told the minister you were unwell so he doesn't expect to see you.'

The house was very quiet after Millicent left. Cook was busy preparing the evening meal, Thirley had gone to a service in the parish church, the under housemaid had the day off to visit her parents.

Filled with a restlessness she couldn't control, Jenny went out again. This time, driven by some impulse she didn't analyse, she walked out of the grounds towards the town. There was no one about – either the inhabitants of Galashiels were at church or, if they weren't churchgoers, they were working in their gardens or sitting down to their early evening meal.

She walked past the silent mill of W & D Thomson, down to the Mill Lead, and without stopping to think why, she crossed on the narrow footbridge to the long path that led to the end of the High Street. On the left, just before the paved road, there was a row of small finishing works at Weir Haugh, silent in the peace of the Sunday evening. Alongside stood a cottage, formerly inhabited by the foreman of the fullers.

This was where Franz lived. On the ground floor he had his office, where on weekdays he employed a clerk-book-keeper. Above were his living quarters – spartan, one supposed, for the cottage had only one room and a kitchen downstairs, and two rooms above.

She stood in the lane. In a room above, a lamp had been lit, for the cottage was in the shade of old beech trees.

What was she doing here? She should turn and hurry home.

Home to wait an hour for her mother. To share the dull evening meal and listen to chat about Dr Dall and his stern views on morality. To go at last to her lonely bed, to lie wakeful and desolate.

Why should she deny herself the happiness that existed, only a heartbeat away? She had tried, she had truly tried, to live within the conventions of her world. She had wanted to be a dutiful wife, mistress of a household, mother of children.

But it seemed to elude her, that ordinary happiness. There was no one to respond to her – except Franz.

Franz offered her love. Right or wrong, he loved her, he valued her. And she wanted him – wanted what he could give, the bliss of forgetfulness, the joy of belonging, the ecstasy of fulfilled need.

At the top of the beech trees a rook landed, ungainly for a moment, flapping his wings and then folding them to poise, sombre as a clergyman.

He cawed. He seemed to say, 'Go! Go!'

She almost obeyed. She half-turned, ready for flight.

But the way back was long and shadowed and lonely. There was nothing for her at the end of the path but an empty house.

She turned back, stepped up to the door, and let the knocker fall resoundingly on the solid panel.

Chapter Fifteen

It is very easy to hoodwink someone who is without suspicion. Mrs Corvill was a million miles from believing her daughter could ever do anything dishonourable. Even in business, she was confident Jenny never stooped to deceit: the cloth made by Corvill and Son was not 'raised' or 'shorn' or over-milled to give it a false appearance of excellence, but was in fact excellent. So with Jenny – she was in her mother's opinion what she appeared to be: a clever, good, hardworking girl.

That first Sunday, Jenny had reached home a little after Mrs Corvill got back from church. It was easy enough to allay any anxiety by saying she had been out for a breath of air. And then, next evening, simple to say that she had a meeting with a few other employers to see if any of them could lend her a dye foreman to replace Ronald Armstrong temporarily.

Her meeting was with Franz, in the room upstairs in his cottage, with the thick wooden shutters closed to seal them up from the eyes of others, with the soft lamplight glowing on warm limbs and cool sheets. Eager, quickly snatched joy, and then long moments of languor as they lay in each other's arms exchanging little kisses, murmurs, minute caresses.

They could only meet infrequently. Jenny had social engagements she couldn't shirk, and her mother would have protested if she had spent too many extra hours at the mill. Moreover, Franz had his own work, both in Galashiels and the other wool towns. It was his travels that gave them one golden interlude. He had to go to Ayr for a week. He chose to come back via Carlisle. Jenny had business there concerned with the carriage of goods.

They met at the station, went together to the Crown Hotel

where they registered as man and wife. Jenny was unknown in the town and in any case, in her mourning gown and appropriate heavy black veil, she was unrecognisable. They spent a long evening and a whole night in each other's arms.

In the morning they parted. Jenny saw her carriers, settled her difficulties, took the train back to Galashiels. Franz went north to Moffat, whence he returned to Galashiels by mail coach two days later.

So September passed and October came, and with it the darker evenings. Jenny now had a new foreman of the dyeing department but she could tell her mother she needed to go back to the mill to work on the handloom. She was making samples of cloth for the spring pattern books, and Old Jamie was too unwell to work. Soon everything would be even easier for the double shift would end at the close of October. It was thought unsuitable to ask mill girls to go home after the late shift in the full dark of winter.

Mrs Corvill had an engagement in a neighbouring parish at a meeting of the Committee for the Rehabilitation of Female Offenders. Jenny was actually forbidden to accompany her mother: the discussions were thought to be unfit for the ears of unmarried ladies. She saw her mother off in the carriage after an early evening meal. She worked for a while at her desk. Then, at about eight o'clock, she set off from Gatesmuir.

It had been a sombre day, and was now almost completely dark. She hurried, thinking of Franz waiting in the cottage. She turned a corner, and came across the lamplighter.

'Good evening, Mistress Corvill,' he said.

'Good evening, Leerie.' This was the affectionate nickname given to all lamplighters.

'Where are you off to this dark nicht?'

'Oh, I'm going to the mill to fetch some papers I should have taken home at six.'

'I'll walk wi' you,' he said companionably, shouldering his lamplighting pole. 'That is, if you've no objection to walking wi' a workman.'

'Oh. Of course not. But I don't want to take you out of your way – '

'It's no out of my way. I have to light the lamps at the Cuddy Green yet. And how are you, mistress?'

'I'm well, thank you. And you?' There was no help for it. She fell into step with him. She knew little about Tam Willis. He was employed as lamplighter only in the season of long nights, during which he came out at dusk to light the gas lamps and again at a quarter after midnight to turn them out, it being the firm conviction of the town fathers that no decent citizen would be out and about after that hour, except at New Year.

He told her he went round helping on a cart in summer, selling fruit and vegetables. 'I like to be out and about, I like to see life going on,' he told her, with a glance of unexpected shrewdness.

At the Cuddy Green he should have stopped to light the lamps. Instead he trod on at her side. 'I'll see you to the mill door,' he said.

'It's not necessary – '

'Aye, aye, I can spare the time.'

The mill was at work. As she was leaving him at the entrance under the big clock, out came the day foreman of the carding-room, shrugging on his jacket. 'Mistress! What are you doing here?'

'I've come to fetch some papers I forgot. What are *you* doing here?' For the work in the evening should have been under a charge-hand.

'Och, you remember the engineer came to see to that fault in machine Number Four – he asked me to stay on to point out the snag.'

'A happy chance,' said Leerie. 'You can see Mistress Corvill to her home again.'

'Not at all. Off you go, Mr Ainsley – '

'Och aye, if you're only picking up some papers, I'll wait and see you home, Mistress Corvill.'

'Good gracious no, your wife – '

'I sent her a wee note saying it'd be eight or mebbe half past afore I got home. I'll gie you my arm back to Gatesmuir.'

'But that's a fair step past your house, Mr Ainsley – '

'And why should he not step it in a good cause?' said Leerie. 'I'll bid you goodnicht, then, mistress.' He nodded and walked away, hefting his pole. Jenny had a strange feeling he had arranged an escort for her on purpose.

Trapped, she fetched some documents for which she had no use, put them in the satchel she was carrying, and rejoined Ainsley in the hall. He put on his cap, she pulled her jacket collar against her neck to ward off the night chill, they set off.

They were at High Street when Jenny saw a well-known figure moving towards them under the lamplight.

'Good evening, Miss Corvill,' Franz said.

'Good evening, Mr Lennhardt. Mr Ainsley here is kindly escorting me home,' she said, so that he could understand her difficulty.

'Good evening, Mr Lennhardt,' said the foreman. 'What brings you out in the night?'

'Oh, exercise, exercise,' said Franz. 'I've sat all day at my accounts. May I walk with you, Miss Corvill?'

He fell into step on her other side. At the gates of her home the lamp was shining over the carriageway. They all paused.

'Goodnight then, Mistress Corvill,' Ainsley said, touching his cap.

'Goodnight, Miss Corvill,' said Franz.

Ainsley waited to walk back down the road with the gentleman, as good manners dictated. There was nothing to be done. The two men moved off.

Jenny went up the drive towards the house, disappointed and yet ironically amused at how things had turned out. She saw a slight movement at the drawing-room window. She frowned, but walked on to the front door. It opened before her hand could touch it.

'Good evening, mistress,' Thirley said.

Jenny passed her, unbuttoning her jacket. A frisson went through her. Thirley had been watching out of the window. Watching for her?

She whirled. The housemaid was moving sedately away towards the kitchen quarters.

Foolishness, Jenny told herself. She was in there mending the fire, tidying magazines – any of a hundred chores could call the housemaid into the drawing-room. She went in, to look about and think what Thirley might have been doing. Immediately her eye lighted on the tea-tray, neatly put out on a low table by the fire, lacking only the teapot. Of course.

Yet Thirley had been by the window.

Well, it was nothing. The maid had a perfect right to go and glance out of the window. But it would have been reasonable for her to say, 'I saw you coming up the drive,' when she opened the door.

That night Jenny's sleep was troubled. Her meeting with the lamplighter went through her mind. Had he looked askance at her? He had said he liked to be out and about to see life going on – had he seen her before, flitting through the town, thinking herself invisible?

At about two in the morning she sat up in bed. Clear-headed in the chill of the night, she said to herself, I'm heading straight for disaster. It's impossible to keep anything hidden in a town this size. Sooner or later Franz and I will be discovered.

Their plans for that evening had been set awry. It was necessary to make a fresh assignation. She couldn't see him on the forthcoming night, she had to go to the provost's house to dinner. Franz had a business colleague coming to him from London on the following day, to stay two days.

They met at last at a gathering at the mill for buyers. Jenny had completed the spring pattern books, had given a first sight to the Russian agent Mr Ross, and now threw them open to any buyers who could accept her invitation. She offered Madeira wine and plain biscuits in the afternoon in the visitors' room at Waterside Mill.

Under cover of studying a page with her, Franz said in a low voice, 'It's been so long, Jenny.'

'I know.'

'When can we meet?'

She shook her head. Mr Ross, who had accepted the invitation although he had already seen the patterns, stopped beside them. 'Colours are becoming less bright, I note, Miss Corvill.'

She agreed. 'Of course, for a special order, I can make some of the patterns in brighter shades.'

'That might be well. St Petersburg will like the more subdued colours, but I fancy the merchants of Moscow will want brighter tones.' He began to elbow Franz aside. Franz, annoyed, refused to give way.

The two men turned towards each other. 'Excuse me, Lennhardt, I would like to discuss this with Miss Corvill.'

'Miss Corvill and I were engaged in a conversation!'

'If you have a firm order to offer, well and good – '

'Sometimes one speaks of other things than trade – '

'Gentlemen, gentlemen!' For heads were turning in the room to find out what the two men were at odds about. 'Gentlemen, there's no need for raised voices. Orders won't be taken now, in any case. This is a purely social occasion.' With a bow, she walked away, leaving Franz shamefaced and Mr Ross put out.

Later Franz came up to her quite openly. 'I apologise for quarrelling with Mr Ross,' he said, in a voice that anyone could hear if they wished to listen. 'I find him rather . . . I don't know the English . . . *anmassend.*'

'Pushy,' suggested another of the buyers, munching biscuit.

'He has a difficult market to cater for – he must think of aristocrats following the royal whims, and also the ordinary buyers,' Jenny said.

'Huh, everyone has problems. May I take another glass of Madeira, Miss Corvill?'

'Please – the waitress will serve you.'

When he had gone Franz went on more quietly, 'When can we meet?'

'This evening. I'll come straight from work. But I can only stay a moment – we're having London buyers to dinner.'

He frowned, but accepted it.

When she slipped into the cottage a little after six that night, he snatched her into his arms and kissed her hard. *'Du lieber Gott*, how I have missed you! It seems a century since you were here last.'

'Franz, I only have a moment – '

He stopped her words with kisses. She wrenched herself free. 'Franz, listen! Listen, we must be much more careful. The other night . . . the other night I was nearly caught.'

'Caught?'

She explained how she had met the lamplighter.

'But good heavens, my darling, what does it matter if a labourer – '

'Dearest, don't you understand? I came across him at the corner of High Street. I might just as easily have been in this lane when we met.'

'But it could never happen again.'

'That's not true. Anyone could see me, everyone knows me.'

'But when it's dark – '

'Besides, I think one of the maids suspects.'

'Then dismiss her.'

'On what grounds? Besides, if she were dismissed without good reason you can be sure she'd tattle her suspicions – '

'What can she possibly say? Don't let yourself become nervous, dear one – '

'I am nervous, Franz! And your behaviour this afternoon only made me more so.'

He flushed. 'I'm sorry. I didn't mean to speak like that to Ross – '

'You spoke as if he were a rival. I don't know how much other people understood but it sounded strange.'

'No, no, you're over-anxious – '

'Franz, I'm scared.' She was shivering. 'Suddenly I feel we're heading straight for disaster. It would break my mother's heart if there were a scandal.'

'There won't be, there won't be.' He put his arms round her, drew her close, and stroked her cheek. 'Dearest Jenny, we shall be careful. I bow to your better sense. Even if I die during the intervals, we'll see each other less often.'

'Oh, Franz . . . Thank you . . . I wasn't sure if you would agree . . .'

'Of course I agree. It shall be as you wish.'

'Now I must go,' she said, turning in his arms.

'No, just a moment longer – '

'No, I absolutely must – '

'You don't love me!' he burst out. 'You avoided me all week and now you want to rush away – '

'It's not that, my darling! You know it isn't!' She was shocked at his reproach.

'All these silly little ideas about being seen – it's a way of keeping us apart. You don't really love me!'

'Franz, don't speak to me like this!' Tears brimmed, she felt herself weakening. Next moment she would have let him lead her upstairs to their heaven of happiness – except that her eye caught the little clock on the office wall. It was past six-thirty.

'Franz, I *must* go. Our guests are arriving in an hour and I have to bathe and change.'

'Why wasn't I invited?' he demanded, his voice full of jealousy.

'Franz, it's two of the London buyers. What reason could I give for including you?'

'You could have thought of something – '

She went to the door, opened it. 'There's no talking to you when you're in this mood,' she said, and was about to go out when he seized her and turned her around.

'Forgive me, *mein Schatz*,' he murmured, drooping his head against her breast. 'I love you so much. I can't bear to be parted from you, to think of you with other people while I'm shut out – '

She kissed him and soothed him and at last hurried away. As she went she found herself thinking, He's too possessive. He's getting beyond discretion . . .

Once she'd got over her rush and her anxieties, the evening was pleasant enough. But while it went on she was thinking of Franz in some inner recess of her mind. And she came to the conclusion that she must end the affair with him before calamity befell them.

How could it be done? He would never let go voluntarily. He had persuaded himself she was the great love of his life. He sometimes quoted Heine to her: *Ich liebe alleine, Die Kleine, die Feine, die Reine, die Eine.* He told her it meant he loved her because she was small and fine, pure and the only woman in the world for him. She had been flattered at the time but now it alarmed her – his romanticism could lead him to rashness.

She had hurried away without making any further arrangement with him. She felt it in her bones that he would come to the mill next day – it would be perfectly in order, he would want to look through the pattern books again. She must ensure she kept her head clerk with her in the visitors' room.

Next morning everything was suddenly changed. There was a letter for her by the early post. The handwriting was that of her sister-in-law Lucy.

That in itself was enough to alarm her. Lucy never wrote

to Jenny, only to her mother-in-law. It must be something serious if she chose to address Jenny.

Dear Sister-in-law,

I write to you because I can't alarm Mother with this besides she wouldn't know what to do nor do I I am at my wits' end. Ned is behaving very badly, I can't control him and in my condition you know I might lose the baby and he is so strange at times and I have had a hint from Mrs McVeigh that the other tenants have complained and we may be asked to leave which would be very hard on me in my delicate state as I wouldn't want to make a journey to Galashiels for it would make me sick as I have been grately troubled with sickness since my condition began. Come at once Jenny I really need you.

The last sentence rang with desperation. Lucy must be in a bad way to appeal to Jenny for help.

Mrs Corvill had not yet come down to breakfast. Jenny put the letter away, rang for Thirley, and said, 'Tell Baird to pack for me – clothes for a few days.'

'Going away, are you, mistress?' said Thirley in surprise. And then with a faint smile, 'On business?'

'My sister-in-law writes to say my brother is ill. I'm going to Glasgow.'

She went up to tell her mother, with utmost gentleness, that she'd had a letter from Lucy saying that Ned was a little indisposed. 'I think Lucy feels lonely for female companionship, Mother. So I'm going for a few days just to see her and cheer her up.'

'I'll come too,' said Millicent, throwing back the bedclothes as if she would leap out and dress for the journey at once.

'No, dear, it's better if I go alone. Besides, you have a meeting of the Church Charitable Committee tomorrow, haven't you? And the Misses Doone coming to spend the afternoon the next day?'

'Oh, yes . . . But I can put it all off.'

'No need, Mother. I can go in a moment and be back in a day or two.'

'But the mill?'

'Everything is going forward. The new pattern books are out, the clerk can take any new orders, the orders in production are going smoothly. I can take a day or two.' She smiled. 'To tell the truth, I need it.'

Within an hour Baird had packed a valise for her, and a hackney was at the door to take her to the town. She stopped at the post office first to put a letter for Franz in the box then went to the mill to give last-minute instructions. 'If anyone calls in person, tell them I had to go to Glasgow on a family matter.'

'Yes, mistress.'

Franz would come today, receive this message, and then by last post would receive her letter of fuller explanation. While she was in Glasgow she would write again, setting out her feelings that they should break off their affair while they were still able to do so without scandal. She'd been given a respite, unexpected but all the more to be seized because of that.

The apartment in which Lucy and Ned were living was in a tall and very handsome building in Hanover Street, from which the statues of Scott and Moore in George Square could be seen. Their flat was on the first floor, reached by a splendid stone staircase with a wrought iron banister of fine workmanship. A maid, middle-aged but in a very fancy uniform that included a lace collar, opened the door.

'Mrs Corvill is lying down, miss, and is not to be disturbed. Mr Corvill is out.'

'Tell Mrs Corvill her sister-in-law is here.'

'Miss Corvill! Oh, excuse me, please, I didn't know – '

She ushered Jenny in, taking her valise. Then she led the way along a rather dark passage lit by elaborate wall brackets. Through open doors Jenny glimpsed a large sitting-room, furnished in the gilt reproduction Louis Quinze that Lucy admired, with, opposite, a parlour with piano and loo table, then a surprisingly lofty dining-room. There were one or two closed doors, at the last of which the maid tapped before entering.

Jenny heard her voice announcing her arrival, very low. There was a cry of joy from within. The maid reappeared, throwing the door wide open. In the half-light of lowered lamps Lucy lay on a chaise-longue, her hair loose, her face pale. She was wearing an elaborate peignoir of blue satin and cream lace tied with broad ribbons.

She half-raised herself, stretched out a hand to Jenny. Even as she saw the real tears on Lucy's face, Jenny felt that there was something theatrical about the gesture.

'Oh, Jenny! Oh, how glad I am to see you! Oh, Jenny, if you knew what I've been going through!'

Jenny turned to dismiss the maid, who had been hovering, looking sympathetic yet avid.

'Yes, go, Maggie,' Lucy ordered, 'go and make some tea or coffee – or would you prefer a glass of wine? And something to eat?'

'Some hot soup with toast would be very welcome,' said Jenny. 'And what about you, Lucy – will you share it with me, or is it soon to be dinner?'

'Oh, I couldn't swallow a morsel,' Lucy cried. 'Not a bite have I eaten all day. I am so sick all the time, Jenny – you can't imagine.'

'But I thought, my dear, that morning sickness passed off after a month or so?'

'That's what I thought, but it's not true. Oh, having a baby is terrible, you've no idea! Had I known – !' She lay back, waving Jenny to a chair. Jenny took it, brought it to the side of the chaise-longue, and sat down while taking Lucy's hand.

It was true that Lucy was thinner, except for where the child thickened her. She looked miserable, her forget-me-not eyes large in her white face, her pink mouth down-turned. Jenny was filled with pity.

'Lucy dear, have you seen a doctor?'

'Oh, that old fool – he just tells me I must bear the suffering as women have always done.'

'Then find a better doctor, dear – there must be some way of alleviating the sickness?'

'Not that I can find.'

'I'm so sorry, Lucy. And you've been like this all the time, and with no one to help you – '

'Oh, I wrote first to Mama, and she came over from Edinburgh, but she was no help, she wanted to go out shopping all the time and she quarrelled with Ned – '

'Where is Ned?' Jenny asked.

'God knows! He went out at mid-afternoon, when he had cured himself of the shakes enough to shave his chin and comb his hair – '

'Lucy!'

'He's been drinking like a fish. I knew he liked a dram, but I had no idea he – '

'But after Father died, Ned gave up the drink almost completely.'

'Ha!' cried Lucy. It was a sound of contempt, almost of hatred. 'We hadn't been here a week when he began to invite his new friends – long sessions when they talked and talked, and though I didn't like the smell of tobacco smoke and stale whisky in my sitting-room, all the same I . . . well, it wasn't too bad. But they battened on him, you know – sprawling about, smoking his cigars, drinking the decanters dry.'

'Who are these people?' Jenny demanded in indignation.

'Oh, writers they call themselves, poets, journalists.' Lucy clasped her hands in emotion. 'I thought they were very clever at first – one of them is a lecturer at the University, you'd think he'd be respectable!'

'But if you were hostess, Lucy, you ought to have been able to – '

'I told Ned, I told him, "You don't bring those men here any more if they're going to drink till they can hardly find the door to go home." And he . . . he . . . he began to go out without me. I couldn't go, you see, I was often so sick once my condition began and I would have to rush out of the box at the theatre or leave the party – '

'When will he be home?'

'After the public houses have closed, I imagine – if he comes home at all! He may stay at his club. He was elected member of one of the gentlemen's clubs, he's slept there sometimes when he was too drunk to get home. Many's the night I've been left all alone while he's off who knows where.'

'Lucy, this all sounds very bad – '

'You don't know what I've suffered! I thought Glasgow would be such fun; so much to do and so many fashionable people – but they avoid us, Ned is so unpredictable.'

217

'What church do you attend? Have you asked the minister – '

'Church! Ned insisted the first two or three Sundays – we went to some poky little hall, worse than that one in Galashiels – and then Ned wouldn't get out of bed one morning and I *certainly* wasn't going to go on my own, kneeling on boards, listening to all that thunder about vanity and show – and the preacher staring straight at my new bonnet.'

'So, in fact you aren't in touch with a minister – '

'I asked my doctor to speak to Ned, I told him, "My nerves won't stand it, you must tell him to behave," but Dr Laggan just said he never interfered between husband and wife.'

Maggie came to say that the snack Jenny had asked for was ready, and where should she serve it. 'Bring it here, Maggie,' Jenny began, but Lucy interrupted.

'No, no, the smell will make me sick. Eat in the dining-room, Jenny. Come back when you've finished.' She lay back on her pillows, closing her eyes. Though there was still an element of drama in it, she did in fact look poorly.

Jenny took the chance to speak to the maid. 'Does she manage to eat anything, Maggie?'

'Oh, aye, she takes beef tea wi' a drop of sherry in it and dry toast and plain biscuit and the like o' that, and whiles she'll have a good day and she'll eat cold meat and a milk pudding. She's no entirely starving. But, poor leddy, being in the family way is hard to her.' She shrugged. 'Her personal maid could tell you more.'

'Send her to me, please.'

Lucy's maid was called Fordyce, once again in a very fancy uniform with braid and a lace collar. 'I do my best,' she said, in affected tones and with some hauteur, in response to Jenny's inquiries. 'I didn't know when I took the post that Madam would be enceinte so soon. I know nothing about nursing, miss, it's not my place to say what I think about Mrs Corvill's health.'

'Does she sleep well?'

'Oh, she has a sleeping potion from the doctor, her nights are fair enough except when Mr Corvill causes a disturbance.'

'Does she get out for fresh air?'

'Carriage outings on a fine day, but the weather's been poor lately and she doesn't like the cold. I haven't had time to let out her winter gowns. I must say, if I had known, I might not have been so keen to come here, though it's a good address. I've sat sewing until my eyes are ready to drop out.'

'I'm sure you do your best, Fordyce. Thank you.'

These conversations weren't very heartening. Maggie was well disposed but uneducated, the personal maid thought of herself as equivalent to a French maid suited to a lady of fashion. There was no use looking to them for help – and besides, it was not their duty to do anything.

Revived by the food, Jenny returned to her sister-in-law. Lucy was glancing through a fashion magazine, but threw it aside at Jenny's entrance. 'Did you have enough to eat? Just tell Maggie whatever you want, Cook can do most things. Maggie is a treasure. She gets Ned to bed sometimes.'

'Lucy!'

'Well, who else is there? I've no men servants, I didn't think I'd need any with only one set of rooms to run and cabs and messengers at the door as soon as you send for them.' She glanced about, complacency in her gaze. 'It's a smart place, don't you think, Jenny?'

'Oh, very.'

'That's why,' Lucy said, her voice gathering complaint as she thought of it, 'I don't want to be turned out! But the tenants of the other flats are very respectable – Lady Bligh is in the one below, and there's a High Court judge and his wife above us.' She paused. '*We* are respectable too, it's just that Ned . . . Oh, if he causes us to be thrown out, I'll never forgive him!'

'Lucy, it's more important to get him back on the track again. His health will suffer – '

'Oh, he's as strong as an ox! Drink all night, sleep all morning, out again to see a boxing match or a play in the evening and drink all night again.'

'It's dreadful! I can't think how you could let him – '

'Let him? I have no control over him! Why do you think I sent for you? You're the only one he ever listens to in the family! You must make him behave, Jenny. I can't have my reputation as a hostess ruined for ever just because while I'm in a delicate state I can't keep my husband within bounds.'

219

'But your reputation as a hostess isn't the point – '

'It is to me!' Lucy exclaimed. 'I didn't come to Glasgow to be trapped with a baby coming and a drunken husband! I came to take a place in society.'

Seeing that it was no use discussing it at the moment and that her sister-in-law was upsetting herself, Jenny let the matter drop. Instead she inquired about the baby. Lucy had felt movements from the child, who was now four months on the way. Dr Laggan told her this meant the baby was doing well despite her bouts of sickness.

They chatted about this and innocuous matters until bedtime. Jenny's brother still hadn't appeared. Lucy took the sedative draught prescribed for her by her doctor and went to bed.

'I shouldn't stay up for Ned,' she told Jenny with some self-righteousness. 'It may be two or three o'clock before he gets in.'

Jenny stayed up till midnight but there was no sign of him. Maggie, yawning, came in from time to time to look after the fire or to ask if Jenny needed anything. In pity she told the woman to go to bed, and did the same herself.

Somewhere in the early hours she heard stumbling movements outside in the passage. There was a thud as someone fell against her closed door. Then mumbled words, continuing footsteps. A door opened and closed at the end of the corridor.

Presumably Ned had come home and was putting himself to bed.

Jenny rose early. She got herself a makeshift breakfast, then went out for a walk. Glasgow was still only half-awake around her. She found the Exchange, and the great clumsy cathedral looming over the ravine on the other side of which she could see the Necropolis in the mist of early morning. She walked home by way of George Street and the Andersonian building. People were about now, in the pale light from the still-glowing streetlamps. She could see why Lucy wanted to live in Glasgow. The city was rich, full of activity, there were bills advertising theatres and music halls, shop windows with fine goods . . .

Lucy was up when Jenny came in, but in another peignoir.

'It's going to be a fine day,' Jenny said. 'Would you like to go out after breakfast?'

'Breakfast! Don't speak to me of breakfast! I've been so sick!'

'I'm sorry, dear. I've been told that if you sip hot water or eat an apple – '

'What nonsense! What could you possibly know about it?'

Jenny held her tongue. She found that a proper breakfast had been prepared for her so she sat down again in the dining-room, ate porridge and drank tea. Afterwards she passed the time starting a letter to her mother, although she felt she couldn't say much until she had seen and spoken to Ned.

Ned got up about eleven o'clock. He could be heard moving about, going into the bathroom, groaning to himself. He rang the bell for the maid, who took him some kind of restorative drink. At close to midday he came into the sitting-room.

'Well, Jenny,' he said, 'Maggie told me you'd arrived. Lucy sent for you, I suppose?'

He looked terrible. His skin had a pallor like clay. His eyes were sunken and bleary. Even his hair was lank and dull. His hands trembled as he took out a cigar and attempted to light it with an appearance of nonchalance.

'Ned, what have you been doing to yourself?' Jenny said in dismay.

'Sister dear, don't preach at me. I didn't ask you to come. In fact, I wish you hadn't . . . You . . . you . . . Don't look at me like that!'

To her horror, he began to cry; deep, racking sobs that shook his body. The unlit cigar tumbled to the floor, the matches were scattered on the carpet. Jenny leapt up and ran to him. She knelt, she put her arms around him.

'Jenny,' he wept, 'Jenny . . . why is life so awful? Oh, I can't bear it . . .'

She hushed him and rocked him. After a little he seemed to grow quieter. She raised her head to look at him. He was staring at a corner of the room with a fixed, terrified gaze.

'What is it, Ned? What's the matter?'

'It's here again! It's here – I told Maggie to dust it down. It's here – Oh, God, don't let it come near me!'

'What, Ned? What?' She was looking about, trying to fix

221

her eye on what he saw. All she could perceive was a corner of the ceiling-moulding, ornate, with roses and acanthus leaves.

'Coming out of the leaves – it shouldn't be there – No, no, I can't – don't!' He hid his face against his sister's shoulder. He was trembling so violently she could hardly hold him.

'But I don't see anything, Ned – '

He threw himself on the floor, hunched over, covering his head with his folded arms. He rocked to and fro. 'A spider! A spider! It's too big to squash, I've tried, and there are more if you squash one, they come out of the ceilings – oh, God help me, they glare at me, don't let them see me, hide me, Jenny!'

She tried to make him rise, to get him to a chair. Maggie came running in, frightened by the noise. 'Shall I get him a dram, miss? That sometimes quiets him.'

'No – no more drink,' Jenny cried, trying to soothe her frantic brother.

But it was no use. Nothing she could say had any effect. He thrashed about on the floor, hitting himself against the legs of the furniture, gashing his head on the edge of the fender.

'Call a doctor, Maggie,' she gasped. 'This is beyond anything I can manage.'

She was still struggling with him when the door opened again and Lucy appeared on the threshold. She was pale and scared. She drew her lace dressing-gown about her as if to preserve herself from some infection.

'You see?' she wailed. 'I told you! He's impossible to handle.'

Jenny tried to still the awful wails that were coming from her brother's gaping mouth. She was terribly afraid. It seemed he had gone mad.

Chapter Sixteen

Maggie returned breathless, with the news that Dr Laggan was engaged with a patient but would come as soon as he was free. For the moment Ned was relatively quiet. He simply huddled on the floor, shuddering with terror at who knew what. Jenny had a cut lip from one of his flailing hands.

Lucy had retreated to her boudoir. Fordyce came to say that she was faint and sick. 'And no wonder,' she said, with a stare of disapproval at Jenny and her brother.

The bell from downstairs rang. Maggie rushed to let in the doctor, who came hurrying up the staircase with his bag clutched to his chest.

'What's amiss?' he demanded as he came in. 'The maid said *Mr* Corvill – she meant Mrs Corvill – ?' He broke off on the question, seeing his patient in Jenny's arms.

'My God! What's been going on here? It looks like a battlefield!'

'My brother has had some sort of fit,' Jenny explained.

Ned looked up. 'Who're you?' he asked in a frightened voice, peering at Dr Laggan. 'Can you make the spiders go away?'

'What spiders?'

'There, man, there!' Ned swept out an arm to point to the corner of the ceiling. 'You can't miss them – they're so big, and they have dark red heads.'

Lucy came to the door, having heard the doctor arrive. 'He's mad,' she said. 'That's all it is, he's mad. He keeps seeing things that aren't there.'

'Help me get him in a chair,' the doctor said. With the aid

of Jenny and the maid, Ned was hefted up. He threshed out in protest.

'Don't, I'm safer on the floor, they can't get at me there.'

'You say he keeps seeing things, Mrs Corvill?' the doctor asked.

'It's happened once before.'

'When was this?'

'Two days ago.'

'Lucy,' Ned said, looking at her where she stood in the safety of the doorway. 'Lucy, make them dust the room properly. I want the spiders cleared away.'

'There are no spiders, Ned,' Jenny soothed. 'Truly, there's nothing there.'

'There are, there are! Why do you pretend you can't see them?'

Dr Laggan bent. With difficulty, as Ned shrank back from him, he looked in his eyes and tried to take his pulse.

'Hm. Does he drink much?'

'Like a fish,' Lucy said.

'I see.'

'But he's not drunk now, he's had nothing this morning except some eggnog,' Maggie put in.

'You may go now,' Jenny said to her. 'Thank you for your help, Maggie.'

'Should I no stay, miss? In case he gets violent again?'

'You can go,' the doctor said. When she had left he beckoned Lucy into the room, then closed the door. 'I'm afraid, Mrs Corvill,' he said, 'that your husband has had an attack of alcoholic dementia.'

She drew back. 'You mean he really is mad?'

'No, my dear, not in that sense. He has been poisoned by a long association with alcohol – I take it he has been drinking for a long time?'

'Since he was sixteen,' Jenny put in.

'Ah. Heavily?'

'Well, at first, no . . . It was more in secret defiance of my father – we were very strictly brought up.'

Lucy gave a shaky laugh. 'All that churchgoing and praying from the old man, and all the time Ned was – '

224

'The point is, your husband is in a very serious state, Mrs Corvill. He'll kill himself if he's allowed to go on like this.'

She began to cry. 'Let him! I don't care! He's mad and horrible and I want nothing more to do with him!' She wrenched the door open and fled to the safety of her own room.

Dr Laggan started after her, then changed his mind and once again closed the door. He wanted to discuss his patient in decent privacy and calm. 'Well,' he said, 'when Mrs Corvill asked me to speak to her husband I refused. She said he was being "difficult", I thought it was the usual marital quarrels . . . husbands don't understand women's moods when they're pregnant. If she had explained properly . . .'

'What's to be done, doctor?' Jenny asked.

'Just tell them to get rid of the spiders,' Ned implored. 'I'll be all right if only you'll take away the spiders.'

Laggan cast him a glance of pity. 'He really thinks they're there,' he said. He patted Ned on the shoulder. 'I'm sorry, my friend, I can't get rid of the spiders. You're the only one who can do that.'

'But I can't, I daren't go near them.'

'Now, be a good man and take this.' He had opened his bag and now shook a pill out of a dark phial. 'Come on now, it'll quiet you down.'

Jenny fetched a glass of water from the kitchen, where the servants ceased talking on her entrance and watched her silently until she left. Ned took the pill without protest. He seemed dazed.

'What is the pill, doctor?' Jenny asked.

'It's laudanum, a very good depressant, but it's only a temporary measure. Your brother needs long-term treatment, Miss Corvill.'

'I understand that,' Jenny said, standing behind Ned's chair with a comforting hand on his shoulder. 'How should it be done?'

'You don't live here with the young couple?'

'No, in Galashiels with my mother.'

'No men in the family?'

'No, my father is dead.'

'Uncles?'

'My mother's brother – but he lives in Dornoch. They keep in touch only by letter.'

'I see.' Dr Lagan played with the watch-chain stretched across his rather dusty black waistcoat. 'The situation is this. Alcohol is poison to your brother's system. He must give it up – utterly, completely. Someone must keep watch on him at all times to see he doesn't get hold of it and that is quite difficult because, I have to tell you, victims of this disease can be very cunning in deceiving their nurse. He would need to have attendants, male attendants, one for night and one for day – can you manage this in his home in Galashiels?'

Jenny had been picturing it even as he spoke. She imagined her mother's grief and horror when she saw her darling son in this state. The shock would overset her completely. And then the quiet house turned into a prison, two strangers as warders. The town talking, her mother avoided and ostracised as it became known that Ned Corvill was mad.

'It's hardly possible,' she said. 'We could do it, but at the cost of great distress to my mother. She has no idea that Ned . . .'

'I understand. This is only too common. Parents are often the last to know.'

'I can't understand it!' Jenny cried. 'Other men drink more than Ned, I've seen them – '

'It's one of the mysteries. Spirits are a great restorative, I like a drop of brandy myself at night after a hard day's work. And as you say, some people can swallow it and go on without harm, or at least without noticeable harm. Your brother's constitution somehow makes him vulnerable to alcohol. In this case, the harm is not only noticeable, it is dangerous – he can have other attacks such as you've seen today, he can develop extreme neuritis, or apoplexy. He must really stop while there is a chance to make a decent life. How old is he?'

'Twenty-five.'

'He mustn't throw his life away,' Dr Laggan said gravely. 'You must see that he gets treatment.'

'How is it to be done? I could speak to my mother and we could perhaps arrange – '

'I don't think your household sounds a suitable one for

226

home treatment. In any case, it is better done in an institution with medical supervision by a specialist.'

'An institution!'

'Believe me, Miss Corvill, it's best. It sounds harsh, but I know of a nursing home run by a medical missionary – '

'I don't understand you – a missionary?'

'Dr Murdo. He served in Africa for ten years but on coming home on leave he saw so much that needed doing here in Glasgow, he decided to stay and work in his home town. He runs a private sanatorium for nervous diseases, mostly cases of chronic alcoholism. His regime is strict but considerate. I do assure you, Miss Corvill, it is the best thing for your brother.'

'I don't know . . . I don't know . . .'

Ned had let his head fall back against her as the laudanum took effect. He roused himself to look up at her. 'Is that you, Jenny? What are you doing here? Did Lucy send for you?'

'Hush, dear, go to sleep. Everything is all right.'

Ned smiled. 'I'm glad you're here, Jenny. I haven't been well, I think.'

'We'll make you better.'

'Yes, I know you will. I know you'll help me, Jenny.'

'The best help he could have,' the doctor said across Ned's head to Jenny, 'is complete absence of alcohol, chloral or bromide in measured doses, and complete rest.'

'But it's so awful . . . to put him in a kind of prison.'

'It's for his own good, Miss Corvill.'

Jenny shook her head. 'It's too cruel.'

'What's the alternative?' Dr Laggan said. He gestured at the wrecked room. Gilt chairs were overturned, the veneer on the loo table had been scratched, a handsome palm had been dragged out of its pot and lay broken.

'I could take some small place, look after him – '

'Give up your life to him, you mean?' He studied her. 'Didn't Mrs Corvill tell me at one time, you are the great Miss Corvill of the cloth firm? You run the family business?'

'Well, I . . .'

'Who would do that if you focused your entire attention on your brother?'

'I could find someone to take over – '

227

'Immediately? I think not. And, meanwhile, your brother is not receiving proper care, and your sister-in-law . . . You must think of the coming baby, too. She could be in danger when he is violent, you know.'

'Ned would never hurt anyone – '

'No?' He came to her, touched the split lip. 'So who did this to you?'

'It was an accident – '

'Exactly. You want to do all you can for your brother, I quite see that, but your sister-in-law's safety must be considered. Moreover, she has a right to take part in this discussion – we can't settle anything without her agreement.'

Jenny looked down at Ned. He had dropped asleep, his head drooping on the tapestry cover of the chairback. He looked so peaceful, so much himself, compared with the madman who had devastated the room.

'We could leave him now?' she asked.

'Yes, he'll sleep an hour or two. Perhaps we could have a talk with his wife now.'

She led the way to the room where Lucy lay on her chaise-longue. Fordyce was tending her but, on a sharp command from Lucy, left them.

'Where is he?' she demanded.

'Asleep in the sitting-room. Have no fear, dear lady, the attack is over for the time being.'

'For the time being. It can happen again, though!'

'Quite so.' The doctor went through the argument he had just had with Jenny. 'It's my opinion that your husband would be much better off with Dr Murdo in his sanatorium – '

'Oh yes, yes, I agree! Anything to get him away from here!'

'Lucy!' Jenny cried in protest.

'Oh, it's all very well for you! You haven't lived here with him these last few weeks! I can't go on like that. He's got to go somewhere where he'll do no damage.'

'Lucy, the first aim is to get him a cure.'

'You can't cure a drunkard, everyone knows that! And I don't care, anyway, so long as he's safely locked up!'

'My dear young lady, you're overwrought,' Laggan said with kindness. 'You don't mean quite that. All the same, you are right in saying that your husband would be better under lock and key. It *is* possible to cure alcoholism and his best chance is in an institution.'

'Very well, I agree.'

'It's not quite as simple as that. There are papers that have to be signed.'

'Bring them, I'll sign them.'

'Lucy, you can't!' Jenny begged. 'I forbid it – '

'Who are you to forbid it? I'm his wife.'

Dr Laggan was nodding. 'Mrs Corvill is correct, Miss Corvill. You have no status in law in this matter. If Mrs Corvill agrees to commit her husband to a medical institution on the advice of his doctor that is her prerogative.'

From the moment Dr Laggan mentioned Lucy's prerogative, Jenny knew the battle was lost.

The doctor left, to return in two hours' time with Dr Murdo. He proved to be an old giant of a man who looked as if he might burst out of his formal frock coat and checked trousers. He had weathered skin and a fringe of white whiskers. His manner was amiable and brisk.

He was greeted by Lucy with a fervent plea for help. He and Dr Laggan went to have a talk in her boudoir. Jenny was excluded. She sat with her drowsing brother in the sitting-room, wondering what his wife was saying about him.

She had set the room somewhat to rights but the signs of disturbance were still there – soil from the plant pot incompletely brushed away, the scratch on the table, and her own cut lip. How she regretted that cut – her lip was swollen and noticeable.

The two doctors came into the sitting-room. Ned roused himself, sat erect. He rubbed his face. 'I feel rotten,' he said. Then he noticed his sister. 'Oh, hello, Jenny. Oh, yes, you were here this morning . . . What's been going on?'

'My dear young man, you have had a very severe attack of delirium tremens,' Dr Laggan said in a formal, forthright manner. 'My colleague Dr Murdo has come with me to persuade you to go voluntarily for treatment.'

'What? Treatment?' Ned looked vague. 'Delirium . . . ?'

'You've heard of it, I'm sure, Mr Corvill. It's the result of addiction to alcohol.'

'I'm not addicted – '

229

'You are, my dear sir,' Murdo said, speaking for the first time. 'You have all the signs. Look at the tremor in your hands.'

'That's only because . . . because . . .'

'Because you have had an attack of alcoholic mania.'

'No!'

'Yes. You attacked your sister.'

'I didn't!'

Murdo nodded towards Jenny. Ned staggered out of his chair to stare at her in the cold afternoon light. 'I . . . cut your face?'

'It was an accident, Ned – '

'I quite allow that it was an accident. But think of the damage you might do next time,' Murdo said.

'I don't know what you mean! Next time?'

'You've had two attacks.'

'No.'

'Yes. Remember the spiders?'

Ned went very pale. 'Don't,' he gasped.

'Both times, you've seen the spiders.'

'No. Yes. Don't talk about it.'

'It will happen again unless you stop drinking.'

Ned glanced from one to the other. The two men were impassive, Jenny was looking at him pleadingly. If he had to have treatment, and she saw he must, then she wanted him to go voluntarily, not signed away like some chattel by his wife.

'I don't feel well,' he said, trying to put off decision.

'No, of course you don't, and you'll go on feeling like this after every attack, and you'll have other attacks, believe me. You must have treatment,' said Dr Laggan. 'My colleague Dr Murdo can provide that treatment, under excellent conditions for a complete cure.'

'Think of it, man,' Murdo said with hope and encouragement in his hearty voice. 'No more spiders.'

Ned turned to his sister. 'Jenny?'

'I think you must, Ned. You need help and I don't know how else . . . how else . . .' Her voice broke.

He came uncertainly towards her, put his arm round her. Much though she loved him, she had to steel herself not to wince, for he smelt of stale drink and some odour to do with illness.

'Don't cry, Jenny. I'll go if you think I ought to.'

'Ned, I can't tell you what to do. It's your decision.'

He looked at Laggan. 'What does my wife say?'

'She's strongly of the opinion you should go into Dr Murdo's sanatorium.'

'How long . . . ?'

'Two months? Three? We must wait and see, Mr Corvill. But give me your cooperation and you can be a new man.' He paused. 'I'm told you had a religious upbringing.'

'Yes.'

'Then with God's help we will conquer your affliction.'

'I don't think God is there any more,' Ned murmured.

'God never leaves us,' Murdo said, in the tone of full belief. 'It's we who leave him. I'll help you find him again, Mr Corvill.'

'Yes.'

'You'll come to me?'

'Yes.'

'First you must sign these papers.'

He took from his breast pocket some printed forms. Ned looked at them, squinting, but in the confidence inspired by Murdo's presence he was ready to accept anything. The forms were laid on the scratched table. With trembling hand he took the pen Murdo offered, and signed.

'I will give you a draught to take,' Murdo said. 'Then I have to go and arrange for your admission to the home. I'll send a conveyance for you. Please pack a few things – clothes for leisure and comfort, and night attire.'

'I'll see it's done,' Jenny said.

'Perhaps, young lady, you could ring for a tumbler with some water in it, about half full.'

She did so. Maggie came, was instructed. 'Bring it to the bedroom,' Murdo interjected.

'Yes, sir.'

'It will be better if you take this and lie down, Mr Corvill. It is a sedative; you won't sleep but you will feel lethargic.'

'All right.'

231

They went along the passage. Dr Murdo made for the door of the master bedroom, which stood half-open.

'No,' said Ned, 'this one.' He led the way into what was clearly a dressing-room, where a narrow bed was neatly made.

'Oh, I see,' said Murdo, and entered, almost filling the space with his old muscular frame.

The water was brought, and Murdo produced from his bag a bottle from which he measured liquid. The water turned milky. He handed it to Ned, who drank it obediently.

'Lie down now. Let yourself relax. My assistant will come for you in about an hour. You and I will do good work together, Mr Corvill.'

Jenny saw the two men to the door. 'May I go with him to the home, Dr Murdo?'

'Of course. And you and Mrs Corvill may visit him when you like for the first day or so when he will feel ill at ease in new surroundings, and restless for lack of a drink. But then we must get down to serious work, Miss Corvill, and his time will be taken up with tasks that I shall give him – he will work in the garden, row on the Clyde, take up some hobby, carpentry perhaps, who knows. There will be prayer and meditation. His time must be completely occupied and he must have as little reminder as possible of the outside world until he is strong enough to go out in it without wanting whisky.'

'It sounds . . . strict.'

'Strict, but humane. It's the only way, dear lady.'

'I understand.'

Dr Laggan glanced behind Jenny, as if expecting someone, but Lucy made no appearance to bid farewell. 'Say good afternoon to Mrs Corvill for us,' Laggan said, with a look of faint perplexity.'

'Yes, I will.'

She set about packing for Ned. Night things were in the drawer of the lowboy, and toilet articles on the shelf, but the selection of clothes in the press wasn't right for the kind of life Murdo had sketched. She went to the master bedroom.

She was looking on the shelves of the mahogany wardrobe for woollen jerseys when the connecting door opened and Lucy appeared from the boudoir. 'What are you doing in my bedroom?' she challenged.

232

'Packing for Ned.'

'Oh.' Taken aback at the reasonable answer, Lucy paused.

'Perhaps you'd rather do it?' Jenny suggested.

'He can't need much. I'm told he's going to be locked in for at least six weeks.'

'And you can think of it without regret?'

'Regret? *He's* the one who should be feeling regret. He absolutely ruined our chances of being accepted in polite circles in Glasgow.'

Jenny found what she was looking for, and turned to go through the opposite door.

'What's he doing now?' Lucy asked.

'Lying down. Dr Murdo gave him a draught.'

'When's he going?'

'Any moment now, I should imagine. Dr Murdo said he would send someone.'

'The sooner the better.'

Ned appeared from the dressing-room, roused by their voices. 'Lucy . . .'

'Go back and lie down,' Lucy said.

'Lucy, I'm going to a sanatorium.'

'I know. Go and lie down till they come for you.'

'I don't know where this place is . . . Do you know, Lucy?'

'No, but it will be all right, you'll like it.'

'Shall I? I don't know . . . I feel funny. Everything seems to be happening behind a pane of glass.'

Lucy looked irritated, began to turn away. Ned said desperately, 'Lucy, don't go. Stay with me. I need you.'

'Jenny will look after you.'

He moved lethargically towards her as if he would catch at her hand. She jerked out of his reach. He looked hurt.

'Come and lie down, Ned,' Jenny said quickly. 'Doctor said you were to lie down until – '

The bell rang from downstairs. Maggie went to open the door. There was the sound of men's heavy footsteps on the staircase, in the passage. A young man came into view, in a semi-uniform of blue serge with black braided fastenings.

'Mr Corvill?' he asked.

'Yes.' Ned looked uncertain. The uniform was somehow disturbing.

233

'Dr Murdo sent me. The ambulance is downstairs.'

'Ambulance?'

'It's all right, Ned,' Jenny soothed. 'Dr Murdo said he would send it, remember? And you said you would go.'

'Yes, but – '

'I'm coming with you, dear.'

'Lucy too?' he said, resisting the urgings of the sanatorium attendant to lead him to the door.

Lucy was about to say no. 'Come,' Jenny whispered, 'at least just down to the cab.'

Unwilling, but agreeing so as to see him gone, Lucy went with the group to the outer door. Maggie handed Jenny a shawl for Lucy as they went out on to the staircase. Slowly they descended. Night had come down now, the lamps in Hanover Street were casting pools of light on the pavement.

At the kerb stood a four-wheeled van, painted a dark blue. It had windows but the blinds were down. It opened at the back. Another attendant stood there, waiting. Somehow it was not reassuring.

'No!' cried Ned, throwing himself backwards to avoid being ushered in.

'Now, sir, please dinna cause a fuss,' said the attendant.

'I won't go in that – '

'Please, Ned, you agreed to go,' Jenny said, through tears she couldn't check.

'No, no – Lucy, don't let them – ' He threw himself on Lucy for protection. She turned away, avoiding his weight. He staggered, regaining his balance by windmilling his arms.

The two horses harnessed to the van shied at the figure silhouetted by the street lights. The more nervous of the pair reared up. The van moved grindingly against its brake, rocking.

Lucy, nerves already stretched, shrieked in fright. She turned to fly from the rocking van.

Her foot caught in her floating peignoir and the falling shawl. She went headlong on the hard pavement.

'Lucy! Lucy!' shouted Ned, beside himself with concern for her. The attendants stepped up, wrestled with him efficiently as they had learned to do with many a violent patient, and pushed him towards the van's entry. He went suddenly limp. Afterwards Jenny wondered if she had seen a little black implement momentarily wielded at the back of his neck.

But her main concern was for Lucy, who had come down with a terrible impetus. She got down on her knees beside her. Maggie came flying to help her. Together they turned Lucy, raised her head. Her eyelids fluttered. She was alive, and in a moment she was conscious. She looked at Jenny with frightened eyes.

The driver had quieted the horses. The attendants had closed the back door of the van. One had gone inside with Ned, the other now came back to the women. 'Is the lady a' richt?' he asked.

'I think so – '

'We'll be off then, better no to hang aboot.'

With a clatter and a rattle the van pulled away from the kerb, the assistant climbing on the box beside the driver. Its square black shape with its tail lantern disappeared up the street.

Maggie and Jenny between them got Lucy upstairs again. Without consulting they took her straight into the bedroom, laid her on the bed. 'Sal volatile,' Maggie said, and went for it.

'Jenny . . .'

'Yes, dear.'

'Jenny, I've got a pain.'

'You're bruised – '

'No, not that. Jenny, I – Oh!' She gave a moan, half raised herself, and wrapped her arms about her middle, twisting in agony.

Jenny ran out, to meet Maggie in the passage with the restorative. 'Never mind that, Maggie, run for Dr Laggan. I think Mrs Corvill is losing her baby.'

Chapter Seventeen

In thirty-six hours it was over: the baby boy had entered and left the world for which he was so ill prepared.

Lucy was weak from shock and loss of blood but in no danger. She slept and woke, took the beef tea and brandy prescribed by Dr Laggan, wept a little from time to time, but was undoubtedly recovering by the Sunday.

'If you feel well enough to do without me,' Jenny said, 'I'd like to go out for a while.'

'Go out?' Lucy said jealously. 'Where to?'

'To Dr Murdo's clinic to visit Ned.'

Lucy had the grace to blush. She'd almost totally forgotten Ned in the drama of her own situation.

'You'll tell him about the baby?'

'Not yet, Lucy. I don't think it would be good for him. I'll ask Dr Murdo. Would you like to write a note for Ned?'

'What on earth would I say to him?' Lucy cried, tears springing. 'I don't want to write to him! It's his fault I lost my baby.'

'No, no, Lucy, it was an accident.'

'It was his fault! I don't care what you say! I don't care if I never see him again – I hate him!'

Jenny felt that it was weakness and self-pity forcing the words from her sister-in-law. She shook her head in silence and went out.

In a conference with Dr Murdo, she was advised to tell Ned the truth. 'Nothing is to be gained by lying to the patient,' he said. 'It does away with trust – and if he doesn't trust me he will never accept my treatment.'

Ned seemed well but very passive, which she put down to

the chloral he was prescribed. He became more alert when he asked if Lucy would be coming to visit. 'I'm only allowed one more day of visiting, you see. Then the treatment begins in earnest and the doctor has explained to me I must concentrate on that and not see anyone for at least a month.'

'I understand, Ned. Lucy won't be coming to see you. She's . . . not well.'

'Sick again because of the baby? Poor darling.'

'She had a miscarriage, Ned,' Jenny said, taking his hand. 'It's all over about the baby.'

'No!'

'I'm sorry, brother. It is so.'

'She was upset because I had to go away,' he said, looking as if he might weep. 'I blame myself. She's so sensitive – it upset her.'

'Perhaps it was that,' Jenny sighed. No matter what Dr Murdo said, she couldn't bring herself to tell him Lucy wasn't the sensitive flower he imagined.

She promised to come back next day. When she got home, she let herself in quietly in case Lucy was resting, then herself lay down on her bed. She seemed to have had no sleep for days. Yet she couldn't find ease in an afternoon nap, she lay awake trying to compose the letter she must write for the evening post, the letter telling her mother what had happened.

She became aware of sounds in the passage. Her door was a little ajar, left so in case Lucy called for her. She heard the maids moving about near the big press at the end of the passage nearest her room, where superfluous garments were stored until needed.

Lucy's maid Fordyce said, 'Well, I shan't have to let out the rest of the winter gowns after all.'

'Aye, that's one good thing, if aught good can come of what's happened.'

'Oh, come, Maggie – she's better off without the baby, if its father was to be shut up in a madhouse.'

Maggie was apparently catching up with some housework. The sound of a broom on the corridor carpet could be heard. 'The poor man,' Maggie said, pausing. 'He was aye decent enough to me. Sad to lose his liberty and his wain.'

'If it *was* his.'

'Miss Fordyce!'

'Well, oftentimes she was flushed and excited when I'd be doing her hair to go out. Don't tell me she was excited over the master – it was more likely the handsome gentleman that came a-visiting when he got back from abroad.'

'Mr Brunton? Aye, there was a charm about him. But it couldna ha' been him. He's never been nigh nor bye these six weeks.'

'And why would he, Maggie? He didn't strike me as the man to enjoy a woman full of morning sickness and self-pity.' There was a pause, then Fordyce said in a lower tone, 'We'll see if she can get him back now she's lost her little burden.'

Jenny threw an arm over her eyes to blot out the picture they had conjured up. Archie and Lucy . . .

Of course she knew Archie had returned to Scotland. It had been reported in the social column of the *Galashiels Record*. He was now living in Edinburgh, where his mother had joined him so as to have easier treatment for her vein inflammations. The big house at the Mains had been let to a gentleman tenant.

Lucy's whereabouts were just as easy for Archie to ascertain. The young Corvills would have figured in newspaper accounts of social functions in Glasgow. It only needed one or other to make the first move – a hostess-like note to Archie to invite him, a letter from Archie to Ned recalling old acquaintance . . .

Could it have been Archie's child?

Perhaps not even Lucy herself could say. Better not to think of it at all. That was all in the past. But, for the future . . . ?

Ned was shut up out of the way in the sanatorium. Lucy would soon be on her own in Glasgow, for Jenny would have to return to Galashiels. Archie Brunton was a few miles away, an easy journey by passenger train.

Jenny lay wondering what she should do. Should she in fact do anything? Had she any right to interfere? Formerly she had had some role – she was the prospective fiancée of Archie Brunton, considered so by his mother and all the rest of the community. But now . . . she had dissociated herself from Archie, she had no right to moralise over his conduct. And as for Lucy . . .

Jenny felt she had no right to condemn Lucy considering what her own behaviour had been recently.

She gave up the attempt to sleep. She got up and paced about her room. Maggie, coming in to dust, drew up in astonishment. 'Losh! I thought you were out visiting the master!'

'No, I got back a while ago.'

Maggie went red, no doubt wondering how much, if anything, Jenny had heard. 'Can I get you aught, Miss Corvill?'

'No.' Jenny suddenly made up her mind. If she stayed she might end up quarrelling openly with Lucy, and nothing was to be gained by that. 'I'm going to pack and go home in the morning as soon as I've visited Mr Corvill again.'

'But what about the mistress?'

'I'll send a pre-paid telegraph message for her mother. Perhaps my sister-in-law would be better off with an older woman as companion at the present time.'

'I see what you mean, miss.'

Lucy wasn't pleased when she heard her mother had been sent for. 'I wish you hadn't taken so much upon yourself, Jenny. I don't want my mother here.'

'At a time like this, surely – '

'No, we don't really get on. But since you've done it she'll come. I can put up with her for a few days, I suppose.' There was no attempt to retain Jenny as a companion. They both knew they'd be glad when they parted.

Mrs Morrison duly replied that she would come at once. Jenny packed, went one last time to see Ned, and set off for the Borders with her mind full of the encounter with her own mother yet to come. How much should she tell? Only what concerned Ned, only what her mother had a need to know.

To her astonishment Millicent took the news with less shock and dismay than she expected. 'I sometimes wondered, you know, Jenny . . . I was closer to Ned than your father ever was. I had to go in and rouse him in the mornings when he didn't get up, and there were times . . . I thought . . . But I didn't want to believe my own son was a drunkard and it would have been such a blow to your father . . .'

'Oh, Mother, I wish we'd confided in each other! We might have been able to help him before things got so bad.'

Millicent sighed. 'Yet you know what it says in Proverbs: "A fool uttereth all his mind, but a wise man keepeth it in till afterwards." Ah well, it's afterwards now – we must do all we can to make this new start when the time comes.' She thought a moment. 'Was Lucy very upset about the baby?'

'Of course.' Yet while Jenny gave this conventional reply she was already thinking, She'll get over it quickly, she's not the maternal type.

Her mother seemed to echo the thought when she spoke again. 'I was very pleased at the idea of a grandchild, but you know, Jenny, I never could quite picture Lucy with a baby . . .'

It was Tuesday morning when Jenny got back to Waterside Mill. In some mysterious way, the news had gone before her – she had been to Glasgow, her brother was sick and in a nursing home, her sister-in-law had lost her baby. Everyone was kind, sympathetic.

Everyone except Franz.

'You did not write to me! You said you would write from Glasgow but you did not!'

He had waylaid her as she hurried down Market Street towards the printer who was producing her first catalogue of tartans for distribution abroad.

'I'm sorry, everything happened all at once. I simply didn't have time.'

His eyes flashed with anger. 'You have been gone a week! Surely you could have found a moment – '

'Oh, Franz, please don't be angry. I can't bear it – everything has been so awful!'

Her obvious distress made him regret his accusations. He seized one of her hands. A passer-by glanced with interest but she had the presence of mind to say, 'Thank you, the cobbles are slippery here.'

It was a very cold November day. The summits of the hills around Galashiels were dusted with snow and the lower slopes had the glint of frost. Jenny held her long jacket close against her to keep out the chill. Franz looked as if he longed to put an arm about her to protect her from the weather and any other ill that might come to her.

She told him what she had told no one except her mother

– the real nature of her brother's ailment. Franz, who remembered the gentle, amiable creature he had met in Hamburg, was horrified.

'My dear! I'm sorry I snarled at you! What must you think of me, to be so selfish when you have such troubles.'

'No, no, Franz, I understand – I should have written. I meant to send a note the moment I got back but my mother – '

'She must be very anxious.'

'She keeps saying she wants to go to Glasgow to be near him, but there's no point in that – he isn't allowed visitors until another three weeks have gone by.'

'But she wishes to go so as to be a comfort to the daughter-in-law, of course.'

'Yes.' She didn't want to go into explanations about Lucy, which in any case would sound unkind and ill-natured. 'I shall take Mother there in good time to be the first visitor to Ned.'

'In the meantime – '

'In the meantime we can write to him, and receive letters from him, only not frequently because Dr Murdo feels – '

'No, I meant, in the meantime, when can we meet, my darling?'

'No, Franz.' They had reached the printer's office, so she had good reason for stopping and drawing away from him. 'I *must* spend time with Mother. She's upset, frightened . . . I can't leave her alone in the evenings.'

'But Jenny – '

'Please, Franz. If you feel anything for me, give me just your friendship for the moment. I need that – I have no one else to turn to.'

This appeal was simple and genuine, but it could not have been better calculated to touch the knight-errant in Franz. He was at once all sympathy and concern, promised to be her good friend, and left her to enter the printer's with an easy mind.

Baird had been getting out the clothes she had put away when William died and Jenny went into mourning, for the year in black was up. She said to her, 'You're thinner than you were, mistress. You should work less and eat more.'

'This isn't the time to work less, Baird. We're busy – and

if I'm to be away again at the end of the month I must get everything in apple pie order so I can leave it.'

The maid tried not to look too eager. She'd been told she would accompany Jenny and her mother to Glasgow, staying on there to look after the elder Mrs Corvill. She was happy at the thought of being in a big city where all the necessities for good appearance were ready to hand – new lace to refurbish a tired gown, trimmings for bonnets, the latest style in gloves. Not that the elder Mrs Corvill paid much heed to such things, but Baird liked to 'turn out' her mistress well.

Letters from Ned, though limited to one page only, had conveyed his progress. He said he had been given the task of helping with the horses, was being taught to mend harnesses, had learned to row in a four-man skiff, and felt well. Jenny thought they were like letters from a boy at boarding-school rather than a grown man. But perhaps that was Dr Murdo's method – to take the patient back to childhood then start him again on a better path.

At the big apartment in Glasgow they found Lucy involved with dressmakers. She too had left deep mourning behind but had decided to have new clothes. Her mother was helping her choose styles, but it seemed to involve more wrangling than pleasure.

'It's almost as if they're quarrelling,' Mrs Corvill said to Jenny. 'It's a strange way of enjoying yourself, surely?'

'Never mind, Mrs Morrison will be gone tomorrow.'

Lucy's mother had let it be known that she preferred Edinburgh to Glasgow, that she had a gentleman friend who pined for her and that she must get back as soon as someone could take her daughter off her hands. She had a money allowance now, provided for her by William Corvill soon after Lucy's marriage: he had felt it unsuitable for any woman relative of his to be running a boarding-house where she had to handle a succession of male lodgers.

As a result Mrs Morrison saw herself these days as a lady of leisure, and had not been best pleased to play nursemaid to her daughter. Moreover, she was eager to get home before the gentleman friend cooled off, because she had hopes of hearing wedding bells again.

Dr Laggan had prescribed rest and quiet for Lucy. Mrs

Morrison had faithfully carried out his orders, had stayed indoors to play card games and read to her daughter. Visitors had been few and none of them male. Letters of inquiry and sympathy had been dealt with by Mrs Morrison. It was clear from casual conversation that Archie Brunton had not been in touch. Jenny was very relieved.

Relieved, too, that Lucy spoke more kindly of Ned. Perhaps her mother had given her a talking-to, perhaps absence had made the heart grow fonder. Whatever the reason, she said nothing harsh about her husband in front of Millicent, and seemed to accept that he was ill rather than wicked. Millicent took it for granted that her daughter-in-law longed for Ned's complete recovery and restoration to the family. Whether that was quite true, Jenny rather doubted – but she had always doubted that her sister-in-law really loved Ned.

Mrs Morrison left, happy to be conveyed to the station in a private hired carriage and with a handsome present from Jenny for her stint as nurse. The day came for Ned to have a visitor. His mother was eager to go, but took it for granted Lucy would want to be first. Lucy accepted the role, though with a lack of enthusiasm that was noticed even by Millicent, who never thought ill of anyone.

'I expect she's frightened,' she accounted for it to Jenny. 'Hospitals are frightening, and after all this is a kind of private hospital.'

They had driven past it several times to let Millicent see where her son was staying. It was a large house, a mansion almost, in its own grounds and with access to the shore of the Clyde by a private path. A pleasant enough place until you noticed that there were bars on the windows, that the gate was guarded by a sturdy attendant in uniform.

Lucy went to make her visit wearing one of her new gowns and looking exceedingly pretty despite the grey foggy day. She returned looking perplexed.

'How was he?' Millicent asked eagerly. 'How did he look?'

'He looks different – thicker in body – I think it must be all the physical work he's been doing. Oh yes, he's quite well, very well.'

'What did he say? Is there anything I can take him tomorrow? Books?'

'You had better ask him if he wants books,' Lucy said. 'Now that you mention it, it's odd – he's always surrounded by books as a rule but the only one he had by his bed was the Bible.'

'That's no bad thing,' his mother said, nodding sagely. 'His father always used to read a passage night and morning, you know.'

'He talked a lot about his father,' said Lucy. 'About how he wished he'd paid more attention to him when he was a boy . . .'

'Oh, that's good. It sounds very good indeed, Lucy. And did you speak to Dr Murdo? What does he think?'

'You can ask him yourself tomorrow.'

When she got her alone Jenny said to her, 'What's wrong? What troubled you so much?'

To her surprise, Lucy looked almost tearful. 'He was like a stranger,' she faltered.

'In what way, Lucy? You don't mean he didn't know you?'

'No, no – he was waiting for me when I was shown in, he kissed me fondly; in that way he was as he used to be. But . . . Jenny, he kept talking all the time about repentance, and his duty to God . . . It wasn't like Ned at all!'

Next day was Millicent's turn. She had no fault to find in what she saw. Her late husband had talked often of duty and uprightness and God's will – she found nothing strange in hearing her son speak of these things with fervour. Quite the contrary: she was pleased and reassured. When Dr Murdo restored Ned to his family, she was sure he would be a new man.

Jenny agreed with that. Her visit to Ned gave her an insight into what Lucy had meant. Her brother was different, buoyed up by a new belief in God that had been instilled by Dr Murdo. It seemed to Jenny that religion had been called in to fill the space in his life left by alcohol. Whether it was a good thing remained to be seen. Certainly Ned was changed.

He was full of remorse for past behaviour, full of plans for the future. He would really work on his book about the influence of Greece on Scottish life, but Jenny gathered his view was no longer so favourable. 'Of course, we can't blame them, since they were born before God sent His Son to save us, but the Greek philosophers had some very wrong views, Jenny. They were full of pride in their own abilities.'

His sister, who had never read any Greek, couldn't argue one way or the other.

Although Dr Murdo felt that the visits from Ned's family had been beneficial, he let it be known that enough was as good as a feast. From now on they would be restricted to one visit per week until Ned's treatment ended. Since Jenny had to return to Galashiels she was granted the favour of another visit before leaving.

St Andrew's Day was approaching. The sanatorium was preparing a special celebration. Jenny found Ned engaged in making St Andrew's crosses by fixing white ribbons on blue rectangles, which were to enliven the rather solemn green paint of the clinic's interior.

She bit her lip at the sight. It seemed such a belittling occupation for a man who used to discuss the politics of Athens and Sparta. He told her with evident satisfaction that they would have a reading of Scottish poetry and some songs of Robert Burns, 'although we can hardly be too strong in our approval of a drinker like Burns, poor man . . .'

Before she left, Jenny had a private word with Dr Murdo. 'I don't want to take up your time, doctor – I'd just like to know how you think my brother is progressing?'

'He's doing very well indeed. We've purged his body of the poison and his mind of the craving for it.'

'When do you feel he could return to his family?'

'Well, generally three months is the shortest time. That would bring us to Hogmanay, and I believe you'll agree with me,' Murdo said with a smile, 'that there's too much strong drink available in Scotland at such a time for a newly-emerged abstainer.'

'You are saying my brother must not drink at all?'

'Exactly. His system cannot tolerate alcohol in any form.'

'That's a very severe restriction. Surely he may have a glass of wine – '

'Nothing, Miss Corvill. I assure you, Ned understands this perfectly. He has even accepted that he must not take the wine at Communion – the Lord will understand and uphold him in his vow of abstinence when he closes his lips at the rim of the cup.'

'But surely one sip of communion wine – '

'Could be fatal. One sip, one chance for the craving to take hold again – he absolutely must not take a mouthful of anything alcoholic.'

'And how long must he go on in this way?'

'For ever, my dear young lady. It is a lifetime prohibition.'

'Dr Murdo, I'd no idea he would have to face such an ordeal!'

'Ned understands, that's the main thing. You see, he has not only been very ill, he had a very great fright. He thought he was going mad. Now that he knows the cause of those episodes, and with his renewed faith in God, he will do well, have no fear.'

'But doctor, you speak of keeping him with you until Hogmany is over – there will be a Hogmanay next year.'

'But by then, Miss Corvill, Ned will have another year's strength and experience. Come, don't look so anxious. Your brother has not only his own strength, but the strength of his religion.'

'That's what worries me, sir. My brother was never very . . . devout. In that respect he was a disappointment to my father. I can't help wondering if he has turned to religion out of . . . out of a desire for a prop, rather than a sincere feeling for it.'

'Why should you blame him for using religion as a prop?' Murdo said, wagging a finger at her. 'He's quite right to do so. "Thy rod and thy staff comfort me," as the Psalmist said. And I am sure his sweet young wife and his family will be a support to him too.'

Gatesmuir seemed very empty and strangely cold to Jenny when she reached home. Her mother wrote every day, and Ned once a week: she would read the letters with avidity, longing for someone with whom she could discuss them. But there was no one. Not even Baird, with whom she'd often had a cosy chat: Baird had been left in Glasgow to look after her mother. The other domestic staff would have been very embarrassed if Jenny had spoken to them of personal matters, and the workers at the mill were too much in awe of her to be friends.

Ronald Armstrong had been the exception. Ronald had been a friend as well as a colleague. But Ronald was gone.

It was inevitable that she should turn to Franz Lennhardt. At first it was simply for talk, for human contact. But there was no one at home for her to hurry back to, and to go to Franz's little cottage became so much part of her life that she gave up reproaching herself for it.

Their lovemaking now was different. They were lovers but they were also friends. They would lie side by side and talk for an hour or more, sometimes about inconsequential things but sometimes about deep feelings.

'Oh, if only we could be married,' Franz groaned as he held her close at parting one night. 'We are like man and wife – are we not?'

'But it's not really so,' she reminded him, putting a finger on his mouth as he was about to kiss her again. 'My darling, it will soon be the New Year. My brother writes to say he has decided to come home to Gatesmuir. By the end of the first week of January they will be here – and after that it will be difficult for us to go on meeting like this.'

'We must manage somehow, Jenny,' he insisted. 'We must find a way.'

They both knew that it would be well-nigh impossible. And yet Jenny looked forward to the homecoming of her family. Her mother came first with Baird, saying Ned had stayed behind to close up the Glasgow flat. 'He felt he ought to see to all that himself,' she confided.

'But is he fit for that kind of thing, Mother?'

'Oh, yes, Jenny, he is very well indeed. You'll be surprised when you see him.'

Jenny was indeed surprised. Her brother was the very picture of health. His hair had a deep vital gloss, his eyes were clear and alert, he moved with confidence. His wife, by contrast, seemed to have lost some of her self-assurance. It was as if she didn't quite know what to make of this man to whom she now found herself married.

Ned took a week or so to work himself into familiarity with the old round in Galashiels. Then, over a substantial family dinner at which he as always drank plain water, he announced his plan for his new life.

'I talked this over with Dr Murdo before I left the sanatorium and I have his full backing and approval for my campaign.'

'What campaign is that, dear?' his mother asked innocently.

'I'm going to found a Borders Branch of the Scottish Temperance Society.'

'Ned!' gasped Lucy in dismay.

'Good gracious,' said his mother.

'Are you sure you're up to it?' Jenny asked.

'I told you, Dr Murdo says I am. Working and living with him, I became conscious of how lucky I was. There are so many unfortunates who haven't been brought to the Almighty for the help they need to conquer the Demon Drink. You know it's the curse of Scotland, Mother – there's too much strong drink too easily available to people who ought not to have it.'

'Well, I know it's true that many of the sad cases I deal with in my charity work are brought about by – '

'Exactly!' Ned struck in. 'And who better to show them the error of their ways than a man who has been through all that and been cured. A *rich* man, who admits he has been weak and sinful.'

They listened to him talk. It appeared he planned to go out into the highways and byways of the Scottish Borders displaying himself as an example of how one could sin and yet repent and be saved.

Jenny watched her mother and her sister-in-law. Millicent Corvill was half-apprehensive and half-approving. Lucy looked as if she wished the ground would open up and swallow her. True enough, it would be hideously embarrassing, thought Jenny.

It became clear that Ned expected his family to come with him on his mission. To Jenny's surprise, her mother quietly refused. 'I'm too old for that kind of thing, dear,' she said. 'I honour you for what you mean to do, but I don't think I can take any part in it.'

'But I had such great hopes – ' He broke off. 'Well, at any rate, *you'll* come, Jenny.'

'I think not, brother.'

'But you must! You'll be such an asset on a public platform!'

She shook her head. 'It would sound very odd if I stood up and preached temperance when any business acquaintance would be able to say I offer wine and spirits in my office when I entertain.'

'But you could say you yourself never partake. I allow alcohol here at Gatesmuir for guests, but I can honestly say I never touch it myself.'

'You, of course, can say that, but I must confess I like an occasional glass of wine, Ned. I don't wish to become a total abstainer.'

Her brother went on trying to persuade her but she made it clear she didn't want to be involved in his vocation. Ned sighed. 'Ah well, it must be just you and I, Lucy dear,' he said.

'Me?' cried Lucy.

'As a good wife you'll accompany me to meetings. There are many women, you know, who fall by the wayside because of drink. And many mothers of families where the bread-winner spends his wages on whisky, so that they need our help and advice.'

Lucy tried to say she felt she would be no good at that kind of thing. But she had never been any good at standing up to a man. She had played a role all her life, the role of the gentle maiden, the sweet obedient wife. She got her way in general by wheedling and cajoling and, if all else failed, by secret disobedience. But with this new Ned, it was impossible to wheedle and cajole. He was strong in his conviction and expected Lucy to be the same.

He launched himself into his campaign. Lucy went with him. It was clear to Jenny that her sister-in-law hated it all, yet she hadn't the courage to stand up and say, 'No, I don't want to.' She attended meetings, she sat on platforms, she shook hands with black-clad men and earnest ladies, she listened while her husband beat his breast in public and every day she looked more and more desperate to escape.

They had a party at Gatesmuir for Millicent Corvill's fiftieth birthday. It was the first party since the family's return from Glasgow, so there were a large number of guests. The usual innocent party games were played, there was dancing to a little trio of fiddle, melodeon and flute, and there was plenty to eat and drink.

In deference to Ned's principles, there was alcohol-free fruit cup and selzer water in plenty. But Jenny had insisted there must be spirits for the local businessmen, and there was also a vast bowl of what was known locally as the Captain's Grog. This was a concoction of juices from expensively-imported tropical fruits liberally laced with white rum, a traditional recipe much in favour with the older generation.

Jenny was sitting with the young Corvills at a table in a shadowy corner where the candles were beginning to dwindle in their holders and the light from the ceiling gasolier didn't reach. She was glad of the dimness for she was very tired; it was well past midnight and still the guests didn't seem to want to go.

Ned had been teased a good deal by the young men in the course of the evening. He put up with it with good grace, but Lucy blushed with embarrassment when he was called 'Mr Misery' and accused of being a spoilsport. He was now enthusing over a grand rally he was organising for the following week, when temperance bands from the local area were to meet in Selkirk and be given newly woven banners, these to be borne in procession to the local Free Church where they would be blessed by the minister.

'And you, I suppose, will preach a sermon,' laughed Laurie Menteith.

'Certainly not, sermons are for the pulpit. But the minister has kindly agreed to allow me to say a word about my own salvation.'

Lucy, Jenny knew, was desperately trying to avoid having to go to the event, which promised to be more than usually mortifying to her. In fact, she came as close as she could to saying she wouldn't go, only to be gently admonished by Ned for her shyness and too-great humility.

'We'll be doing the Lord's work,' he assured her, looking around for approval at the others round the table.

Since most of his guests were fond of a drink, this appeal met with scant response. Jenny, half-asleep, let her gaze drop and was just in time to see a hand move Ned's glass of fruit cup away from his plate. In the guttering candle-flame she thought perhaps she had dreamed it but no – the hand reappeared from behind the central flower-arrangement, nudging a different wine-glass into place.

Perplexed, Jenny peered at the glass. It had a shred of pineapple floating on its surface. The glass contained the Captain's Grog.

She thought: Someone's trying to play a cruel joke on Ned, someone's trying to get him drunk.

Jerking awake, she glanced up. Her eye met Lucy's. And a flush of guilt ran up under Lucy's pale skin.

It was Ned's wife who had wanted to get him drunk. And it was no joke.

Chapter Eighteen

Anyone who wanted to avoid Jenny in the morning could easily do so by breakfasting late. Jenny was always out of the house by eight o'clock, though she returned at midday for lunch. Anyone wishing to avoid her at lunch could do so by being out when she came home.

Lucy's tactical information was insufficient, however. When she came down at eleven on the morning after the party, having breakfasted in her room, it was to find her sister-in-law in the drawing-room with the household cat purring on her lap.

Lucy turned to go out faster than she had come in. 'Don't go, Lucy,' Jenny said, 'I want to have a chat.'

'Er . . . I can't stop – I'm going out on a morning visit.'

'I'll come with you,' said Jenny, rising and putting the indignant cat on the settee.

'Oh, no, I'm visiting Mrs Lyall – you know you don't like her – '

'All the more reason why I should come,' Jenny said. 'I don't play enough part in the family calls.'

She rang the bell, and told Thirley to have the carriage brought round. She accompanied Lucy upstairs while she got her bonnet and fur pelisse. She waited at the bedroom door for her, meanwhile sending Baird to fetch her thick promenade jacket and a hat.

There was no escape for Lucy. They were helped into the carriage, the coachman flicked the reins at the bays, and off they went on the road towards Clovenfords, a distance of some three miles round the slope of Meigle Hill on a bad road.

It was a mild February day, but drizzly, so the carriage was closed up against the dampness. There was no danger that the coachman would hear what was said between the ladies.

'Now,' Jenny said as soon as they had left the driveway of Gatesmuir, 'what were you doing last night?'

'Doing? I don't understand you.'

'When you switched Ned's glass for someone else's.'

'I did no such thing.'

'Lucy, we both know you did. What was your intention? To get him drunk, to break his spirit, to put him back in the sanatorium with Dr Murdo? Or perhaps you wanted to achieve more – perhaps you see yourself as the pretty young widow of poor Ned Corvill who drank himself to death?'

'No!' It was a cry of protest.

'Very well, let's say you didn't actually intend a murder. What did you have in your mind?'

'I didn't do anything – ' Lucy gulped and burst into tears.

'Cry if you must. It won't have any effect. I'll wait until you recover to get my answers.'

'You . . . you're hateful!' Lucy sobbed. 'You have no feelings! And you've never liked me!'

'When you came to Gatesmuir after pushing Ned into a secret marriage,' Jenny said drily, 'none of us were exactly delighted with you. But we could have forgiven you everything – the secrecy, the lies – if only you'd really loved Ned.'

'Lies? What lies? How dare you!'

'Oh, Lucy . . . You're such a fool.' She said it without scorn, simply as if stating a fact. 'Because you don't know how to get at facts, you think no one else can do it. But of course I learned within a week or two that there was no heroic young lieutenant called Morrison who died with the China Squadron.'

'What? Of course there was – my father – '

'Your father's name doesn't appear anywhere in the Navy List. It's such a silly lie.'

Lucy's tears had ended as her anger began. 'Only someone like you would even think of checking!'

'Quite true. Now you know that I did check, and that I've never been taken in by your tales about your father.'

Lucy mopped her eyes to peer at her. 'You told your mother? Your father?'

'No, no one. I couldn't see how it would help. You've made a legal marriage with my brother and he loves you. That's why it's so despicable of you to try to undo all the good of the nursing home. He doesn't deserve that, Lucy. It was a very mean thing.'

Lucy clenched and unclenched her hands over her lace handkerchief. 'Oh, you don't know what it's like!' she burst out. 'He makes me go to those horrid, horrid meetings and I have to sit on the platform and hear him tell everyone how low he sank, and it's so *sordid*, and then I have to smile and be nice to those awful people, they're so *dull* or else they're fervent and strange – wild-eyed – and they expect me to know what to tell them, they say things like, "Do you find prayer helpful?" or "How should I get my husband to reform?" as if *I* would know, and they're the kind of people no one of any *breeding* would want to know and I can tell everyone is laughing at me behind my back because of it . . .'

The outburst ended as she ran out of breath. It had been uttered with perfect sincerity and feeling. Jenny had no doubt she was hearing the truth.

'Are you telling me you tried to wreck Ned's recovery just to avoid going to a meeting?'

'There's this terrible rally in Selkirk. Ned actually wants us to head a procession through the High Street, in front of everybody. He wants me to hold a banner! I only thought . . . I only thought . . . if he had a relapse we wouldn't have to go.'

Jenny closed her eyes. And for this – to avoid being publicly embarrassed – Ned's wife had been prepared to toss him back to the terrors of delirium tremens.

When she looked up again Lucy was watching her in anxiety. 'You won't tell Ned what I did?'

'Of course not. Once I'd put the glass beyond his reach – '

'Because if you tell him I'll deny it and it'll only be your word against mine.'

'I shouldn't dream of telling him, Lucy. It would break his heart.'

A faint colour came up under Lucy's pale skin. 'You say that as if he cares a lot for me but it's not true, he drags me with him to – '

254

'Lucy, all you have to do is say, "I won't go".'

'I tried that – I explained I didn't like it and all he said was, "You must believe that God has called you and all will be well." So another time I pretended I had a headache and I didn't have to go, but after that I couldn't think of an excuse so I had to –'

'You don't have to go, you don't have to have an excuse. Just tell him you don't want to do it.'

'But I can't . . . he thinks it's all so important, I can't just tell him I don't agree, I don't know how to say that to a man . . .'

Jenny felt, not for the first time, an impulse of pity for Lucy. She was so utterly trapped in her own view of herself as gentle and good, like an ideal heroine of some Sir Walter Scott poem.

'Would you like me to tell him for you?' she said.

'Oh, would you, Jenny? Would you? Explain to him – my health won't stand up to it – my nerves –'

'I'll tell him,' Jenny said, mentally making a vow to invent nothing about Lucy's nerves.

They made their call on Mrs Lyall, who was so delighted by the unexpected honour of seeing Miss Corvill as well as the young Mrs Corvill that Jenny's conscience was smitten. She really ought to do more in the domestic circle. It was wrong to leave it all to others – and think of the damage it had done, in Lucy's impulsive act last night. With no one to turn to for help, her sister-in-law had almost committed an unforgiveable act.

Perhaps it was unfortunate that Mrs Lyall was so gushing to Jenny. It was clear Lucy resented it. On the way home she was silent. At lunch time Ned appeared, glowing with health, having spent the morning sawing up logs at the far side of the woods. Millicent Corvill had been to see an exhibition of handwriting at the Subscription School. The chat over the meal was about small, household matters. Lucy went up to her room immediately it was over, avoiding her husband's suggestion of a long walk now that the drizzle had cleared up.

'Let me walk with you, Ned,' Jenny said. 'I'm going down to the works in any case.'

'Very unlike you, taking a morning off,' he remarked, as

255

he offered her his arm on the slippery surface of the steep drive.

'I thought it was permissible,' she said with a laugh. 'It's the first time I've taken time off for anything except family matters or business.'

'That's true. You do too much, sister.'

'Not at all. You know I enjoy my work. But that's what I want to speak to you about, Ned. Enjoyment.'

'Enjoyment?' He checked in his stride to give her a puzzled look. 'That's a strange topic!'

'You enjoy working for the Temperance Society, don't you?'

'Oh, Jenny, you can't imagine! It's changed my life! For the first time I feel there's a reason for my existence.'

She hugged his arm. 'It's certainly made a great change in you. But you know . . . you used to be a very tolerant man, brother.'

'Tolerant! Tolerance is merely an escape route for a man without true convictions.'

'My word! Is that your own thought, or a quotation from someone?'

'Dr Murdo said it, in fact.'

'Yes, Dr Murdo. A fine man.'

'A man in a million.'

'He has no wife, I think.'

'She died on the mission station in Africa.'

'I see. That's sad. She shared his convictions, then, if she too was a missionary.'

'Of course.'

Jenny drew a deep breath. 'What I wanted to say to you, Ned, was that all wives don't necessarily share their husband's views. And if others differ from you, you must be prepared to tolerate it.'

'I don't understand you, Jenny,' he said, and she could tell from his tone that he was a thousand miles away from guessing she was speaking about himself and Lucy. 'I accept naturally that some people don't share my views, and those who have no problem with the Demon Drink are entitled to – '

'Yes, entitled to their own opinion. So you ought to allow Lucy to have an opinion of her own.'

'Lucy?' Consternation rose in his voice as he said the name. 'Lucy? What has Lucy to do with this?'

'Lucy doesn't like it when you force her to share in your work. She doesn't – '

'I don't force her!'

'You do, Ned. She's . . . she's accustomed to pleasing people and she can't bear to irritate or disappoint you – but she hates going to your meetings.'

'That's not true.'

'It is true, brother.'

'But she plays her part so very well. She sits there looking so earnest and . . . and almost saintly, and people take to her . . .'

'Is that what you want her for? Window-dressing?'

'Jenny!' He was greatly shocked.

'Lucy doesn't have your vocation to take the message of temperance out to the rest of the world. She finds it embarrassing and it makes her miserable. If you have any mercy on her, you'll leave her at home.'

'Mercy?' her brother said faintly. 'You can't think I want to be cruel to my own sweet little wife?'

'I'm sure you don't mean to be. Your enthusiasm for your work has perhaps blinded you a little to Lucy's unhappiness. She has tried to draw back, I believe?'

'No, never, except, for what I took to be a natural modesty, humility . . .'

Jenny almost said, Take if for what it really is, a great desire not to look a fool in front of people she wants to impress. Aloud she said, 'You will think about what I say?'

'Of course. I can scarcely believe . . . I'll discuss it with Lucy.'

'No, brother, don't discuss it. Lucy is the kind of girl who can't argue her own case against a man. That's why she confided in me – she couldn't bring herself to discuss it with you. Just tell her that she needn't come with you.'

Ned tried to cope with this sudden new outlook on his partnership with Lucy,. 'I shall miss her very much. It's been a joy to me to have her with me.'

'But your faith is strong,' Jenny said, thinking that she was using flattery and that it was all very wrong, but somehow she had to rescue her sister-in-law from her undoubted misery. 'You can stand alone on a platform, brother.'

'With God's help, I can.'

She almost said, If God is so quick to help you, why didn't He tell you your wife wanted to get you drunk last night? But she dared not argue with Ned. She felt that, for all his protestations, his faith was precarious. Perhaps that was what made him so loud about it.

'I'm sure you will be strong even without Lucy.'

'And you know, if she feels the call, she can come to it again later.'

'Yes, if that happens, she can certainly change her mind,' Jenny agreed, knowing it was the most unlikely thing in the world.

It seems to be the way of life that when you've solved one problem, another rises to take its place. Lucy, set free from any compulsion to go with Ned on his temperance campaigning, was for a week or two full of blithe good spirits and energy. But Galashiels in late winter wasn't the most entertaining place in the world.

By mid-March boredom had set in again. She couldn't be given the task of redecorating Gatesmuir again because it had taken Jenny and her mother six months to get it comfortable after her last effort. She didn't want to join the Mothers' Union or the Ladies Charitable Sewing Circle. She didn't enjoy outdoor pursuits such as skating or riding to hounds. The parties, the concerts by local amateurs, the bazaars and fairs for good causes, the exhibitions of weaving products – they had too little sophistication for her taste.

Ned was away on his meetings and rallies, often overnight. Archie Brunton was long lost to her. For the one or two rather raffish male friends she'd made in Glasgow while Ned was out drinking she had no use; it was too risky to summon them up, even if they would come.

She studied her social circle in Galashiels looking for agreeable masculine company. And her eye lighted on Franz Lennhardt.

Chapter Nineteen

'Is your sister-in-law a little odd?' Franz asked Jenny.

'Odd? How do you mean?'

'Flirtatious . . . artificial . . . ?'

Jenny might have said that she thought Lucy all of these things, but it never did any good to speak unkindly without good reason. 'Why do you ask?' she inquired.

They were at a gathering in Peebles to hear a lecture by a former Inspector of Factories on possible changes in the law regarding the employment of child labour. This important matter was being continually discussed, yet neither Jenny nor Franz would have chosen the lecture hall as a meeting place. But it was so difficult for them to see each other these days that they grasped any opportunity.

So here they sat, Jenny in Row G of the auditorium and Franz in Row H. An intermission had been called during which refreshments could be obtained in the lobby. Franz and Jenny had decided to go without so as to have a moment's private conversation.

'Why do you ask about Lucy?' she repeated, for she was always on the alert where Ned's wife was concerned.

'I think she is trying to make me into an especial friend. Last week at that concert of songs – you remember, where Mr Kennet's son sang so badly? – she engaged me in a long conversation about German music.'

'Well, she is interested in music. She plays a little.'

'But why does she pretend? She was clearly under the impression that Schubert's *Die Schöne Müllerin* means *The Jolly Miller*. I found it hard not to laugh. Anyone who has

259

ever listened to the music knows there is nothing jolly about the songs.'

'Franz, you didn't say anything to her about that? She might take offence very easily.'

'No, of course not, it would have been impolite. But I can't imagine why she is bothering to talk at such length to me on subjects she knows nothing about.'

Jenny found it easy to imagine the reason. For Lucy, Franz was an ideal target. He was young, handsome, and well-educated. Then followed the reasons that troubled Jenny's conscience when she thought about their own liaison. He was alone, far from home, vulnerable – very likely to respond to friendly overtures from a pretty woman. Lastly, he was married – there was no danger he could take things too seriously if Lucy flirted with him.

Jenny couldn't say any of this to Franz. But she wanted to put him on his guard. 'Dearest, please be careful. Lucy doesn't like me – '

'Doesn't like you? But why not?' To him, it was impossible not to like Jenny.

'It would take too long to explain – mostly it's a family problem. All I'm asking is that you don't take Lucy lightly. If she found out about us . . .'

'What would she do? Cause a scandal? Surely not.'

'I don't know,' Jenny said, deeply troubled.

'In any case, what is there to find out? We meet almost as strangers these days. And our past is gone, melted away with December's snow.'

People began to filter back into the auditorium. Jenny turned to greet a colleague. The chance to talk was over.

But she had been put on the alert, and now she noticed that when Franz was one of the gathering Lucy always tried to arrange for him to be close to her. Franz was polite but not warm. Lucy became a little puzzled. Why wouldn't he like her?

She began to watch him at every opportunity. And soon she saw what no one else would have noticed – that Franz had a deep interest in Jenny. Although he didn't always sit near her at a party, he seemed always to be aware of where she was. If she needed anything – a glass of wine, a fan, a pencil to write down a card score – Franz was ready with it.

'Anyone would think that young German was on the mash for you,' she remarked softly to Jenny, watching him approach across the Cuddy Green as they walked back from church on the last Sunday of March.

Jenny went cold. 'Who do you mean?' she asked. playing for time.

'Mr Lennhardt, of course – what other young German gentleman do we have in Galashiels.'

'Mr Lennhardt? What makes you speak of him?'

'Because I see him walking towards us at this very minute – and what he's doing here except putting himself in the way of meeting you, I can't imagine.'

Luckily Franz was provided with an excuse that had nothing to do with Jenny. He wanted to have a word with Ned about how to obtain fishing rights on the upper Tweed. Ned made it clear that he couldn't possibly discuss such a thing early on the Sabbath but nevertheless invited Franz to the Sunday meal that evening, at which hour he might feel more free to talk about sports and pastimes.

'He arrived here soon after we left for Glasgow last year, didn't he?' Lucy inquired when he had bowed and gone on his way.

'Yes, if I remember rightly.'

'Oh, I'm sure you remember, sister-in-law. It's unlikely you'd forget the arrival of such an asset to Galashiels society.' Lucy's tone was teasing, but it had an undertone.

'Jenny won't let me invite him to the house very much,' Millicent put in from behind Lucy. 'She says we mustn't show favouritism to any of the buyers.'

This gave Lucy pause. If she had been in Jenny's place she'd have invited Franz at every possible opportunity. So perhaps after all it was one-sided – the handsome foreigner might be on the mash for Jenny, but Jenny wasn't interested in him . . .

This was heartening. A man who had an eye for a lady who wasn't interested might very well be persuaded to change direction.

Lucy put herself out to be very kind to Franz that evening.

Since it was Sunday, there could be no playing of the piano or singing except for hymns, which Lucy hated. So there was no chance to shine by sitting at the instrument looking poetic over Chopin. On the other hand, while her husband read aloud from *Tracts for the Times* it was possible to have a low-voiced conversation on the far side of the room.

Franz, trapped with this young married lady whom he didn't much like, behaved well. He replied as briefly as he could to Lucy, tried to attend to Ned, and leapt up to help when the tea things were brought in at eight o'clock.

Ned was putting away his text, turning instead to the record of fishing rights on the local stretches. Franz carried tea to Millicent and Jenny, then after taking his own sat down beside the elder Mrs Corvill. 'And how is your little boy?' Millicent asked kindly.

'Very well, thank you. He was one year old this month.'

'And you didn't go home for the birthday? Oh, how sad.'

'I sent a present, of course,' Franz said. 'I sent him a doll dressed as a Highland soldier – but he is too young for that, I know.'

'You should have asked my help, Mr Lennhardt,' Lucy called. 'I would have been delighted to help you choose a present.'

'Thank you, you are very kind.'

'Have you a picture of the little boy?'

'Yes, I carry one in my pocketbook.' He produced it – the same one he had shown at first to Jenny and her mother.

Perforce he had to go back across the room to show it to Lucy. She detained him: he sat down and talked about the latest news of his son, about his home in Hamburg of which he had a little sketch showing the house and the linden tree in the street outside.

'You must long to go back,' Lucy suggested.

'No,' Franz said, 'I am happy enough here in Galashiels. I have made good friends here.'

'Ah, friends . . . Who is there to be friends with here? A very dull crowd, don't you find them?'

'Not at all,' Franz replied unwarily. 'I have made good friends here. I am honoured to have the friendship of Miss Corvill.'

'Oh, business friendship you mean. But that's a very shallow thing. Jenny never makes friendships of any depth, you know.'

'That is quite untrue!' he exclaimed.

Ned looked up from the fishing record. Millicent turned her head to stare. Franz coloured. 'I'm sorry,' he said. 'I didn't mean it in quite that way.'

'I should hope not,' Ned remarked with a smile. 'You sounded as if you were quarrelling with my poor little wife about something.'

'I assure you, not in the least. We were saying how charming it was to have friends.'

Jenny had studiously avoided being drawn in. Perhaps too studiously, for as he made his farewells Franz said to her aside and in an anxious tone, 'You weren't hurt by what Lucy said?'

'I didn't even hear, Franz.'

'I am glad of that. She is an unkind lady.'

'I told you to be careful.'

'She made me angry.'

'Please take care in the future.'

'Yes.' He pressed her hand as he turned to take his coat from Thirley.

Lucy had watched it all from the door of the drawing-room. She couldn't hear what passed between them but she saw that her sister-in-law looked anxious and that Franz pressed her hand in leave-taking.

She had plenty to occupy her mind for the rest of that Sunday evening. As she went upstairs at bedtime she had an impulse to go into Jenny's room and see if she could tease a little more out of her.

Jenny had made ready for bed. She was by her bureau in the light of the lamp selecting a book from the row that stood there, to soothe herself for a few minutes before settling down to sleep.

As soon as ever she first gathered together some money in Edinburgh Jenny had bought herself a secondhand copy of the *Vestiarium Scotium* of the brothers Sobieski-Stuart. She had felt it was a necessary tool of her trade though it had cost more than she could afford. In it were notes about clan tartans that she had gathered herself, and a few mementoes of important moments – a scrap of the Royal Stuart tartan she

263

had shown to the Prince Consort at Balmoral, an envelope of a letter from the Tsarina.

Lucy's entry surprised Jenny. She started. Something fell out of the book.

It was a dried flower, the blossom of the hoya that Bobby Prentiss had picked for her in the dusty conservatory at Balmoral that day six years ago.

It lay on the floor. She stooped to pick it up. Lucy did likewise and it was her hand that fell on it first.

She looked at it, handed it to Jenny. 'A keepsake from a sweetheart?' she said lightly.

Jenny went crimson. She cursed herself for the weakness but she knew she had shown far too much emotion – and there was nothing to be done about it.

'My goodness,' Lucy said with a laugh, 'I seem to have touched a tender spot.'

'Did you want something, Lucy?'

'I only dropped in to say I think I was right after all about that young German. He *has* got a mash on you.'

Jenny shook her head. She accepted the flower from Lucy, put it back in the book, closed it, and set the book in the row.

'Aren't you going to read the book?' Lucy asked.

'I think I'm too tired. Goodnight, Lucy.'

'What do you think about Mr Lennhardt?'

'I think you're letting your imagination run away with you.'

'It would be very shocking if he really were to be in love with you. He's a married man.'

'I'm quite aware of that.'

'Yes, it's the kind of thing you can't really forget, isn't it. Well, goodnight, Jenny. Pleasant dreams.'

When the door had closed behind her Jenny sank down on the chair by the bureau. Good God, what had she done? Clearly Lucy thought the dried flower she had so foolishly kept was a memento from Franz. That stupid fit of blushing had given her what she thought of as proof.

Ever since she had been caught red-handed exchanging Ned's wine-glass, ever since Jenny had fought the battle for Lucy's freedom that Lucy couldn't fight for herself, her sister-in-law's resentment had been almost palpable.

She had wanted to get her own back for being shown in

such an unfavourable light. And now Lucy had found a weapon. What she would do Jenny couldn't predict. But she would use the weapon.

Jenny buried her face in her hands. Why, why, did everything have to be so difficult, so complicated? Why couldn't Lucy be content instead of always grasping for what she couldn't have? Why couldn't she herself live her life solitary, without needing love, since it seemed it must be denied to her?

She slept badly, and faced the new day with suppressed anxiety. But nothing happened. Lucy made no reference to the dried flower.

If anything, her sister-in-law seemed rather more considerate than usual. She dropped in on Jenny in her office to bring a magazine Jenny expected in the post. She offered to give a dinner party for Jenny's business acquaintances when the pattern books were opened to them. Franz was among those who came but Lucy made no special effort to single him out.

There was only one moment that Jenny was later to think of as significant. When the guests had gone, Lucy said playfully to the others: 'Which of them all do you like best?'

'Why, I like Mr Kennet,' said Millicent. 'But then I know him best.'

'I rather like Hailes,' Ned confessed. 'A hard character, but direct.'

'Jenny likes Mr Lennhardt best, don't you, Jenny?'

Jenny laughed. 'I see you've made the choice for me, Lucy.'

'Well, he's the one *I* would choose – he's the one I should miss most. Such a delightful man.'

The next ten days were a very busy time in the Borders. Mills were showing their winter patterns, buyers and agents of cloth wholesalers were hurrying from one wool town to another to see what was on offer. In the midst of this Jenny had to make a trip to Edinburgh to argue with her insurers over an export order lost at sea.

When she sat down again in her office late on a Wednesday to catch up with what had been happening she saw to her surprise that Franz had put in no order on behalf of Gebel's Warehouse. 'Mr Muir, what happened about Gebel's?'

'Eh? Oh, you havena heard, Mistress Corvill? There'll be a delay on that,' said the chief clerk. 'Their Mr Lennhardt has gone.'

'Gone? To Kelso or Hawick, you mean?'

'No, mistress, to Hamburg.'

'What?'

'Aye, a sudden summons by the telegraphic cable. Something amiss wi' his child, I hear.'

When Jenny had first come into her office she hadn't turned up the oil lamp on her desk. She was glad now, for her features would not be clear. She knew she had lost colour at his words.

'When did he go?'

'Let me see . . . It would be the day before yesterday. The same day you set out for Edinburgh, I think, aye, that was it. He was in muckle haste to get to Newcastle for the North Sea Packet so he hadna time for leavetaking. That clerk of his, Jameson, came round wi' regrets and a message that his order will be in as soon as possible.'

'I see.' She stared down at some papers, to look as if she was working. 'When will he be back?'

'That I canna say. Jameson himself doesna ken. His instructions are, "Hold the reins" so he's holding, but not urging the horse on.' Pleased with this little quip, the chief clerk waited with his pencil over his notebook. 'What would you like to start on now, mistress?'

She looked at the fob watch on the bodice of her gown. 'I think it's over late to start work this evening – it's past eight.'

'Aye, it's gey late at that.'

'Let's away home then,' she said.

'Shall I call you a hackney? You'll be tired, after all your journeying.'

'No, I'll walk. The boy can bring my valise up to the house tomorrow – there's nothing in it that I need.'

She went out, with Muir thankfully putting away his silver pencil and closing his book.

It was a chill March evening. Darkness had come down but there was a faint light from a young moon decked with a drifting veil of cloud. She walked head down against the breeze, trying to recover from the surprise of Muir's announcement. That Franz had had to leave at once she understood.

But she couldn't believe he hadn't found just a moment, at Newcastle, say, to scribble a line to her.

She was quick to scold herself for her selfishness. If his child were sick, he'd be too worried.

Sighing deeply, she collected her thoughts. He was gone, perhaps for a long time – it depended on the wellbeing of the little boy. She would have to do without him among her circle of friends. But that was not so new to her as once it might have been. For some time now the bond between them had been loosening. There was still a deep fondness, but the ardour had gone – and perhaps that was just as well. It had always been a wildly dangerous thing to do, to meet Franz as a lover in this close little community.

When she reached Gatesmuir she was ready with news of her journey and her success with the insurance firm. Her mother mentioned Franz Lennhardt, the alarm about his baby. 'Poor man, it's terrible to be so far away from your child at a time like that.'

'Yes, indeed. I hope he got to Newcastle in time for the packet.'

'He might have got a cabin on a cargo ship otherwise,' Ned suggested.

'Oh, he'd certainly find some way to get across,' Lucy said. 'I know what he must have been feeling – the thought of losing a child . . .'

Ned put his hand on hers. 'Yes, my love, you know that grief,' he murmured.

'No one can understand what it's like.' Her head drooped, there were tears brimming.

Yet Jenny had the feeling her eyes were watchful under the fair downcast lashes.

A week later a letter came to the office, bearing foreign postmarks and marked 'Personal'. She recognised his writing. She told Muir she'd look through her correspondence and would like to be undisturbed. The moment the door had closed behind him she tore open the envelope.

It was dated three days earlier, had been neatly timed to catch the packet from Hamburg. The letter sounded more stilted than Franz ever had when he spoke. Perhaps that was because it was a difficult letter to write.

My Always Beloved,

I write quickly so you shall receive this before Herr Tabbler
arrives. He is my replacement, middle-aged, greatly experienced in cloth. He shall bring with him his wife and ten-
year-old son for whom he wishes good English learning at
the Border Academy.

My Jenny, there was nothing wrong with my son. It was
a ruse to bring me home. Yet I must confess I was grieved
when I saw him because he was afraid of me when I wished
to pick up him. I was a frightening stranger.

My wife Elsa had received an anonymous letter in
English. Since Elsa speaks no English, she had to give it to
her brother to translate, and this has caused much conflict
in our families.

The letter said she had better look to her marriage because
her husband was in the toils of an unscrupulous woman.
Hans didn't know what means this phrase about toils but
he looked in a dictionary at the University. The letter
suggested she should come to Galashiels and see for herself
but this Hans forbidded and instead she sent word to me
that Wilhelm was very sick.

I do not know who sent the letter but I suspect. I vowed
to Elsa that it was wicked lies and I think she is believing
of this. But yet she wished very much for me to stay in
Hamburg. She is sorry for the coldness that came between
us and wishes to try again to have a good marriage.

I must confess to you – and I am both ashamed and not
ashamed of it – that I want to stay. It hurt me much that
my son had tears when I wished to take him in my arms.
He is a fine little boy, Jenny, I feel I cannot lose him again
by going away.

Perhaps in any case it was ending for us. I love you, I
always shall, but there was a change in what we felt and
perhaps it is right now to say farewell, though I find my
heart aches very much to write this to you. Forgive me,
Jenny. I am torn in two, but I cannot leave my little boy.

This is a long letter but it is the last I shall ever write to
you. You used to laugh when I quoted our German poets
to you but I will this last time quote: 'When love conquers

pain, A new star gleams in the sky.' You will always be my star, Jenny, and when the pain of parting is too great, I will look up into the night and be grateful for what we had. Always yours, though I shall never see you again,

Franz.

The words in their spiky lettering ran together in front of her eyes. She let the paper fall on her desk. For a long time she sat unseeing, breathing shallowly as if to prevent herself from feeling the hurt.

He was never coming back. That must be accepted. Even though she had said to herself that their love affair was already in the past, she felt a wounded sense of loss. Never to see that bright glance across a room, never to hear his voice catching up some argument. Never to hear it whisper gentle, loving words. Never to feel his hand in hers.

She put her knuckles against her lips to prevent herself from sobbing. Tears – what use were tears? They had been parted from one another by a cruel trick and she ought to feel anger, not grief.

An anonymous letter. It could have been from no one else but Lucy.

Her first thought was, I'll strike back, I'll hurt her.

She could hurt Lucy – easily, easily. She could tell her family about the lies, the non-existent naval lieutenant who in reality had been a third-rate actor. She could tell them about Archie, about the meetings in the Gatesmuir summerhouse, about the child that might have been his. She could tell them the callous things Lucy had said when she heard Ned was ill with alcoholic mania.

She could destroy her. She could have her banished from the family circle, sent away to live on a tiny allowance that would not permit the kind of airs and graces she found so necessary.

Easily. Hurt her. Kill her dream, make her poor and a nobody. Let her see contempt and dislike where before she'd seen admiration and love.

And what good would that do?

Franz was gone. It was over. And perhaps it was best so. The little boy needed his father, Franz needed his son. There was a marriage that ought to be preserved, built up. Franz was where he belonged, with his wife and child.

And she? She was here, alone again – but she was accustomed to that. She had been alone before and though she couldn't enjoy it she could bear it. She had much to be thankful for – her mother and her brother loved her, she had work she enjoyed, she was liked and respected by the community.

Oh yes, all that was true. But it didn't prevent the tears from spilling out on to her cheeks when she thought she would never see dear, loving, impetuous Franz again.

To prevent herself from drowning in self-pity she folded the letter and put it away. She turned her attention to the business letters that had come by the same post. She tried to work, making notes of what she would tell her chief clerk to do concerning this and that. But she found herself seeing Franz's face, picturing scenes they had shared.

It was an hour later before she rang for Muir. She gave him a little pile of work. 'I'm going out now – '

'But it's only nine-thirty, mistress.'

'I know, Mr Muir, but I want to speak to the station-master about greeting the deputation from the Turkish Board of Trade. I don't want any pointing and staring when they get off the train.'

'Well, you can give orders to the station staff, but you canna do much about the passers-by, mistress, and they'll stare at dark men in Arab robes – '

'Mr Muir, they are going to be wearing ordinary frock coats!' She swept out, looking indignant, and walked briskly through the entrance hall and out to the front courtyard. But her mind wasn't on the Turkish delegation, though she did indeed go to the station and ask Mr Gowan to ensure good manners.

She walked on, to the bridge over the Gala Water. When she came to the centre, she paused, leaning on the balustrade. She gazed down at the river running so strongly as the winter snow came down in the spring warmth. The birch and alder were hung with catkins, brownish purple in the weak sunlight.

She took out of her pocket the letter from Franz. She tore it across and across, then again, until it was only a handful of small squares. She reached out over the water, opened her hand.

The pieces fell like heavy snow, catching in the eddy where the water was divided by a floating log. For a moment they swirled, borne along by the current. Then they became saturated. One by one they disappeared under the sherry-brown surface, and were gone.

Herr Tabbler arrived three days later. As Franz had foretold, he brought a wife and a young son. They were immediately acknowledged as a great asset to the neighbourhood: Mrs Tabbler played the piano to perfection and sang in a good steady contralto, Mr Tabbler liked to go shooting and was interested in the game of golf, just beginning to be popular outside its native ground. The son went off to the Border Academy where he stood up to the teasing that was thought necessary by bloodying a few noses.

'He's a fine sturdy boy,' Millicent Corvill said with muted approval. 'I think he's over-ready with his fists but perhaps that will pass.'

'Ach, you've got to stand up for yourself,' her son said. 'But Mr Tabbler is a man after my own heart. He agrees with me that this book by Mr Darwin is just the raving of a madman.'

'Has he read it?' Jenny asked with interest, for all the efforts of the Corvill family to obtain a copy had failed.

'No, but you don't need to read the book to know it's nonsense – the reviewers have made that plain enough.'

'But surely, Ned, Mr Lucas in *The Times* – he talked of a solid bridge of facts, or some such phrase.'

'Mr Tabbler tells me that a friend of his in London has it on good authority that the review in fact was written by Professor Huxley, a friend of Darwin's, so you see it isn't to be believed for a moment.'

'Oh, Ned dear, don't let's talk about it. From the moment it appeared it seems to have done nothing but cause argument.'

'But we must talk about it, Mother. The man seems to be saying that the Bible does not contain the truth.'

'He can't say that, dear,' Mrs Corvill said with a smile.

'I don't even understand what the title means,' Lucy said, looking up from her fashion magazine. '*The Origin of Specials?*'

271

'*Of Species*, dearest. It means, where the different kinds of living things came from.'

'Oh, well, there was no need to write a book about that. Adam named them in the Garden of Eden.'

'If we believe Mr Darwin, there was no Garden of Eden.'

'Now, son, please don't go on about it,' Mrs Corvill said in reproof. 'It's all wicked nonsense and I don't wish to hear it discussed.'

The subject was changed, Ned was persuaded to read to them from *Idylls of the King*, Jenny sketched out a few new ideas for lightweight plaids, and the evening wound its sleepy way to its end. Jenny had no idea how important the subject was going to prove to her brother in the months to come. But then few people had any idea of how Charles Darwin's book was going to shake the foundations of religious faith.

The next day was Sunday. At church the minister delivered a rousing attack on the heresies in this strange new book. He himself – like everyone else in Galashiels – had not read it. But he was sure it was a very bad thing, and said so.

'It's going to be terribly boring if people go on and on about it,' Lucy said, as they set off for home.

'Boring? I'd hardly say it's boring, Lucy,' Jenny said. 'It's terribly important, by all I can gather. I do wish I could get hold of a copy so as to know what the man really said.'

'You don't really want to read dreadful things like that?' her sister-in-law said in horror.

'I like to face things,' Jenny said.

'Ah . . .'

Millicent came up, after having paused for a chat with one or two of the ladies of the congregation. 'Ned has stayed behind to talk to the elders about that awful book.' She sighed. 'I hope it's not going to upset him.'

They strolled on. Spring had come to the borders, the grass on the Cuddy Green was brilliant as emeralds, the birds were singing in full throat as they set about nest building.

'I thought *you* seemed a little upset recently,' Lucy said to Jenny.

'Me? What have I to be upset about?'

'Perhaps I was wrong. But I've had the notion this last week or two that you seem very quiet.'

'Lucy's right, Jenny,' her mother said. 'Are you quite well?'

'Perfectly, thank you, Mother.'

'I think you're working too hard,' her mother said, taking up a constant refrain.

'Not at all – '

'You came home absolutely exhausted after those terrible foreign people were here – '

'The Turkish delegation, you mean. I admit it wasn't much of a picnic trying to talk cloth manufacture through an interpreter. And they didn't like having to deal with a woman.'

'I thought you were surprised and upset at Mr Tabbler coming to replace Mr Lennhardt,' Lucy suggested.

'Oh, that was sad,' Millicent put in. 'Very sad, about his little boy. I wonder how he is?'

'Have you heard, Jenny?' Lucy asked.

'No. But we could ask Mr Tabbler for news.'

'So we could,' Millicent agreed.

Jenny knew Lucy had been pricking at her like a picador in a bullfight. She had taken care to show no response to the veiled hints. Nothing was to be gained by letting her sister-in-law know what she felt.

That afternoon, going up to her room to fetch a shawl, she found Lucy standing at her bureau, hand half-outstretched as if she were about to choose a book from the row in the bookrest.

Lucy swung round. She tried to smile, but her momentary fright had been visible.

'Were you looking for something?' Jenny inqured.

'I . . . just wanted something . . . something to read.'

The idea that Lucy would ever want anything more solid than a fashion journal was absurd. Jenny felt anger sweep through her. 'This is the book you wanted,' she said. She picked out *Vestiarium Scotium*. 'This is the book with the pressed flower in it.' She flicked over the pages. The flower lay on the open page.

Lucy looked at it. She had coloured up.

'And here,' Jenny said, 'is a scrap of the tartan I sold to the Queen and the Prince Consort. And here is another piece, the tartan I sold to the Tsarina. You're quite right, Lucy – this is where I hide my keepsakes.'

'I . . . I'm not interested in your keepsakes.'

'Then why are you here prying? What did you hope to find?'

'I'm not prying – '

'Is this what you were looking for?' Jenny said, holding out the dried hoya blossom. 'Here, take it – it's silly to keep it.'

'Ah no,' Lucy said in a sharp tone. 'You won't part with that! Franz gave it to you.'

'He did? How marvellous. Where did he come by it? There isn't a hothouse anywhere in the Borders that I know of where hoya is being grown. But by all means go and look for one – it will give you something to do.'

'Of course Franz gave it to you,' Lucy taunted. 'Why else were you keeping it?'

'Franz didn't give it to me.'

'Why bother to lie about it? You wouldn't keep it for any other reason.'

'Shall I tell you where it comes from?' Jenny said, wanting to wipe the smile of triumph from Lucy's face. 'It comes from the conservatory at Balmoral. It was given to me the day I went there to show the Stewart tartan to the Prince.'

'From Balmoral? Oh, come now – '

'From Balmoral. It was given to me as a memento of the day by the Prince's equerry.'

'I . . . I . . .'

'So you see, you made a bad guess – '

'You think you can hoodwink me! But I know you're breaking your heart over Franz Lennhardt.'

'No.'

'Oh, don't deny it – '

'Lucy, I don't want to waste my time denying things you've invented. What's wrong with you, that you want to meddle and pry like this?'

'That's right, try to make out I'm the deceitful one, while it's really you – you're the one – '

'No, Lucy, you're the one. You're the one who for some strange reason wants to do harm. Let me warn you: you shouldn't make an enemy of me. I know too much about you.'

Lucy tossed her blonde head. 'What can you know? You think you're so clever – '

'I know you've done some things you wouldn't like Ned to know about – '

'What does that mean? If you're saying I had anything to do with Franz going – '

'I never said that. Why should it spring to your mind? Guilty conscience? You know, I could write to Franz, as a business acquaintance keeping in touch; I could ask him why he decided not to come back.'

'No!'

'Would I find out something you'd rather keep hidden?'

'I've nothing to be ashamed of.'

'We both know that isn't true. I warn you, Lucy, you shouldn't make an enemy of me. I want peace in the family but if need be I would speak out. And now I'll ask you to leave my room and never come back into it unless I expressly invite you.'

Rather pale, Lucy obeyed. Jenny followed her. As they came downstairs to take the air in the garden Ned said cheerfully, 'Well now girls – been sharing secrets?'

'Yes,' Jenny said in a voice of sadness, 'secrets.'

Chapter Twenty

That spring brought a change to Jenny. There had been an ending but she felt it also as a new beginning. She looked at herself in the mirror and she thought, I'm not a girl any more. In a few months I shall be twenty-four.

And then she thought, If I really am going to be an old maid, I shall be a stylish old maid.

Formerly she hadn't paid too much attention to her appearance. To look pleasing, to wear clothes that were suitable and perhaps to shine a little on a special occasion – that had been her aim. She knew she had good looks but she had done little to emphasise them.

Baird, the personal maid, had to divide her services among the three women at Gatesmuir. Jenny had never called on her much except for the care and repair of clothes, preferring to dress and undress herself and do her own hair.

Now she called her in to review her wardrobe. She decided to develop a style of her own. She bought some very good lace to replace run-of-the-mill trimmings, she chose from the Waterside pattern book some pale, dignified tartans for her own particular use and had them woven not only in various grades of wool but in silk and poplin also. She got Baird to study the ladies' magazines for instructions on how to do the latest hair styles, and chose at last a very simple plain coiffure with a centre parting and a high chignon at the back.

'You're unco elegant, if you want my opinion,' Baird said, after she had helped her get ready for a summer party. 'Do you know the ladies are asking in the dressmakers for the Jenny Corvill fashion?'

Jenny viewed herself in the cheval glass. She was wearing

a gown of grey and blue plaid silk and a Mechlin lace shawl. 'I think, Baird,' she remarked. 'I'll have some parasols made in the tartans I use.'

'Parasols! There's no enough sun in Scotland for parasols!'

'But I think a parasol would be amusing . . . And then the ladies can go into the umbrella-makers and ask for the Jenny Corvill parasol. It's good for trade, Baird!'

Lucy watched the transformation with interest and something like respect. Between the two women there was a sort of careful truce – Lucy minded her manners, Jenny concealed her opinion, and no one guessed they had a seething dislike between them.

Ned was out and about on his temperance preaching as summer drew on. He addressed open air meetings, drew large crowds, began to be reported in the newspapers. His friends ceased to tease him, his neighbours began to view him as something of a celebrity – the more so as the argument over Mr Darwin and his book grew hotter.

Charles Kingsley, clergyman and popular novelist, believed that religion and the theory of evolution could be made to fit into one pattern. But that was not the opinion of most churchmen, so that they were eager to call in every supporter. Ned was a strong upholder of religion. He had to be – it was the lifeline that held him safe from alcohol.

He ran his temperance meetings somewhat like a debate. He would make a speech, recounting his own experience and begging the audience to follow his example in asking for God's help in fighting against drink. He would then call on them to 'witness' if they felt the call. This opportunity was sometimes seized by young men who wanted to attack bigoted religionists. 'What about Darwin?' they would shout. 'How can the Bible help you if it's a pack of lies?'

They had no idea how their taunts tortured Ned. 'They're laughing at something that has been the pillar of our society for two thousand years,' he said to Jenny one Sunday afternoon as they sat in the garden enjoying the peaceful sunlight.

'Perhaps they're not really laughing, Ned. Perhaps they're as worried as you are. It *is* a strange idea – that we've believed in something all these years that may not be true.'

'It is true!' Ned exclaimed.

Jenny put out a soothing hand to touch his sleeve. 'Perhaps one ought not to take it all as absolute fact,' she murmured. 'Some of it is perhaps based on legend – not to be taken quite literally.'

'How can you say so, Jenny! It's the word of God.'

'You used not to believe it so entirely, Ned.'

'That was before Dr Murdo brought me to see the sin of intellectual arrogance. I had no right to question – '

'Forgive me, dear, but I must disagree a little with that. Can you honestly say you don't question, even now, the literal truth of some of the things in the Old Testament? Do you *really* believe that God turned the Red Sea into dry land so that the Israelites could go over? Do you *really* believe ravens brought bread to Elijah?'

'Yes, of course, utterly.' But it was said with too much fervour. 'You don't seriously have doubts?'

'Well . . .' She could see he was very upset. There was a look of great strain about him. 'I don't know enough to speak on anything so important.'

'But I feel I must talk to someone, Jenny. Mother just smiles and waves it all away – how I envy her simple faith! And the church elders – they don't have the kind of quick mind that some of my questioners have. You see, I have to answer when people challenge me at the meetings, and I don't know what to say . . .'

'Why don't you go to Glasgow and have a talk with Dr Murdo?'

His face lit up. 'Yes! Why didn't I think of that! The doctor will know how to treat Mr Darwin and his wild theories.'

He made a space in his programme of meetings, and went to Glasgow with Lucy eagerly accompanying him. The trip was unusual enough to make his mother wonder about it. 'Why should he need to see Dr Murdo, Jenny? Is he feeling unwell?' She meant, had he been drinking.

'Oh no, Mother, he just needs to talk to Dr Murdo.'

'Talk about what?'

'About the religious reaction to Charles Darwin.'

'Oh, that,' Millicent said, with a smile and a shake of her head. 'Why is everybody so perturbed about it? Even if what the man says is true and we're here because nature picked out the best ones, somebody had to put the plan in action, didn't He? It's plain as the neb on your face.'

Jenny laughed. If only Ned could see it in such simple terms, what heartache he would save himself.

Lucy had insisted they must stay in Glasgow for at least a fortnight and have some enjoyment as well as religious reassurance. At the end of the trip she came home looking satisfied. She had spent a lot of money, bought a lot of clothes, seen a lot of plays, and met a lot of people. It had been a pleasure to her to find that the young Mrs Corvill was courted by good society. Ned, too, had been greeted with respect, when she went with him to one or two serious events.

'By the way, Jenny, I'll tell you who we met . . . That man, what was his name . . . My love, he was at that meeting of the Glasgow Scientific Society that you took me to.'

'I beg your pardon, Lucy? I didn't catch . . . ?'

'That man you spoke to at the lecture on the German thing about what's-its-name – you know, about all the different colours.'

'Spectrum analysis, dear,' Ned replied.

Jenny smothered a laugh. 'You found spectrum analysis fascinating, Lucy?'

'I didn't understand a single word,' Lucy confessed, with a deprecatory glance at her husband, 'but Lord Dearglen invited us so of course we had to go. He's the president of the society, you know. But what I was going to tell you was – remind me of that man's name, dear?'

'Who?'

'The man you spoke to – the man that used to work for you.'

'Oh, you mean Armstrong? Yes, what do you think, Jenny? We met Ronald Armstrong.'

It was strange how the name affected her. She felt a sudden shock, then a pleased and eager interest. 'You spoke to him? It's a long time since he left. How was he?'

'Oh, very well, I imagine. He'd been in Germany, he told me.'

'In Germany!'

'Yes, in Berlin. Something to do with dye-stuffs. You know, he's a very superior type of workman. He's studious – wants

279

to know more about underlying principles. Of course, the lecture about spectrum analysis wasn't strictly in his line because it's to do with optics, not chemistry, but he said he'd found it very interesting.'

Jenny's interest was more in the man than in the lecture. 'What is he doing now?' she inquired.

'I believe he said he was working with Pullar's of Perth. A very good firm.'

She found herself thinking, I could write to him, in care of his employers. I could ask him to forgive me for that awful blunder, and to come back. It would be so good to have him back – someone to depend on, to talk to . . .

But he wouldn't come back. She knew him well enough to be sure of that. His pride had been too deeply offended for him ever to forgive her. So there was no use in writing.

She longed to ask if he had mentioned her, but with Lucy there to catch every nuance she didn't dare. She waited until she got her brother alone and then said, 'Did Mr Armstrong send any message?'

'Message?'

'I'd have thought politeness would prompt him to send his respects.'

'Now that I come to think of it, Jenny, he didn't. But then, you parted on bad terms, didn't you?'

'What?' she said faintly. Surely nothing had been said by Ronald about their last meeting.

'Well, he walked out at a minute's notice, didn't he? Or you sent him packing on short order. I'd forgotten that.'

'It was a misunderstanding,' she heard herself saying. 'And it was all my fault. I wish he'd come back, Ned. Luchar isn't nearly as good with the dyes as Ronald Armstrong was.'

'Oh, I doubt he'll come back. He seems very well satisfied with his post at Pullar's. Never mind, Jenny, by and by you'll find a man for the dye department who's as good as Armstrong.'

She didn't believe it. But she kept the thought to herself.

In August came a message from someone much more important than Ronald Armstrong. Her Majesty's secretary wrote to say that the Queen would be leaving London at the beginning of September for a stay at her home in Balmoral and requested the pleasure of meeting Miss Jenny Corvill again, at Berwick-upon-Tweed on the royal train.

It was Lucy's first actual encounter with a letter from the Royal Household. She took it from Jenny's hands with awe. 'She actually wants to see *you!*' she breathed, when she had read it. 'I never truly understood before that you had met her face to face.'

Everyone in Galashiels soon knew that Jenny was to go to meet the Queen. The ladies became intensely interested in what she would wear, so that they could copy it as soon as possible. The men tried to find out if there was something on offer from Corvill and Son to the Royal Household and were rather disbelieving when told there was not.

'We must all go to Berwick-upon-Tweed!' Lucy declared. 'It would be too mortifying to be left behind, wouldn't it, Ned?'

'I wouldn't go quite so far as that. But I should certainly like to go to Berwick for the occasion – wouldn't you, Mother?'

'No, no, I'm no fond of travelling,' Millicent said comfortably. 'But go you and Lucy – it'll be a nice excursion and though you won't meet Her Majesty, you'll see her, and that's a pleasant thing.'

Jenny saw Lucy's face fall at the idea she wouldn't meet the Queen. 'Surely, as the wife of the owner of the firm . . .'

'But I'm not asked to meet Her Majesty,' Ned pointed out. 'The letter was to Jenny specifically.'

This didn't deter Lucy from speaking of the matter as if she and Ned were included in the party invited to Berwick. Jenny decided not to correct the impression that had been given. When she was taken to the Prince Consort's private secretary in Berwick on the day, she asked him if she might request a great favour.

'Let me hear it, Miss Corvill,' General Grey said with affability, smoothing his whiskers.

'My brother is the actual owner of the firm of Corvill and Son, for whom I have acted as representative on past occasions. He and his wife are with me in Berwick. It would be a great honour if they could be presented to Their Majesties.'

'Ahh, that is difficult, Miss Corvill. There are a number of town dignitaries and so forth who have already received notice that they will be presented. I hardly think . . .'

Jenny held back a sigh. 'I qute understand, General. I had no right to ask, only that my sister-in-law is so keenly interested in everything to do with the royal family.'

The general gave her a look with his head on one side. He approved of her – she had an air of quiet distinction in her pale gown and bonnet. Her dark hair shone from under the dove grey hat brim, her dark eyes looked up at him undemandingly. He thought it would be pleasant if more of the people he had to deal with were as reasonable as the beautiful Miss Corvill.

'We'll see what we can do,' he said. 'This, after all, is an informal occasion – a royal progress, true, but in holiday spirit. Perhaps it can be managed. Your brother and his wife are hard by?'

'Oh, yes, sir – they are in a carriage a few yards from the station entrance.'

'I'll send someone to bring them into the waiting-room. If Their Majesties are not too pressed, they may perhaps agree.'

The Corvills had spent the night at the King's Arms on Hide Hill. They had slept badly because of the excitement in the town and had been up early – like everyone else – arraying themselves in their best clothes. The royal train had come into the station on the beautiful viaduct during the night, and had stood there while the royal family breakfasted and made ready to receive the notables of the borough.

Jenny was taken to the train after only a short wait. The carriages, lent for royal use by the London and Northwest Railway until special conveyances could be built, were elegant, with lace curtains tied back and flowers in silver holders. There was a 'bed carriage' further back, its windows discreetly veiled, but the carriage into which Jenny was conducted was what had until recently been called a 'posting carriage', in other words a saloon.

The Queen and her husband were sitting on a velvet-padded sofa, with a mahogany table in front of them. There was scarcely room for Jenny to make her curtsey. General Grey bowed and withdrew – perhaps to leave some space.

'Sit down, Miss Corvill. I am happy to see you again,' said the Queen, smiling and nodding. 'You are well, I hope?'

'Yes, thank you Ma'am. May I express my great sense of honour at your invitation – '

'Yes, yes, Miss Corvill, but we had a motive!' said the Prince, something that was almost vivacity lighting up his pale face. 'My good young lady, we wish to call in your expert abilities.'

'Oh, Your Highness, anything I could do . . .'

The royal couple smiled at each other. This was clearly something that pleased them both very much. 'We have decided,' Victoria announced, 'to have a regiment formed in honour of His Royal Highness. It is to be called the Prince's Scottish Regiment. This is to denote our great pleasure in and our gratitude to the Scottish people, for all the joys we have known in their country.'

Jenny was touched. There was something sentimental yet genuine in their attitude. 'I repeat, anything I can do for Your Majesties – '

'Miss Corvill, the planning is quite well advanced. But before we make a public announcement we should like to have drawings of the uniform and accoutrements to give to the press. The uniform has been designed by my dear husband,' said Victoria, with a glance of loving admiration at Albert. 'However, he has not been able to make a tartan that pleases him. To tell the truth, his time is so limited . . .'

'My dear, it is not a matter of time so much as talent. I can make a household tartan, but this is something much more important.' He turned to Jenny. 'Can you design a tartan for my Scottish regiment, Miss Corvill?'

'I, sir?'

'Don't look so astounded. You have made many good patterns. I have seen them. And the one you gave to us for the children – that was extremely pleasing.'

'But that was – '

'I know, it was a variation of a genuine plaid. This is something more difficult. You will have to start from nothing. But you have done that many times for the public.'

'That's different from making a tartan for a regiment, sir.'

'I agree. But I should like you to try. Will you do that, young lady?'

'Why, Your Highness, of course I will try . . .'

'That is all we ask. The matter is fairly urgent – I should like to announce recruitment for the regiment in the spring, and soon after that we shall want to issue kilts to the men. So that gives you . . . shall we say three months to bring us designs and three months to make the cloth after we have chosen?'

'Your Majesty, I shall do my very best. But supposing I don't produce anything to your liking . . . ?'

'Then I suppose we delay the announcement and ask some other designer to try.' The Prince shrugged. 'Don't worry too much, Miss Corvill. We shall undoubtedly find a tartan to suit the need, but the Queen and I would be very pleased if it were your design. We feel we have a long-standing interest in you.'

'Your Highness is too kind,' Jenny said, hardly knowing how to find words to respond to so much benevolence.

The Prince picked up a leather folder in which there were several sheets of paper. 'These are the thoughts of the Queen and myself on the grounding of the regiment. It shall be recruited in the Highlands, mainly, and shall have as its motto "Steady of heart and stout of hand", from Sir Walter Scott – '

'*The Lay of the Last Minstrel*', Jenny murmured.

'Ah! You see, we were right!' the Prince said with a laugh, turning to his wife. 'She catches the thought at once. Well, look through these papers, Miss Corvill. The regiment will probably be based at Grantown, where we have had so many happy visits and viewed such glorious scenery. If you think of that district, its mountains, its moors, its lakes and rivers . . .'

'Yes, sir, I understand.'

'And now I believe your relations are coming to be presented.'

Jenny could do no more than curtsey and murmur thanks. The honour of the commission to design the tartan had been quite enough to overpower her: the kindness in sparing time to see Ned and Lucy was too much. To her own dismay and annoyance, she felt tears brimming at her eyes. Absurd . . . Yet it was a great occasion, and she had been singled out.

Ned came in, knocking his head on the low ceiling of the carriage. Lucy followed, looking angelically fair and fragile in her pale blue velvet gown. The Queen smiled, the Prince bowed, Ned bowed, Lucy curtseyed.

'We are pleased to receive you,' said Victoria.

'Thank you, Ma'am,' muttered Ned.

'Yes, thank you, Ma'am,' gasped Lucy.

Next moment they had been quietly ushered out, and the royal audience was over.

The locomotive had been quietly hissing steam for some minutes. The station-master advanced, stovepipe hat clasped over his bosom. The door of the royal saloon carriage was closed, steps were carried away, attendants leapt into carriages at the rear, doors slammed. The wheels began to turn.

The crowd on the platform cheered. The people lining the track waved. Below on the River Tweed the paddlesteamer *Susan* tooted its siren. The bunting blew in the brisk breeze coming from Holy Island, and gulls swooped overhead screaming inquiry at all the turmoil.

In a few moments the royal train disappeared on its way north. The Corvills turned to one another. 'I met the Queen!' Lucy said, lips parted in blissful amazement.

'Was there a special reason why she sent for you?' Ned asked his sister.

'You might say so.' Suddenly Jenny was filled with excitement and pride. 'She's asked me to design a new tartan for a new Scottish regiment!'

285

Chapter Twenty-one

Though it was a Sunday, the King's Arms had set on an eight-course luncheon in honour of the day. The town's notables were gathered there celebrating their moment of fame. The Corvills were welcomed among them as people of equal consequence. They had a place of honour at one end of a long table at the head of which sat the Provost and the Town Constable.

Lucy was in her element. Through the *consommé* she talked to the chief magistrate and when the *filet de saumon monarque* was brought she turned to her other neighbour, the stationmaster, to discuss rail travel.

Dishes were placed before Jenny and removed almost untasted. Her thoughts were already engaged on the problem set for her by Victoria and Albert. Colours and shapes were forming and dissolving before her mind's eye. She had to rouse herself as the *canard sauvage roti* was served, to be polite to her neighbours, two local landowners.

As soon as she could she left the after-luncheon groups. Her departure was unnoticed since some of the town fathers, having missed church that morning, now felt they must sleep off a too-lavish meal to be ready for evening service. She put on her jacket and took a shawl, to walk down Hide Hill and out through the arch to the side of the harbour. The breeze was strong now, full of salt and the tang of seaweed as the tide ran out at the rivermouth.

Mountains and moors, lakes and rivers: grey shale, green moss, purple heather, grey-blue lochs that reflected back the sky, dark brown rivers carrying the peaty water to the sea.

White for clouds, for the silver of fish in the lochs, for the gleam of birch trees on a hillside. Dark green for pines lonely against the sky. Fawn for the hide of the deer, for the pine marten skittering among the branches.

Which? Which to choose? Where to start?

Certainly she must read and re-read the notes Prince Albert had given her about the structure of the regiment. It was to be an infantry regiment, she recalled from skimming through the papers already.

A vision sprang up before her eyes: men marching, making their way through a pass – in some foreign land, for the trees were unfamiliar and there was sand underfoot. Shadows were dark beneath the rocks.

Not too much white in the kilts, then – it would gleam and glint too much, especially if the men were engaged in a night attack.

'Gracious goodness, why are you mooning about out here?' said a sharp voice behind her.

Dragged back from her vision, she felt a moment's actual faintness. She turned. It was Lucy, of course. 'Sister-in-law, what for did you slip away like that? We've been having such an interesting conversation with Viscount Hendry, and he specifically asked for a word with you, and as Ned was off inquiring for a strict protestant church for evening service, I thought I'd better . . . But if I'd known how horrid this wind was, I'd have sent a servant.'

Perforce Jenny turned back along the cobbled road. Boats in the harbour were beginning to tilt as the water ebbed from under them. Their celebration bunting canted over; jagged lines of colour against the weed-draped walls of the harbour. Jenny saw it with pleasure – so different from the quiet stretches of the Gala Water running between its tree-lined banks.

It came home to her that she didn't travel enough. She sought inspiration for her patterns in the world around her, but as she watched the Tweed glide under its bridge and run to the sea she knew she was becoming limited. Galashiels and the hills around it were dear to her now but she ought to see other places. She remembered Edinburgh and its brownish castle-rock, she thought of the smoke-stained buildings of Glasgow – there was inspiration to be found in many places for shades and colours.

But not yet. First she must concentrate on the work she

had been commissioned to do. Three months to prepare a design – time was short.

On the train journey back to Galashiels she read through the notes in the folder. They mentioned the number of companies, the junior status at which the regiment must join the infantry brigade, the possible number of staff officers and the buildings now available in Grantown-on-Spey as head-quarters, notably some sites left when the railway had been completed on through the wilderness of Brae Moray.

Brae Moray. She had never been there. Except for that short trip six years ago to Balmoral she had never been to the Highlands, the home of the cloth from which she made her living.

She made a decision. As soon as she was home she would attend to a few urgent matters and then she would make a trip to the mountains, to see what it was that had bewitched the Queen and her husband so deeply. Without seeing the country that they had seen, she doubted if she could ever capture what it was the Prince wanted from her as the tartan of his regiment.

The carriage was there to meet them at Galashiels Station. She waved the porter to put her luggage in, but turned away from her brother and his wife to have a conference with Mr Gowan, the station-master. 'I want to go to Grantown-on-Spey, Mr Gowan.'

'What? Now?'

She laughed. 'I'm sorry, of course not – in a day or two. Let's see – today's Monday, I've things to do that will take me tomorrow and next day. Shall we say I'd like to travel on Thursday?'

'Whaur to again, Mistress Corvill?' Gowan said, gasping a little as he tried to keep up with her thought processes.

'Grantown-on-Spey.'

'Och, aye, you'll go by the new line, then. Let me see . . .'

'I leave it with you, Mr Gowan. I suppose I must stay overnight at Edinburgh and then travel on?'

'We'll see, we'll see, the connections mebbe will favour a stop somewhere else. Shall I send a wee telegraphic message for a hotel wherever seems best?'

'Yes, for Thursday night, I think. And then the Friday I'll be at Grantown?'

'Aye, ah-huh, aye, I'll sort it for you, mistress, just give me an hour or two wi' the timetables.'

When she rejoined Ned and Lucy she found Lucy fidgeting with annoyance. 'Do hurry yourself, Jenny, I'm dying to get out of this travelling costume.'

'Go you home then, my dear,' Jenny replied. 'I think I'll walk to the mill and see that everything is all right.'

'Don't you want to change first?' Lucy said in amazement.

'No, I'll do fine as I am. Tell Mother I'll be home by four, I shan't work a full day.'

Lucy cast her eyes up to heaven, as if to say, Who in their senses would work even an hour, after a journey in a rattling branch-line train?

At the mill Jenny went at once to the yarn store. She wanted to fill her eye with the colours of wool, to feel the textures under her fingers, to seek from them as she had a hundred times before the inspiration for a new cloth.

Mr Muir, her chief clerk, pursued her with urgent correspondence. Sighing, she went to her office. She worked efficiently for an hour or two then, called again by the inner voice that was speaking to her about the new tartan, she went out into the town.

It was mid-afternoon. The place was quietly busy. She walked west along the mill lane, then up the slope towards Gala Hill. There was a bench by the church. She sat there, looking at the September sunshine on the rose sandstone of the houses, the tint of the trees as autumn laid her fingertips upon them.

The scene was full of colour, of light and shade. But it wasn't the wild light of the northland where the regiment would be quartered. She would see that soon, in a few days.

Millicent was in vehement opposition when Jenny told her her plans. 'Dear sakes, child, you won't have been home long enough to take a wheezing breath! What's the need to go rushing off again?'

'I must see the Highlands. Ned told you what the Queen wants me to do?'

'Aye, and a great honour for all, and very pleasant for Lucy to have such a long chat with Her Majesty – '

'A long chat?' Jenny stared then shrugged. 'Well, no matter. Mr Gowan is making the arrangements for me and I'll be off on Thursday.'

'Then I shall come with you.'

'Mother! Why on earth should you?'

'I could visit my brother in Dornoch – '

'Mother dear,' Ned intervened, 'Dornoch is another eighty miles or so north of where Jenny is going. I don't even know if the railway line goes that far – it might have to be done by stage-coach.'

'Oh,' said Millicent, taken aback. Her knowledge of geography was strictly limited. 'Well, but I must go because it's not fitting for Jenny to go alone.'

'But I've travelled alone before – '

'Not into the wilds of the Highlands, daughter!'

'The wilds of the Highlands! The Queen walks about in the wilds with perfect safety,' commented Lucy.

'The Queen has a husband and John Brown to look after her. It's no use arguing, I'm coming with you, Jenny.'

'But Mother, you always get travel sickness. You didn't even want to go as far as Berwick.'

'Well, I . . . I'll overcome all that.'

'It's a quite unnecessary discomfort for you. I'll take Baird, and you know Baird is a fine dragon.'

When she got her mother alone Jenny put forward another reason, equally good. 'I want you here to look after Ned.'

'Ned? Lucy can look after Ned.'

'Lucy can be a wee bit inattentive. Remember, it was while they were on their own in Glasgow that Ned fell sick.'

Her mother spoke with unexpected severity. 'Ned brought that upon himself. Lucy cannot be held to blame.'

'But she left it very late to call for help, Mother. And he's been very nervy and upset recently.'

'That stupid book!' Mrs Corvill burst out. 'Everyone is in a tither about it. The ladies in the Sewing Circle tell me their fathers and husbands talk about nothing else.' She shook her head. 'I thought after Ned had seen Dr Murdo, his mind would be at rest?'

290

Jenny had asked her brother what Murdo had said about Charles Darwin and *The Origin of Species*. 'He says it's a trial sent by God to test the strength of true believers.'

'Like Job in the Bible?'

'Exactly!'

Jenny forbore to point out that Job reached a point where he cried, 'Let the day perish wherein I was born!' Besides, she couldn't understand why God should put Ned to the test – Ned who was only hanging on by his fingernails against the need for a good glass of whisky.

Ned was still waiting for a copy of the book. The Edinburgh bookseller promised it any day now by post. Jenny was afraid that it would come while she was away and that her brother, in the midst of his temperance campaigning, would find time to read it. What the result would be she dreaded to think. From the reviews she'd read in the journals she gathered it was a well-argued scientific treatise. Ned had until recently always had a very open mind, trained in logic. The book might find a crack in his over-protective shield of faith.

Perhaps she ought to stay at home to help her brother through the crisis. Yet she needed, she really needed, to see the country which might give inspiration for the new tartan – and time was short. She must go now.

She comforted herself with the thought that she'd seen letters in the newspapers from clergymen who pleaded for calm, who said they themselves had been able to reconcile this shatteringly new view of the world with belief in a loving God. Surely her intelligent, well-educated brother could come to a similar conclusion without a sister to soothe him like a child?

Her tickets were brought to the office by a railway porter on the day before she was to travel. She looked them over, glanced at the list of destinations and connections. 'Overnight stay at the Royal George Hotel, Perth.' The place name jarred her eagerness to be on her way.

Perth. Ronald Armstrong lived and worked there now.

She hurried along to the station to speak to Mr Gowan. 'I didn't want to stop in Perth,' she said.

He stared at her. 'What for no?'

'Well, I . . . . I wanted to get further on before stopping for the night.'

'Where to? Dunkeld? Pitlochry? They're wee places, Mistress Corvill – ye're better off at Perth for the comfort and convenience.'

'Couldn't I go on to Kingussie?'

'Oh, aye, I hear there's a fine new inn there – but it would make you nearly two hours later for your supper and bed, and when you're travelling it's ill to be late at the hotel, do you no find that, mistress?'

It was only too true.

'I'd have to send a message immediately to alter the hotel arrangements,' Gowan went on, frowning at her. He didn't want her to upset his beautiful schemes.

'No . . . I see it would be best to go with your plan, Mr Gowan.' After all, she would reach Perth around six tomorrow. At that time Mr Armstrong might very well be still at work in his dye-room and since the city was fairly large, there was hardly the slightest chance that she would run across him. 'Yes, very well, thank you, Mr Gowan, we'll go ahead as we are.'

Baird grumbled and muttered through the first stages of their journey. She had once been to the grouse moors with the family of a former employer, a shipping magnate. 'There's scarcely a level step, it's a' either up or down, and damp underfoot so that there's no keeping a clean hem – '

'Baird, if you hate it so much you can stay in the hotel once we get there! Now, can I have some peace to read my book?'

She was studying a treatise on the history of the British Army. Her chief interest was in the uniform. She had already learned that until after Waterloo British soldiers almost exclusively wore scarlet tunics, which dismayed her at first, for she couldn't envisage the tartan she might design as worn with a scarlet jacket.

But as she read she realised that changes had come about in the present century. The officer's blue greatcoat had been shortened to a frock coat worn on parade and then further to a jacket. More recently some regiments, particularly in the artillery and rifle brigades, had adopted dark green or grey jackets. She wasn't called upon to design anything except the tartan for the kilt – others would deal with the uniform and the accoutrements. Yet it was a comfort to her to think there might be a quiet colour to go with the rather sombre tartan already beginning to weave its web in her mind.

At Perth the porter put their luggage into a hackney. 'Is it far to the Royal George?' Jenny asked.

'It's by the bowling green – you'll see it in a minute in the gloaming, mistress.'

She had to admit to herself she was glad to have fallen in with Gowan's wishes. She was weary of constant motion. The hotel was excellent, spacious and elegant, with the blessing of trees and greenery around it. Glad to change out of her travel costume and to wash the grime of train smoke from her face, Jenny relaxed with Baird over a substantial meal.

Afterwards, since it was still early and she felt in need of exercise, she strolled out to look at the River Tay, which lay just beyond the bowling green outside the hotel. It was a cool September evening. Lamps shone on the bridge to her left. To her right, a ferry was making its laborious way to the Kinnoull Church side. In the distance someone was playing a fiddle, a plaintive air.

She walked towards Sir Walter Scott's monument at the end of the High Street. Here was the commercial centre, all the banks were grouped nearby. Sight of the post office reminded her she ought to write a line to her mother. It was still open. She went in, bought a folding letter, and sat down to write.

'Dear Mother, We have safely arrived in Perth where the hotel is very comfortable. Weather cool enough to hire a foot-warmer for the train but it stays fine.' She paused, thinking what else to say.

She heard a voice she knew. 'Is there a special delivery packet for me, Mr Howe?'

'Ah, Mr Armstrong. Bide a minute, I'll see.'

Jenny was sitting at a desk near the door, with her back to the counter. She turned her head a little.

That unmistakeable tall, angular figure . . . He was leaning with one elbow on the counter, whistling to himself as he waited. He took off his hat to smooth his hair – sandy hair that gleamed in the light from the gas lamps.

Jenny felt her heart lurch at the sight of him. All the blood seemed to rush from her face, she felt cold, almost dizzy. She

293

turned back to her letter, bent her head and leaned on one hand to recover.

'Here you are, Mr Armstrong. "Fragile, Handle with Care" – more dyestuffs, is it?'

'Aye, urgently wanted, Mr Howe. I'm hanging about at the works for them. Good evening to you.'

She could hear his footsteps. He walked swiftly past her, his open jacket brushing her elbow.

She would go after him, call his name, apologise for the past. It was foolish to be in the same town with him, to be only yards away from him, and not take some step to repair their friendship.

She got up to hurry after him. But her knees seemed to buckle under her, she fell back on her chair.

When at last she got out into the street he was gone. Yet all she need do was ask the way to the firm of Pullar's. At the gates she could inquire for him.

She walked a dozen steps up the High Street, almost at random, thinking to find a carriage and be taken to the works.

But then she slowed, becoming aware of the letter in her hand, unfinished.

She must write to her mother and get it in the post before the mail train left.

Anything, rather than face Ronald Armstrong and try to say she was sorry.

Chapter Twenty-two

There were two lengths of tartan cloth, wrapped in blue tissue paper and in a cardboard box made to fit them exactly. It lay on the seat of the hansom cab carrying Miss Genevieve Corvill of Corvill and Son to Buckingham Palace.

The date was Tuesday 11 December. Almost to the hour and the minute, Jenny was bringing the kilt tartan to the Queen. She had already sent two small pattern pieces of the two tartans she had designed, but now she had a sample length of each, hand-woven by herself on her father's old loom and hand-finished to be ready in good time.

She was conducted at once to a room she had not seen before. It looked more like an office than the drawing-room where she had found the Queen on her previous visit. Victoria was alone, reading an official document. She laid it aside as Jenny was shown in.

'Good morning, Miss Corvill.'

Jenny curtseyed, then took from the footman the box she had brought.

'These are the lengths you spoke of in your letter?'

'Yes, Ma'am. It's easier to see what the pattern is like when there is a length giving several repetitions.' With a glance at the Queen for permission, she untied the box, brought out the lengths and laid them on the back of a leather armchair.

The Queen rose. She studied the plaids with her head on one side.

'The Prince is not able to be with us today,' she said. 'He is not quite well.'

'Oh, I'm sorry, Your Majesty.'

'It's nothing, a digestive upset.' But Victoria looked a little anxious. 'However, he and I have discussed the designs you sent, and now that I see them in greater length I realise our choice was correct. The Prince and I were greatly pleased with this one, Miss Corvill.'

It was the one Jenny had known would please them.

She had taken as her inspiration the ancient Montgomery tartan, red and black lines crossing on a purple background. She had replaced the red line with white, and halved the purple background with a dark green mixing check, adding a single brown line to define the perpendicular edge. The effect was austere, sombre, but dignified.

She touched each of the colours now. 'Purple for the heather, Your Majesty, green for the pine trees. Brown for the peaty rivers, black for the rocks as they break the surface of the stream, white for the snow on the mountain tops.'

'You have been there,' the Queen said. 'You have caught the tints exactly.'

'I was there in September. In fact, I saw Your Majesty in Grantown, but it was clear you were travelling incognito so I didn't intrude.'

'Oh, yes, it was so delightful! We called ourselves Lord and Lady Churchill, and General Grey was simply Dr Grey . . .' Her voice was wistful as she recalled that holiday time. 'Well, Miss Corvill, the Prince and I have decided that we shall use this design for the regimental tartan. It shall be called Grantown, for the headquarters barracks. The Prince is designing a jacket to go with it; we think it may be made of the green you have used as the broad check with the purple.'

'I look forward to seeing it.'

'The quartermaster is now set up at Grantown. I should like you to send this sample to him. He will tell you how much he needs for the regimental tailor so that you can at once begin manufacture. He will also forward an invitation to a little celebration the officers are giving to honour their new tartan. I trust you can attend?'

'On what date, Ma'am?'

'I believe it is New Year's Day. They are anxious to come together as a regiment – the officers are, of course, seconded or volunteers from other regiments.' She rose. 'We are very pleased, Miss Corvill. We put our faith in you and we have not been disappointed.'

She held out her hand, Jenny took it and curtseyed; the audience was over.

When the invitation arrived it was addressed to Miss Corvill of Corvill and Son, and was accompanied by a letter from Colonel Alistair Craig inviting Edward Corvill and his good lady as well. Lucy was ecstatic. To be invited to a unique occasion, by order of the Queen herself . . . She launched into a flurry of activity to get a balldress made, only to be stopped in full tilt when Jenny pointed out that the celebration was timed for three in the afternoon on 1 January.

'Well, then, I shall have an afternoon gown of velvet trimmed with ermine! I am determined to be equal to the occasion!'

Though the weather was cold, snow did not hinder their journey. They put up at the Grant Arms, and they found that all the other occupants were the families of the regimental officers. Hogmanay was celebrated rather quietly, with a long evening meal that took them to midnight and a piper to play in the New Year. Guests first-footed each other with gifts of sweets or cake, but there was less drinking than usual because most of the residents wanted to be up in good time for the carriage drive to Grantown Barracks in all their finery.

If Jenny had expected to see a sample of the uniform of the Prince's Scottish Regiment, she was disappointed. The soldiers on duty were in kilts which were a miscellany of tartans worn with black jackets. The officers in the great hall were likewise somewhat motley. They favoured some version of the blue or black frock coat and trousers, with epaulettes still denoting their former regiments, and a white belt.

Colonel Craig was the only man in the Grantown tartan – he had had dress trews made from the sample length Jenny had sent. He grinned and tugged at his moustaches in embarrassment when he saw her eye light upon them. 'What do you think, eh? Smart, en't they? The braid down the side is the Prince's idea. I couldn't get a jacket made in time. But next time you see us, we'll be in full fig, you can rely on it, kilts and sporrans and all.'

The Prince had presented a set of silver drinking cups to

the regiment. These were on display at first and then in use. Whisky was brought in a large flagon, and poured lavishly.

Jenny accepted a glass, as did Ned and Lucy. But they didn't drink. Jenny watched her brother with some anxiety, for in the last few weeks he had been edgy and often had looked tempted when wine was served.

He had at last read the fateful book *The Origin of Species*, but had refused to discuss it with Jenny. That had worried her more than an outburst of anger would have done. She had been quite glad of the invitation to come to the regimental celebration as a way of taking his mind off it.

She was chatting with the quartermaster when she heard her name spoken. She turned, thinking she knew the voice from somewhere in the past.

She found herself facing Captain Bobby Prentiss, former equerry to the Prince Consort.

She went red and then white. When she was able to focus her gaze on him, she found he was smiling ironically. 'Well, Miss Corvill, it's many a long year since last we met.'

She drew a deep breath to steady herself. 'Yes, and under very different circumstances.'

'You two know each other?' inquired Captain Hall.

'Oh, yes, we met ages ago at Balmoral. Didn't we, Miss Corvill?'

There was a taunting note in his voice. She decided to quell him. 'Is your wife with you, Captain?'

'Yes, she's with the Colonel's wife. And it's Major Prentiss now, Miss Corvill. I decided to volunteer for the Prince's Regiment because it was a most encouraging promotion.'

'I thought you hoped for the diplomatic service?'

'Ah yes.' He sighed. 'But that looked more and more unlikely so I decided to return to my army career.'

'You know Mrs Prentiss too?' Captain Hall said. 'I'll fetch her, I expect you two would like to renew old acquaintance.'

Before she could stop him, he had hurried off. And then a toast was called: 'The Queen!' Everyone stopped to raise a glass to the Queen before Colonel Craig launched into his speech.

He spoke fulsomely of the Prince's inspiration in forming a new Highland regiment, asked them to toast His Royal High-

298

ness, invited Colonel McDowell to speak on the training of the forthcoming recruits who were to be mountain infantry. Then he called for a toast to the Highlands and its men.

So it went on. The officers were accustomed to hard drinking. Whisky flowed like Spey water. Jenny glanced round in anxiety for Ned. He was under stress already, and in surroundings like this it must be very hard for him to keep to his vow of abstinence.

She saw him at the far side of the room in the clutches of a hirsute officer who was roaring with laughter at his own jokes. Lucy was flirting coyly with a young lieutenant off in a corner of the draughty hall. Jenny began to thread her way to Ned, to be a support to him.

'Miss Corvill!' It was Laura Prentiss. 'So, here you are!'

'It seems so,' Jenny said, pausing in her move.

'Had I known you were to be here, nothing would have induced me to come!'

Jenny sighed. 'Mrs Prentiss, I am here because I was asked to attend by Her Majesty. I had no idea your husband had volunteered for the regiment but I should not have stayed away even if I knew. I care so little whether I see either of you that it makes no difference to me.'

Laura drew back in surprise. Captain Hall, who had been her escort across the room, caught up with her. 'Having a chat about old times, ladies?' he said cheerfully.

'Excuse me,' Jenny said in some desperation, 'I must join my brother.'

'Ladies and Gentlemen,' called Colonel Craig. 'Another and most important toast. Steward, please see that all glasses are charged. Officers of the Prince's Scottish Regiment, ladies, and guests, I ask you to raise your glasses in honour of Miss Genevieve Corvill, without whose artistic endeavours I should not be wearing these splendid trousers this afternoon. But, in seriousness, my friends – to the honour of the regimental tartan, and to the lady who designed the Grantown plaid of the Prince's Scottish Regiment!'

Jenny had to stand still while everyone called her name and drank with acclaim, except for Laura Prentiss, who ostentatiously turned her back. She could have spared herself the trouble, for Jenny's attention was on Ned. He too raised his glass, an expression on his face that was something like jealousy. Jenny thought, It would have been better if they hadn't drunk a toast to me – it should have been to the firm of Corvill and Son. She tried to move from the group that was pressing in upon her, congratulating her. But she was trapped.

She saw Ned hesitate, pause for a moment, and then, quite deliberately, carry the glass to his lips. He tossed off the whisky. Before she could move, he had held the glass out to be refilled by a passing servant.

By the time the celebration broke off at five, he was very drunk. Lucy was embarrassed, Jenny was aghast, and Bobby Prentiss came to their aid with ironic amusement. 'It seems to me that every time I meet your brother, he's foxed to a stupor,' he remarked.

Jenny hadn't the spirit to reprimand him for his careless tone. 'Please help me get him into the carriage.'

Shrugging, Major Prentiss heaved him in. He helped Jenny in next, and then Lucy. To Lucy he said, 'I hear you're his wife? What a waste!'

A day that should have been a pleasure to Jenny had turned into a disaster. And worse was to come because, even after they at last got Ned home to Galashiels he refused to stop drinking.

'What's the point?' he shrugged when Jenny begged him to go again to see Dr Murdo. 'He's wrong. I think I always knew he was wrong but I needed him so much I made myself believe in him and his Redeemer. But I know better now. It's all a sham, the whole thing – life, the world, the hereafter. It's pointless, useless, worthless.'

As if it weren't bad enough to have her brother drowning himself in the bottle, things were going badly at Waterside Mill. The cloth ordered by the Prince's Scottish Regiment was not coming off the finishing presses in good condition.

Purple, one of the main background colours, had always been difficult to 'fix'. It was little used in the ancient tartans for that very reason. In using it for the Grantown tartan, Jenny had relied on a new dye from Germany, induribinone.

She had asked her dyemaster, Walter Luchar, to provide her with deep purple yarn to the shade she had shown him on her design. Using induribinone, he had done so. She had been satisfied with the colour and when she wove it on the handloom she had been satisfied with the effect. She had had the length of cloth handfinished to save time.

But now that the main pieces from the weaving shop were being finished by steam press and using a much higher temperature than in handfinishing, the colour subtly changed. It took on a reddish tint that was quite unsuitable.

Jenny and her workmen had tried everything they knew to 'fix' the purple. She would stay late at the mill watching Luchar try a larger dose of bisulphite, a smaller dose, more milk of lime, less zinc dust . . . Each time the yarn looked good; a rich, smooth purple. But each time it was pressed in the piece, it took on what Luchar called a 'flush'.

They had been struggling now for three weeks. In two months they were expected to deliver the first half of an order of seven thousand yards of Grantown tartan to the regimental tailors of the Prince's Scottish Regiment.

It was by now almost impossible to fill the order.

It seemed to Jenny there was no peace either at home or at work. Lucy wept, her mother prayed under her breath, Ned ranted against the world in general and his family in particular. At the mill Luchar looked more and more anxious, and became less reliable the more his nerve was shaken. The girls at the looms glanced round as Jenny passed, and she could almost hear them saying. She's bitten off more than she can chew at last!

On a cold evening in early February she came back from the finishing room to her office. Another 'piece' of cloth ruined under the steam rollers. Another twenty yards of disastrous tartan, unsuitable for anything except horse blankets.

It was late. She was very tired. She ought to go home. But if she went home, what would she find except distress and unrest?

She laid her arms on her blotter and let her head droop on to them. She closed her eyes. How quiet it was here in the empty mill. How lovely just to stay here for ever, with all the machines silent and all the people gone. No one to worry her, to demand decisions, just herself and the silent building with its smell of wool fibres and oil and dye.

There seemed to be a sound in the entrance hall. She half lifted her head. Her office door opened, a tall figure came in.

'Well, Miss Jenny Corvill, I hear you've gotten yourself in a bonny fix wi' your grand new tartan?'

There, like an angel from heaven, stood Ronald Armstrong.

Chapter Twenty-three

A thousand phrases of delight and welcome rushed to Jenny's lips. The words she actually uttered were: 'What do you hear, then, Ronald Armstrong?'

'I hear your purple won't press.'

'Who told you that?'

'Walter Luchar has been letting out moans of anxiety for a couple of weeks. Anybody who's interested in the Corvill works has heard about it.'

'Walter Luchar has worked like a Trojan – '

'Och, Trojans only know about wooden horses,' Ronald said with a grin. 'You need somebody that knows about dyes.'

'And you know about dyes, of course.'

'Why else am I here?'

She rose to her feet to come round her desk and stare up at him. 'Why *are* you here, Ronald?'

'I'm here to sort your purple dye for you.'

'You've given up your job at Pullar's?'

'No, I've taken a wee holiday.'

'In February?'

'A free man can take a holiday when he wants.'

'But . . . why should you want?' She laid a hand on his sleeve. Her throat felt dry. 'Ronald, I've wished so often that I hadn't behaved so stupidly – '

'I've had the same thought.'

'Oh, I don't blame you for thinking me an idiot – '

'It's myself I was blaming. I shouldn't have walked out, all stiff-necked pride. I should have listened to what was behind your words.'

'Ah . . . What do you think that was, Ronald Armstrong?'

'Desperation. Nothing else would have driven you to such a course. But I only worked that out a long time afterwards.'

They gazed at each other, black eyes looking up into hazel. At last, colouring, she said, 'I saw you in Perth. I longed to run after you and say I was sorry but somehow . . . somehow I couldn't.'

'In Perth?' he said, surprised.

'I stopped there when I went to the Highlands to catch colours and tints for the new tartan.'

'Aye, the new tartan. You're in a dour corner with it. What's your delivery date?'

'It's less than two months away. We'll never do it.'

'Och aye, we will,' he said with complete assurance. 'It'll cost a bit, and you'll have to put the mill on double shift to get the cloth run through on time, but we'll do it.'

'You really know how to produce a purple that will stand up to the press, Ronald? For mark you, it can't be any of the hard shades – I'm not having magenta or puce!'

'That's an insult,' he said, laughing. 'I can make you any shade of purple you like, soft or hard – show me the colour on your chart and I'll make it.'

'When?' she said eagerly.

'Well, not this moment.' He was almost teasing. 'It needs good light, as you well know. Besides which, I'm tired, I've come all the way from Perth today and I can scarcely see my hand in front of my eyes.'

'Of course! I'm sorry! Have you a place to stay?'

'I dropped my suitcase at the Abbotsford on my way from the station – I came straight on, to see if you were here. I knew you were when I saw the light in the office. I'd have gone on to the house if not.'

'Come to the house now,' she said impulsively, tugging at his arm. 'I suddenly realise I'm ravenously hungry. Come home and have a meal with me, Ronald.'

He resisted her urging. 'Sit down to a meal in your house?' he said.

'Of course, come on, it's getting late.'

She left him to snatch up her cape and bonnet. She turned out the lamp on her desk, turned out the gaslight on the wall. The only light now was in the entrance hall. As they made for the door in the dimness, she felt Ronald pull her towards him.

Next moment she was in his arms. They were kissing each other as if they had known they would come to this from the moment he entered her office.

'Ah, Jenny Corvill, Jenny Corvill,' he murmured as he let her go. 'What a rogue you've been to my peace of mind!'

'You've thought of me, Ronald, man?'

'Every day since I walked out. And cursed myself for a fool as I thought of it. Jenny, did you think of me?'

She hid her face against his shoulder. She had thought of him, but she had tried too hard to forget him.

'Come now,' she said, when she had recovered her senses a little. 'The watchman might walk in on us. I'll just give him a shout to say I'm going.'

He was waiting for her in the cobbled courtyard when she came out. As naturally as if she had done it every day of her life, she linked her arm in his when they set out towards the town. Their walk to Gatesmuir seemed to pass in a flash. They spoke little, but they said much.

When they came in at the house door the parlourmaid hurried to take Jenny's cape. She paused in evident surprise when she saw Ronald, but recovered to take his hat from him.

'We'll have something hot to eat in the dining-room as soon as possible, Thirley. Is my mother in the drawing-room?'

'Yes, mistress, and Mr Corvill and Mrs Edward.'

Jenny led the way. She entered saying, 'Look who I've brought with me!'

Millicent stared, then recognised Ronald. 'Mr Armstrong!'

Ned took a moment longer. He was sunk in after-dinner lethargy by the fire, took time to struggle out of it. 'Who? Oh, Mr Armstrong from the dye department . . . I thought you'd left Galashiels?'

'Aye, for Perth and beyond. How do you do, Mr Corvill?'

'Lucy, this is Mr Armstrong. He used to work for Corvill's.'

Lucy gave a cool nod. She had glanced up with interest from her magazine, but on hearing who he was the interest died. She gave an audible gasp, however, when Thirley came a moment later to say that a meal for two was served in the dining-room.

Out of politeness Millicent came to sit with them. She learned to her delight that Mr Armstrong knew how to solve the problem that had been worrying her poor daughter for weeks now. Gratitude would have made her well-intentioned towards Ronald, but as they chatted through the meal she found herself liking him for himself. He was the plain-spoken, honest sort she'd been brought up with, and if he seemed to laugh at things she thought serious, well, he was entitled to his own view.

Ronald was tired. He was also a little at a loss to find himself a guest of the Corvills. As soon as the meal was over he took his leave, promising to be at the mill by seven-thirty next morning.

As soon as he had gone, Lucy let loose her indignation. 'How could you, Jenny. To bring home an employee!'

Jenny took her sister-in-law by the hand. She led her into the now empty dining-room. 'Lucy,' she said, 'never use that tone of voice again when you speak of Ronald Armstrong. He will come here often, I hope.'

'But he's a *workman!*'

'He's a dye-master, your husband was a weaver, your father was an unsuccessful actor.'

Lucy gasped.

'Did you think I stopped short when I learned there was no Lieutenant Morrison in the China Squadron? Of course not, I found out who your father really was,' Jenny went on remorselessly. 'And that's not all I know, Lucy. Be warned. You'll be civil to Ronald or I'll make you the scandal of the town.'

Pale and shocked, Lucy backed away. 'That's blackmail – '

'I use the weapons you force me to use. Don't try your wrecking tactics between Ronald and me.'

'Ronald and you?' The phrase told Lucy more than a thousand explanations. She frowned, considered for a moment, then shrugged. 'You're a fool, Jenny. What can come of it? There's a yawning gulf between you.'

She was wrong, and Jenny was sure of it when next morning she saw him waiting for her outside the door of her office. Her whole being seemed to come more alive at sight of that easy, angular frame leaning against the doorposts.

The mill was coming into action. Her clerk, having lit the lamp in her office, was setting the first post on her desk. She told him she would be busy elsewhere for the early part of the day, and went with Ronald to the dye-room.

Luchar arrived half an hour later, looking pale and heavy-eyed. He had slept little, trying through the night hours to work out what was wrong with the dye-bath. When Ronald was introduced as an expert called in to help, he practically fell on his neck.

Ronald had brought with him a case in which phials of dyestuffs were carefully ranged in little compartments. He took off his jacket, put on a protective apron, rolled up his sleeves, and looked at Jenny. 'Where's the colour graph?'

'Here.'

He took it from her hand. For the next hour she might as well have been at the North Pole for all the notice he took of her. At length he looked round for a testing vat, and began to measure water and ingredients into it.

'What are you using?'

'It's a thio-indigo – very fast to light once it's fixed. This will take some time, Jenny. Come back in the afternoon. Meanwhile, send me up some newly-spun yarn of the right weight and I'll try a batch.'

'How soon can we weave it?'

'This evening, with luck. You'd best make a test length and then put it through all the processes as quickly as possible – are you cropping before you steam-press?'

'Hardly at all.'

'Right. Today's Tuesday; by Friday we should know if it holds its tone.'

'Ronald . . .'

'Don't worry. It will be all right.'

After the midday break she went to the dye-room. The hanks of yarn hung on a line in a current of warmth to dry them. Already Jenny's practised eye could see that when it had shed all its moisture it would exactly match the shade she had given Ronald.

'You can weave with it in about three hours if you want to,' he said, brushing sweat from his forehead. 'You'll use your father's loom?'

'Yes. I'll fetch the other colours and begin setting up. Bring me the purple when it's ready.'

By five o'clock the old handloom was prepared. Jenny had put a big holland apron over her gown. She sat to the loom, her foot on the familiar treadle, her ear already attuned to the opening and closing of the 'shed' as the weft bobbin went through. The graph of the pattern was on a board at the back of the loom, its squares blocked or empty according to the up and down of the warp. After a time her eyes ceased to see it. She knew the pattern, she could feel its rhythm and see its magical development on the moving frame.

It wasn't the best piece of weaving Jenny had ever done, but then she had never claimed any preeminence in the craft. Her father had been the true master of the loom. But the tartan spreading over the backrest was smooth and good, the colours glowing in their quiet harmony.

She was lost to time. She only knew it was late when she felt a touch on her shoulder and in the pause engendered by it she heard Ronald say, 'It's after eight, Jenny. It's time to stop.'

'No, I want to have enough to send to the fulling room tomorrow – '

'We won't do any fulling. That's not the question we're trying to answer, Jenny. We want to know if the colour will stand the heat of the steam press.'

'That's true. Then I want it to go to the press-room tomorrow. One day to go through, one to dry and breathe, and then . . .'

'Then we'll know.'

She rose from the loom, then all at once came close and leaned against him. She needed the comfort of his touch. 'I'm afraid, Ronald, I'm afraid it will go wrong. And then I shall have to tell the Queen . . .'

'Nothing of the sort,' he said, putting his arm about her. 'Come along now, put on your bonnet and I'll walk you home.'

As they approached the railway station her conscience smote her. Ronald's inn was only a step or two beyond. 'There's no need for you to see me home, Ronald. You've had a long day too.'

'Don't be daft. I'll see you to your door. Unless . . .' He paused. 'Have you eaten at all today?'

She shook her head.

'Come in and let me give you a meal. Then we'll call a hackney from the station to take you to Gatesmuir.'

'Well, I . . .'

'Are you expected? Is there a meal ready for you?'

'No, no, I'd no idea what time I'd be home.'

'Then come and share my evening meal.'

They were standing in discussion under the streetlamp. A passer-by raised his hat, calling good evening as he recognised her. She thought how different things were now. She didn't care who saw her with Ronald. She gloried in his company.

She took his offered arm and went with him to the Abbotsford Inn. But no one was about in the little lobby, and, as if by some previous agreement, they went together up the carpeted stairs to his room. After she had gone in and begun to untie the cord of her cape, she heard him turn the key in the lock.

She flew to his arms. She wanted to wind herself about him so that he could never, never be free. Utterly lost to everything except each other, they made love.

A long time later, when some home-going roisterer roused them from the light sleep that comes afterwards, they lit the oil lamp and studied each other in its golden glow.

He was thin but muscular, with a down of tawny hair on his chest that she found delightful to kiss. She felt his hands caressing her shoulder-blades. When she looked up, she saw his thin lips were curved in a smile of deep amusement.

'What are you chuckling to yourself about, Ronald Armstrong?' she demanded.

He gave a little laugh. 'I was just thinking, Jenny Corvill . . . If you were to ask me to marry you now, I very well might say yes.'

Chapter Twenty-four

Ronald had been so confident of his own abilities that he had
ordered a large enough supply of the necessary dyestuffs before
he ever left Perth. They arrived at the mill on the Friday
morning, the day that Jenny looked at the length of new tartan
on the table in the packing room and knew it was perfect.

The mill at once began work. A large stock of fresh yarn
had to be dyed to replace the batch that had proved imperfect,
and this would take much longer than the time Ronald had
taken to dye the sample on Tuesday. Jenny called in the
foremen of the departments to explain the situation. It would
be a week before they could set up with the new purple yarn.
That would give them less than three weeks to weave and
finish the order for the regiment. It could only be done by
working double shifts – and the tradition forebade evening
shifts during the dark months.

'Ach, we'll thole it the once,' said the weaving foreman.
'The lasses will want to do it for the sake of Her Majesty and
the Prince. Aye, aye, we'll do it.'

All other work was set aside. The mill swung into
production, concentrating only on the Grantown tartan.

The day the machines were switched on with the new warp
ready, Ronald walked through the weaving shed with Jenny.
They came through the double doors at the far end, out into
the fickle sunshine of a March morning.

'Theoretically,' he said, 'I ought to go back to Perth.'

'But you will not,' she countered.

'No, I won't. But on the other hand, what am I going to
do?'

'Stay here and marry me.'

'Och, I take that for granted,' he said, catching her round the waist and swinging her towards him. 'But what am I going to do once we're wed? I canna spend my life being Mistress Corvill's husband.'

She had known this moment would come. 'You must manage the works.'

'But I'm a dye-master.'

'Well, nobody's stopping you from mixing dyes! But you must manage Waterside Mill. And that will leave me free to concentrate on the designing.'

'It sounds as if it's ordained. Is this what you had in mind in the first place?'

'Well, it was a good idea then and it's a good idea now.'

'And what will your brother say?'

'Ned?' The idea that Ned would say anything startled her. In the week that had gone by since they became lovers they had had long talks, confiding in each other. She had told him that he was not the first man she had loved, and he had nodded at the words. 'But I'm the last, Jenny lassie,' he told her warningly.

'The last and best.'

He for his part had confessed a passing liaison with a girl in Perth, regretted now. 'It was only because she reminded me a little of you, my pretty merle.'

When they talked of her family, she had to tell him the secret they tried so desperately to keep – that Ned was a hopeless drunkard.

'So that's why he's given up the great temperance campaign,' he mused, tugging at his chin. 'I realise now, he's not been mentioned in the newspapers for a time or two.'

'Since New Year. He took drink again at the party to celebrate the Grantown tartan. I blame myself – I didn't look after him well enough.'

'Good sakes, Jenny, a 26–year-old man doesn't need to be looked after.'

'He needs something – I don't know what it is. He's had a drink problem since he was a boy. Even then, I tried my best to look after him.'

'I thought that first evening, he looked ill, Jenny.'

'Yes, I think it *is* an illness, but people don't recover from

311

it easily. He took a cure, with a doctor in Glasgow, but . . .'
She sighed deeply. 'If you're marrying into my family you
must understand what you're taking on.'

'Every family has skeletons in its cupboards, my dear.'

Now, as they walked away from the busy mill, Ronald spoke
of Ned again. 'I ought to consult him about our marriage.
After all, he is the head of your family.'

'I suppose so . . . Not that it will make any difference what
he says.'

'Perhaps that's what's wrong with him, Jenny.'

The interview took place that evening, after a family dinner
to which Ronald was invited. Lucy sat at her husband's right
hand being rigidly polite to the guest, Millicent beamed over
all because she could see Jenny had solved her great problem
and Ned, in a momentary spell of self-discipline, drank
nothing but water.

When the meal was over Ronald asked to speak to Ned in
private. Surprised, the master of the house led the way to
what had been his father's reading room.

'What is it you want to discuss, Armstrong?'

'My marriage to Jenny.'

Ned's mouth fell open.

'Jenny would like an Easter wedding – '

'The end of this month?' Ned cried, astounded.

'There's no reason to wait. Jenny and I know our minds.
All I want is your agreement.'

'Agreement! But . . . but . . . this is the first I ever heard
of it!'

Ronald nodded. 'I suppose it takes you by surprise. The
fact is, I've been in love with your sister for years.'

'That's not the point! Look here, Armstrong – you're hardly
the sort of match – '

'What were you hoping for? A rich landowner? A colonel
of the regiment? It so happens Jenny wants me. And I want
her. That makes it a very good match.'

'I'm damned if I think so! Good God, I never thought Jenny
would be fool enough to fall for a man who was obviously
after her money!'

Ronald had been standing by the book table. He came up
to Ned and laid a hand on his shoulder. 'Listen, laddie . . . I

may be about ten years your senior but I'm twice as strong. I'll knock your teeth back into your thrapple if you ever say a thing like that to me again. Is that understood? I don't want Jenny's money. In any case, she doesn't have any – does she? You own the mill. Jenny gets an allowance and nothing more.'

Ned drew back from under the calm touch on his shoulder. 'All right. She doesn't have any actual money. But you . . . you . . .'

'I'm not good enough for her? I quite agree. Who is? But the fact is she wants me, and it's time she had a man to look after her.'

Ned's face flamed. 'I look after her,' he said. 'I'm the head of the family.'

'Are you, indeed? And how long do you think you'll keep the role? In six months or a year you'll have drunk yourself to death.'

'Don't you dare – '

Ronald shrugged. 'If you want to get angry and protest, go ahead. But the first evening I came here you were suffering from a bad case of the shakes, and I hear from the townsfolk you stagger out of the taverns most nights. Why do you do it?'

Ned Corvill turned away from him. 'What business is it of yours?'

'Well, I'm going to be your brother-in-law and, according to Jenny, I'm going to manage your mill. Naturally I'm interested in why you want to pickle yourself in alcohol.'

'Don't speak like that . . . I don't . . . You wouldn't understand!'

'Try me.'

Ned shook his head, wavered, then sat down suddenly with his face in his hands. 'It's all so hopeless,' he sobbed. 'At first I used to find it made everything seem brighter, easier . . . My father had a stern view of life, you see . . . But now I need it because after all, what else is there?'

'Do you mean, as a way of killing yourself?' Ronald said in a conversational tone. 'I'd have thought it was kind of long-winded. If you really want to finish yourself off, come to me. I've things in the dye-room that could see you into the Here-after in ten minutes flat.'

'You see?' Ned cried. 'You make fun of it. But there *is* no Hereafter. It's all a lie, we know that now. Dr Murdo and all he believes in are mere childishness.'

Ronald took a seat, leaning forward so as to glimpse the younger man's ravaged features. 'And if that's true, what of it? Other people have faced it, you know. They see the world is harsh, and perhaps now some of them feel there isn't another world where they'll find compensation for the hardships of this one – but they go on.'

'I don't know how they do . . .' cried Ned.

'I hear you read philosophy at university?'

'What? Yes . . . What of it?'

'Wasn't there a group called the Stoics?'

'What could you know about them?' Ned said, in tearful scorn.

'Oh, I've read a wee bit. Not as much as you, but I think I read they had good laws to live by – '

'But they too were duped – they believed in God – '

'But a god who didn't meddle in human affairs, and because they couldn't call on his help if their corn failed or their ships sank, they lived by . . . what was it called . . . equalness of temperament – '

'You mean Equanimity of Mind.'

'Yes, and the Power of the Will, I remember – that was another one.'

Ned sat up straighter, staring at Ronald. 'You've studied it.'

'Years ago. I don't remember it, really. All I'm saying is that they were men who lived by believing in themselves. It's what you do, if there isn't anything else. Wouldn't you agree?'

The younger man looked as if he might say yes. Then he said, 'You think it's easy. But I can't give up drink by myself. I've tried. Sometimes I'll go as long as two days without a drink. But in the end . . .' He threw up his hand in a gesture of hopelessness. 'And I can't go back to Dr Murdo in Glasgow because he goes on and on about how the Almighty is just at my elbow to help me, and I know now that it isn't true.'

'Ach, man, you're a simpleton,' Ronald said in contempt.

'What? You've no right to – '

'Do you think Dr Murdo is the only man who runs a clinic

for alcoholism? If you really want to find a cure, you can find a better place to go.'

'I do want to!' Ned exclaimed. 'You must believe me, I hate myself the way I am! And I'm so afraid Lucy will leave me.'

'Then use your intelligence. Find someone to help you. And rely on yourself like a Stoic.'

When the two men came down to the drawing-room, Jenny sought Ronald's eye. He gave her a faint smile. Ned for his part looked strange – is if he'd been through an ordeal and come out weak yet the better for it.

'Mr Armstrong, that's to say, Ronald has something to tell you, Mother,' Ned announced.

To Jenny's amazement, her self-possessed lover blushed. 'I thought you would tell them, Ned!'

'No, no, this is your prerogative. Go ahead.'

'Well . . . er . . . I've been speaking to Ned about our marriage. Jenny's and mine, I mean.'

'Marriage?' Lucy echoed in a stifled tone.

'My dear child!' shrieked Millicent, and flew to embrace her daughter. 'Oh, what a fine thing! Oh, I'm so pleased. If only your dear father could have lived to see it!'

'Then we have your blessing, Mother?'

'Of course, of course! Lucy, isn't it wonderful?'

'Oh yes,' Lucy agreed, her blue eyes cold.

'We haven't talked it through, but I think it would be a good move to put Ronald in as manager at Waterside,' Ned went on, smiling on the rest of his family.

Ronald frowned a little. 'I should like to discuss that before you make any announcement, Ned. We haven't talked about salaries.'

'Salaries . . . Oh yes . . .'

'Of course,' murmured Lucy, 'money.'

'I don't think you'll have anything to complain of when we come to the point, Ronald – '

'And what is Jenny going to do?' Lucy inquired with a pricking glance towards her.

'Why, stay at home and raise a family,' Ned cried, delighted with the thought.

Stay at home and raise a family. The sentence echoed in Jenny's mind next day when she watched the first completed

315

piece of Grantown tartan come off the loom. Was that what the future held for her?

She wanted children, of course. She wanted Ronald's children. But did she want to stay at home to raise them? Could she give up the challenge of the work here at the mill, the comradeship of the mill girls, the conversations with men of business, the planning from season to season of something new and different, the daily routine that had filled her life now for six years?

She had fallen headlong as if over a cliff when Ronald came back into her life. She couldn't imagine going on without him. But would the time come when she would regret the price she had to pay?

For Ronald Armstrong wasn't a man who could be wheedled and coaxed as Lucy handled Ned. He was a man with a mind of his own, who would bring different ways to Waterside Mill – changes, improvements perhaps, but differences that she might regret.

Ned had fallen in with the idea that Ronald should be manager. Very well then, he would manage. She would have to subordinate herself to him.

'You won't shut me out entirely when you take over?' she asked him almost timidly.

'What a question! We decided, didn't we, that you would be in charge of the design department.'

'But we haven't in fact got a design department, Ronald. I should like to have a room at the top of the building on the north side, where the light is good.'

'You mean . . . come here?'

'Of course.'

'But you'd be a lot more comfortable at home with your sketching board.'

They had decided for the time being at any rate to live at Gatesmuir. She pictured herself at home with her mother and Lucy. The prospect was not enlivening.

'I shall come here every day,' she said with firmness. 'Let's see if we can find a room that would do.'

They walked up to the fourth floor, the eyes of the workers following them as they used to follow Jenny when she went

316

her way among the departments. Soon they would follow Ronald . . .

I am giving this to him, she thought with a sudden sense of loss. It is *mine* and I am giving it to him, because there's no other way, it seems. Does he understand what a gift it is? It's all I have in the world, except Ronald himself.

On the high floor they found a store room. 'I can have this cleared, and make the window larger. Then with my drawing table underneath I shall be in business.'

'I can't understand why you want to come here at all,' Ronald muttered. 'You'd be far better off at Gatesmuir.'

'But I belong at Waterside . . .' To her own dismay she felt her eyes fill with foolish tears. She turned away so that Ronald shouldn't see them.

But he caught her by the arm and turned her back towards him. With the crook of a finger he caught a tear from her lower lashes. 'Don't cry, Jenny. I know it's a great change, but after all, that's what life is about, isn't it – change and growth. It will be different, I can't help that – there will be good things and bad things, but I promise you there will be more good than bad.'

She saw the room through the prism of her tears. It wavered and changed. A small room, tiny compared with the domain over which she had ruled. And while she ruled she had been Mistress Jenny Corvill of the Waterside Mill. Soon she would simply be Mrs Armstrong. To be Ronald's wife had become part of the dream – or perhaps her dream had changed. The great plan, the ambition to make Corvill the finest name in Scottish weaving – she had achieved that. And found it wasn't enough, that achievement without emotional fulfilment turned the dream to a nightmare.

Yet she was giving up the most important thing in her life so as to become Mrs Armstrong.

She wondered, Shall I resent it? Shall I ever upbraid him with the fact that I gave him my job and came instead to this cubbyhole up under the roof?

She realised she must take care never to do that. It would need forebearance, patience, tact. But then she had used those in running the mill. Surely she could summon them up in running her marriage?

317

Her future was bound up in Ronald Armstrong, she knew that. It was a future she wanted. She knew it might have its pitfalls and crises, that it scared her a little.

But she wanted it.